MARY POPE O...

✦ MAGIC ✦
TREE HOUSE®

AFTERNOON ON THE AMAZON

THE GRAPHIC NOVEL

ADAPTED BY
JENNY LAIRD

WITH ART BY
KELLY & NICHOLE MATTHEWS

A STEPPING STONE BOOK™
RANDOM HOUSE 🏠 NEW YORK

Text copyright © 2024 by Mary Pope Osborne

Art copyright © 2024 by Kelly Matthews & Nichole Matthews

Text adapted by Jenny Laird

All rights reserved. Published in the United States by Random House Children's Books, a division of Penguin Random House LLC, New York. Adapted from *Afternoon on the Amazon*, published by Random House Children's Books, a division of Penguin Random House LLC, New York, in 1995.

Random House and the colophon are registered trademarks and A Stepping Stone Book and the colophon are trademarks of Penguin Random House LLC. RH Graphic with the book design is a trademark of Penguin Random House LLC. Magic Tree House is a registered trademark of Mary Pope Osborne; used under license.

Visit us on the Web!

rhcbooks.com

MagicTreeHouse.com

Educators and librarians, for a variety of teaching tools, visit us at RHTeachersLibrarians.com

Library of Congress Cataloging-in-Publication Data is available upon request.
ISBN 978-0-593-48882-9 (pbk.) — ISBN 978-0-593-48883-6 (hardcover) —
ISBN 978-0-593-48884-3 (lib. bdg.) — ISBN 978-0-593-48885-0 (ebook)

The artists used Clip Studio Paint to create the illustrations for this book.

The text of this book is set in 13-point Cartoonist Hand Regular.

MANUFACTURED IN CHINA

10 9 8 7 6 5 4 3 2 1

First Graphic Novel Edition

This book has been officially leveled by using the F&P Text Level Gradient™ Leveling System.

For Troy Vidal, a great reader
—M. P. O.

For Will Osborne, faithful friend and protector of all
the world's creatures
—J.L.

For Tonka and Puma
—K.M. & N.M.

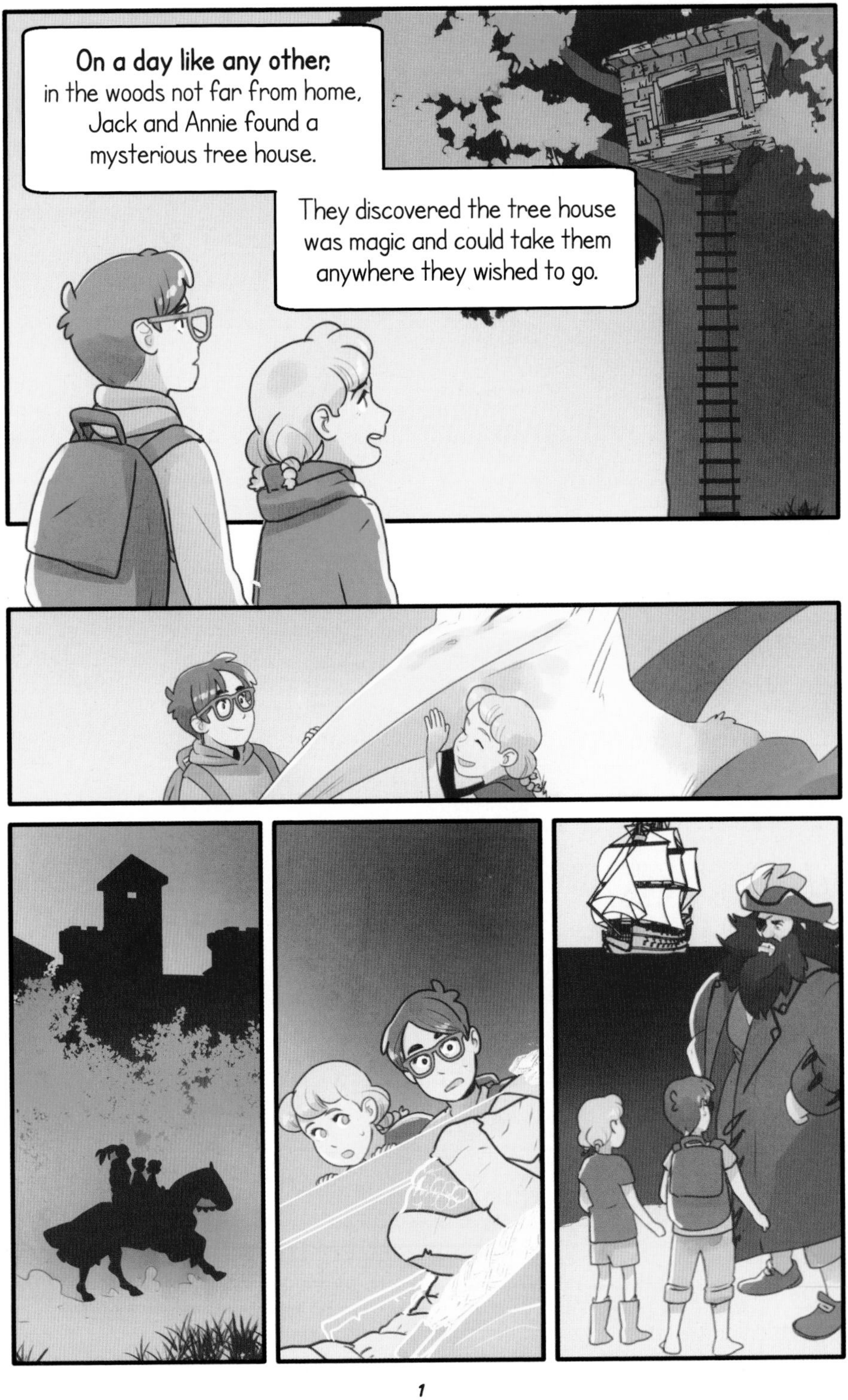
On a day like any other,
in the woods not far from home, Jack and Annie found a mysterious tree house.
They discovered the tree house was magic and could take them anywhere they wished to go.

Along the way, Jack and Annie learned the tree house belonged to Morgan le Fay.

Morgan promised to send the kids on many more adventures.

Jack and Annie are ready for their next adventure!

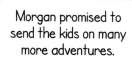

CHAPTER ONE
Where's Peanut?

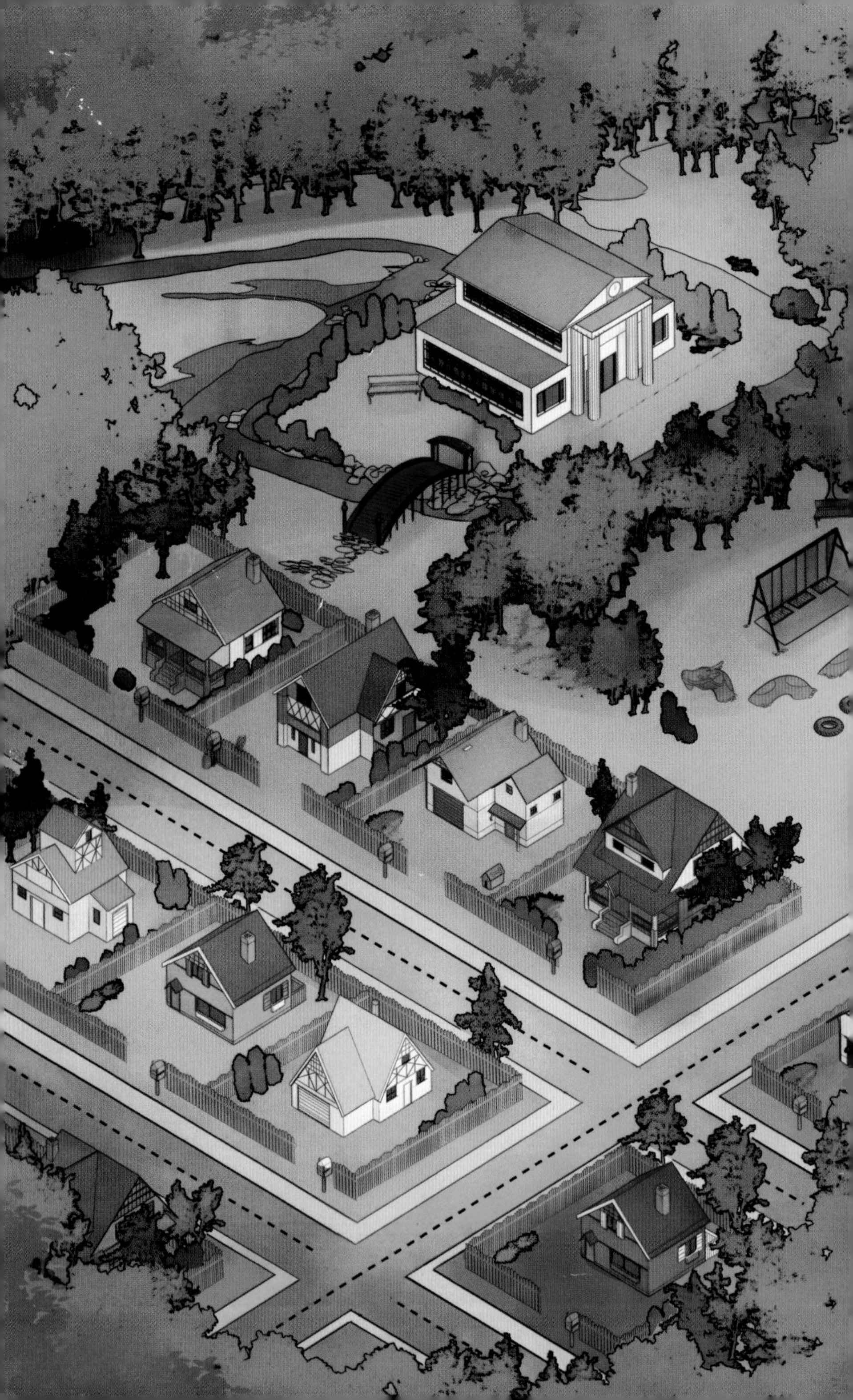

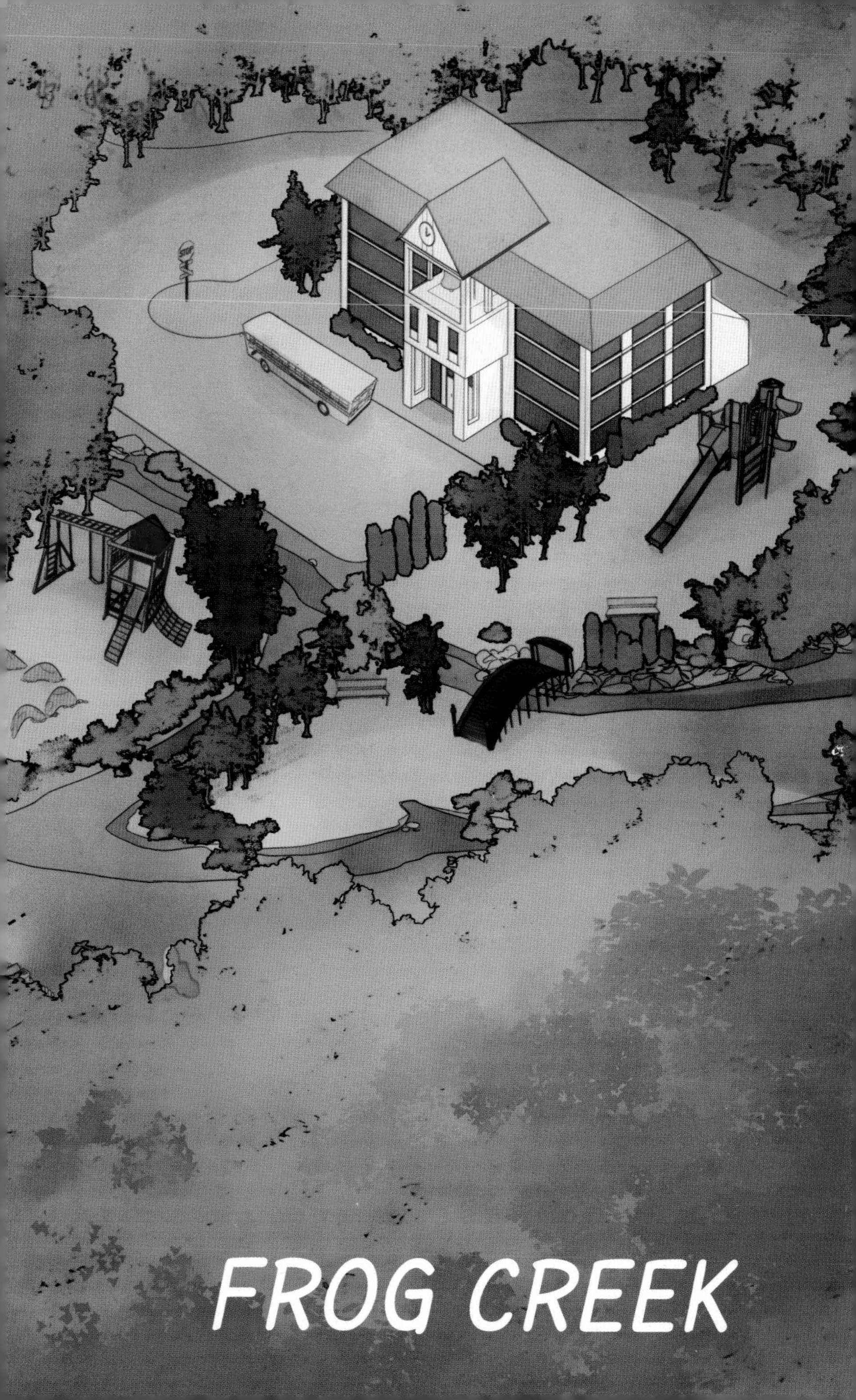
FROG CREEK

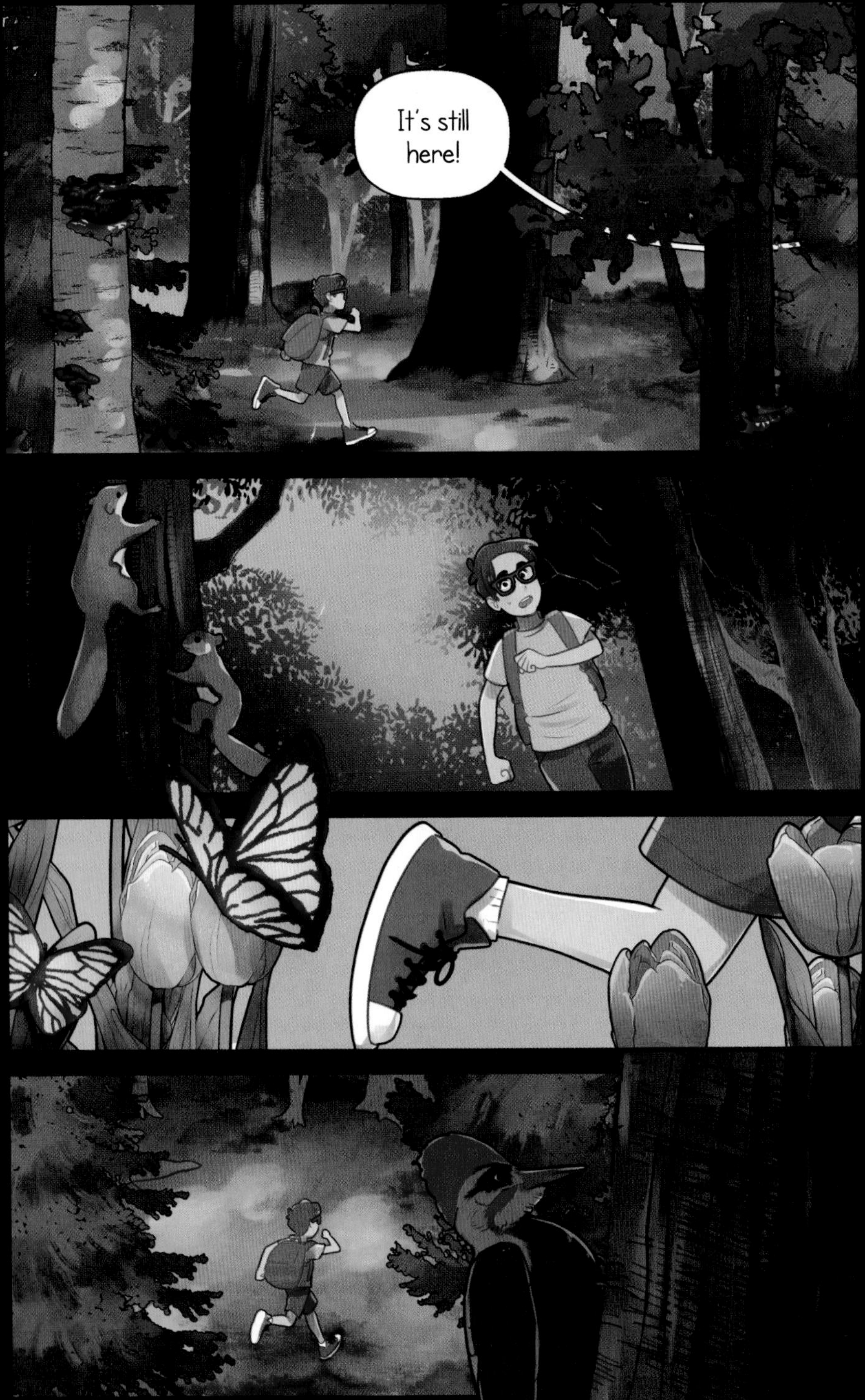
It's still here!

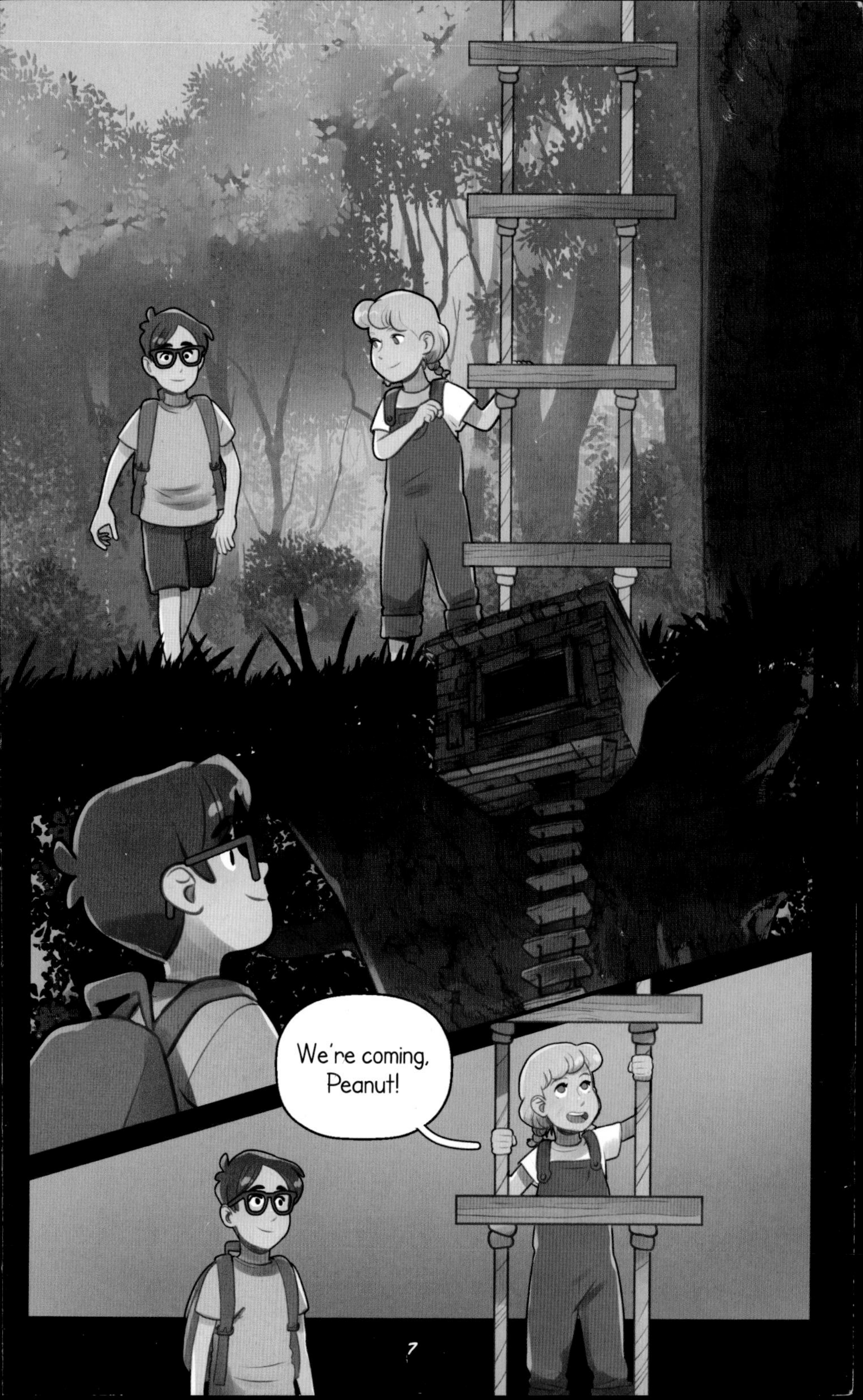
We're coming, Peanut!

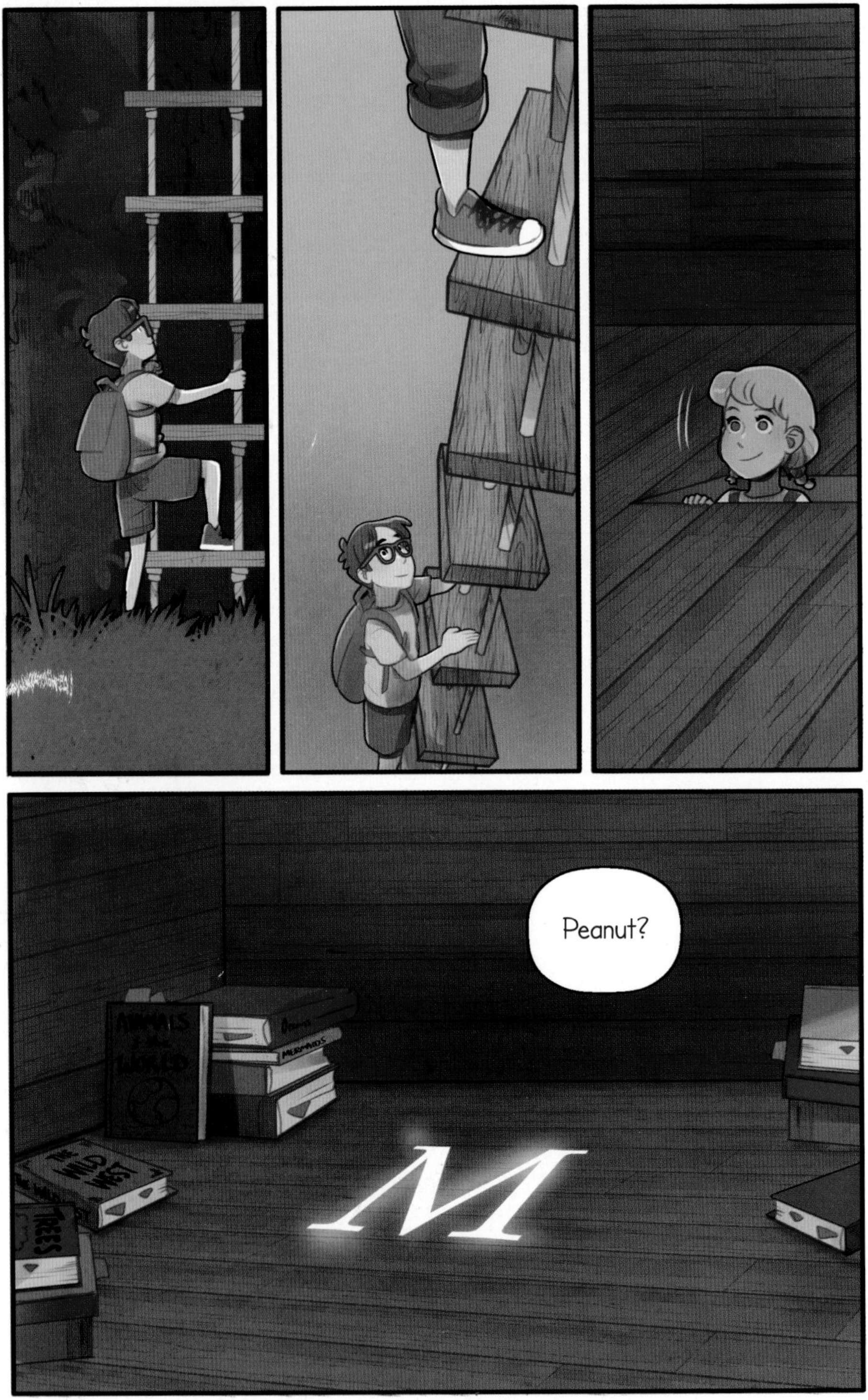
Peanut?
TREES

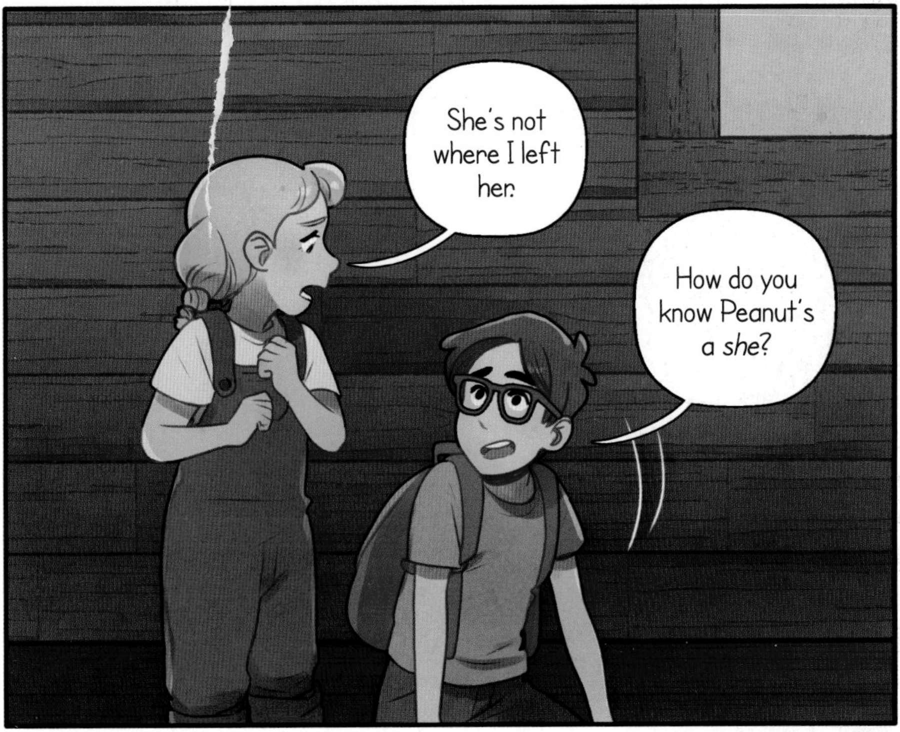
She's not where I left her.
How do you know Peanut's a *she*?

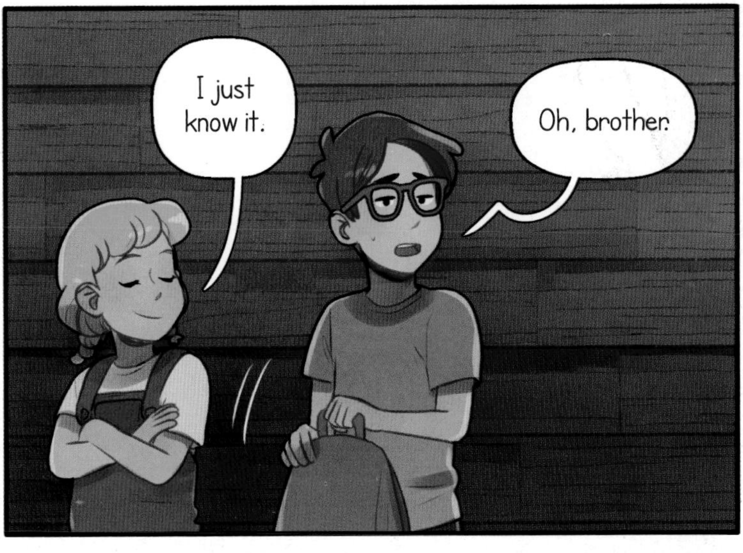
I just know it.
Oh, brother.

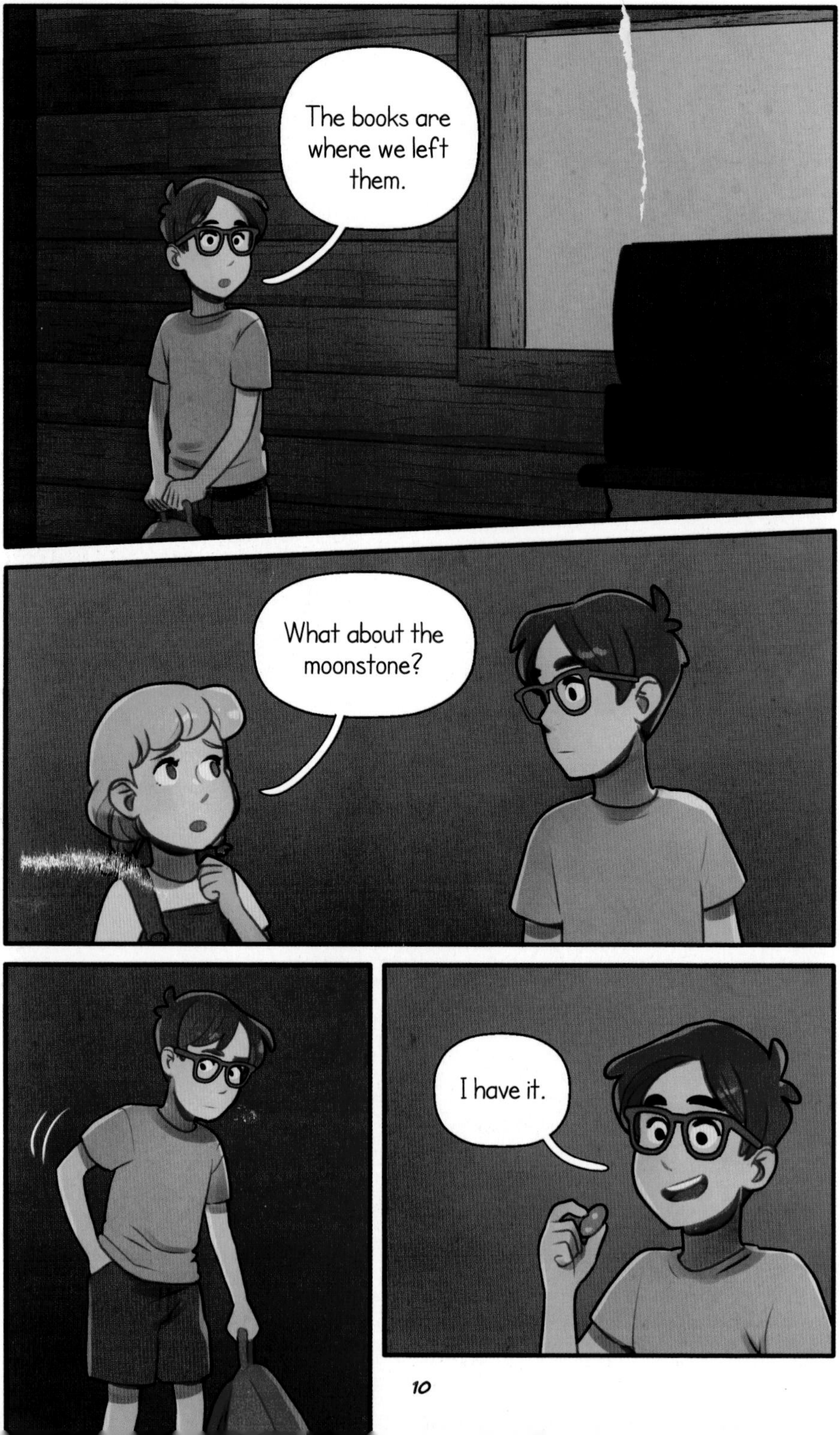
The books are where we left them.
What about the moonstone?
I have it.

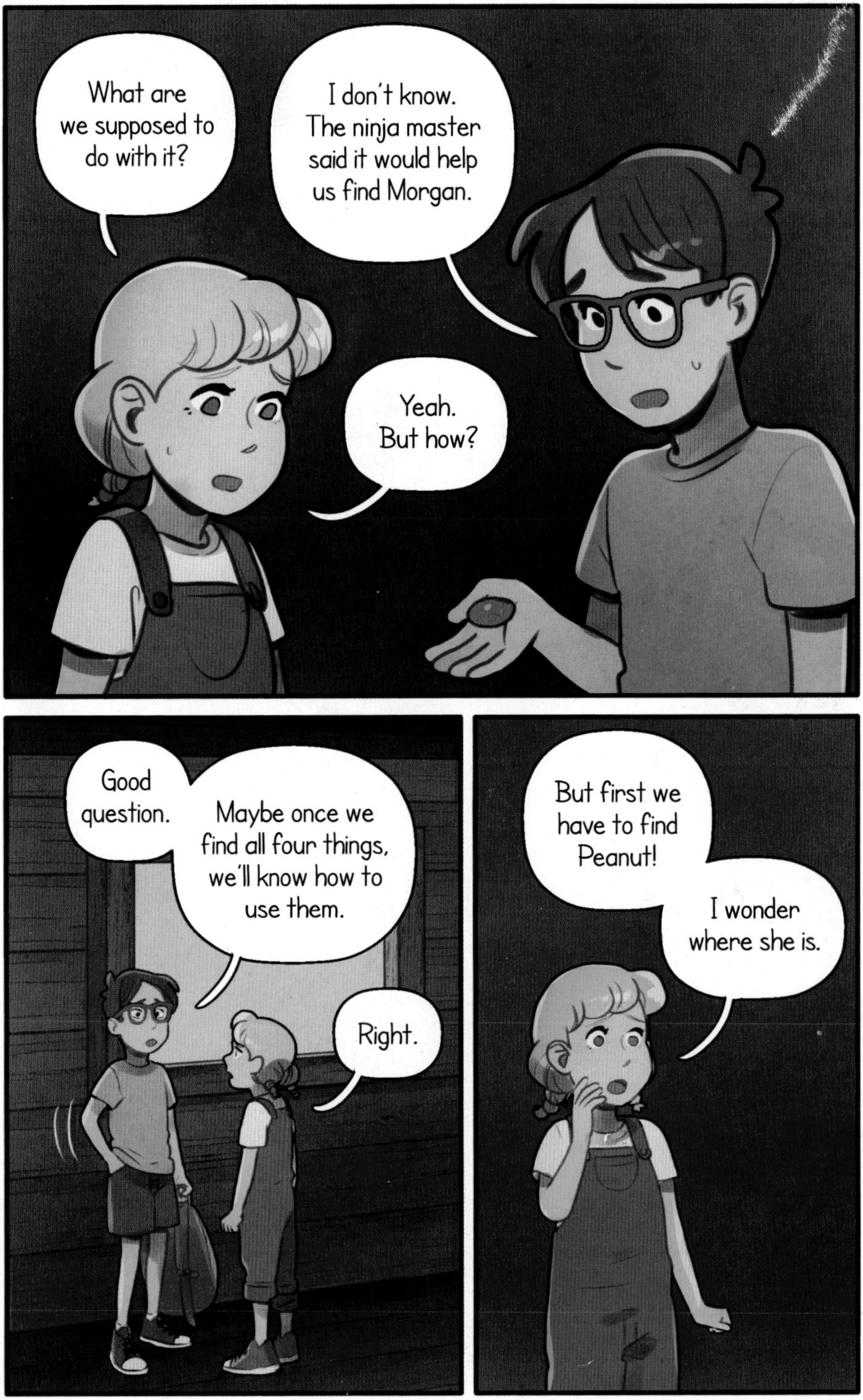
What are we supposed to do with it?
I don't know. The ninja master said it would help us find Morgan.
Yeah. But how?
Good question.
Maybe once we find all four things, we'll know how to use them.
Right.
But first we have to find Peanut!
I wonder where she is.

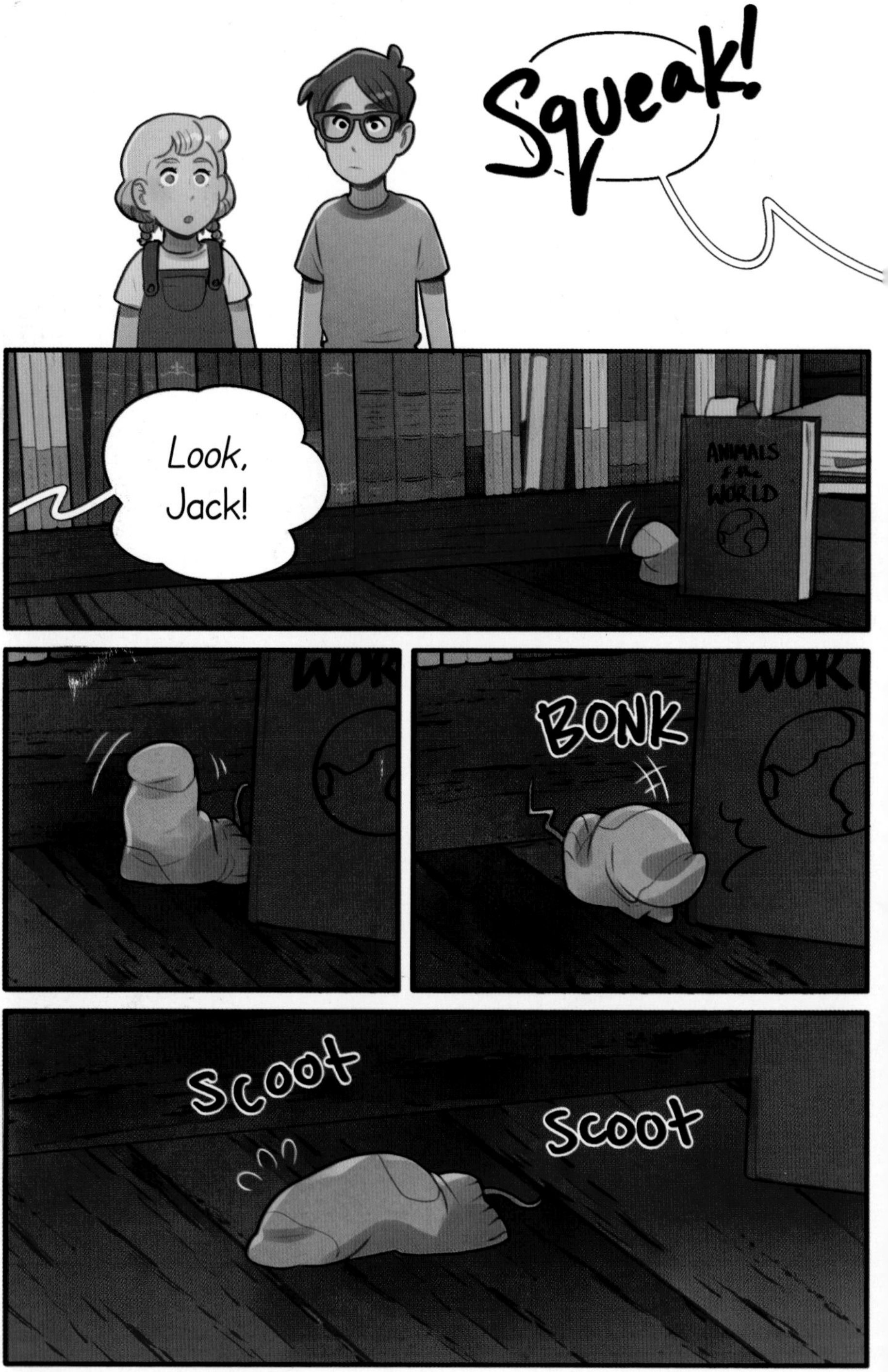
Squeak!
Look, Jack!
ANIMALS of the WORLD
BONK
Scoot
Scoot

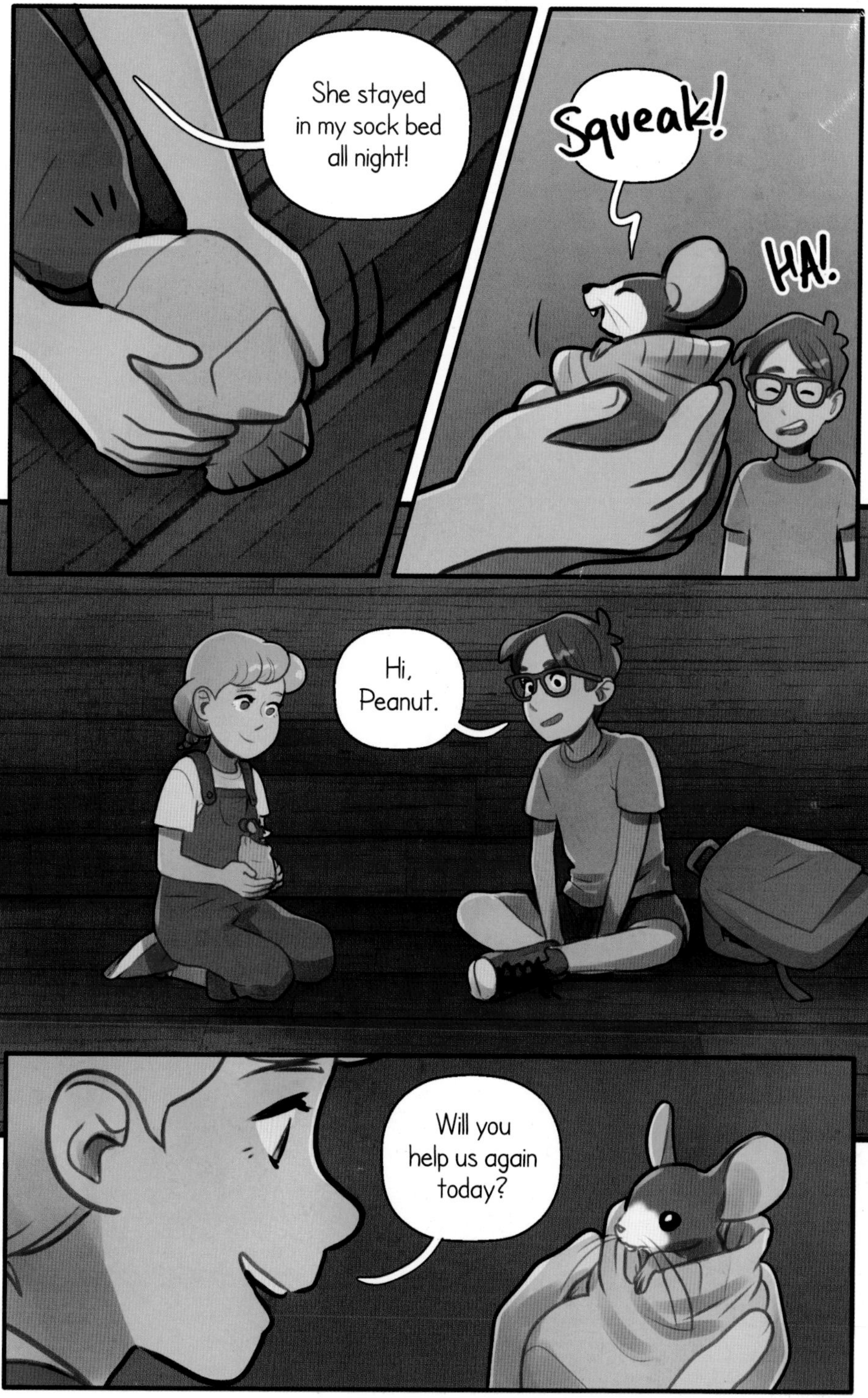
She stayed in my sock bed all night!
Squeak!
HA!
Hi, Peanut.
Will you help us again today?

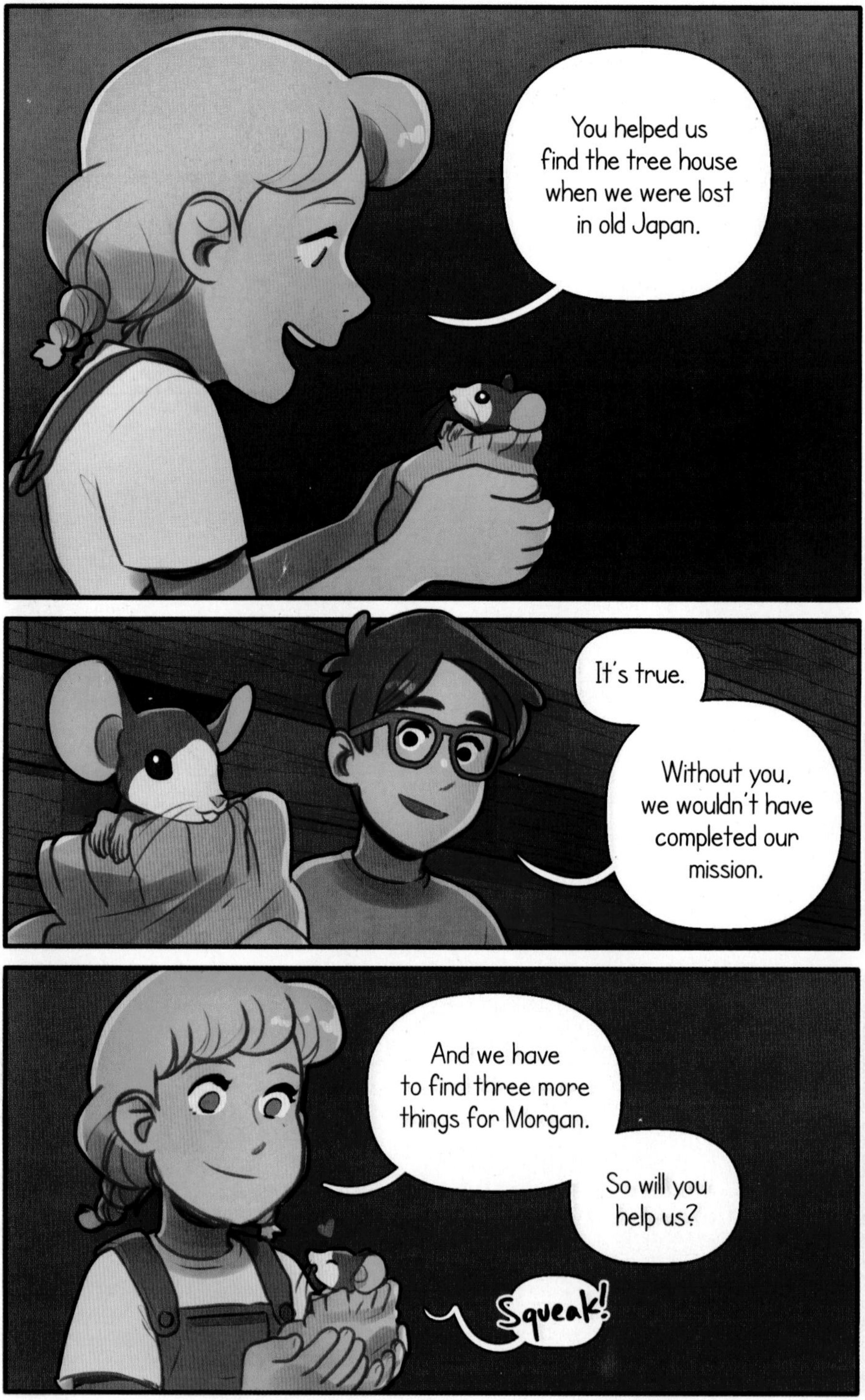
You helped us find the tree house when we were lost in old Japan.
It's true.
Without you, we wouldn't have completed our mission.
And we have to find three more things for Morgan.
So will you help us?
Squeak!

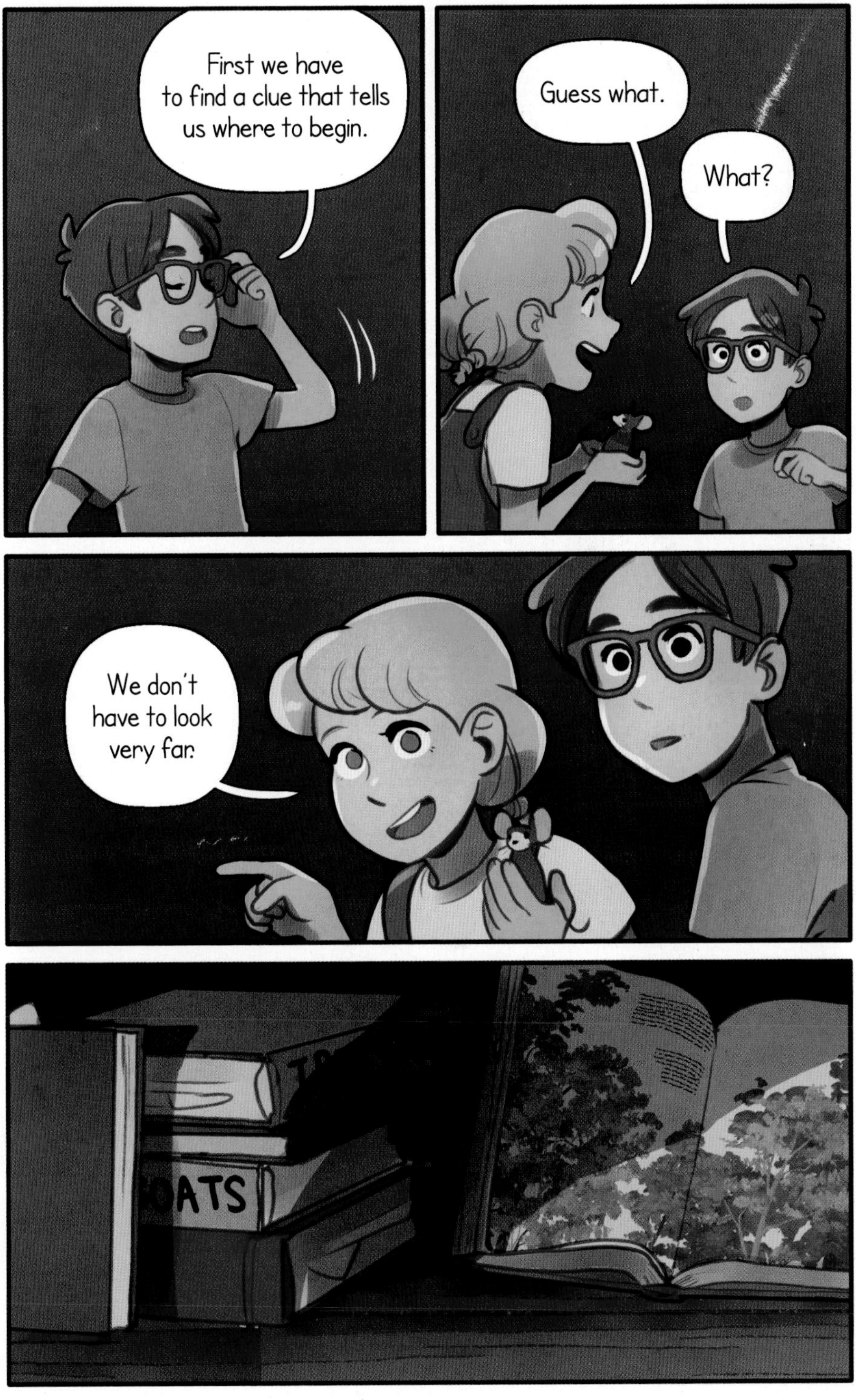
First we have to find a clue that tells us where to begin.
Guess what.
What?
We don't have to look very far.

CHAPTER TWO
Big Bugs

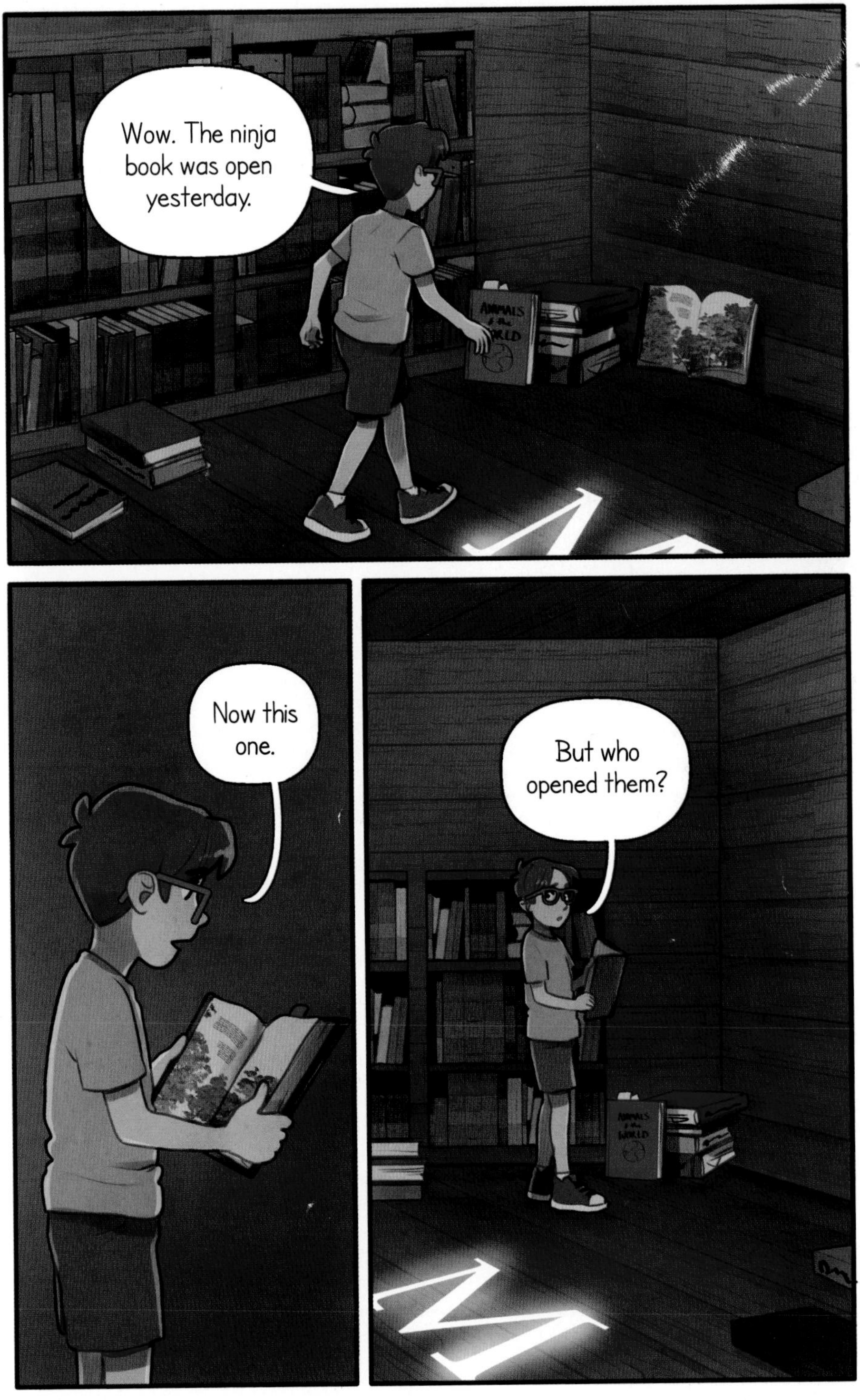
Wow. The ninja book was open yesterday.
Now this one.
But who opened them?

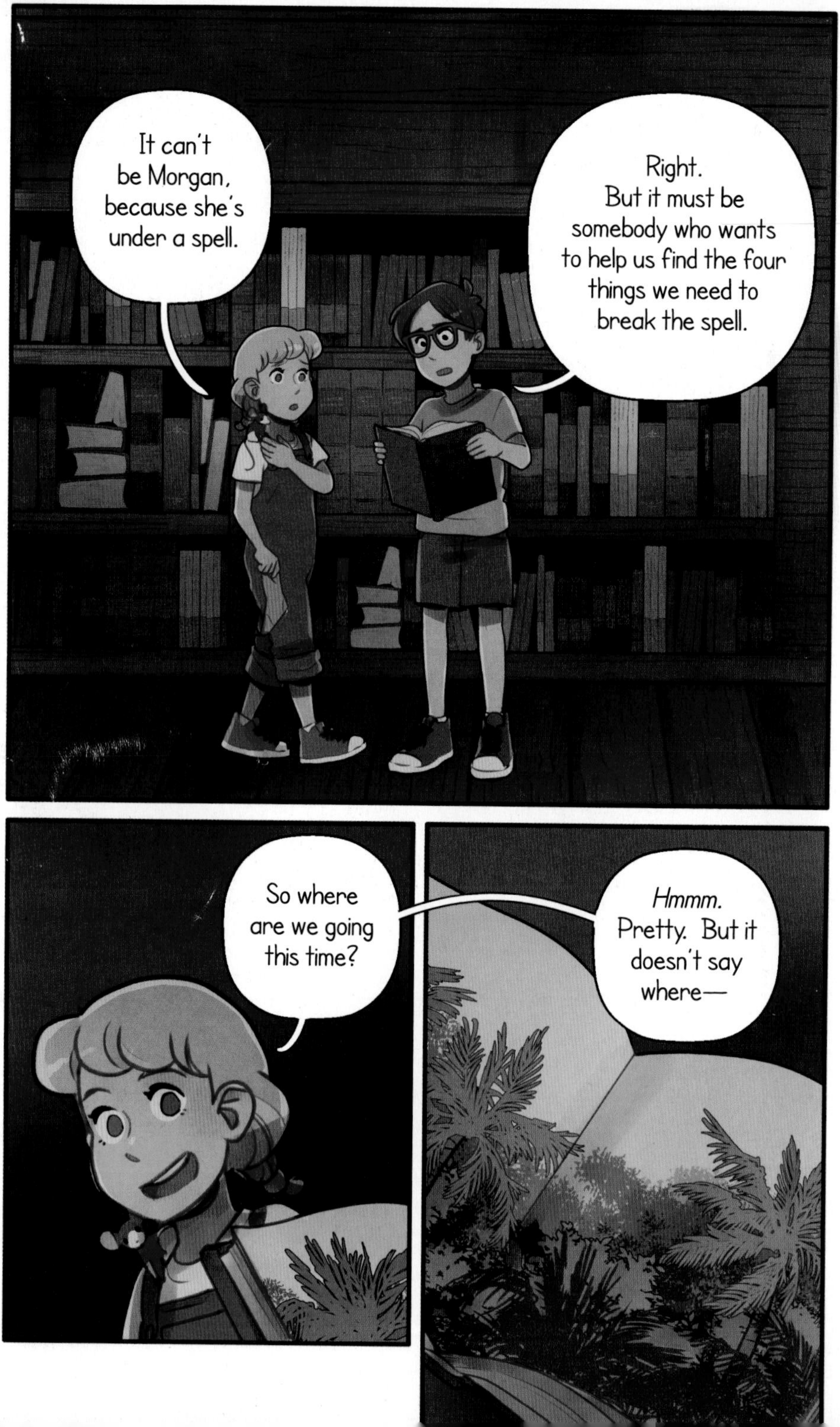
It can't be Morgan, because she's under a spell.
Right. But it must be somebody who wants to help us find the four things we need to break the spell.
So where are we going this time?
Hmmm. Pretty. But it doesn't say where—

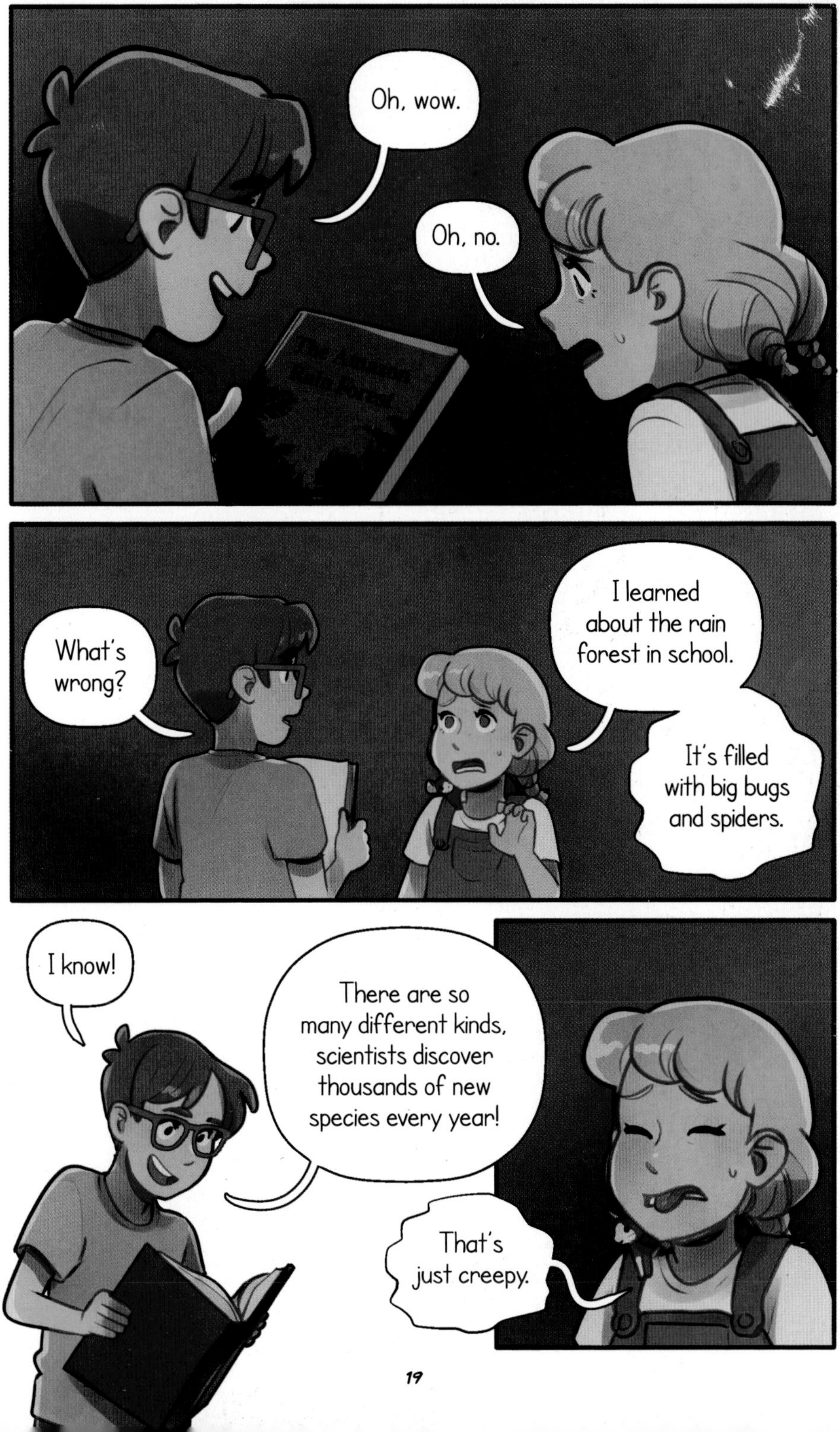
Oh, wow.
Oh, no.
What's wrong?
I learned about the rain forest in school.
It's filled with big bugs and spiders.
I know!
There are so many different kinds, scientists discover thousands of new species every year!
That's just creepy.

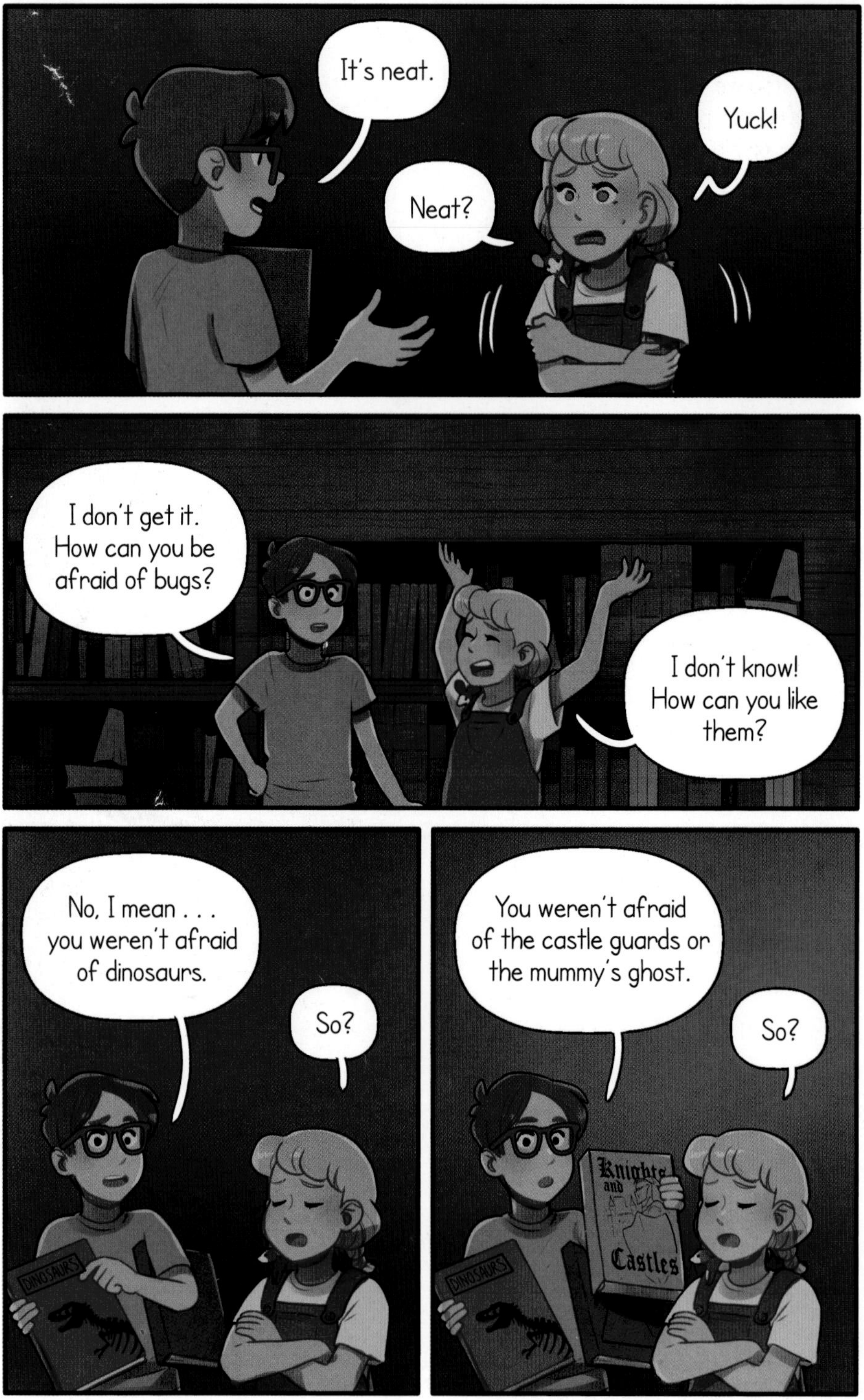
It's neat.
Neat?
Yuck!
I don't get it. How can you be afraid of bugs?
I don't know! How can you like them?
No, I mean . . . you weren't afraid of dinosaurs.
So?
DINOSAURS
You weren't afraid of the castle guards or the mummy's ghost.
So?
DINOSAURS
Knights and Castles

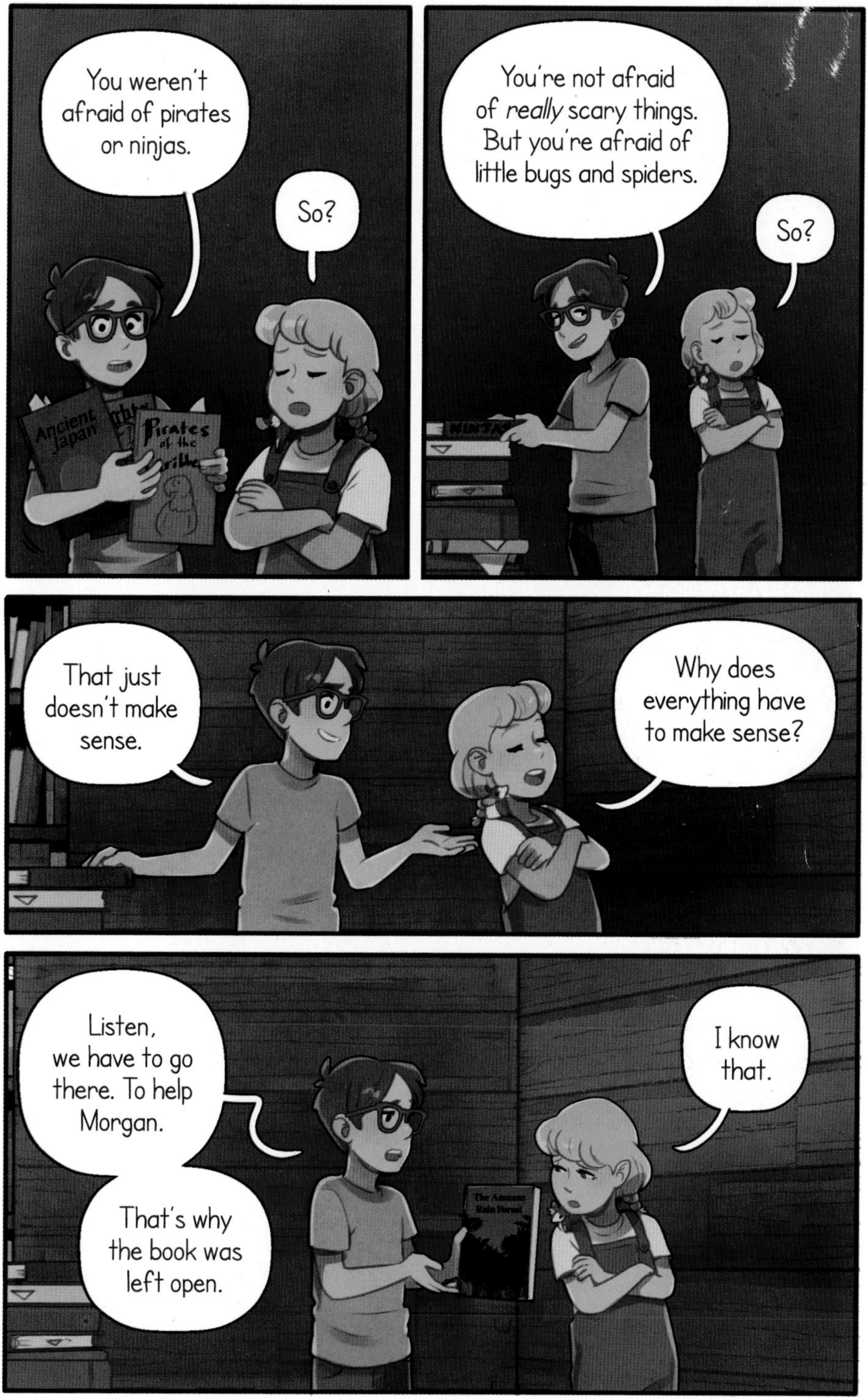
You weren't afraid of pirates or ninjas.
So?
Ancient Japan
Pirates of the
You're not afraid of *really* scary things. But you're afraid of little bugs and spiders.
So?
That just doesn't make sense.
Why does everything have to make sense?
Listen, we have to go there. To help Morgan.
That's why the book was left open.
I know that.

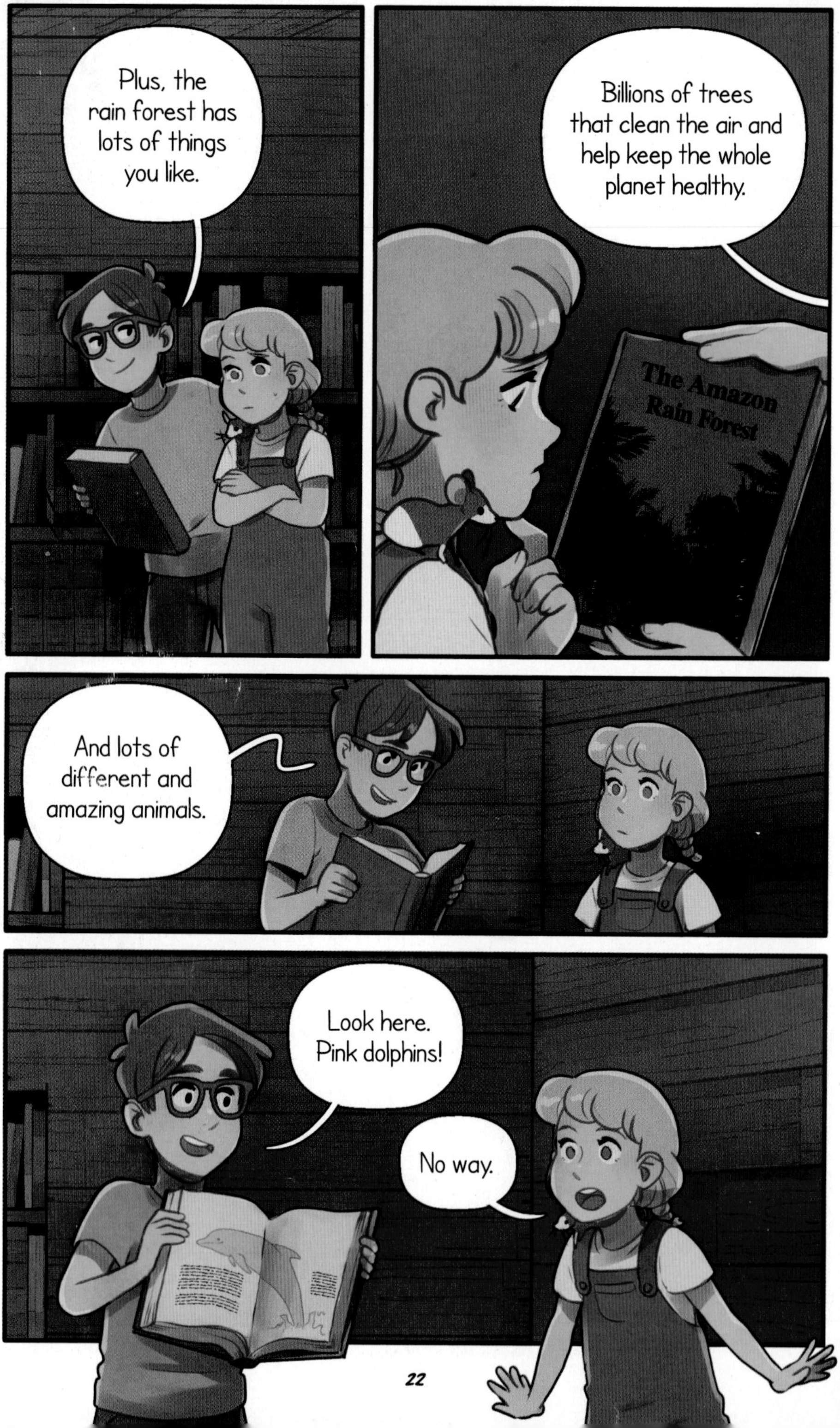
Plus, the rain forest has lots of things you like.
Billions of trees that clean the air and help keep the whole planet healthy.
The Amazon Rain Forest
And lots of different and amazing animals.
Look here. Pink dolphins!
No way.

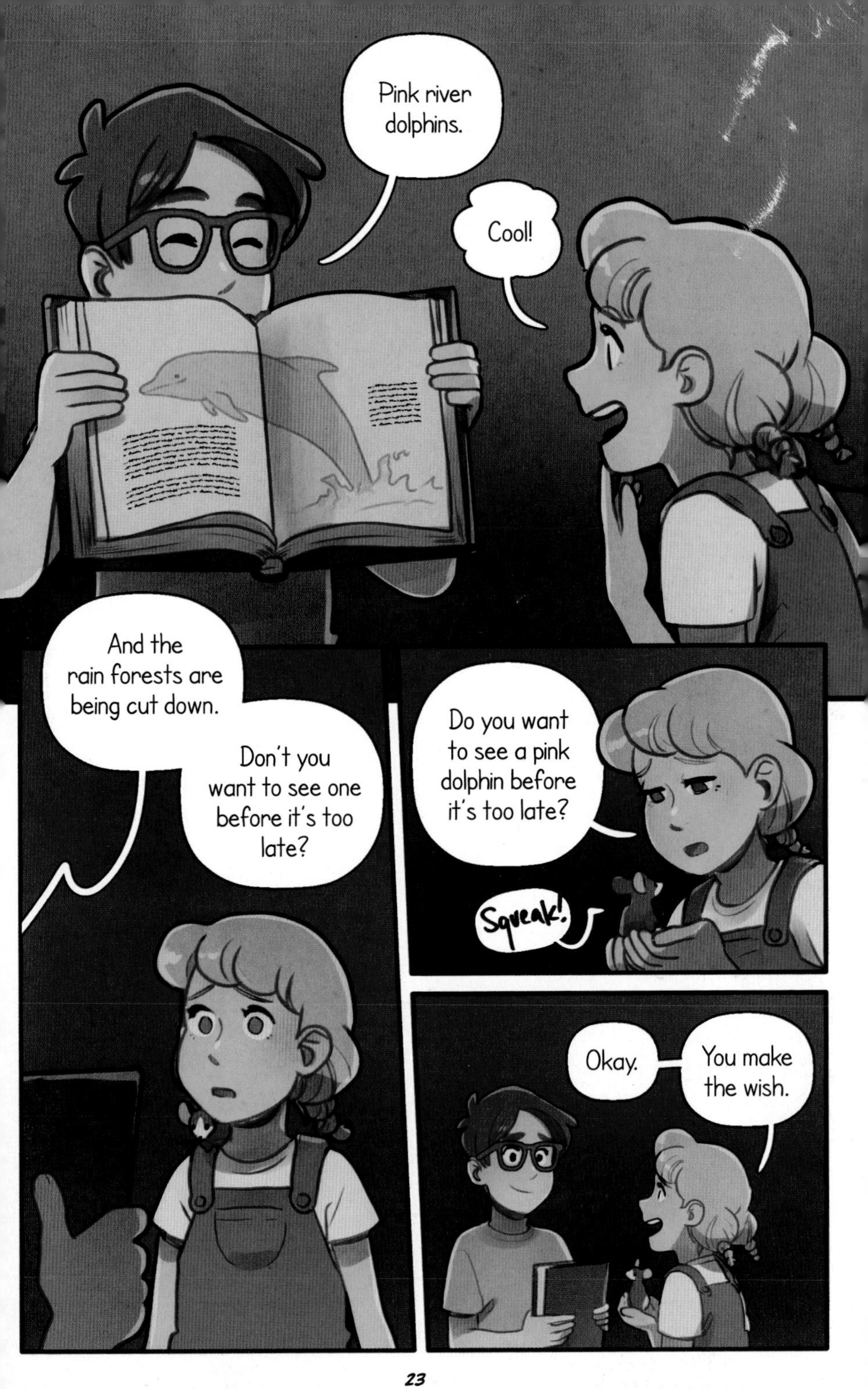
Pink river dolphins.
Cool!
And the rain forests are being cut down.
Don't you want to see one before it's too late?
Do you want to see a pink dolphin before it's too late?
Squeak!
Okay.
You make the wish.

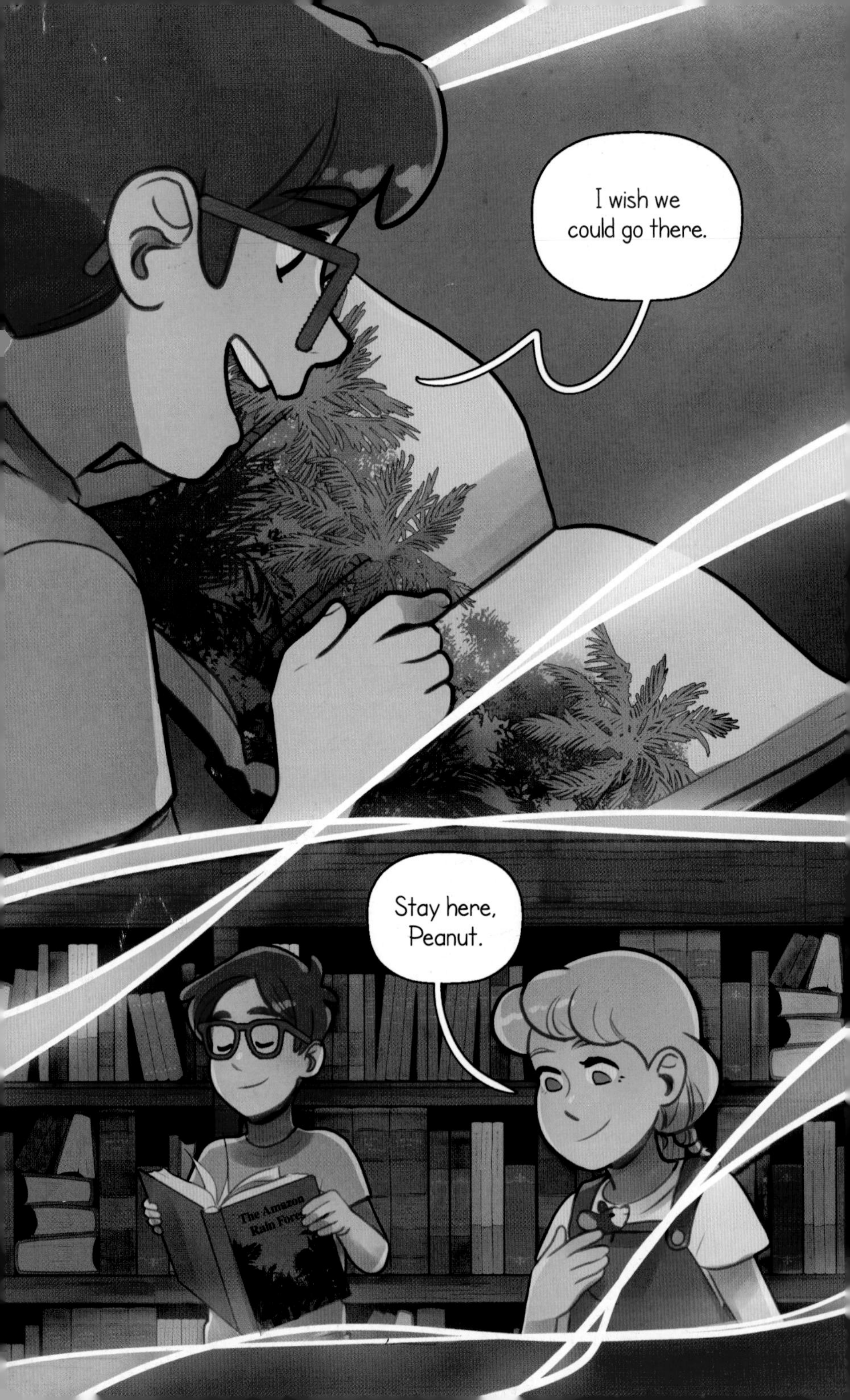
I wish we could go there.
Stay here, Peanut.
The Amazon Rain Fores

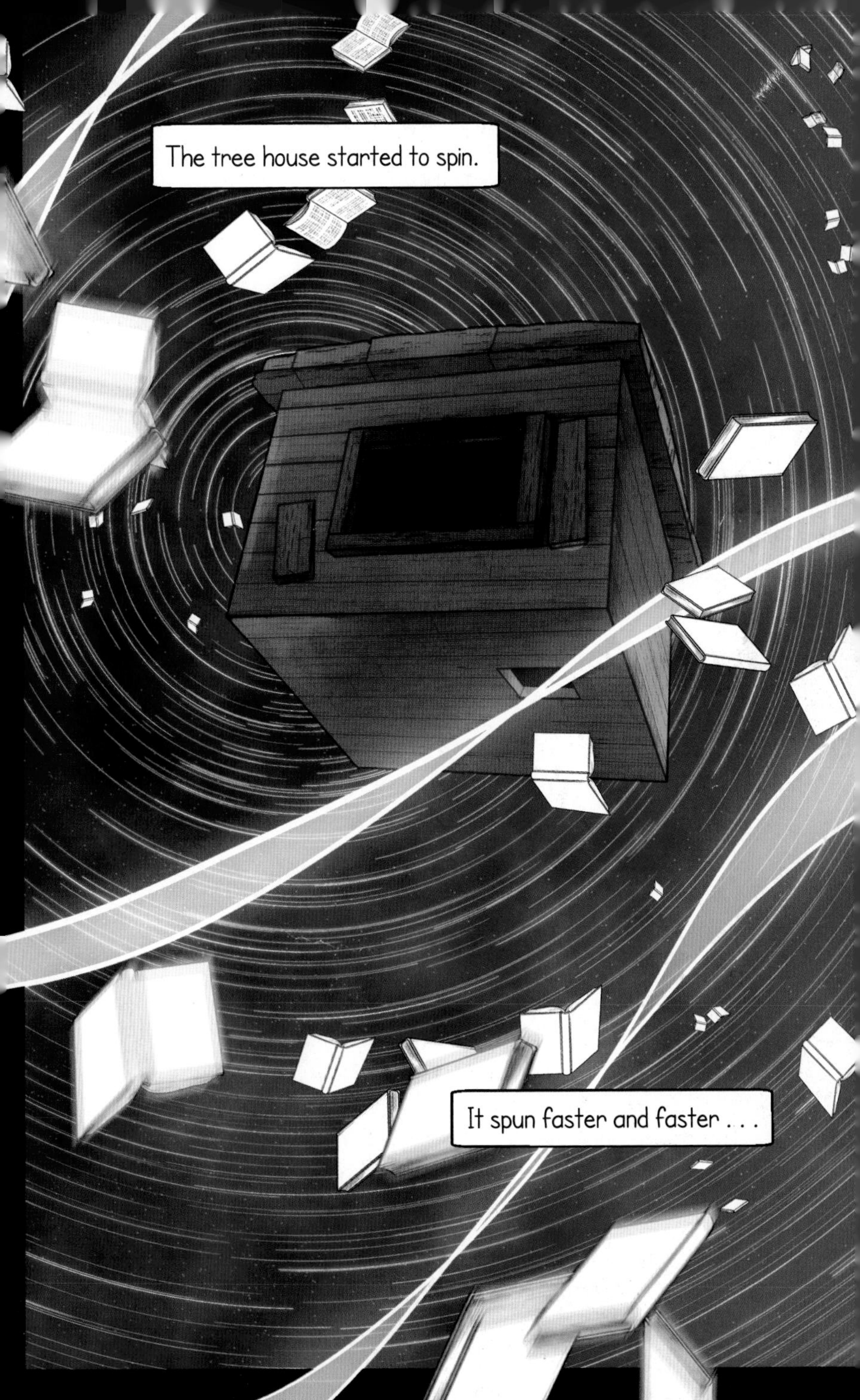
The tree house started to spin.
It spun faster and faster . . .

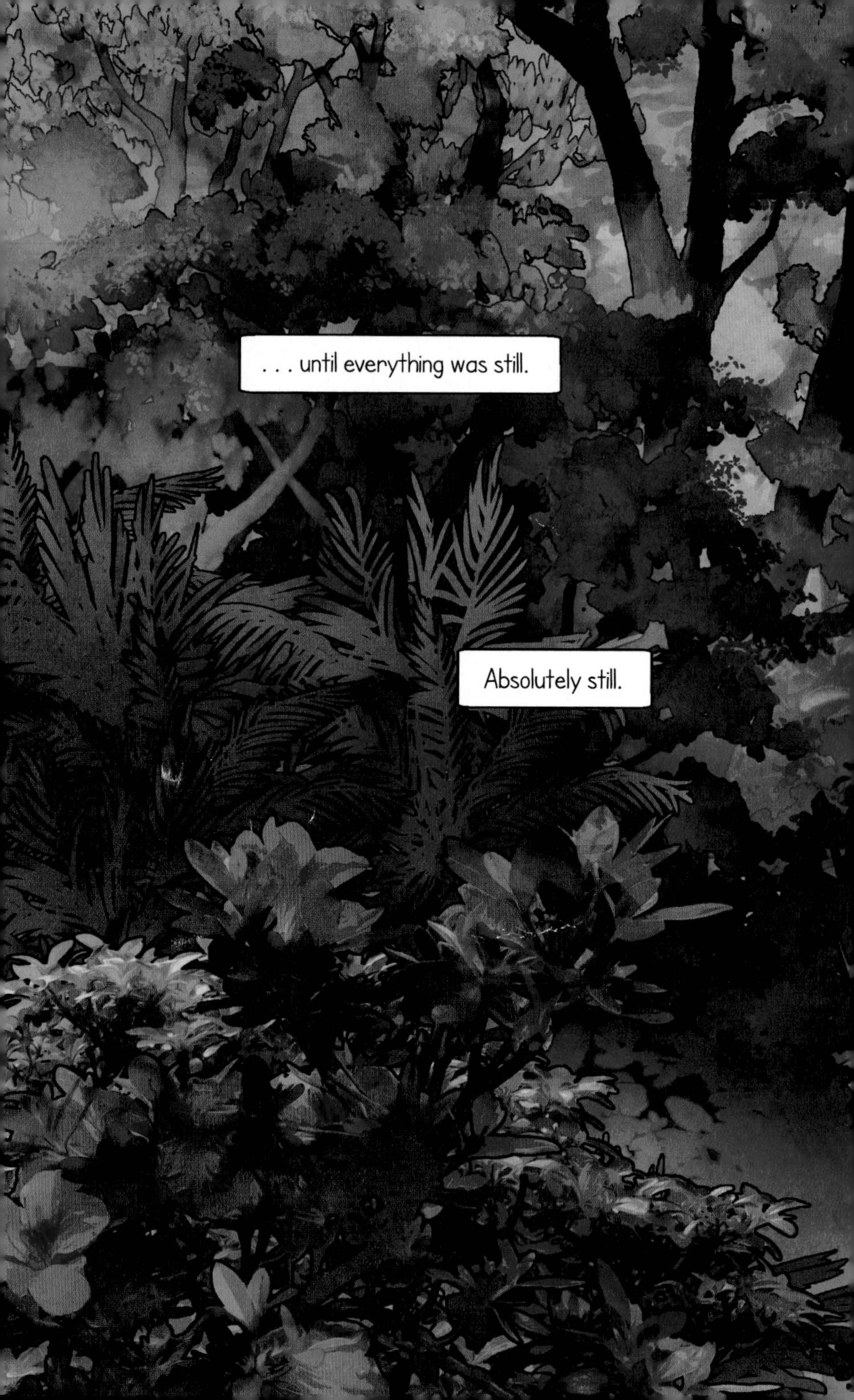
. . . until everything was still.
Absolutely still.

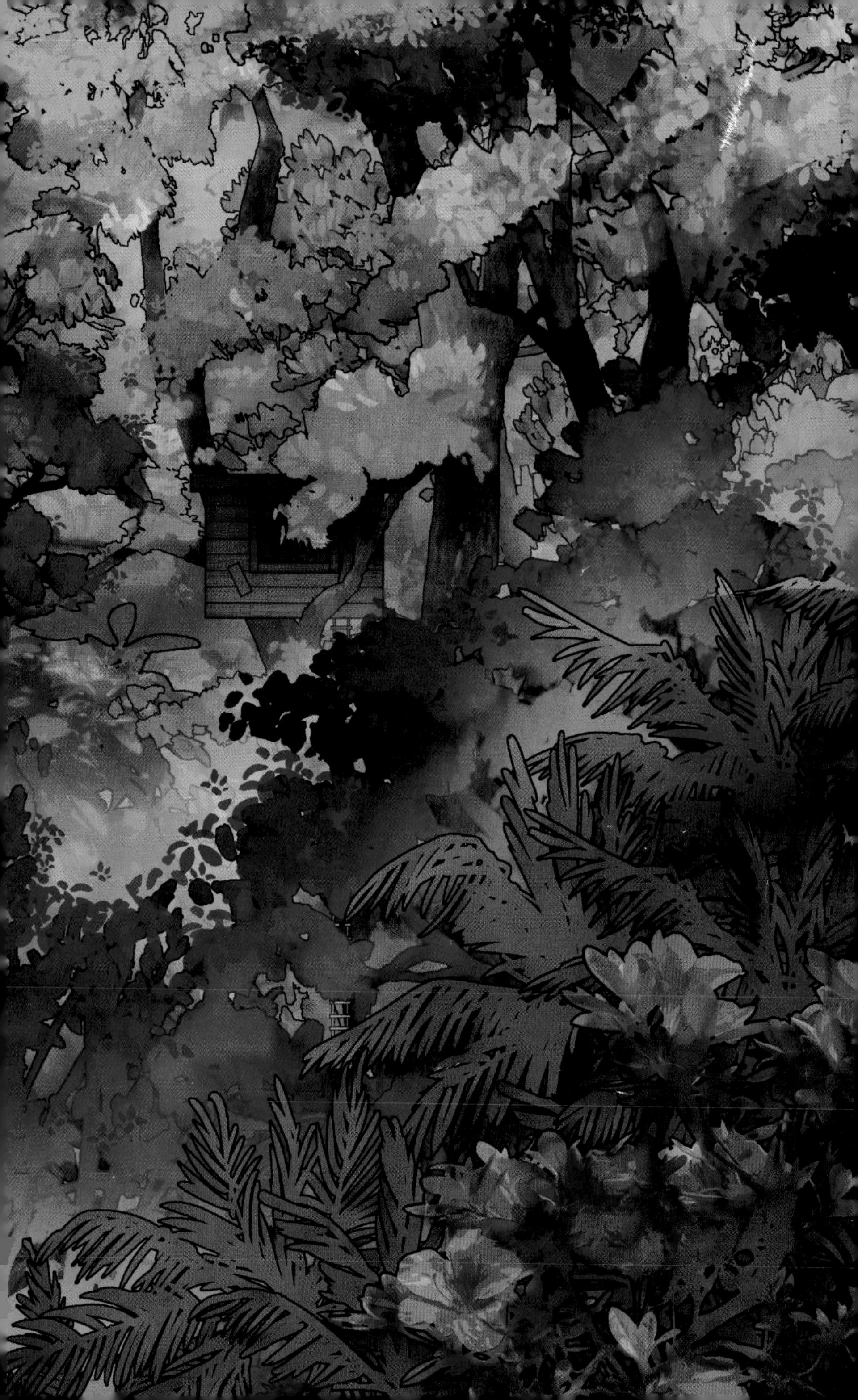

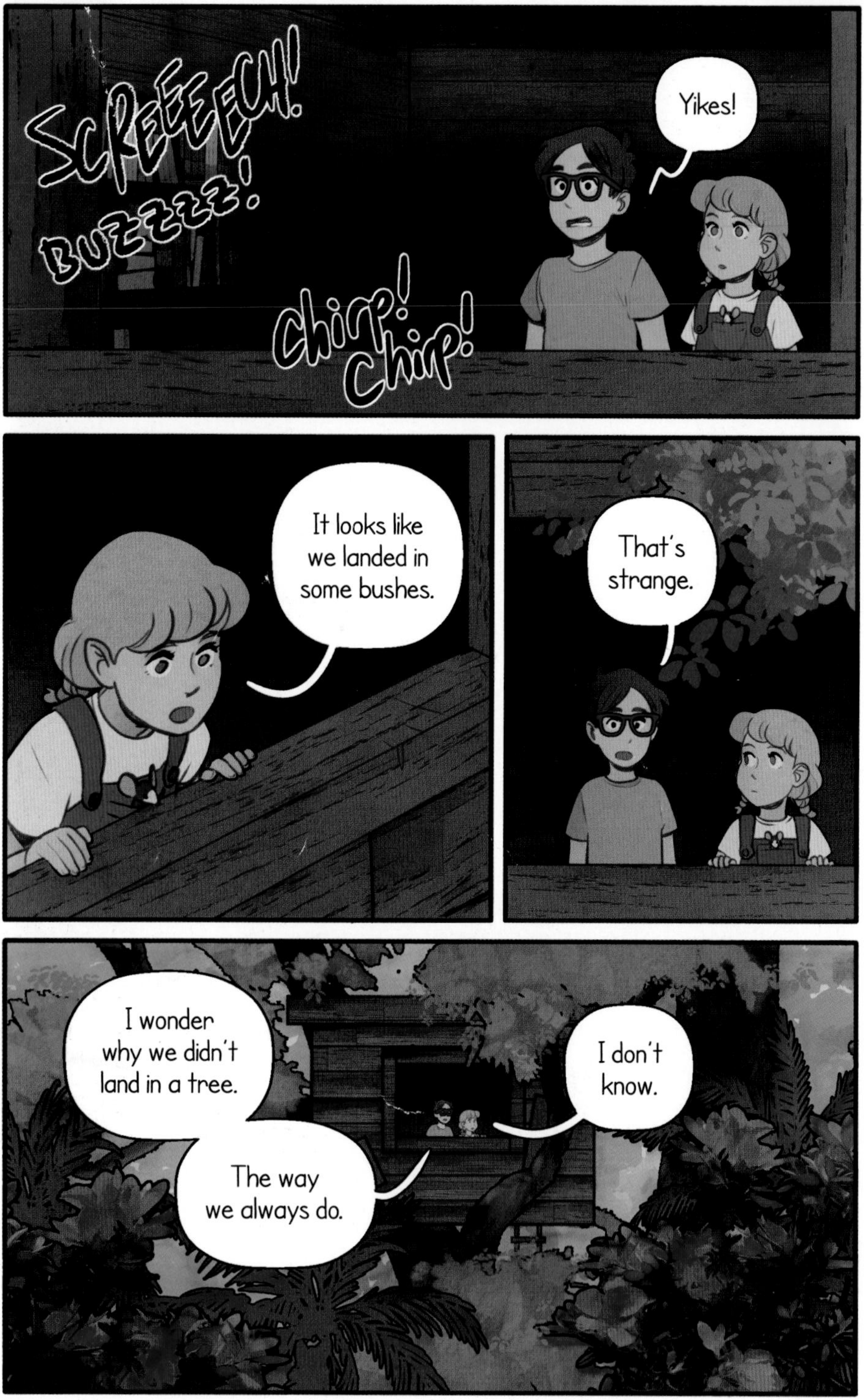
SCREEEECH!
BUZZZZZ!
Chirp! Chirp!
Yikes!
It looks like we landed in some bushes.
That's strange.
I wonder why we didn't land in a tree.
The way we always do.
I don't know.

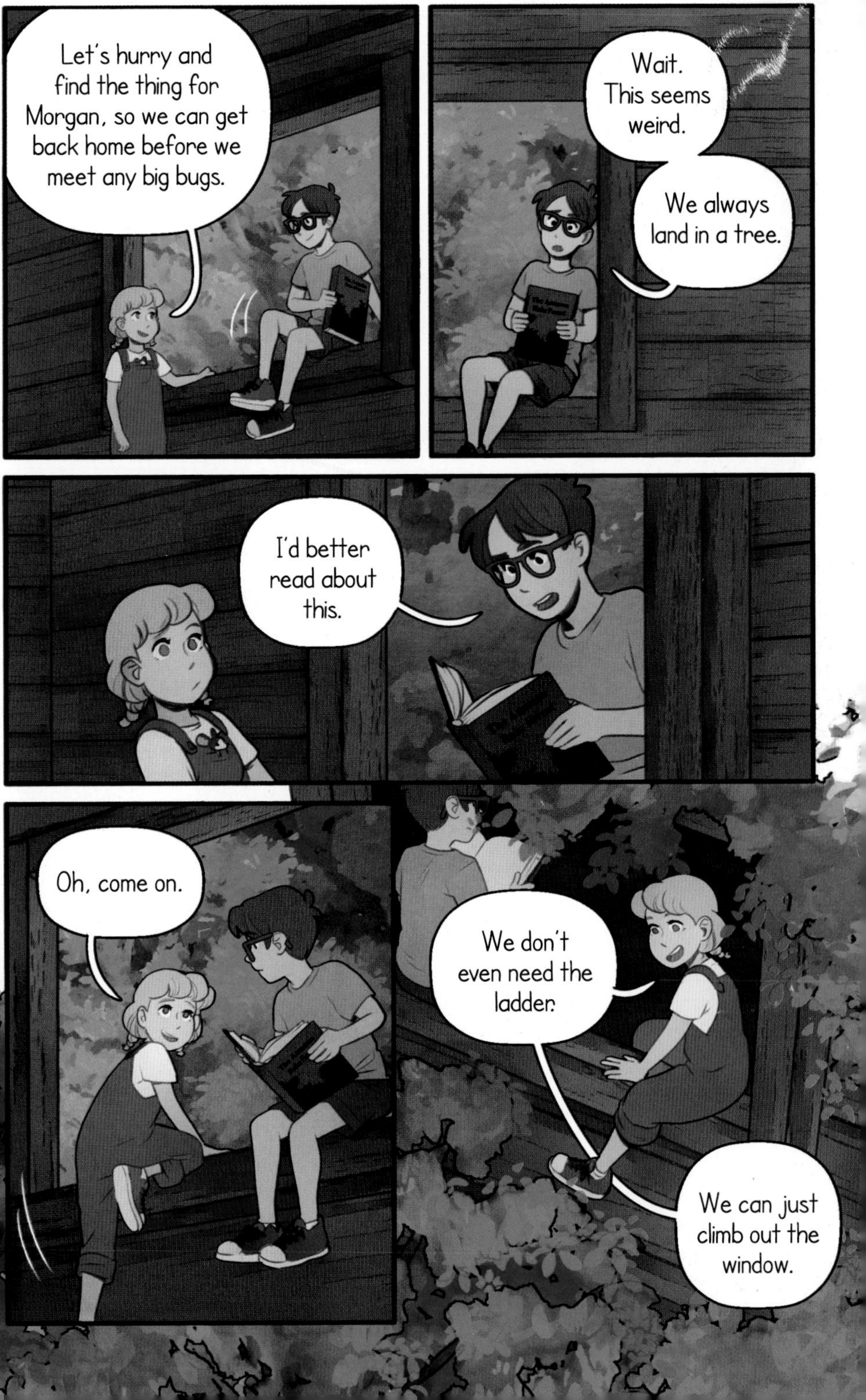
Let's hurry and find the thing for Morgan, so we can get back home before we meet any big bugs.
Wait. This seems weird.
We always land in a tree.
I'd better read about this.
Oh, come on.
We don't even need the ladder.
We can just climb out the window.

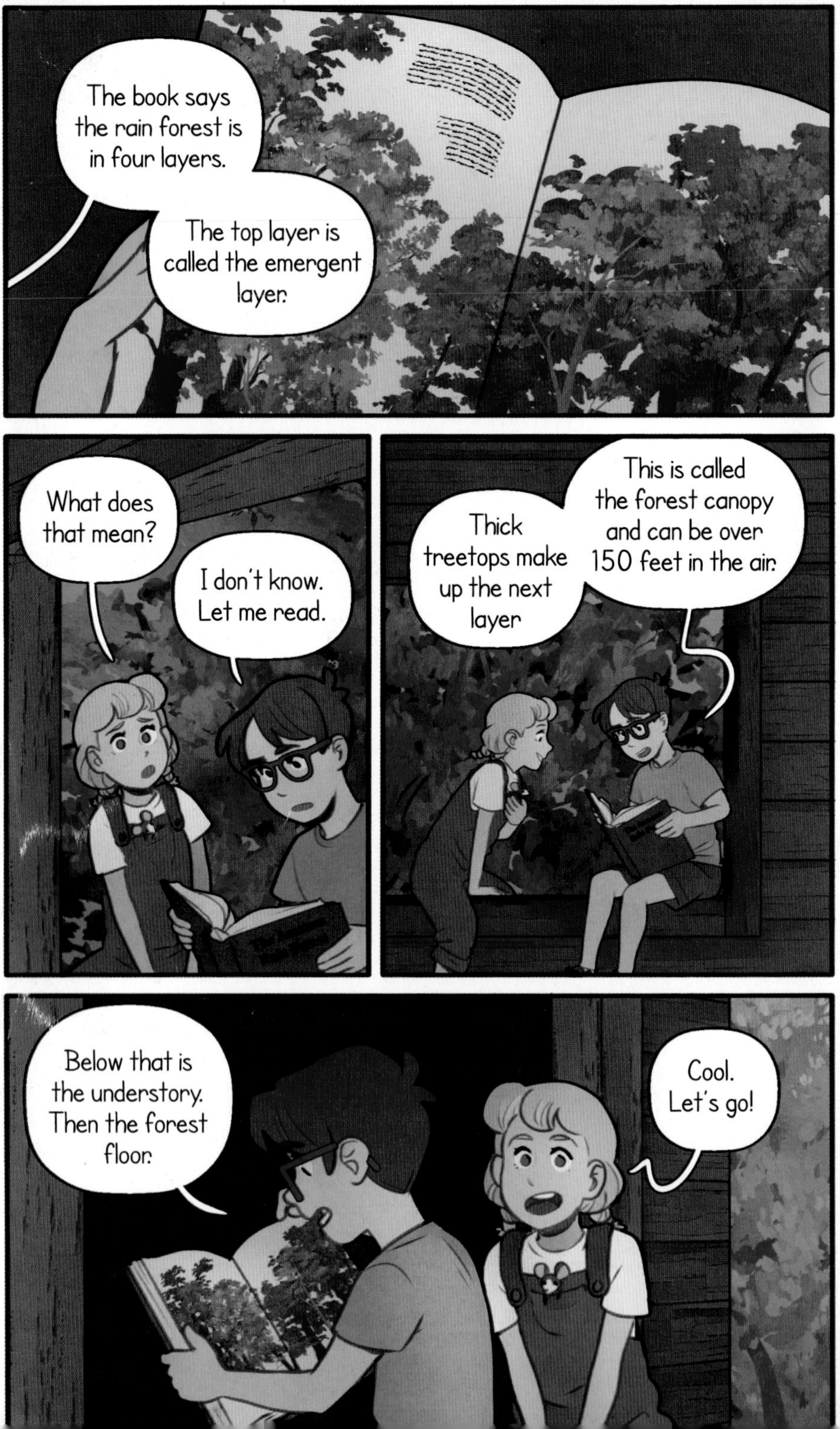

The book says the rain forest is in four layers.
The top layer is called the emergent layer.
What does that mean?
I don't know. Let me read.
Thick treetops make up the next layer
This is called the forest canopy and can be over 150 feet in the air.
Below that is the understory. Then the forest floor.
Cool. Let's go!

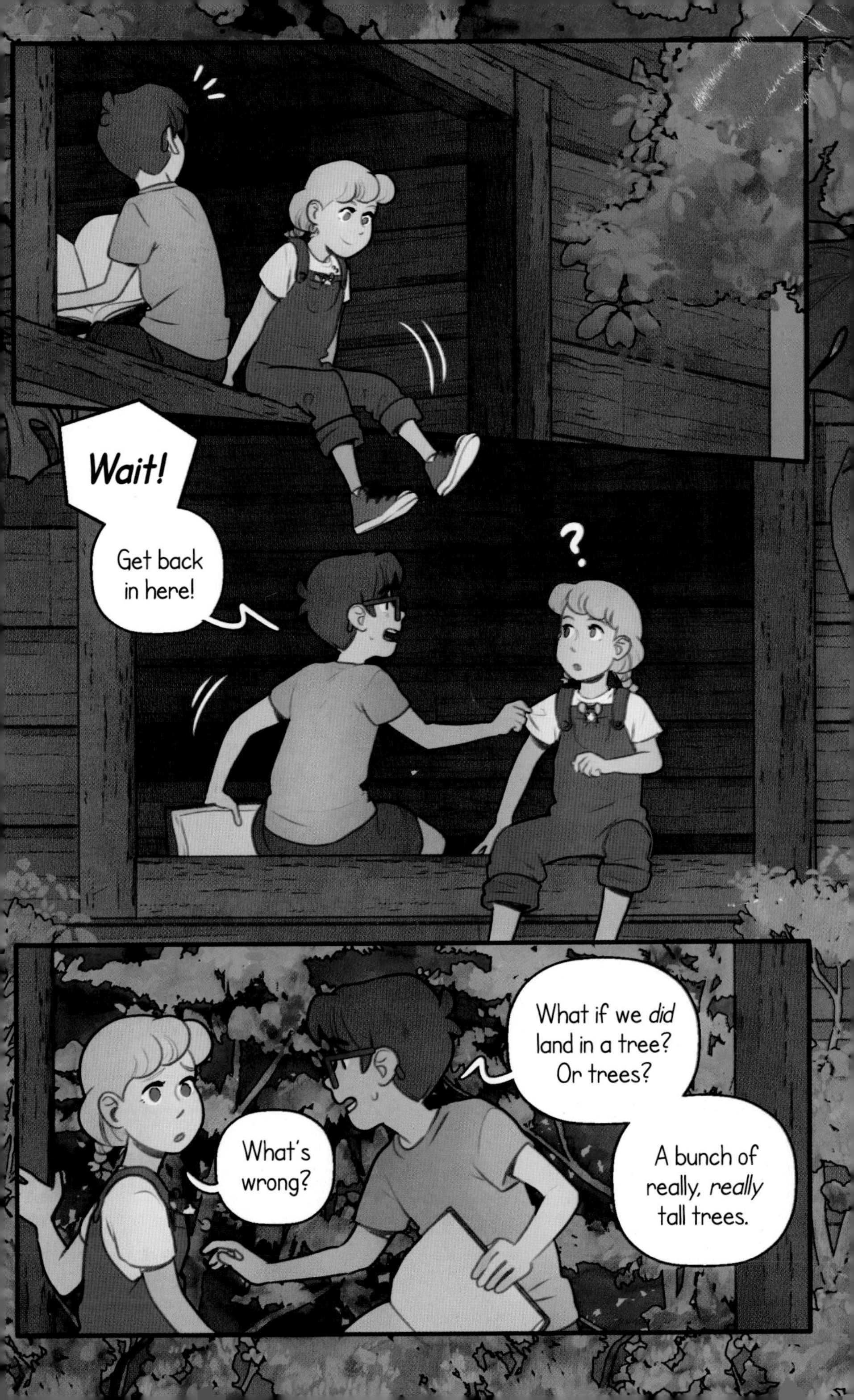
Wait!
Get back in here!
?
What's wrong?
What if we *did* land in a tree? Or trees?
A bunch of really, *really* tall trees.

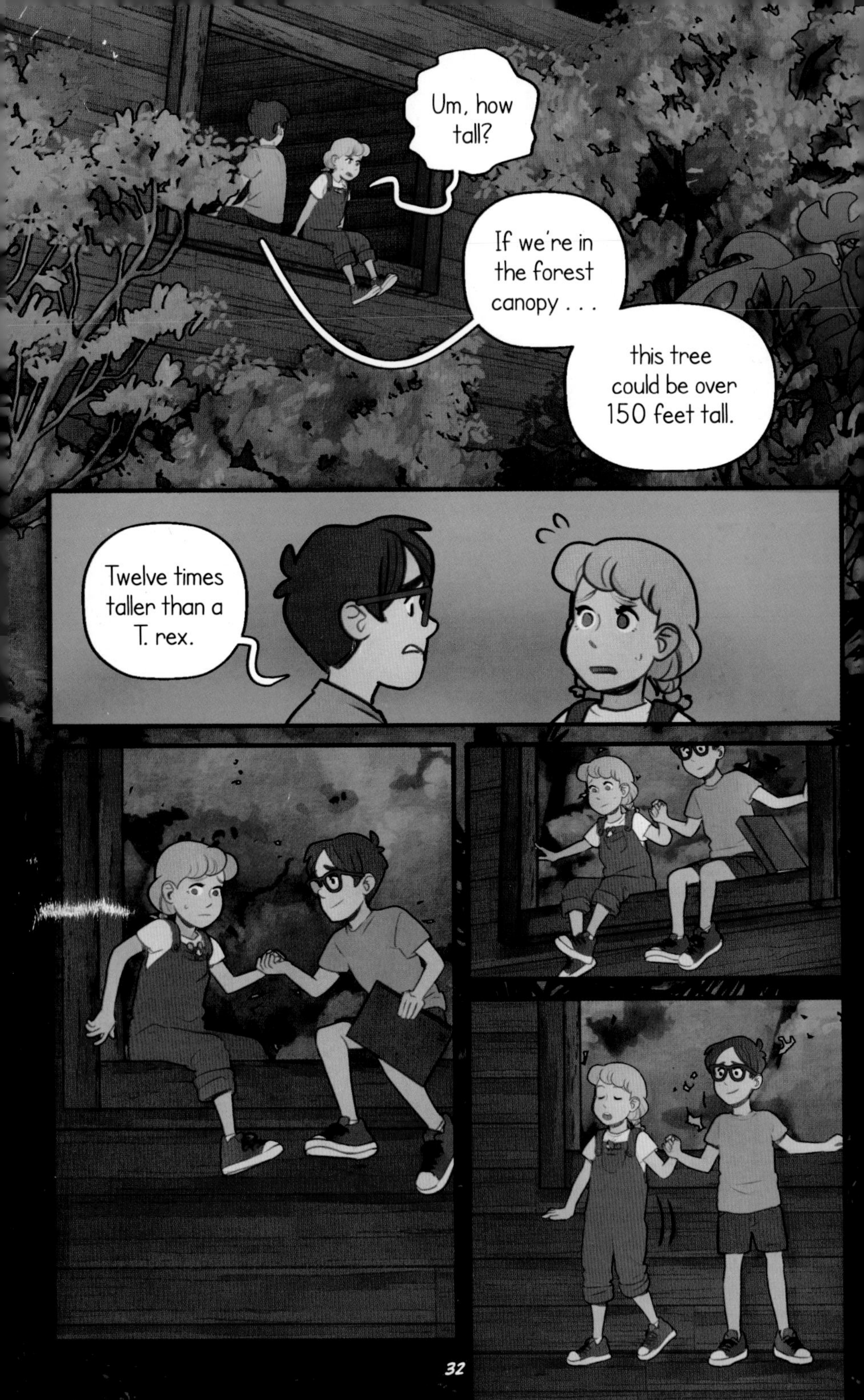
Um, how tall?
If we're in the forest canopy . . .
this tree could be over 150 feet tall.
Twelve times taller than a T. rex.

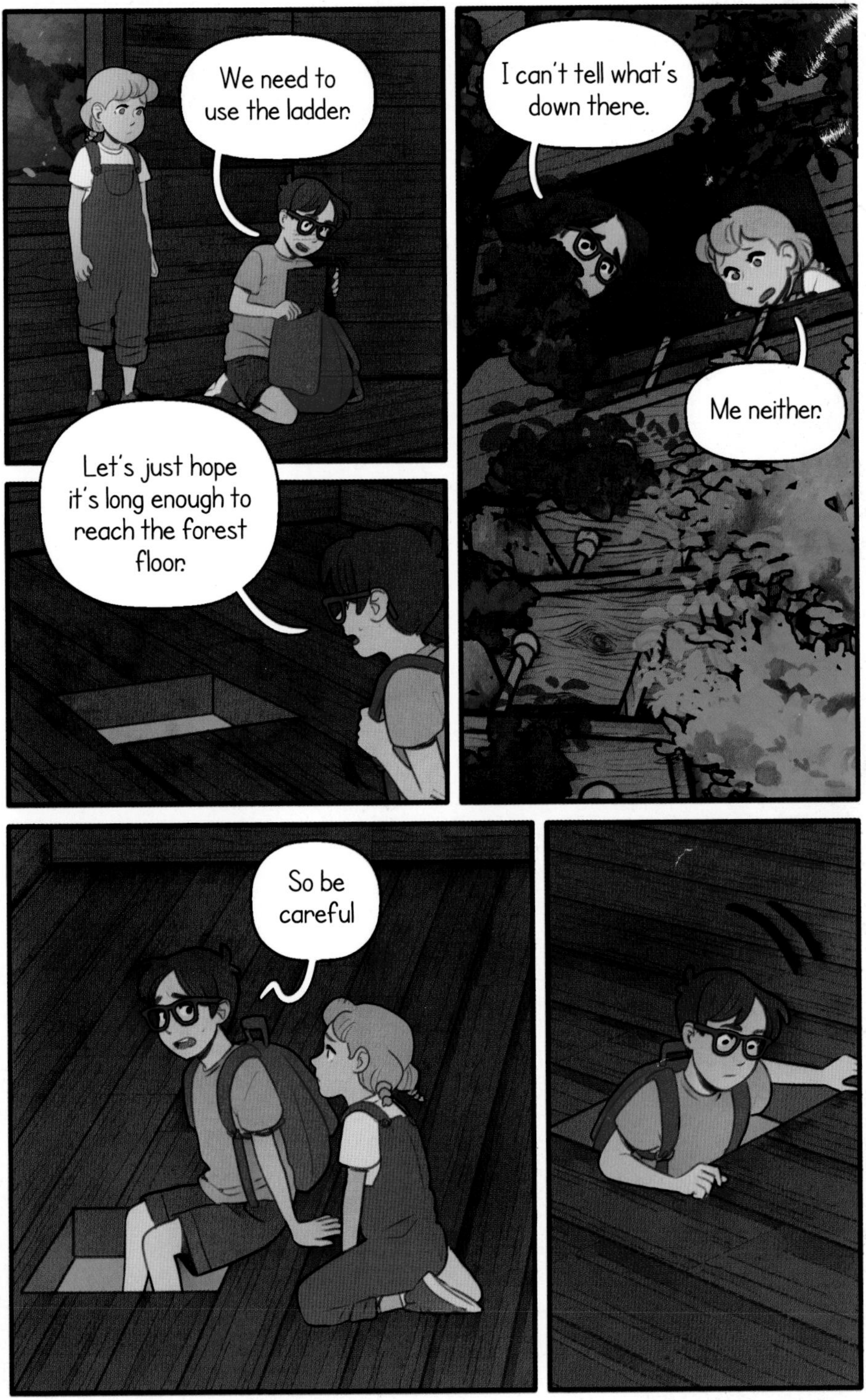
We need to use the ladder.
I can't tell what's down there.
Me neither.
Let's just hope it's long enough to reach the forest floor.
So be careful

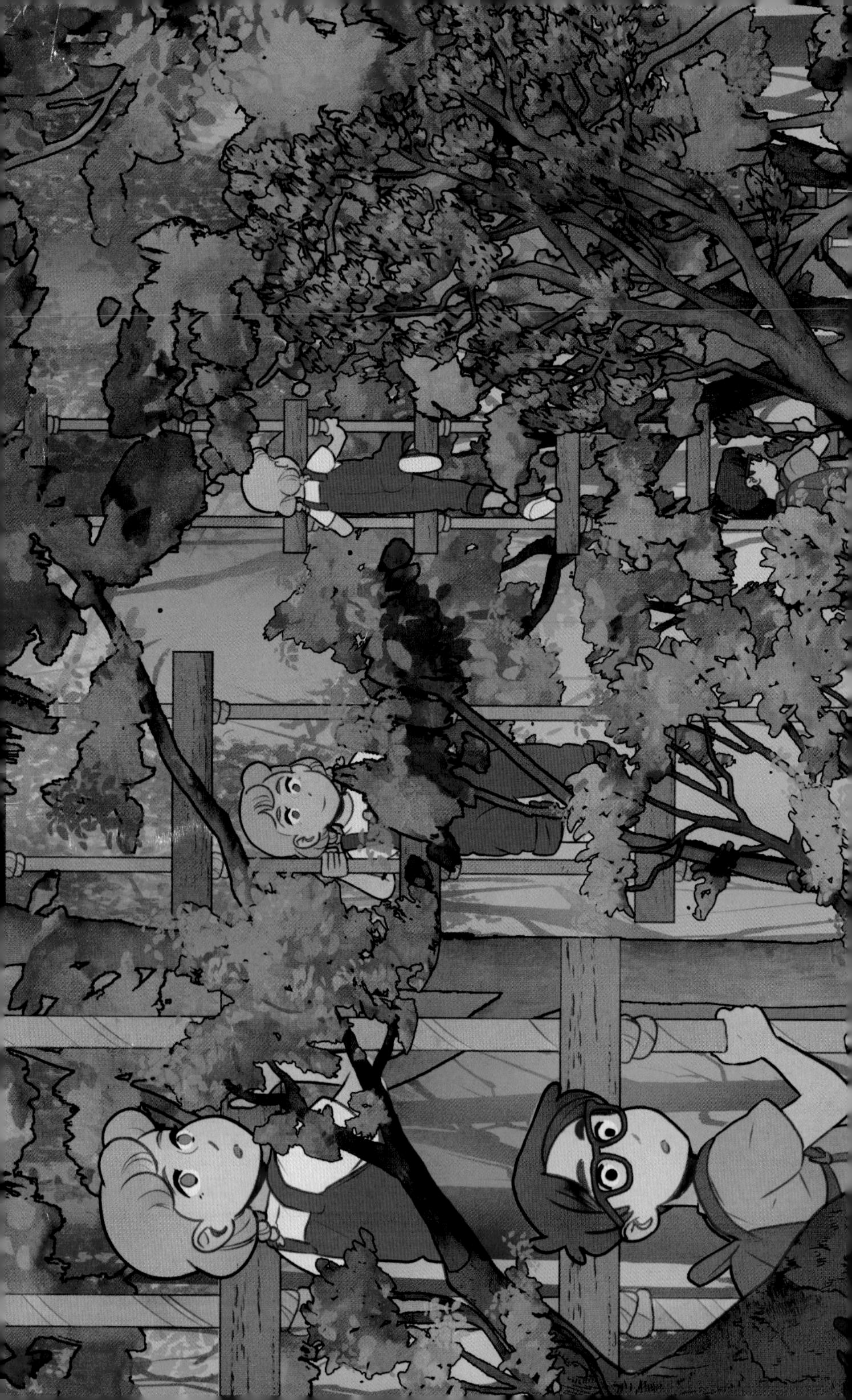

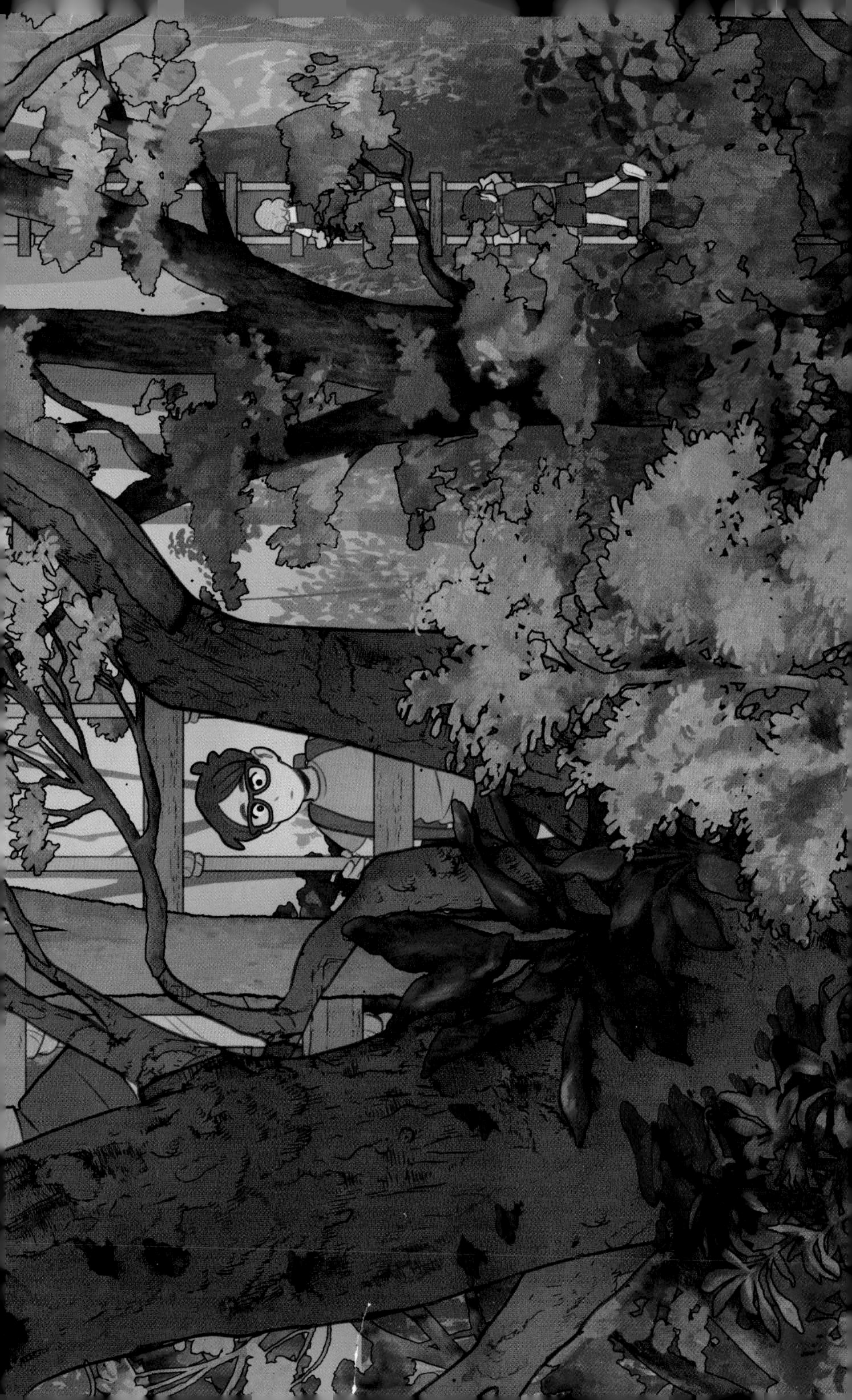

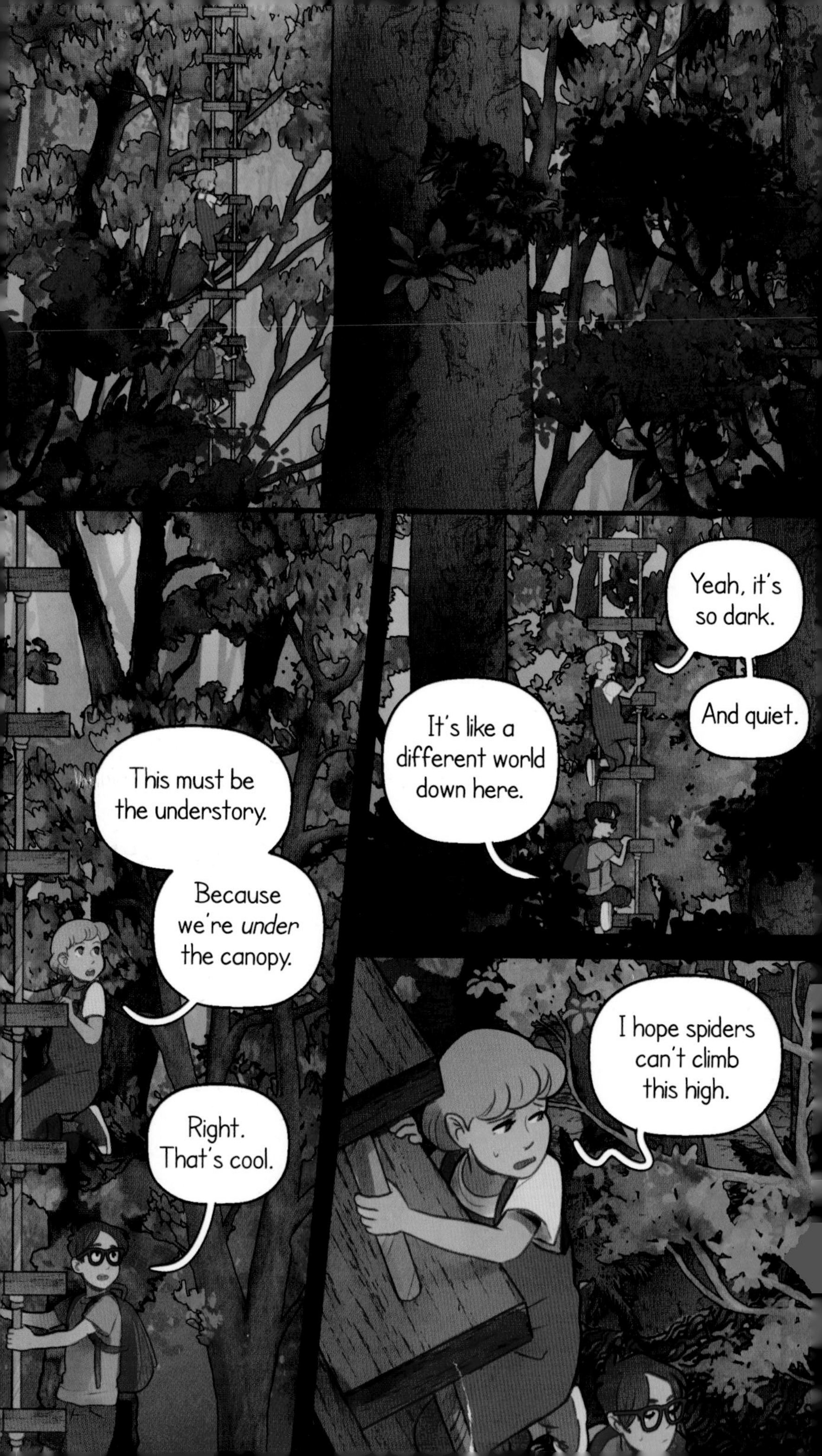
This must be the understory.
Because we're *under* the canopy.
Right. That's cool.
It's like a different world down here.
Yeah, it's so dark.
And quiet.
I hope spiders can't climb this high.

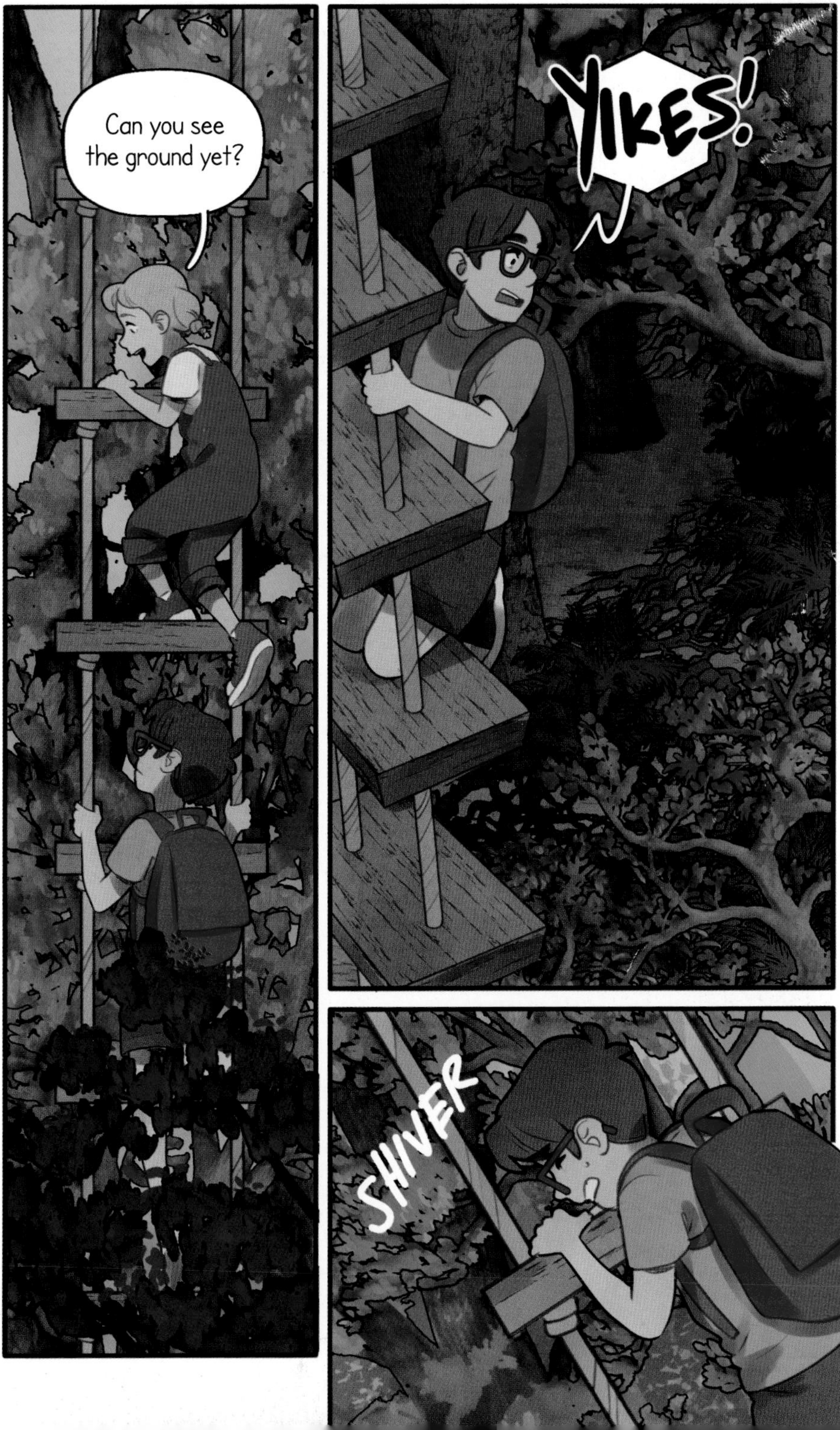
Can you see the ground yet?
YIKES!
SHIVER

CHAPTER THREE
Millions of Them!

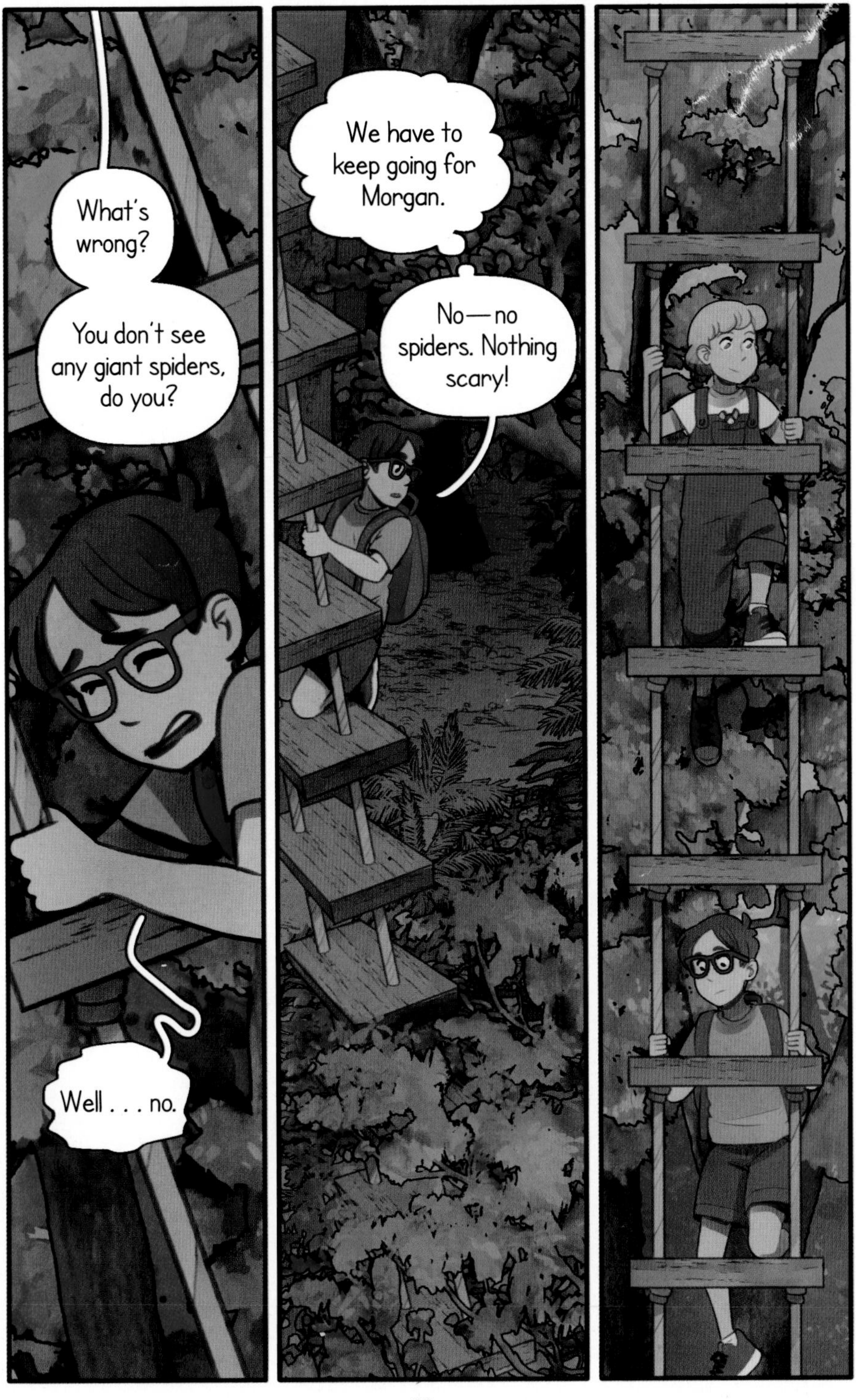
What's wrong?
You don't see any giant spiders, do you?
Well . . . no.
We have to keep going for Morgan.
No—no spiders. Nothing scary!

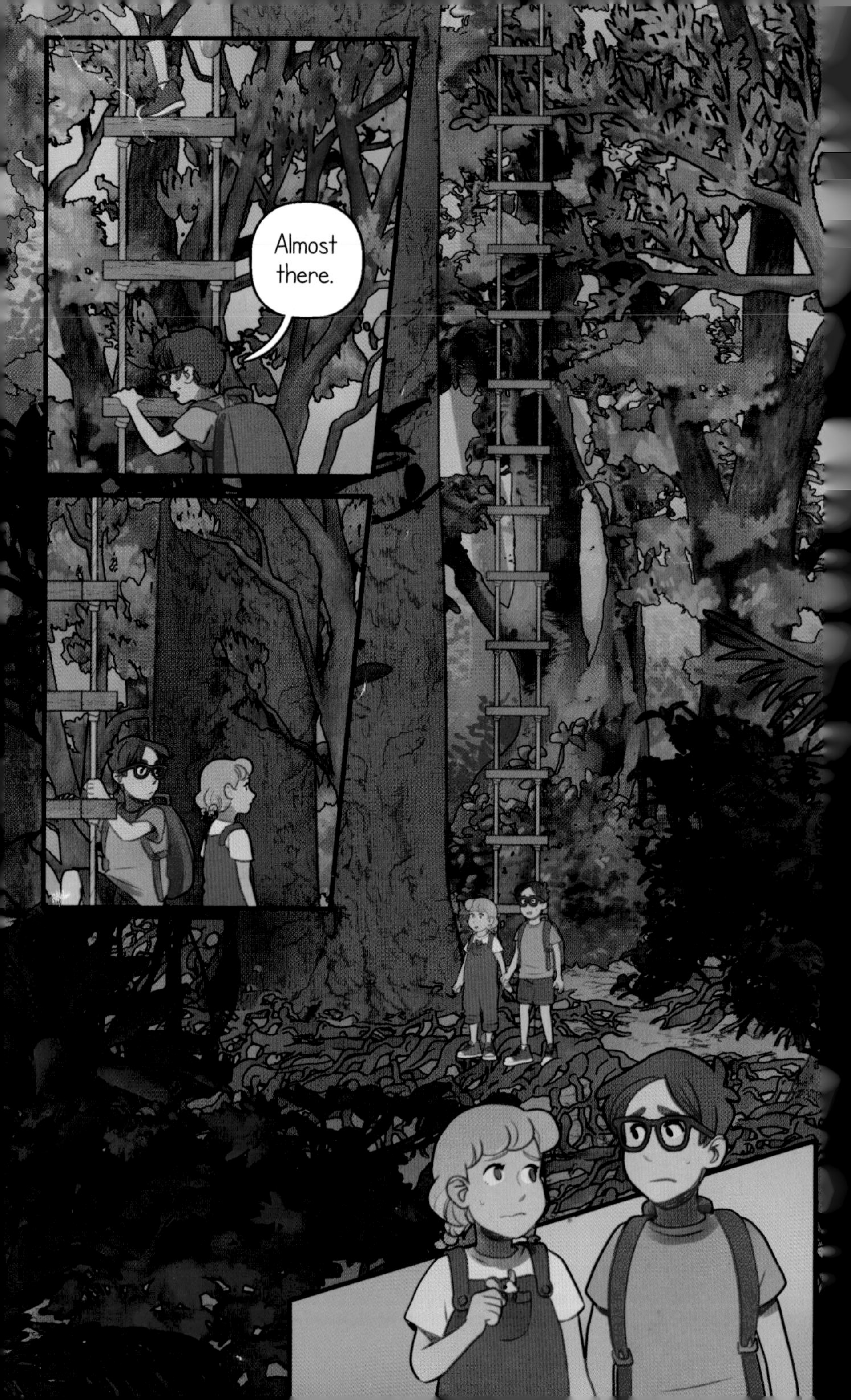
Almost there.

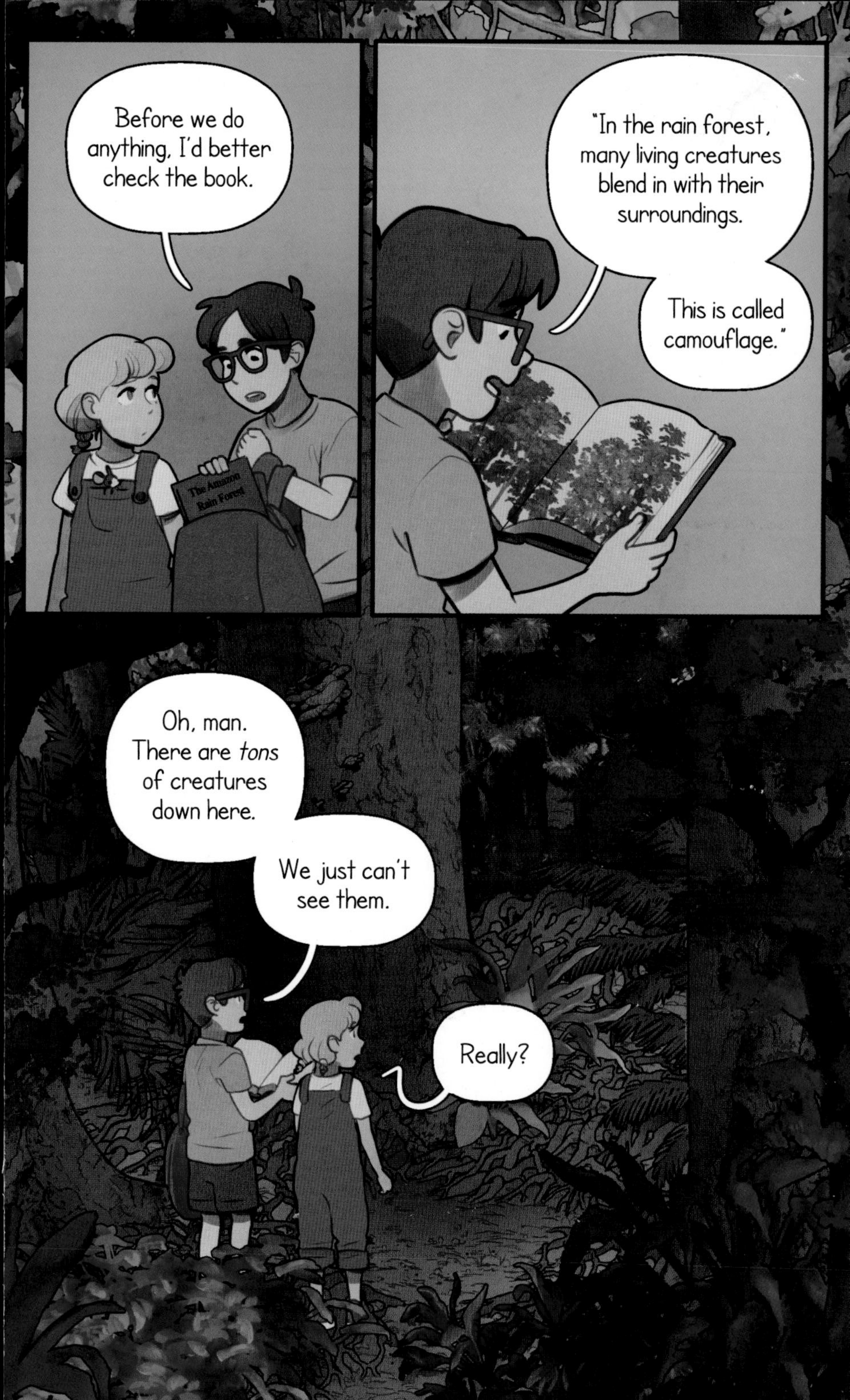
Before we do anything, I'd better check the book.
The Amazon Rain Forest
"In the rain forest, many living creatures blend in with their surroundings.
This is called camouflage."
Oh, man. There are *tons* of creatures down here.
We just can't see them.
Really?

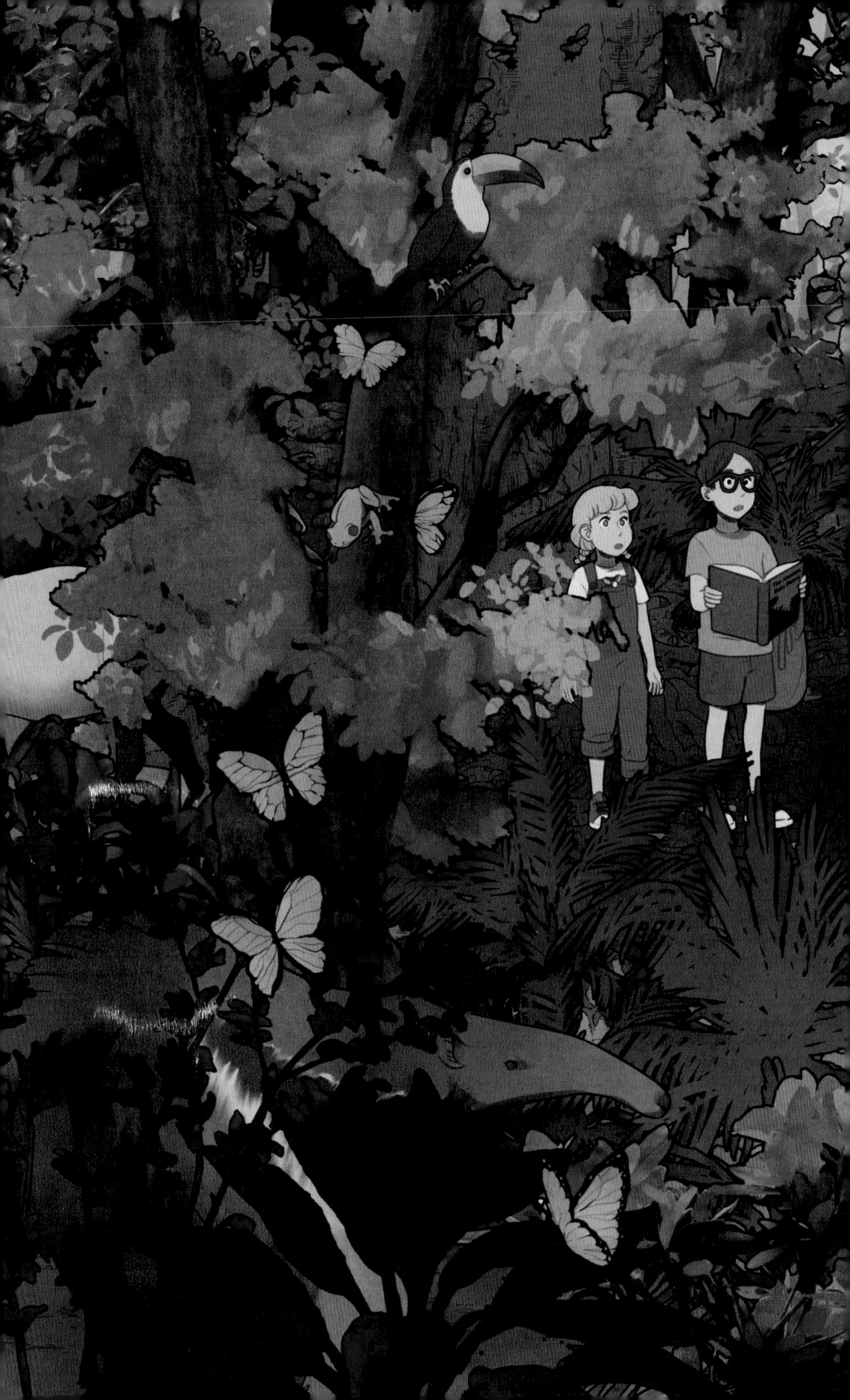

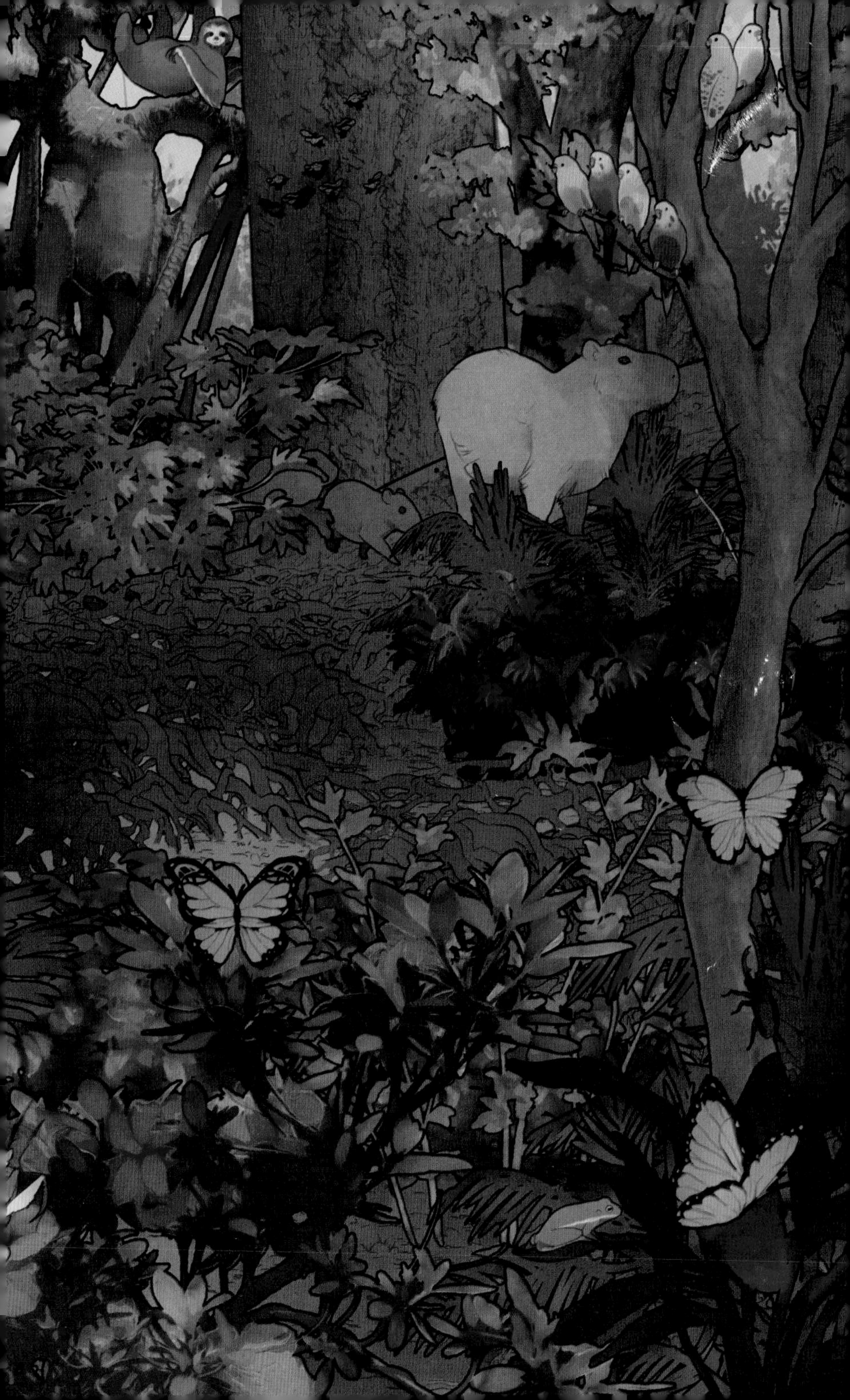

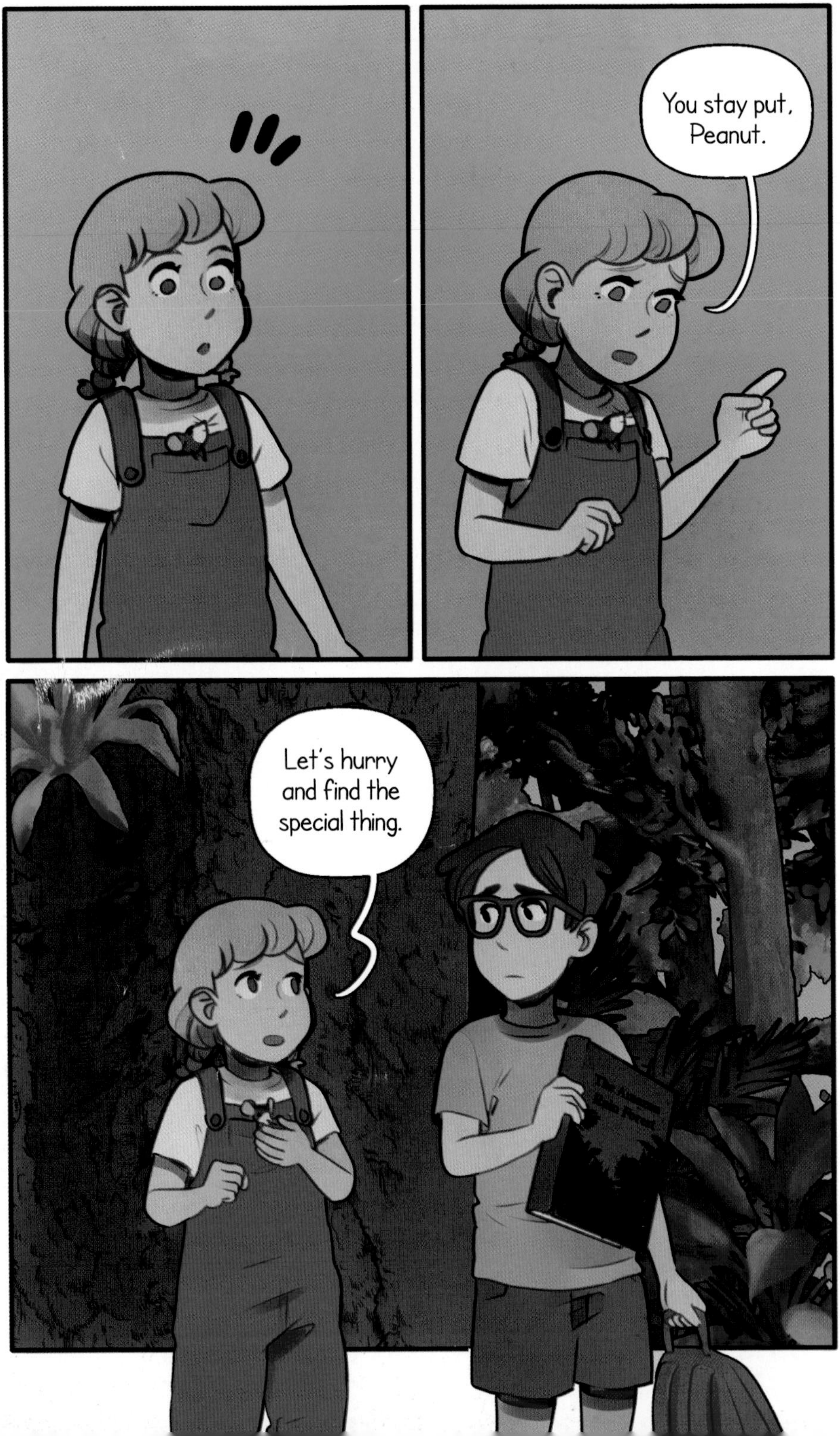
You stay put, Peanut.
Let's hurry and find the special thing.

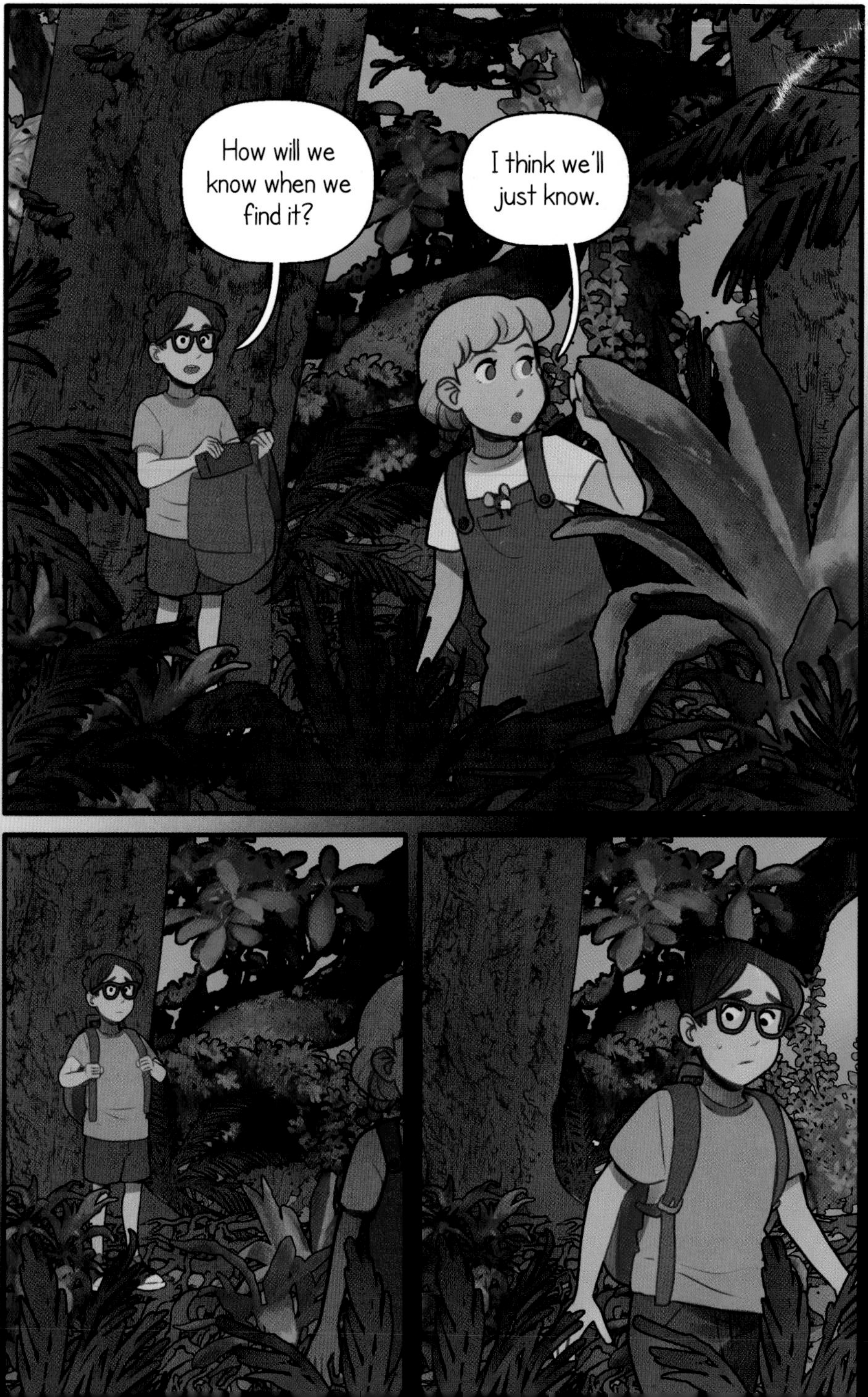
How will we know when we find it?
I think we'll just know.

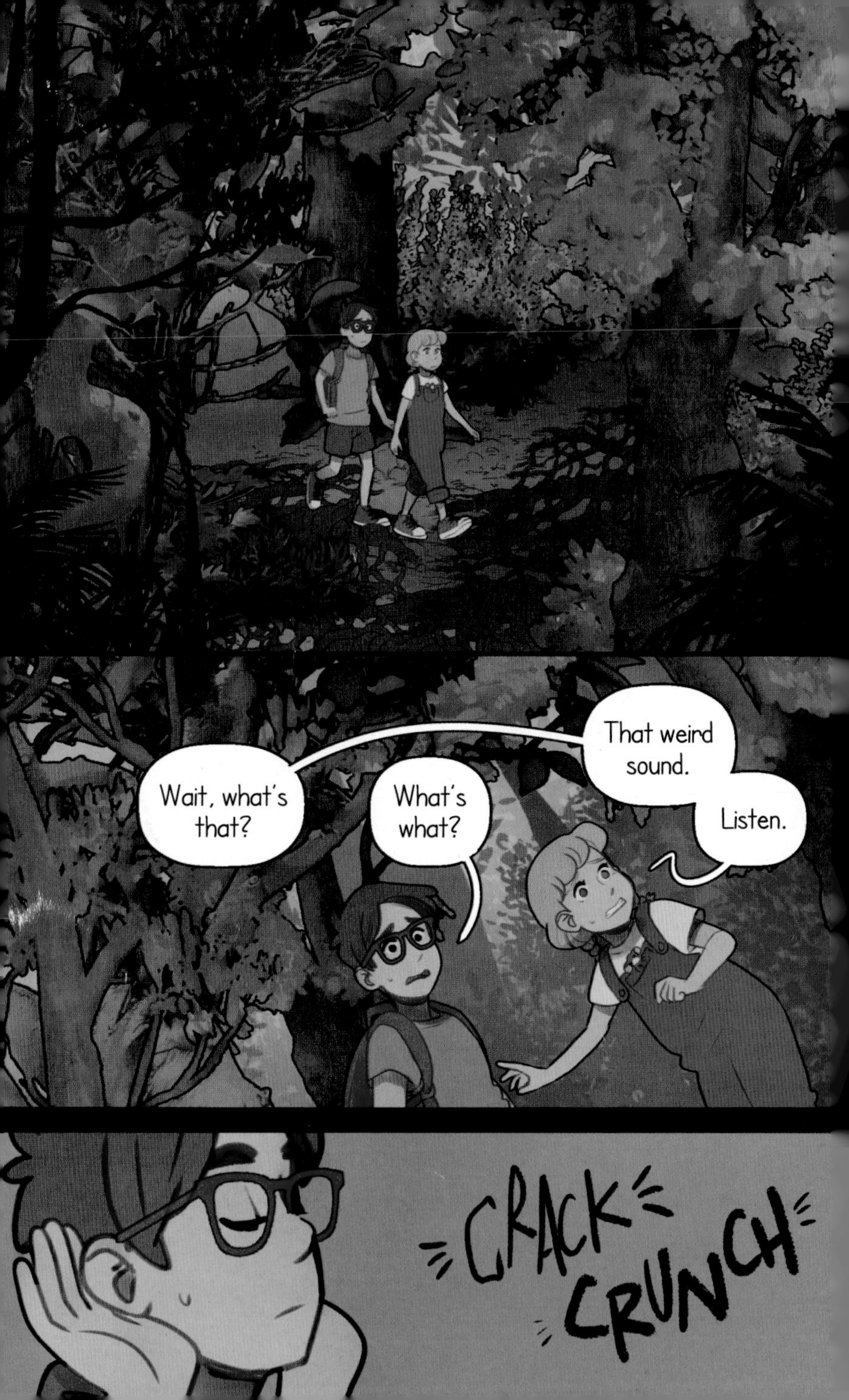
Wait, what's that?
What's what?
That weird sound.
Listen.
CRACK
CRUNCH

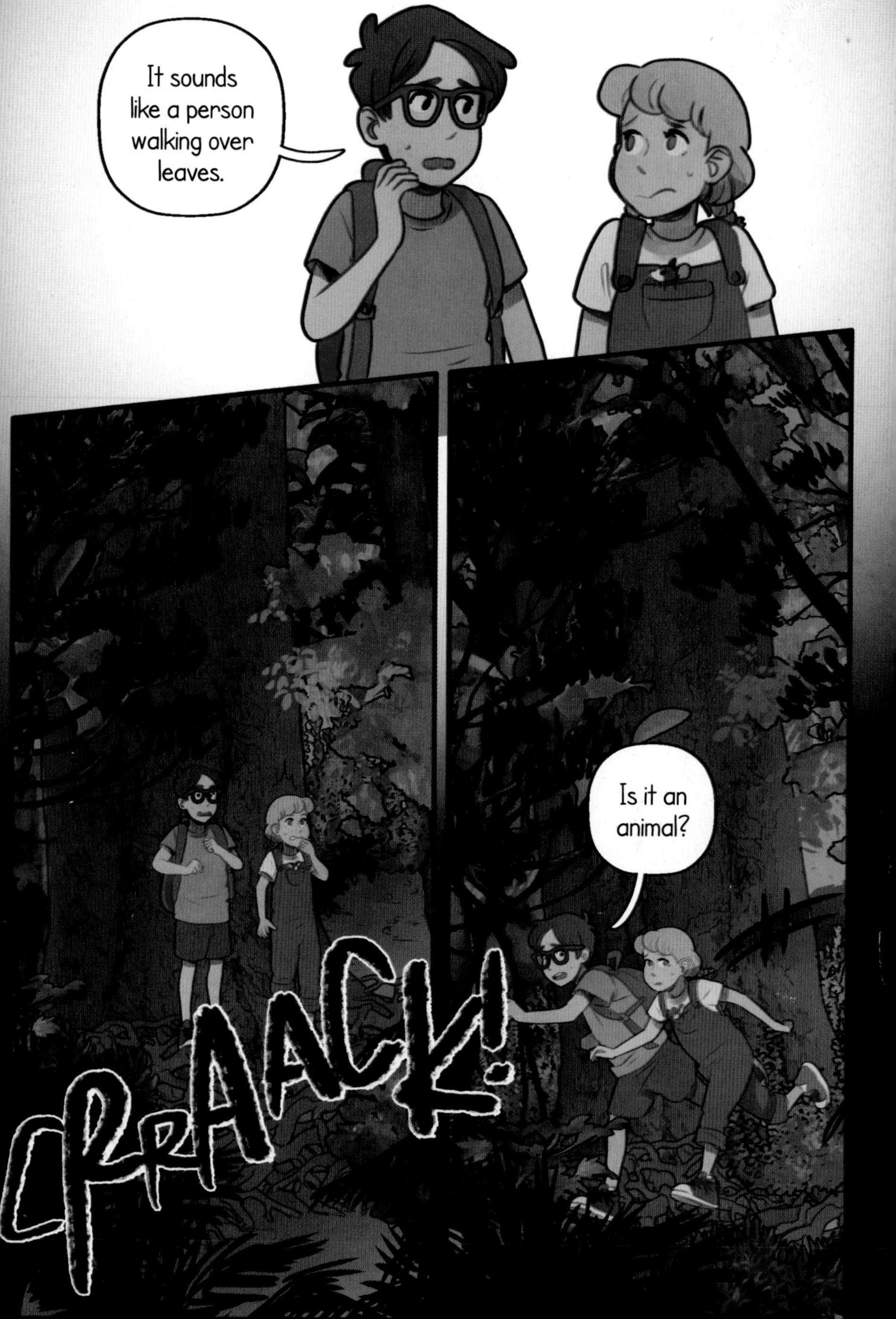
It sounds like a person walking over leaves.
Is it an animal?
CRRAACK!

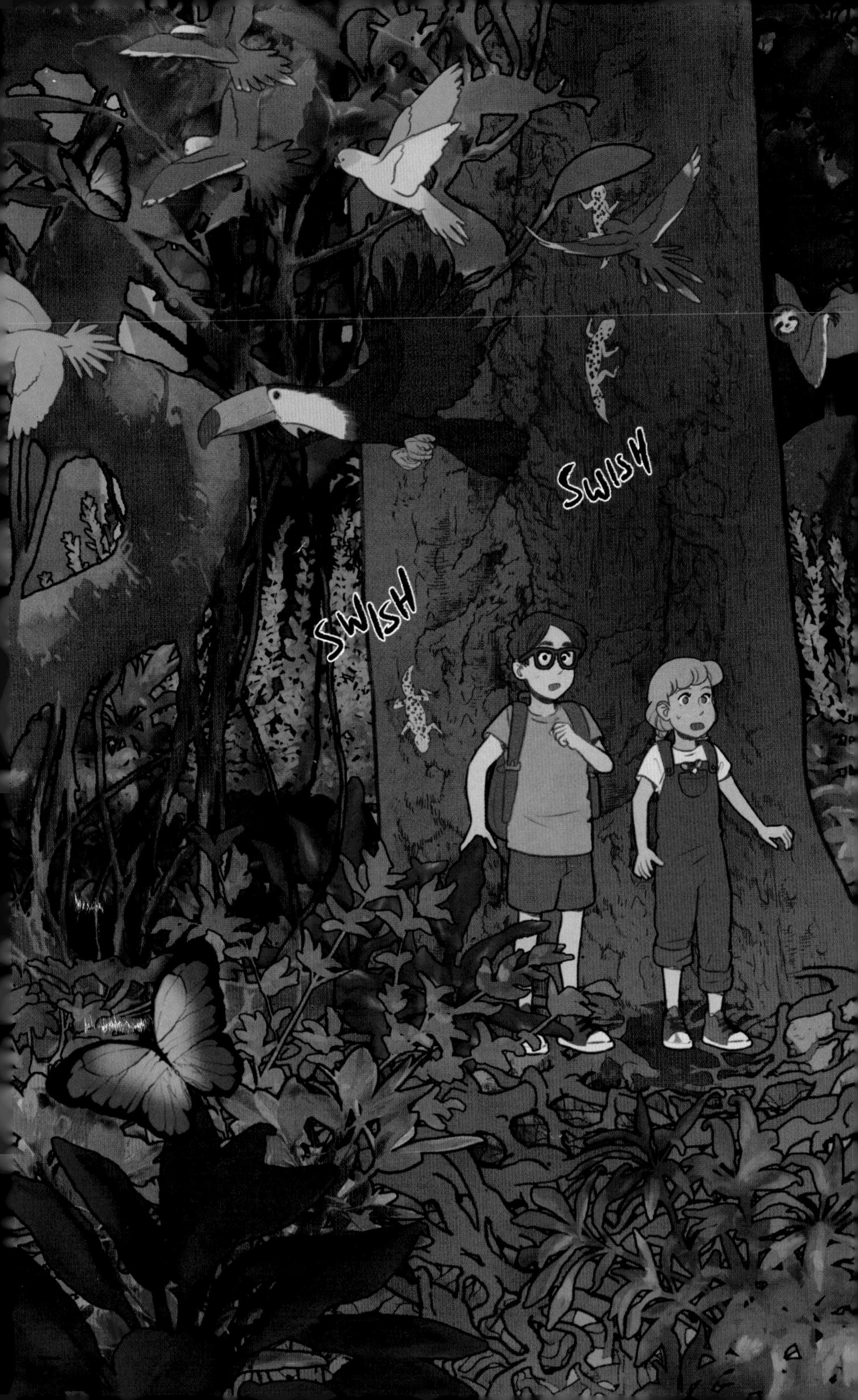
SWISH
SWISH

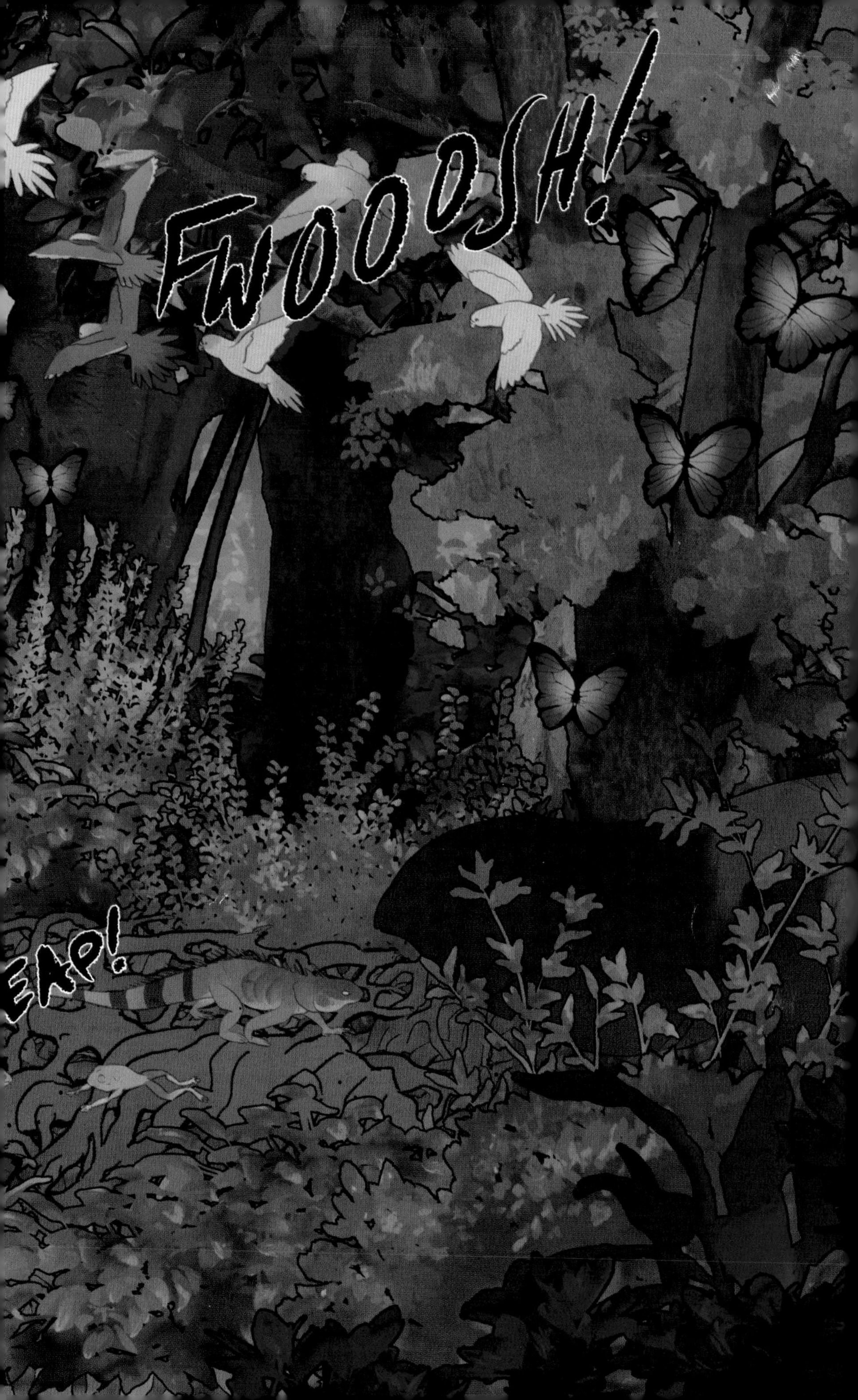
FWOOOSH!
EAP!

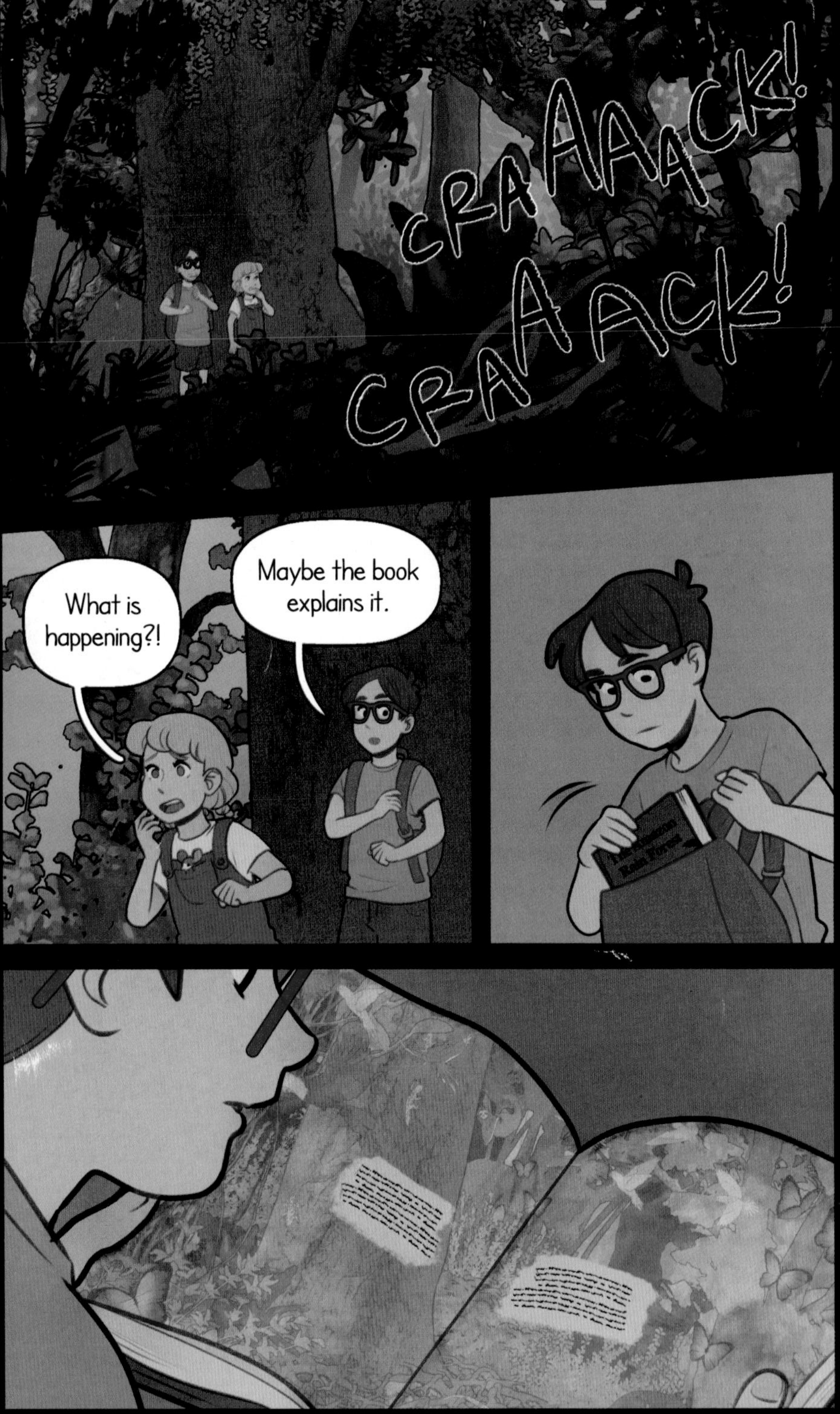
CRAAAACK!
CRAAACK!
What is happening?!
Maybe the book explains it.

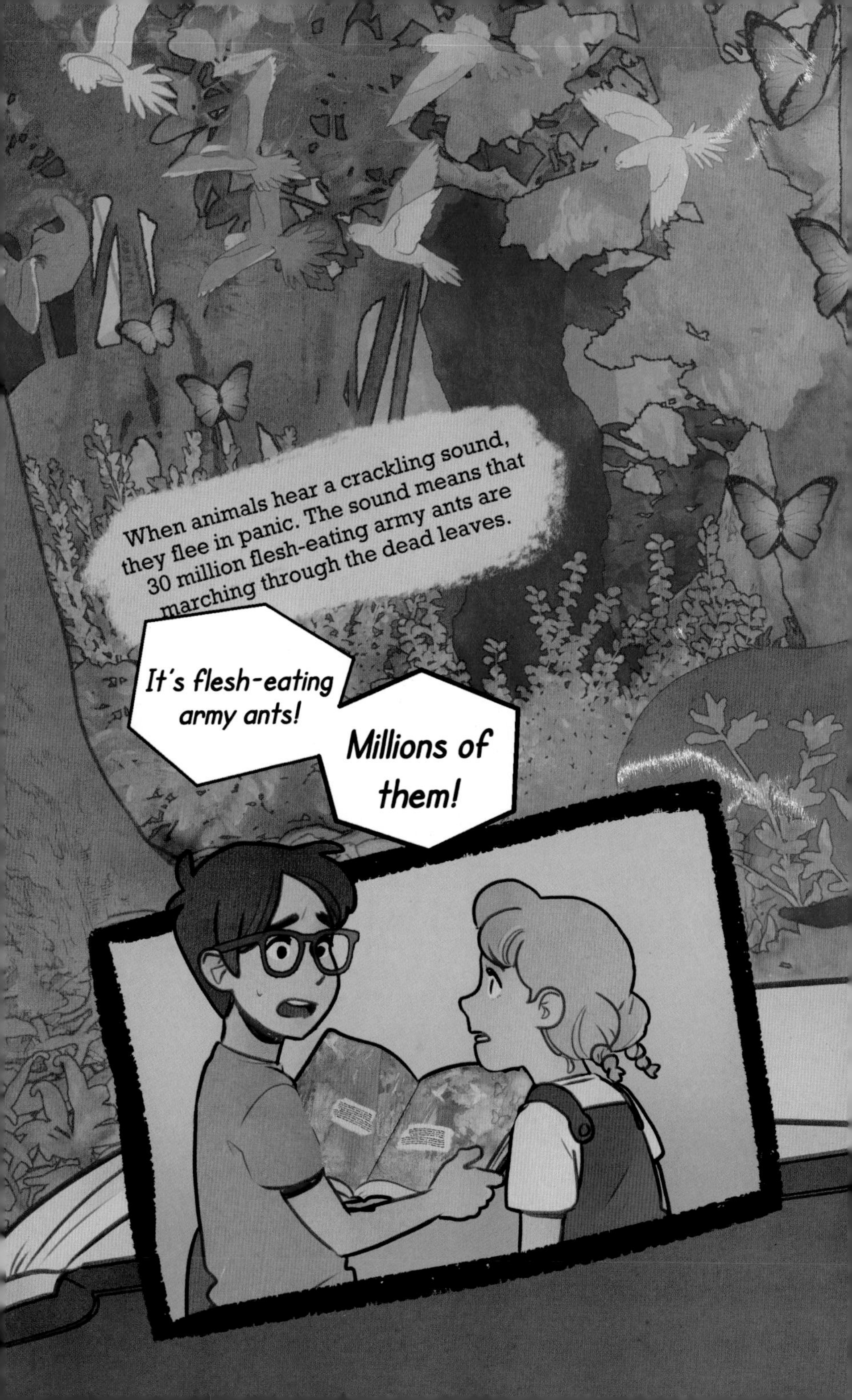
When animals hear a crackling sound, they flee in panic. The sound means that 30 million flesh-eating army ants are marching through the dead leaves.
It's flesh-eating army ants!
Millions of them!

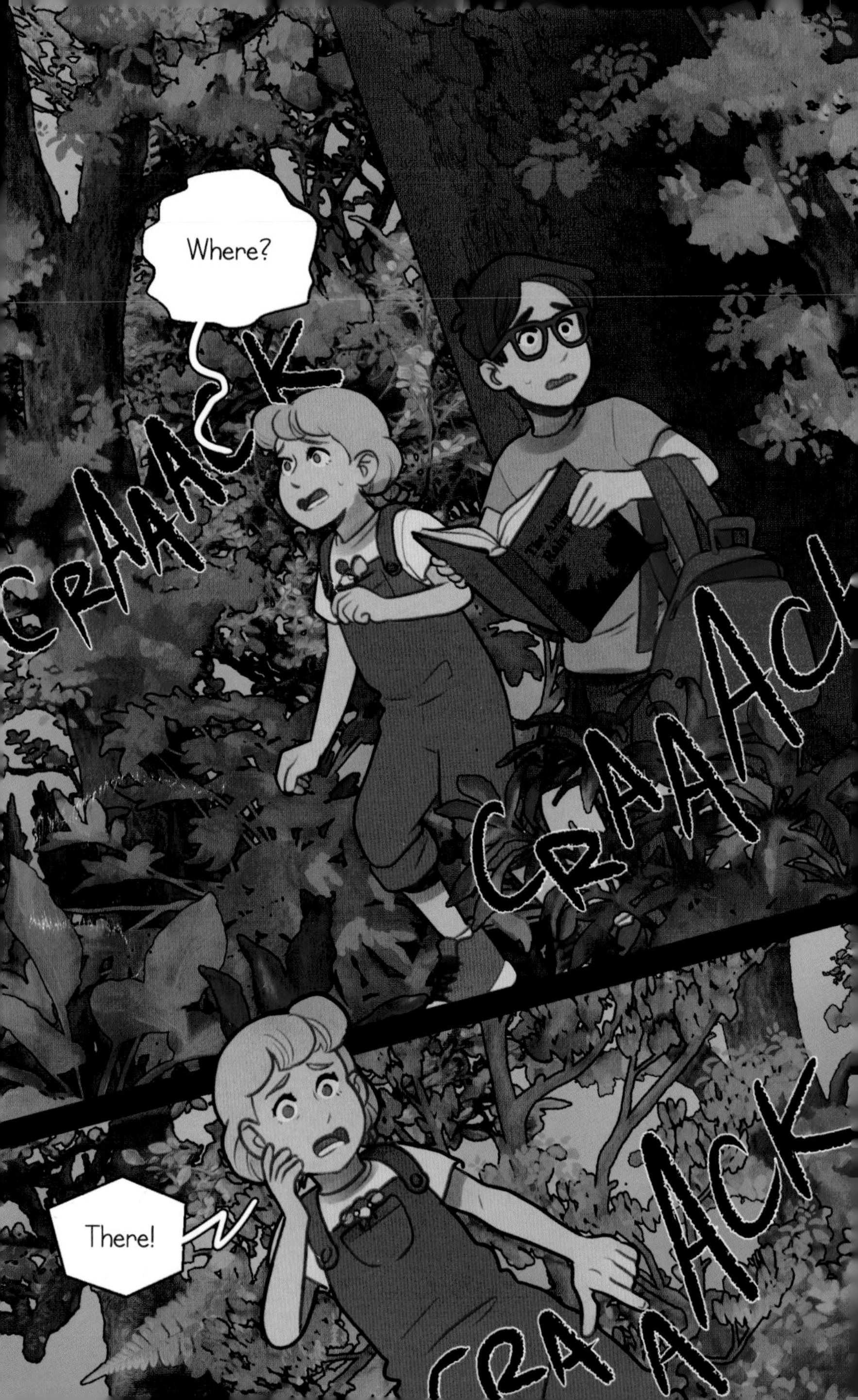
Where?
CRAAACK
CRAAAC
There!
CRAAACK

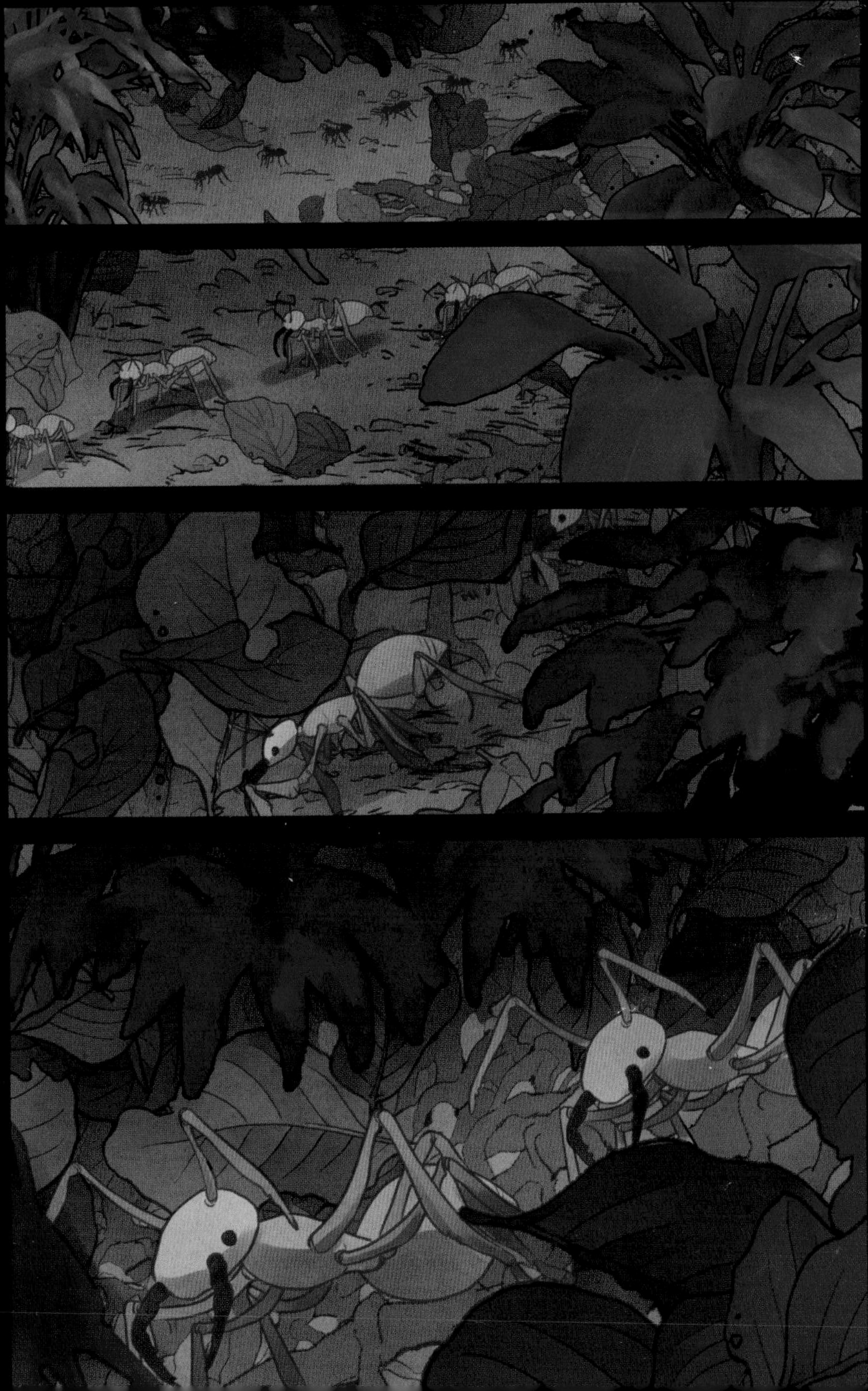

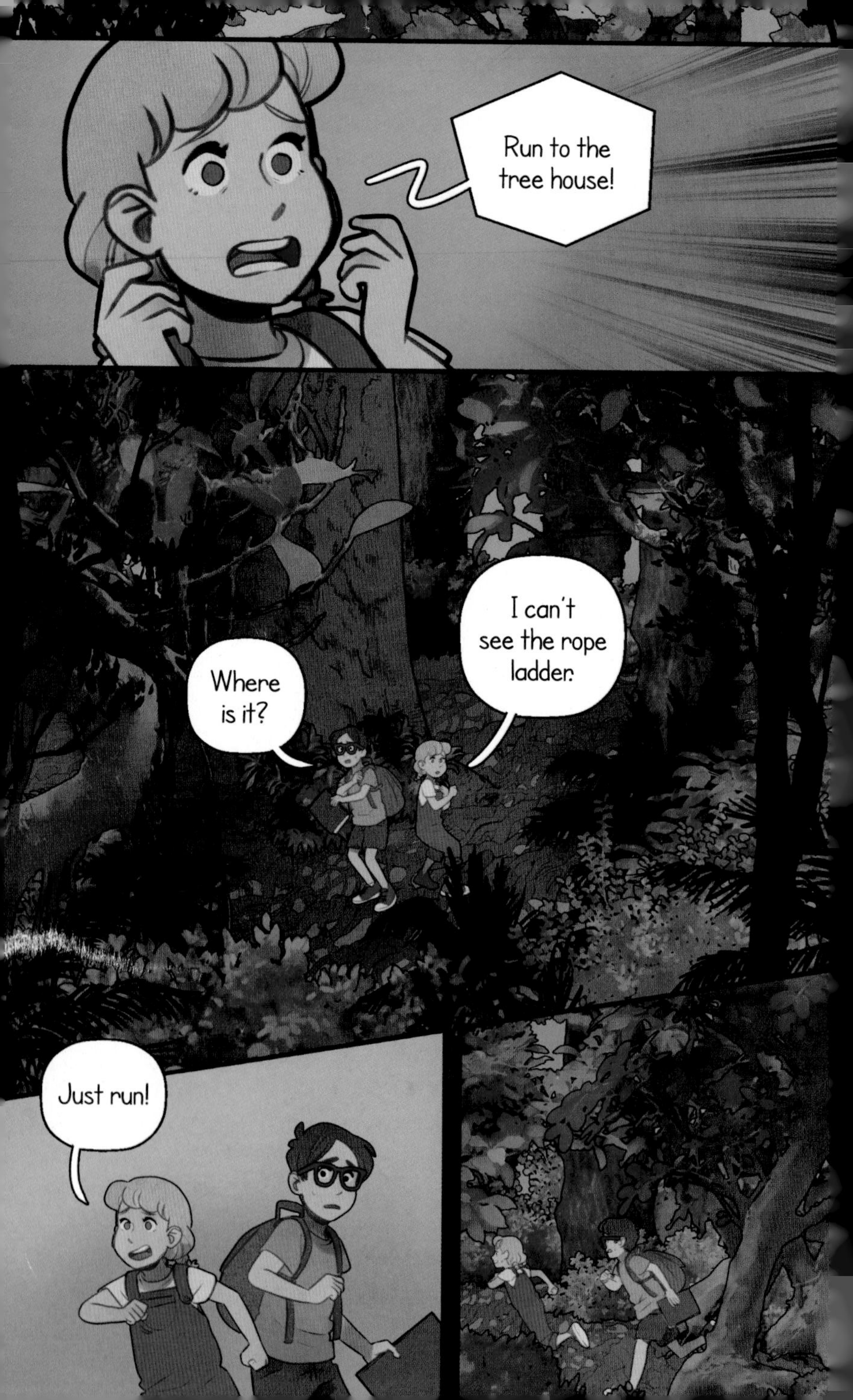
Run to the tree house!
Where is it?
I can't see the rope ladder.
Just run!

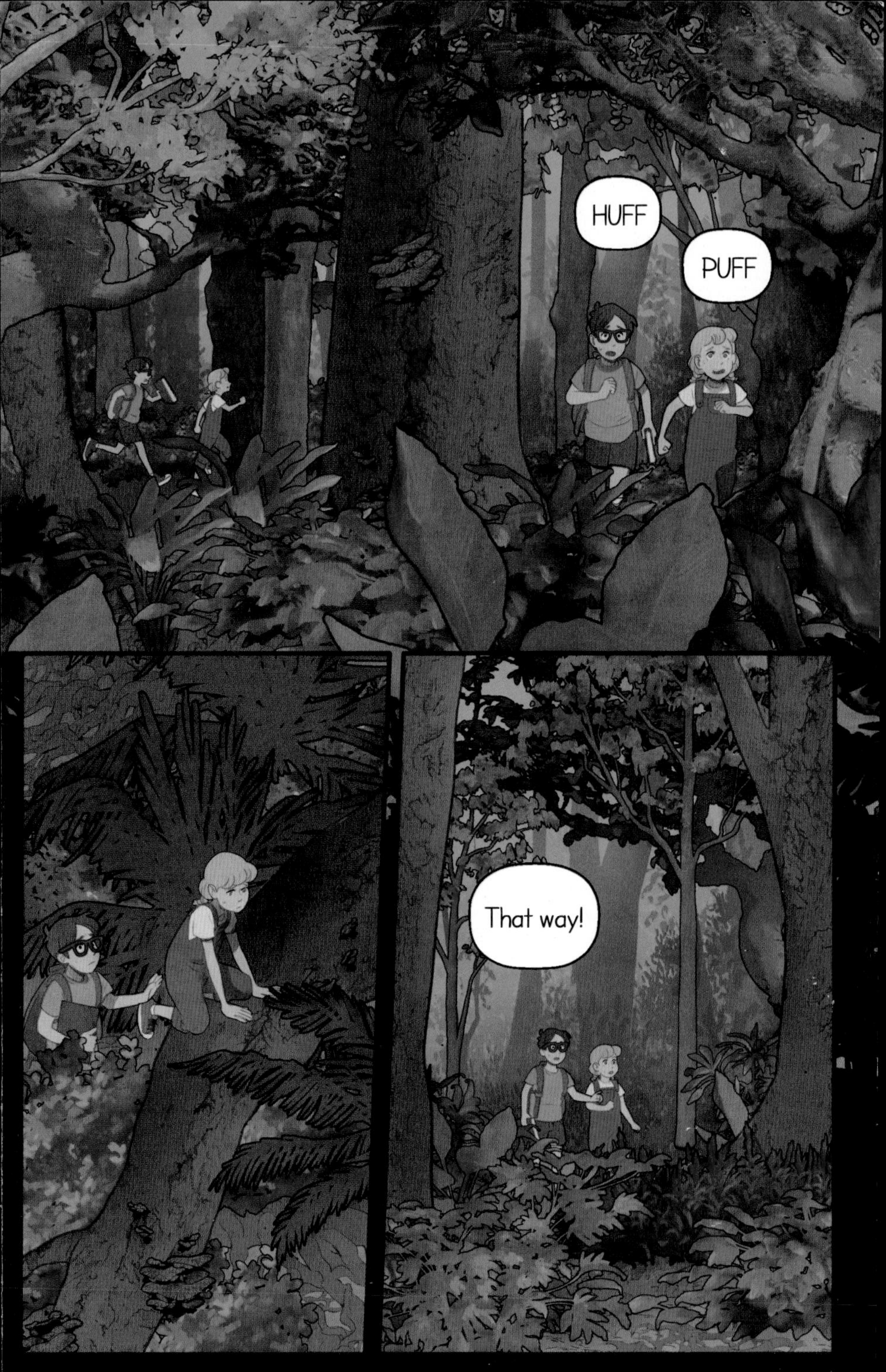
HUFF
PUFF
That way!

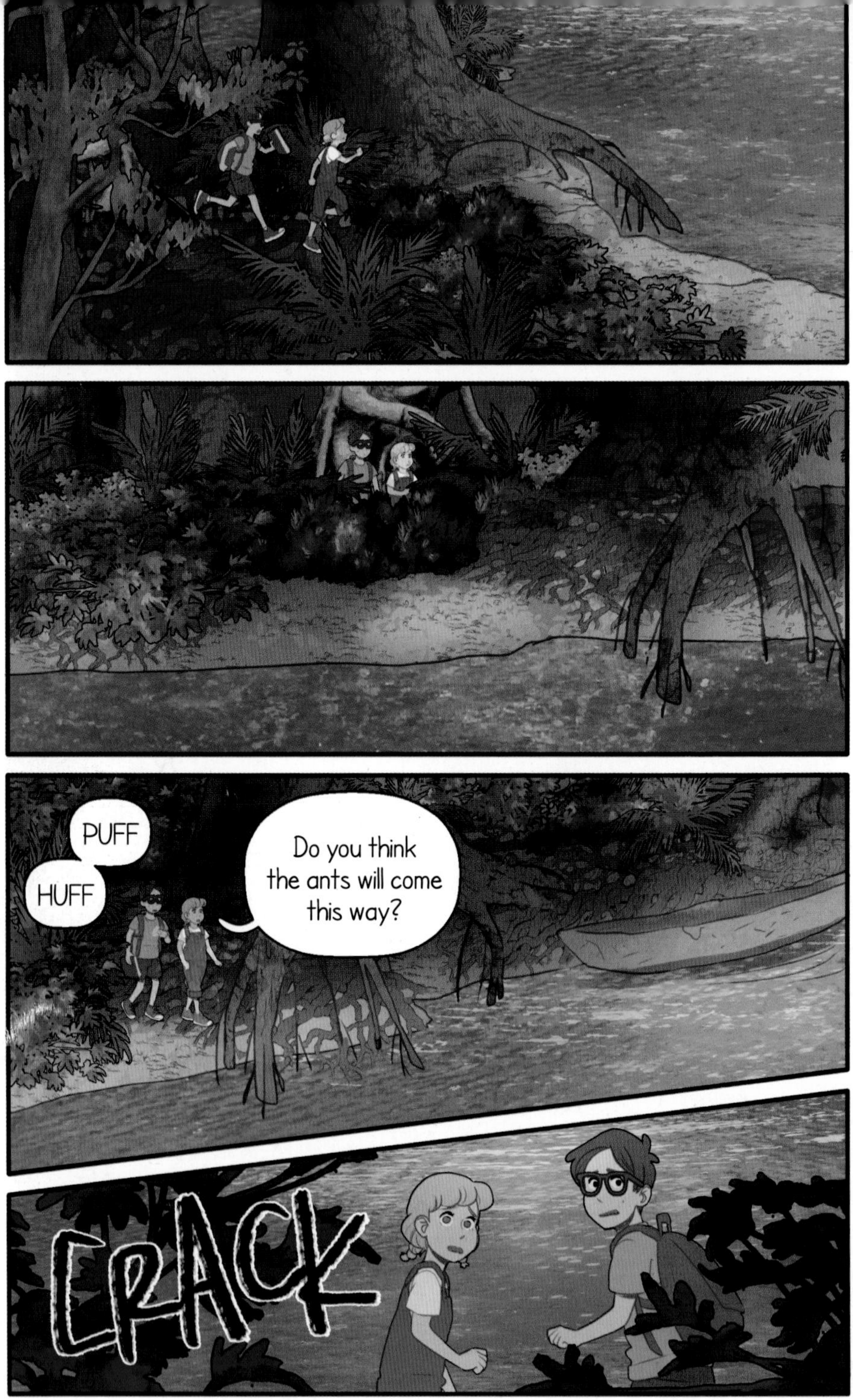
PUFF
HUFF
Do you think the ants will come this way?
CRACK

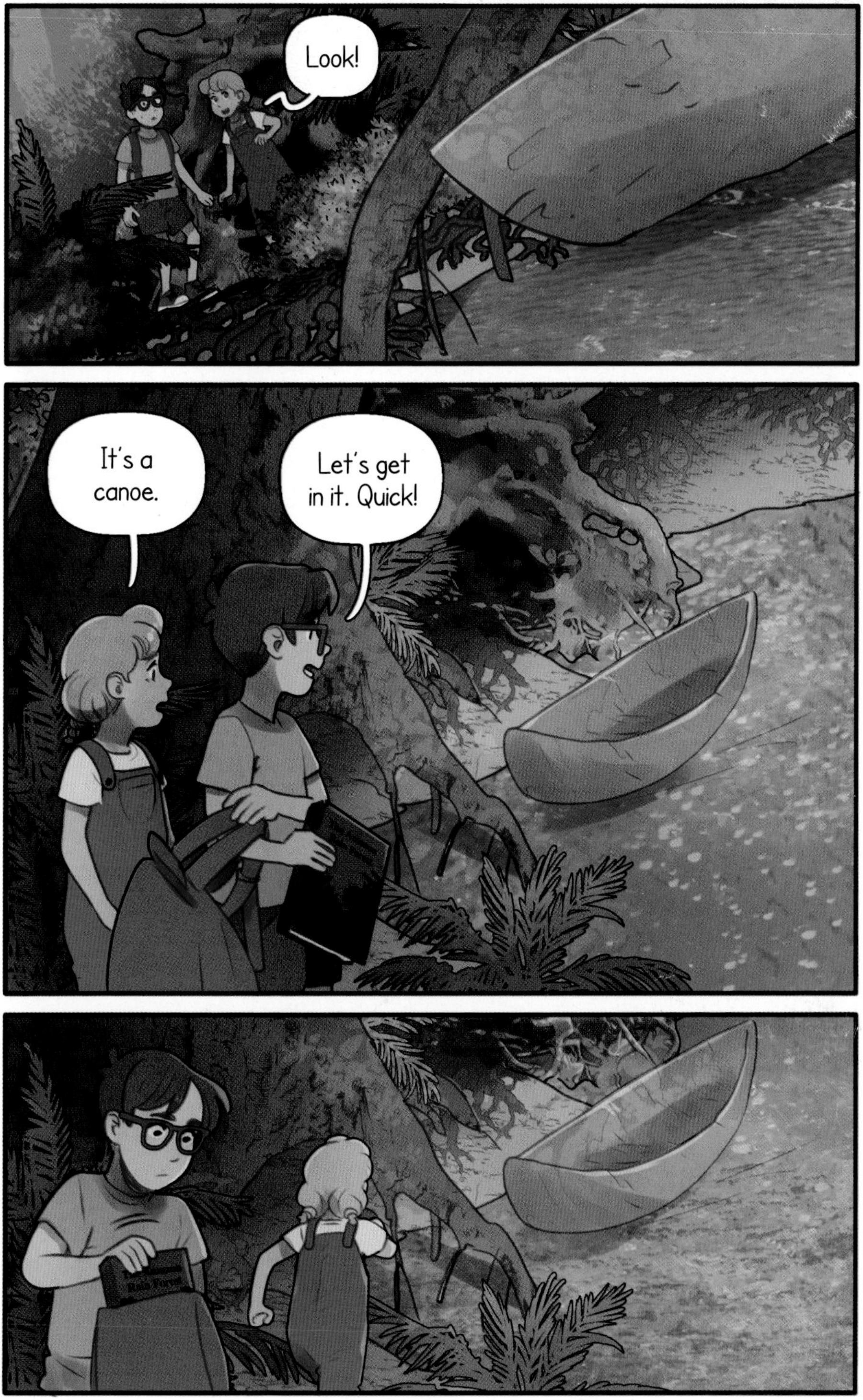
Look!
It's a canoe.
Let's get in it. Quick!

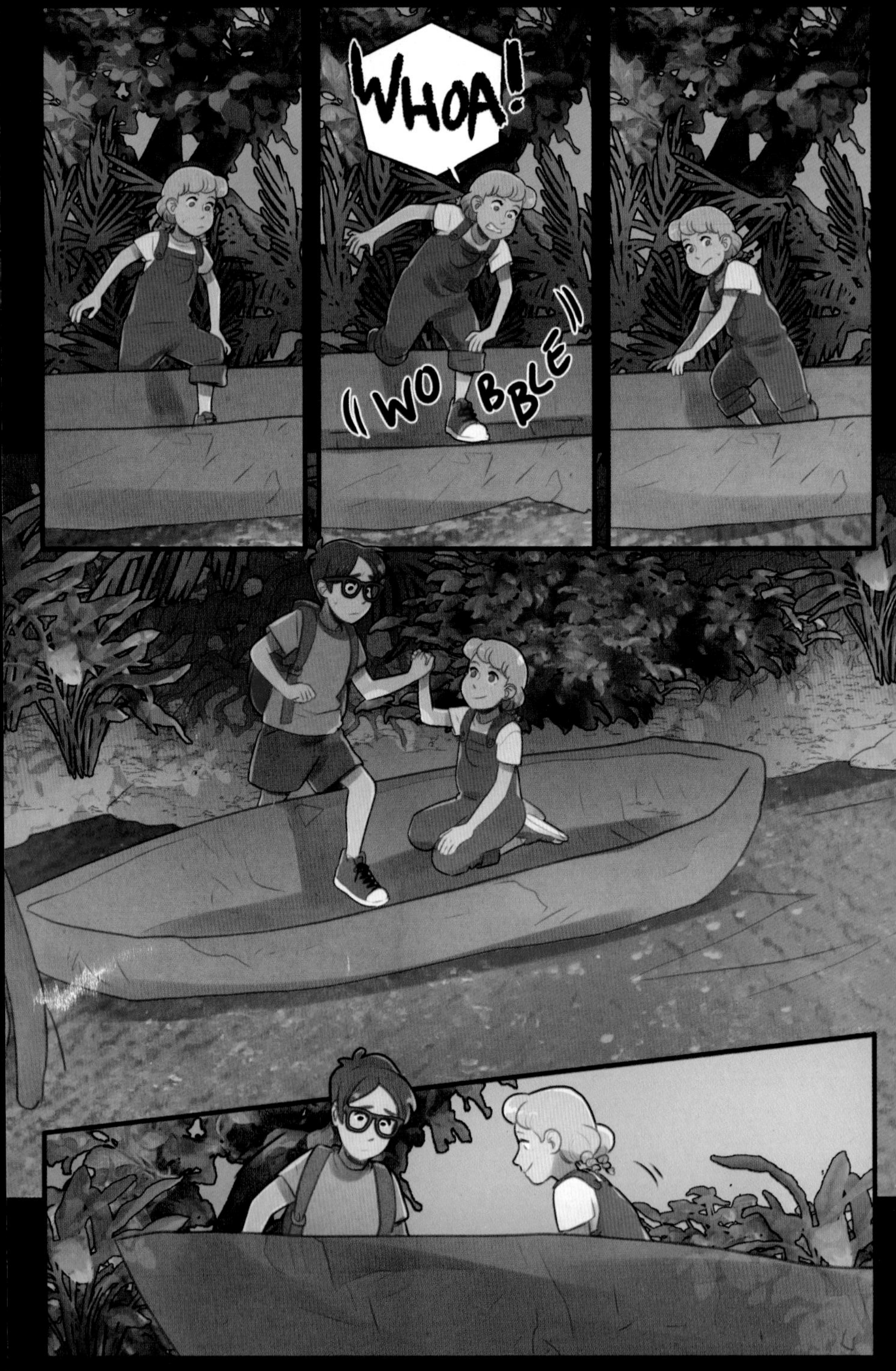
WHOA!
WOBBLE

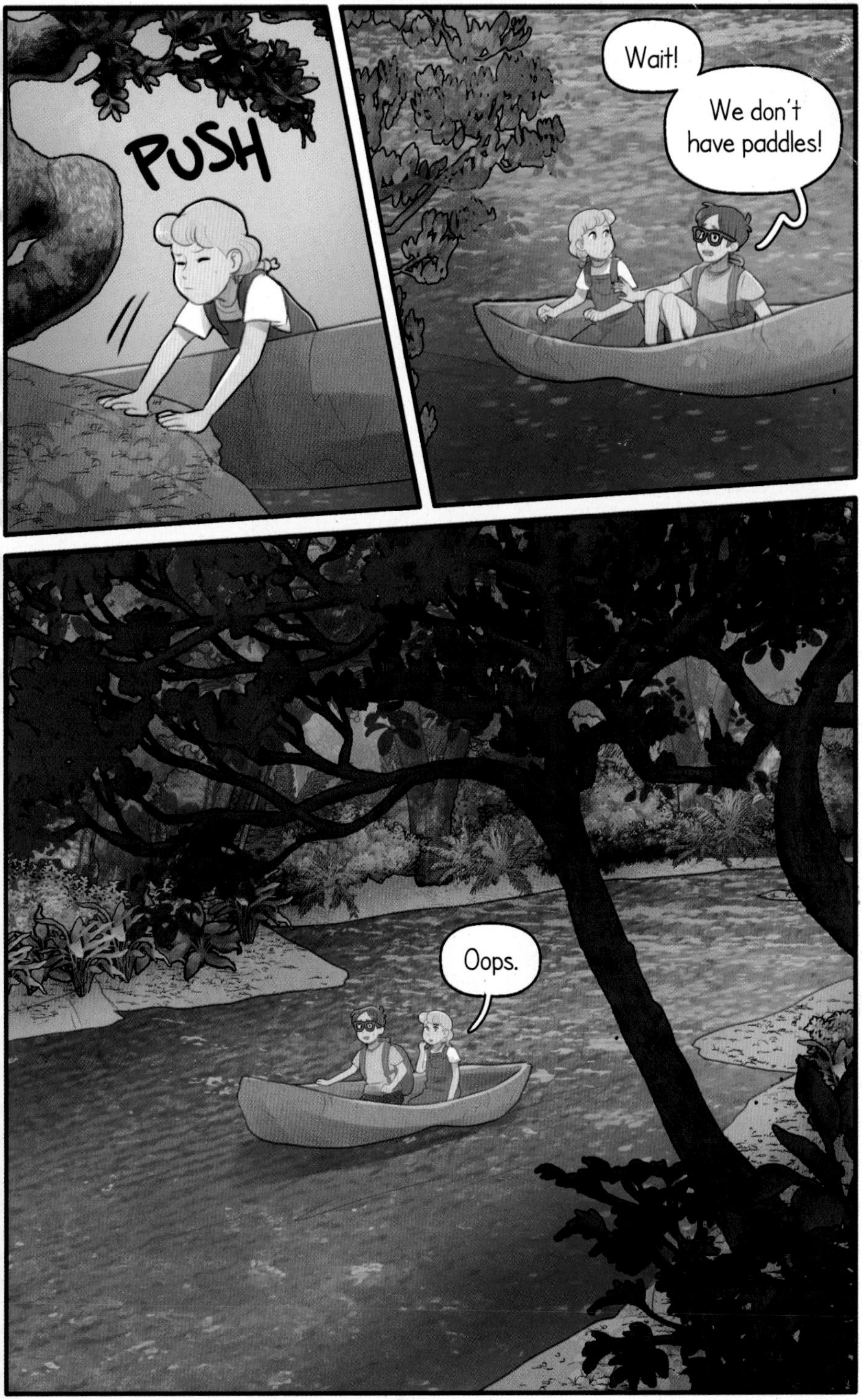
PUSH
Wait!
We don't have paddles!
Oops.

CHAPTER FOUR
Pretty Fish

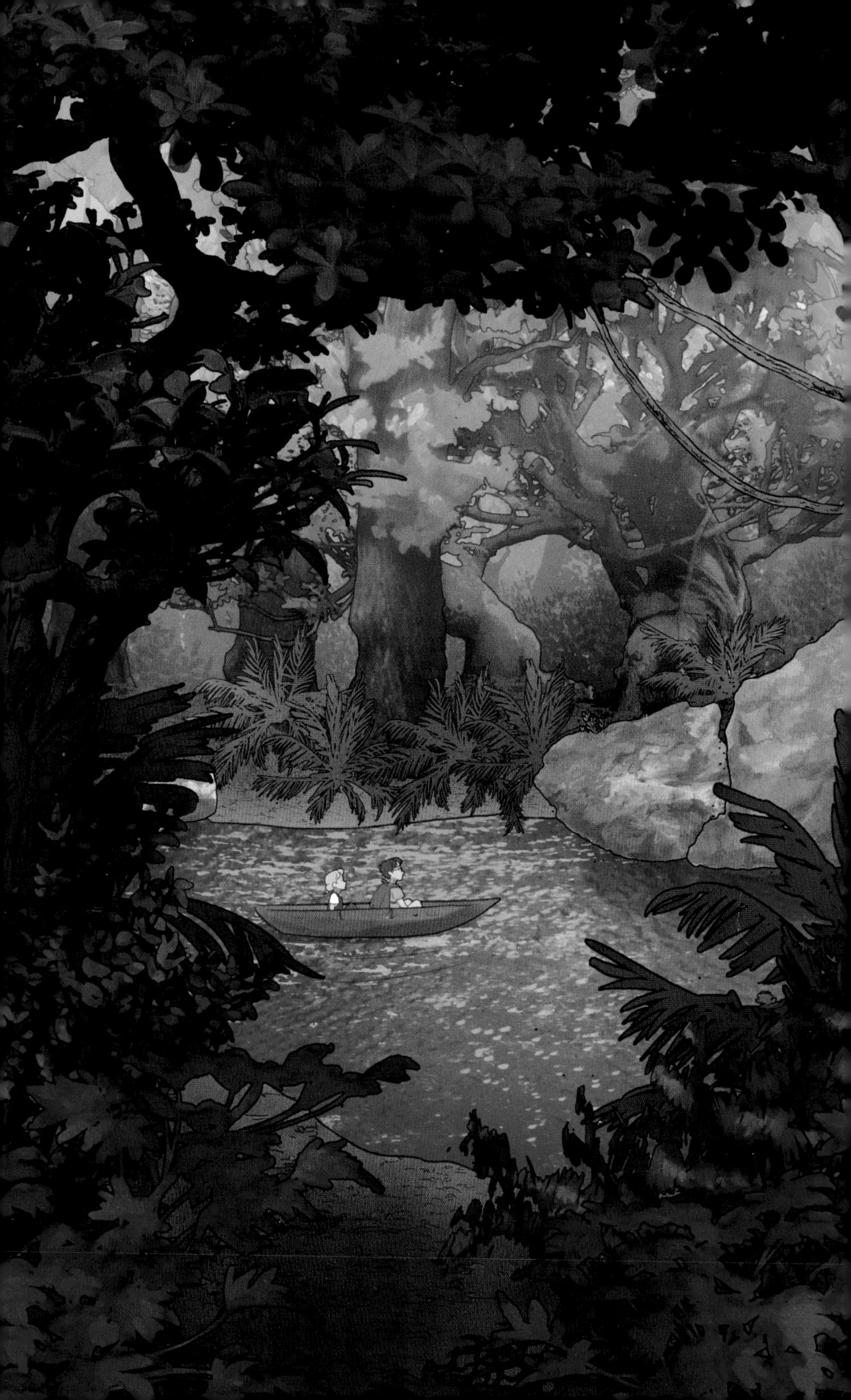

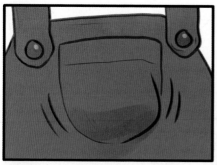

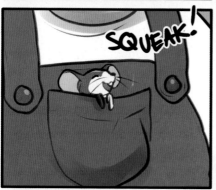

SQUEAK!

It's okay, Peanut. The ants can't get us in the river.

We're safe.

Maybe safe from the ants.

But where is this canoe going?

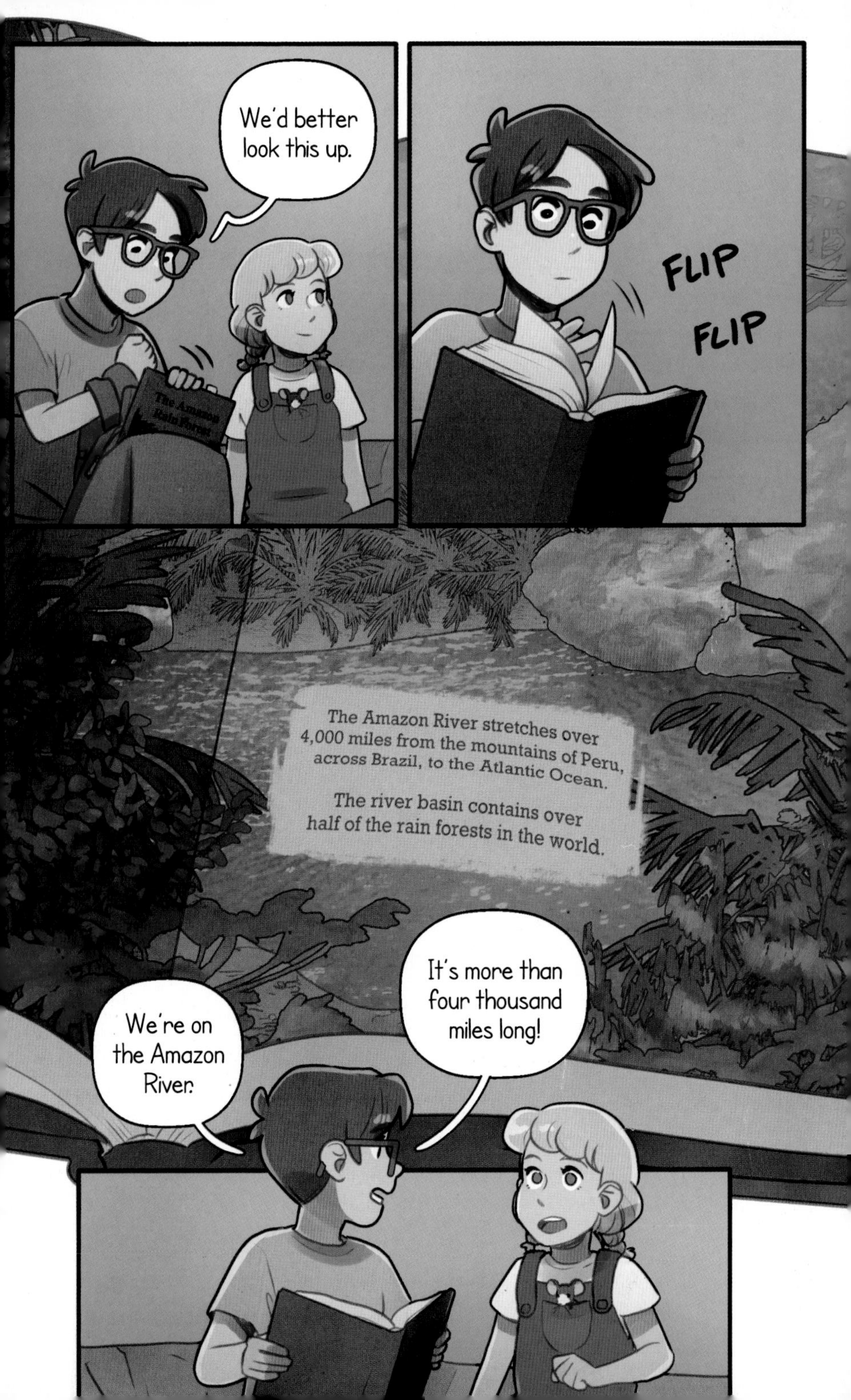
We'd better look this up.
The Amazon Rain Forest
FLIP
FLIP
The Amazon River stretches over 4,000 miles from the mountains of Peru, across Brazil, to the Atlantic Ocean.
The river basin contains over half of the rain forests in the world.
We're on the Amazon River.
It's more than four thousand miles long!

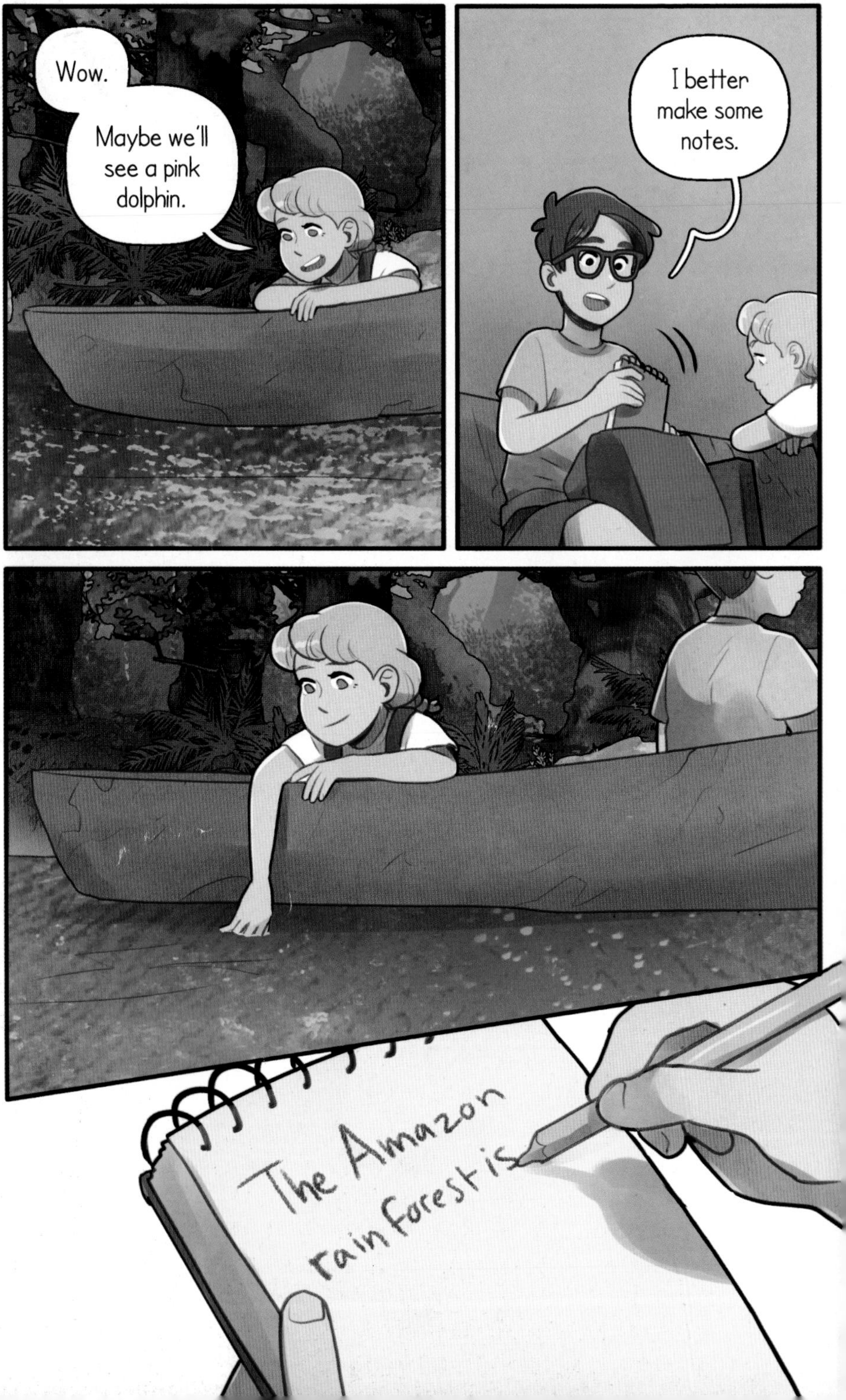
Wow.
Maybe we'll see a pink dolphin.
I better make some notes.
The Amazon rainforest is

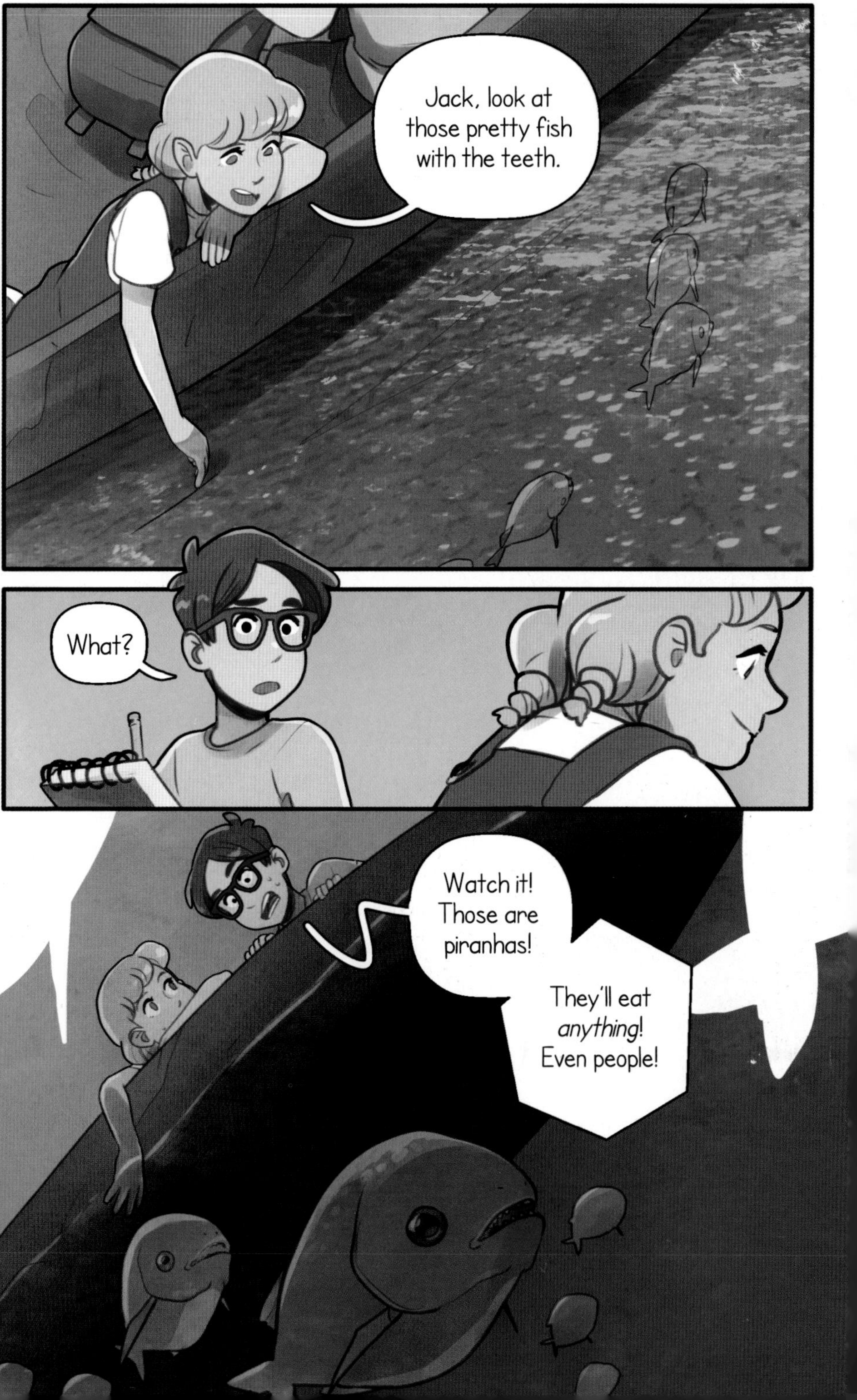
Jack, look at those pretty fish with the teeth.
What?
Watch it! Those are piranhas!
They'll eat *anything*! Even people!

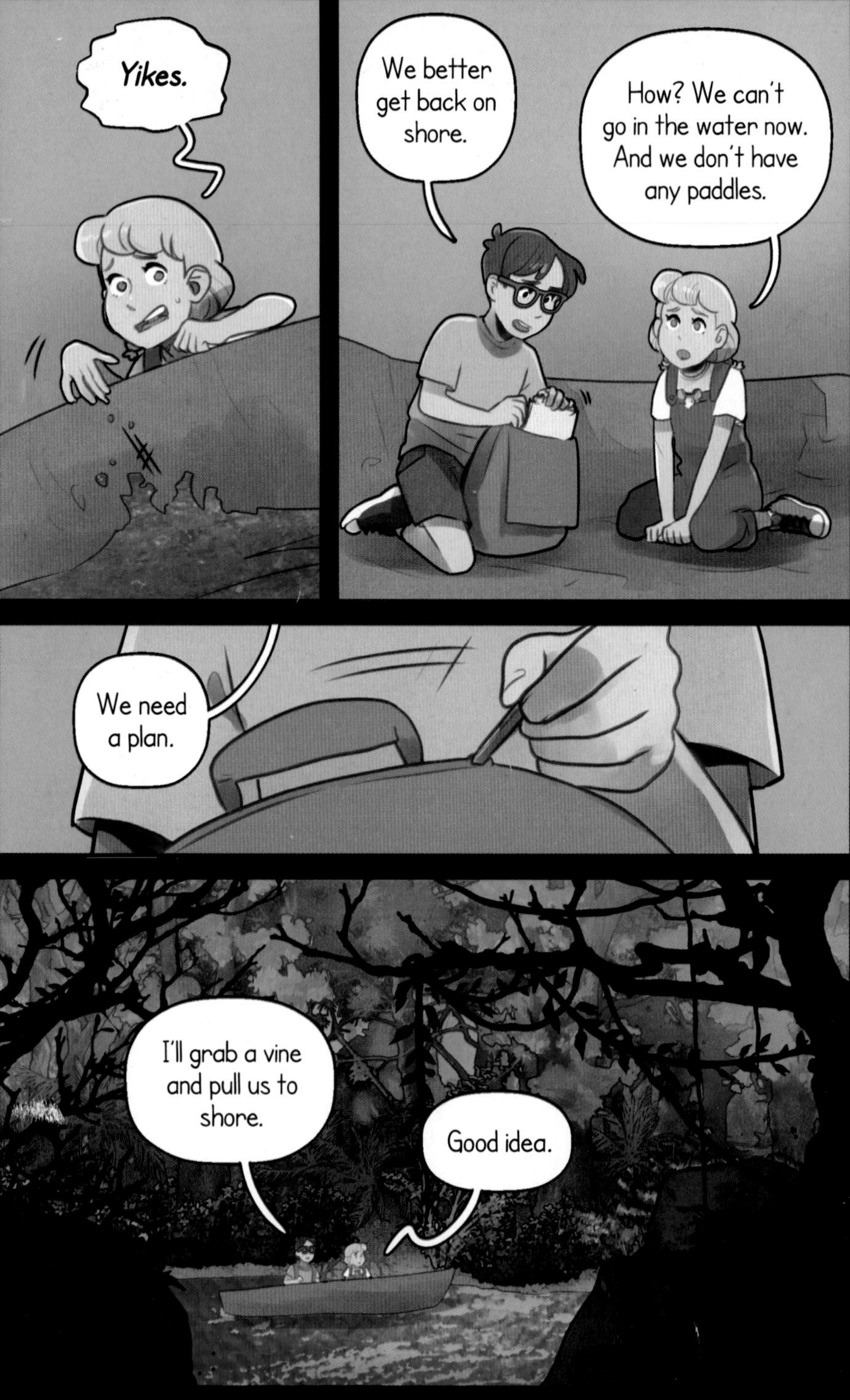
Yikes.
We better get back on shore.
How? We can't go in the water now. And we don't have any paddles.
We need a plan.
I'll grab a vine and pull us to shore.
Good idea.

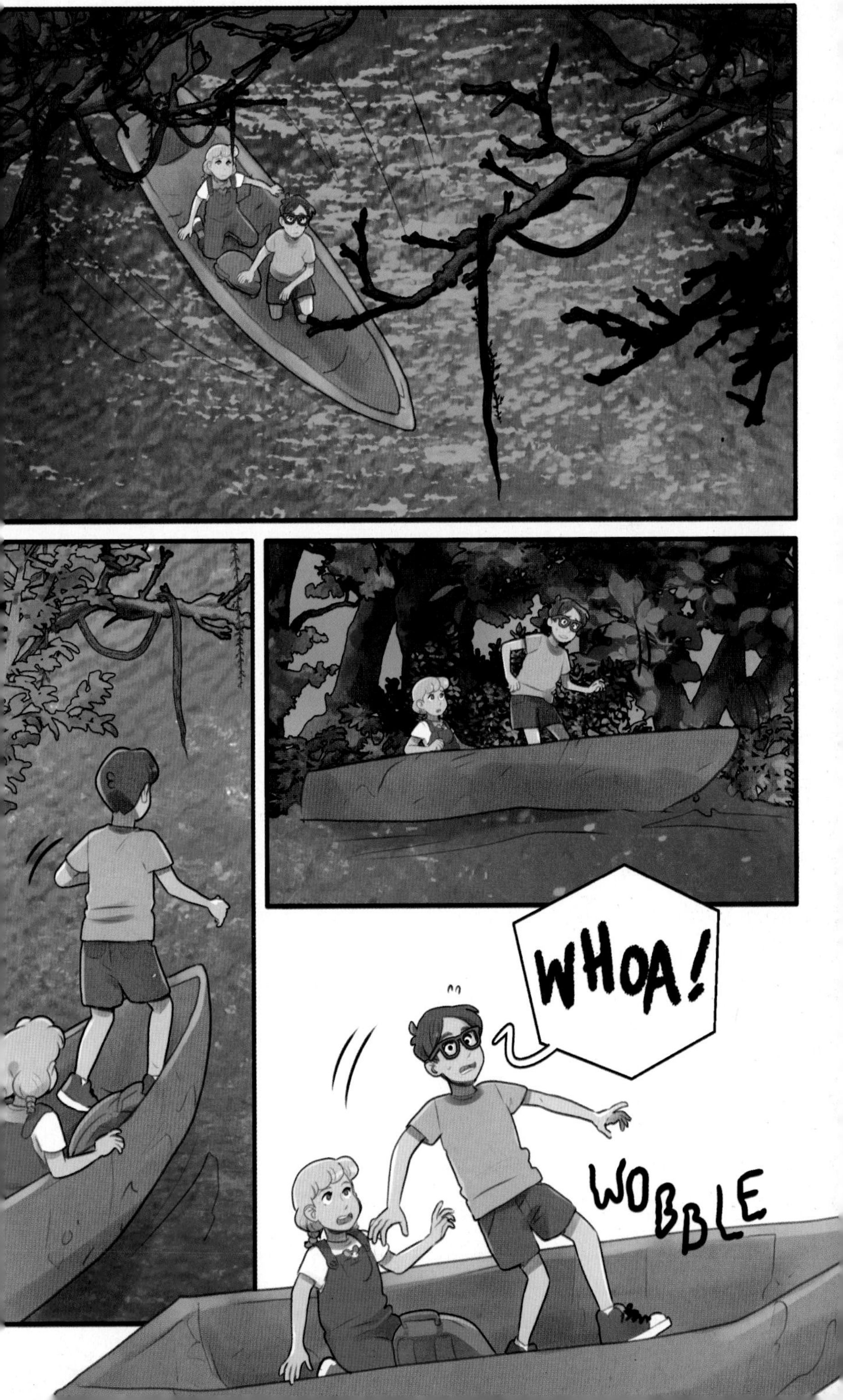
WHOA!
WOBBLE

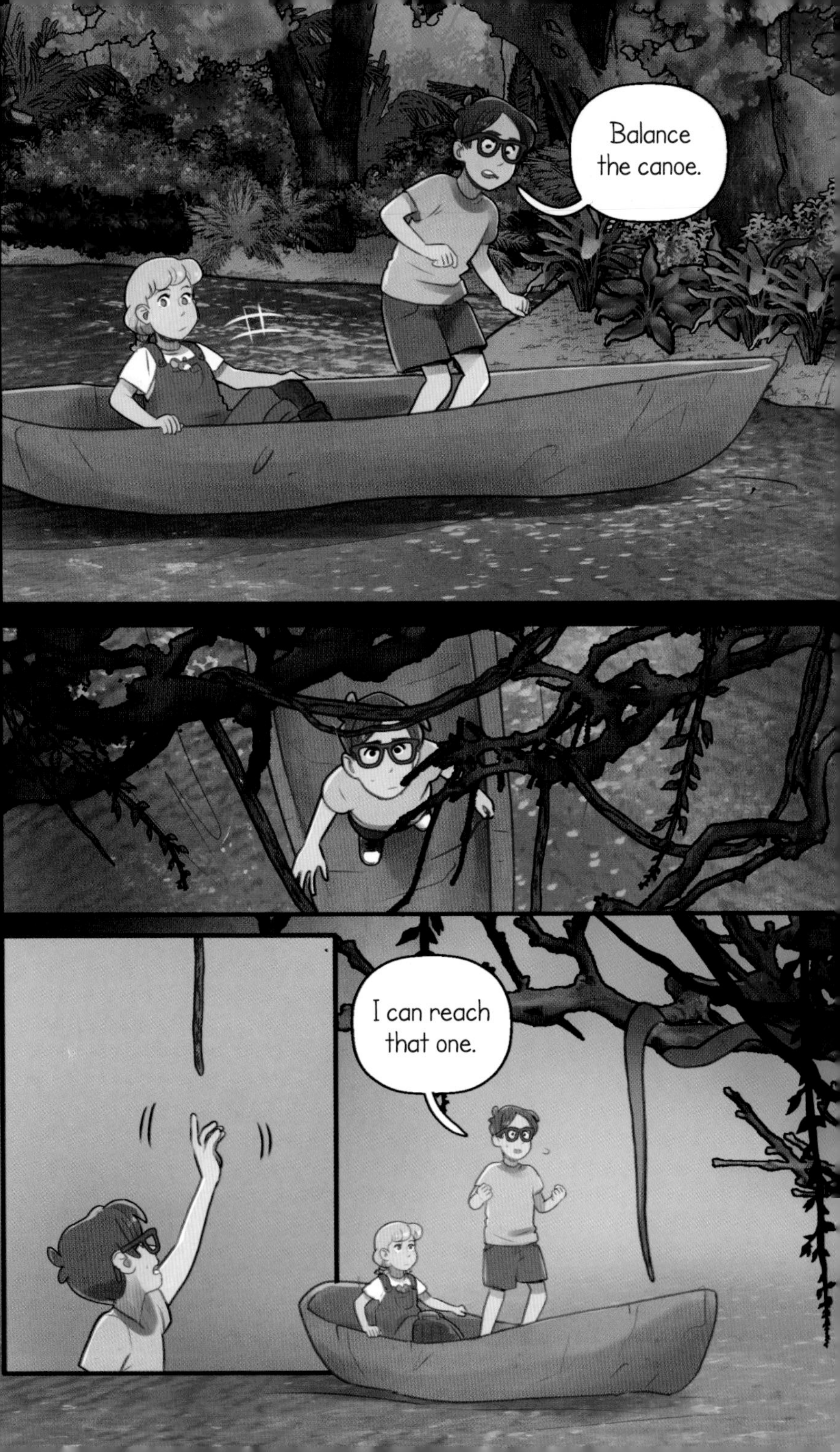
Balance the canoe.
I can reach that one.

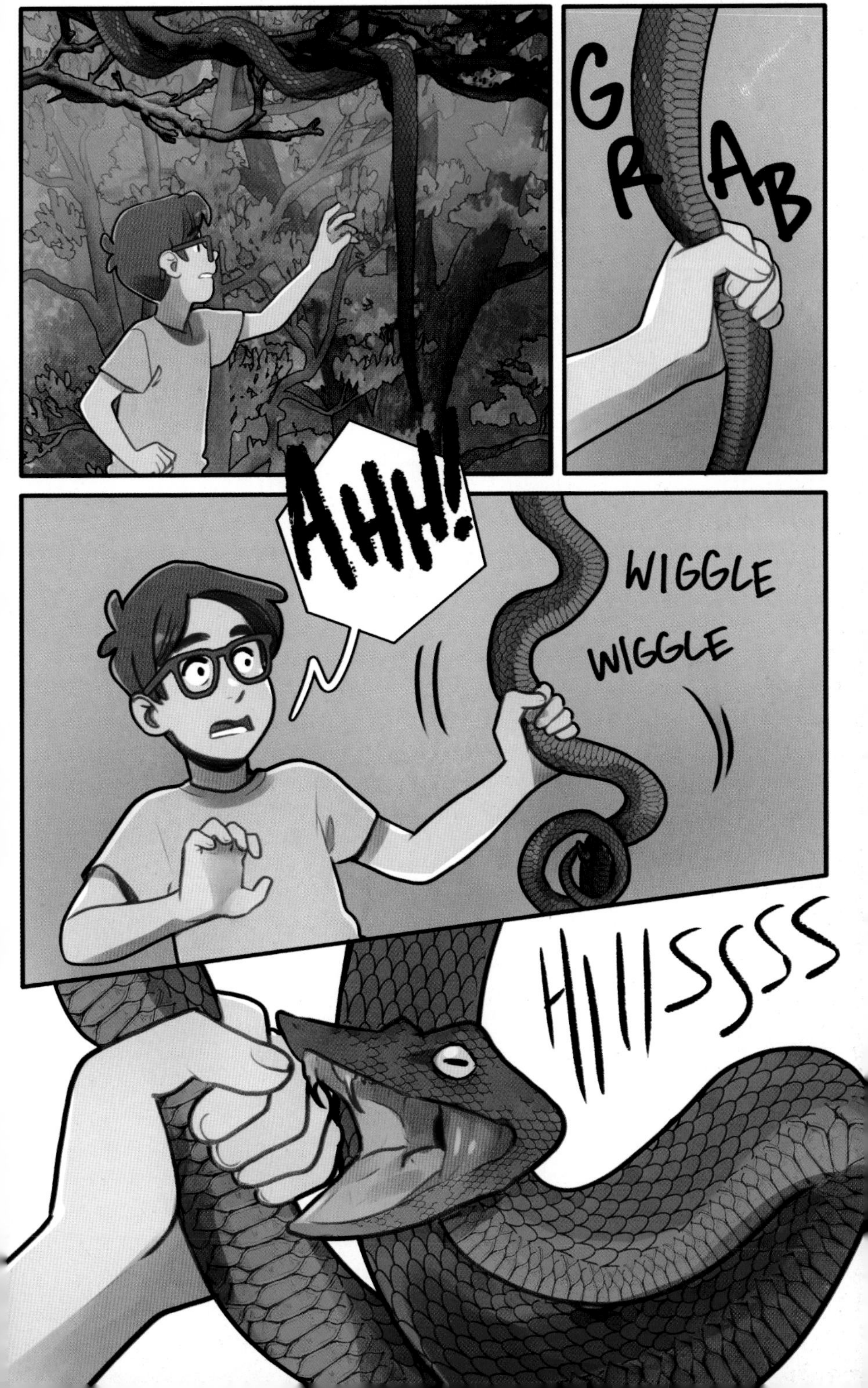
GRAB
AHH!
WIGGLE
WIGGLE
HISSSS

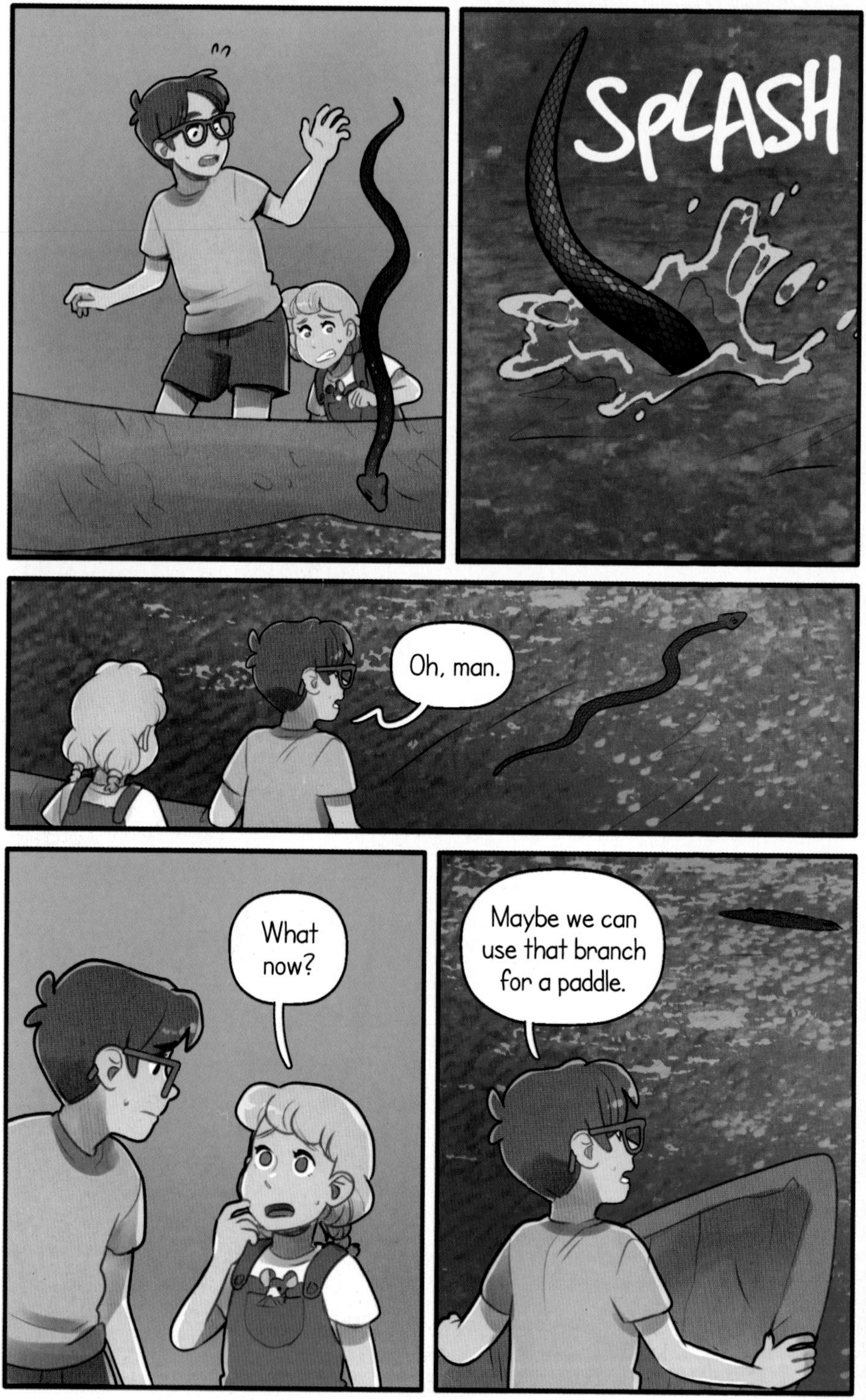
SPLASH
Oh, man.
What now?
Maybe we can use that branch for a paddle.

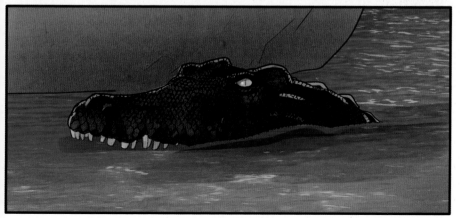

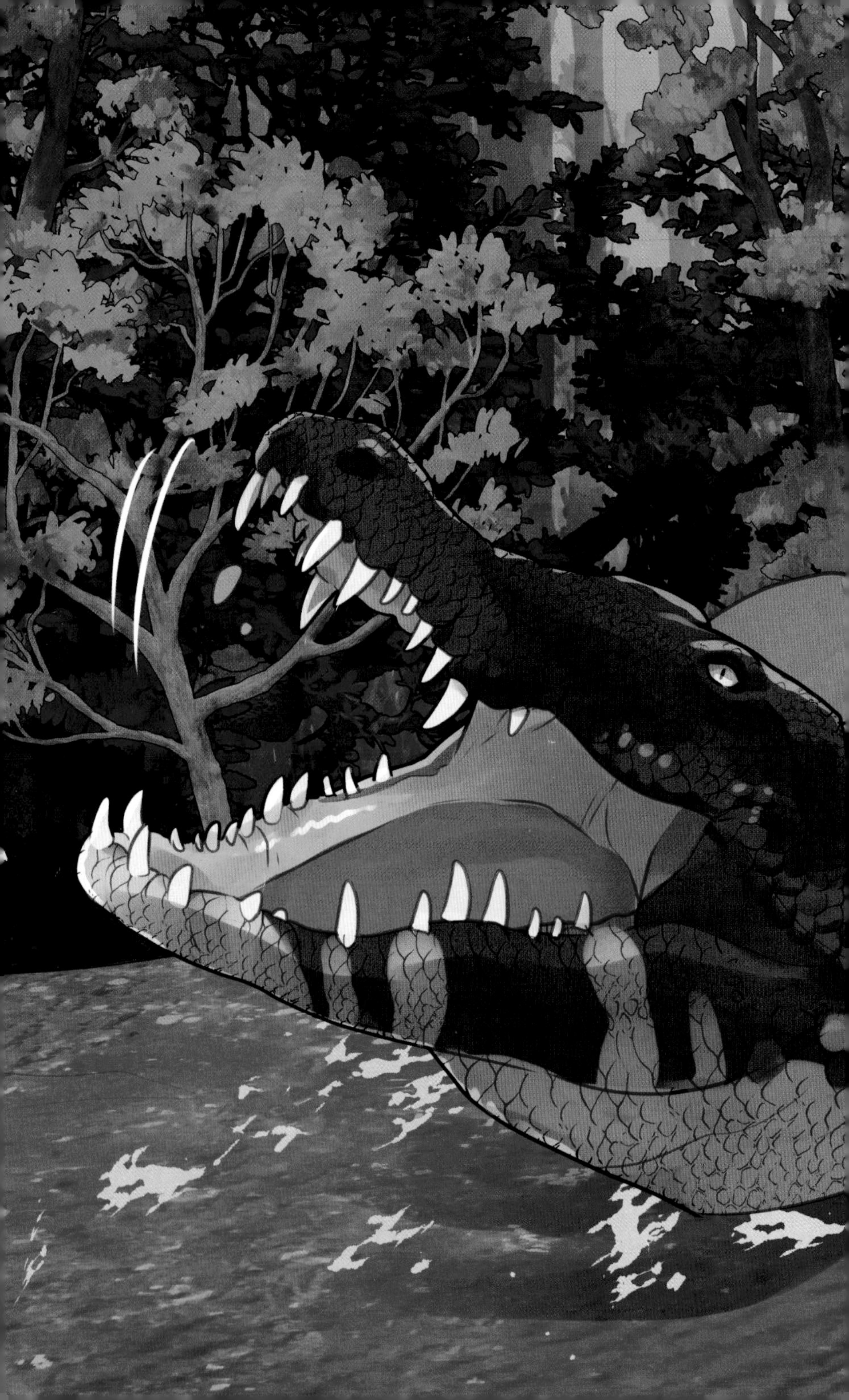

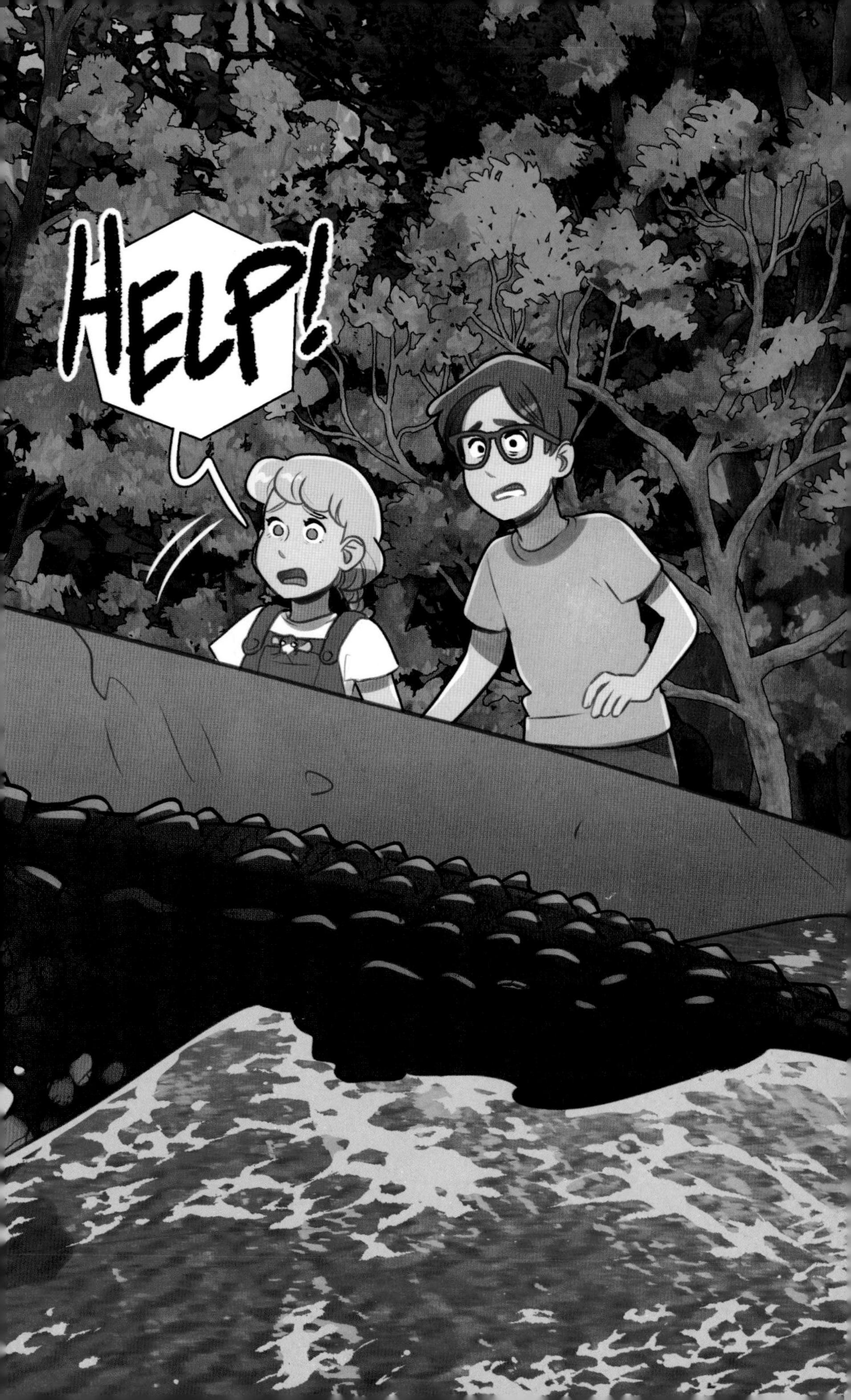
HELP!

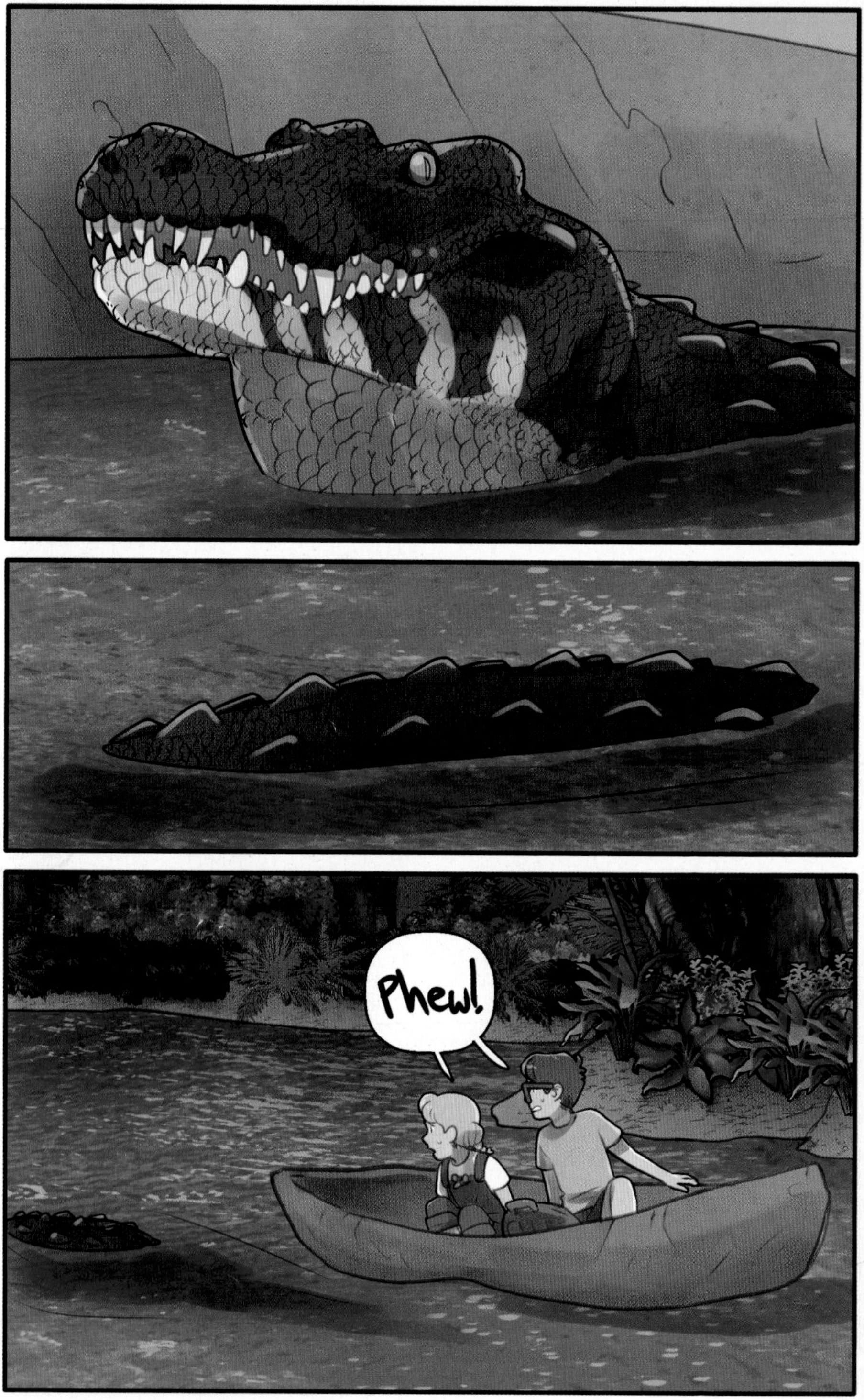
Phew!

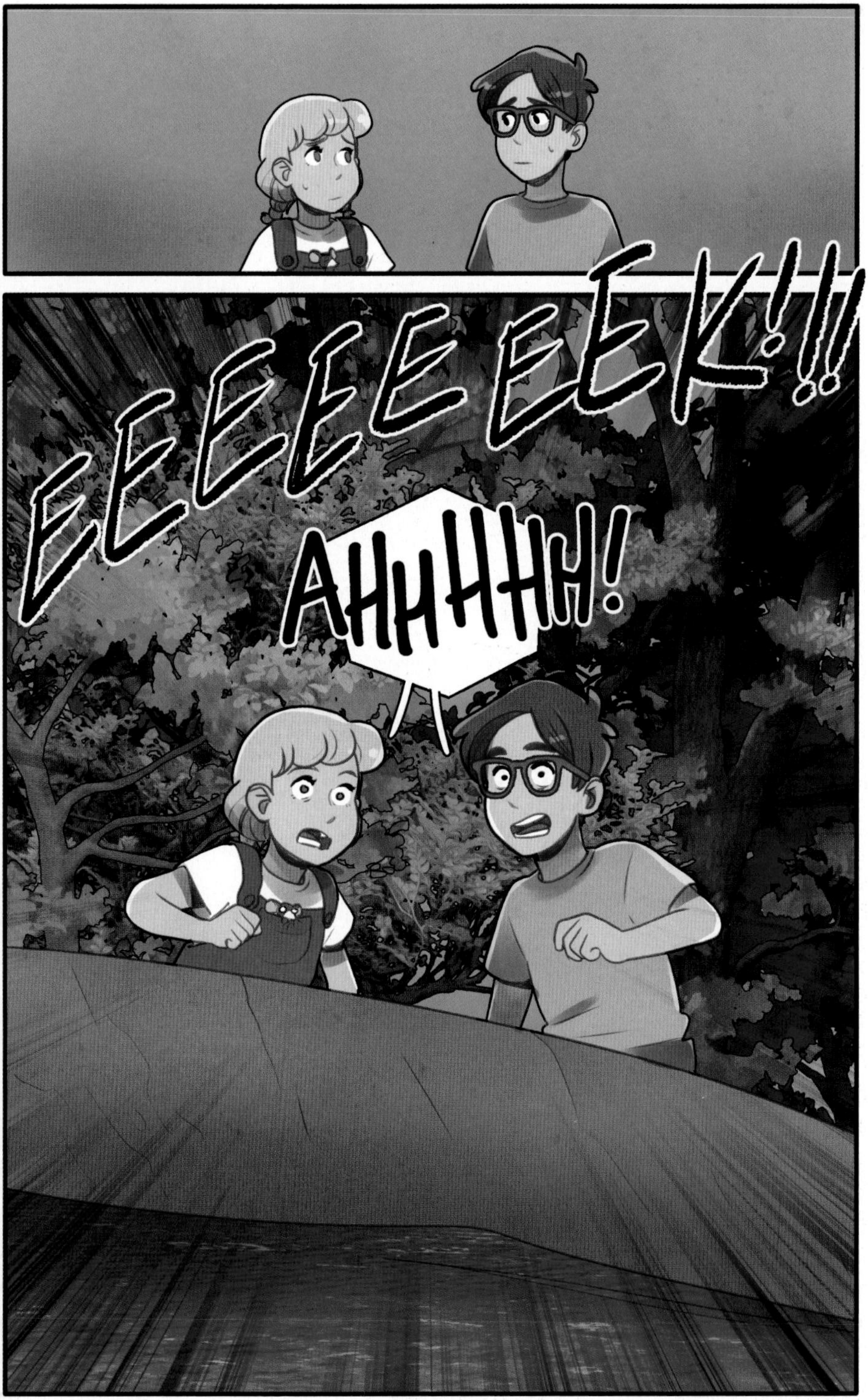
EEEEEEEK!!!
AHHHHH!

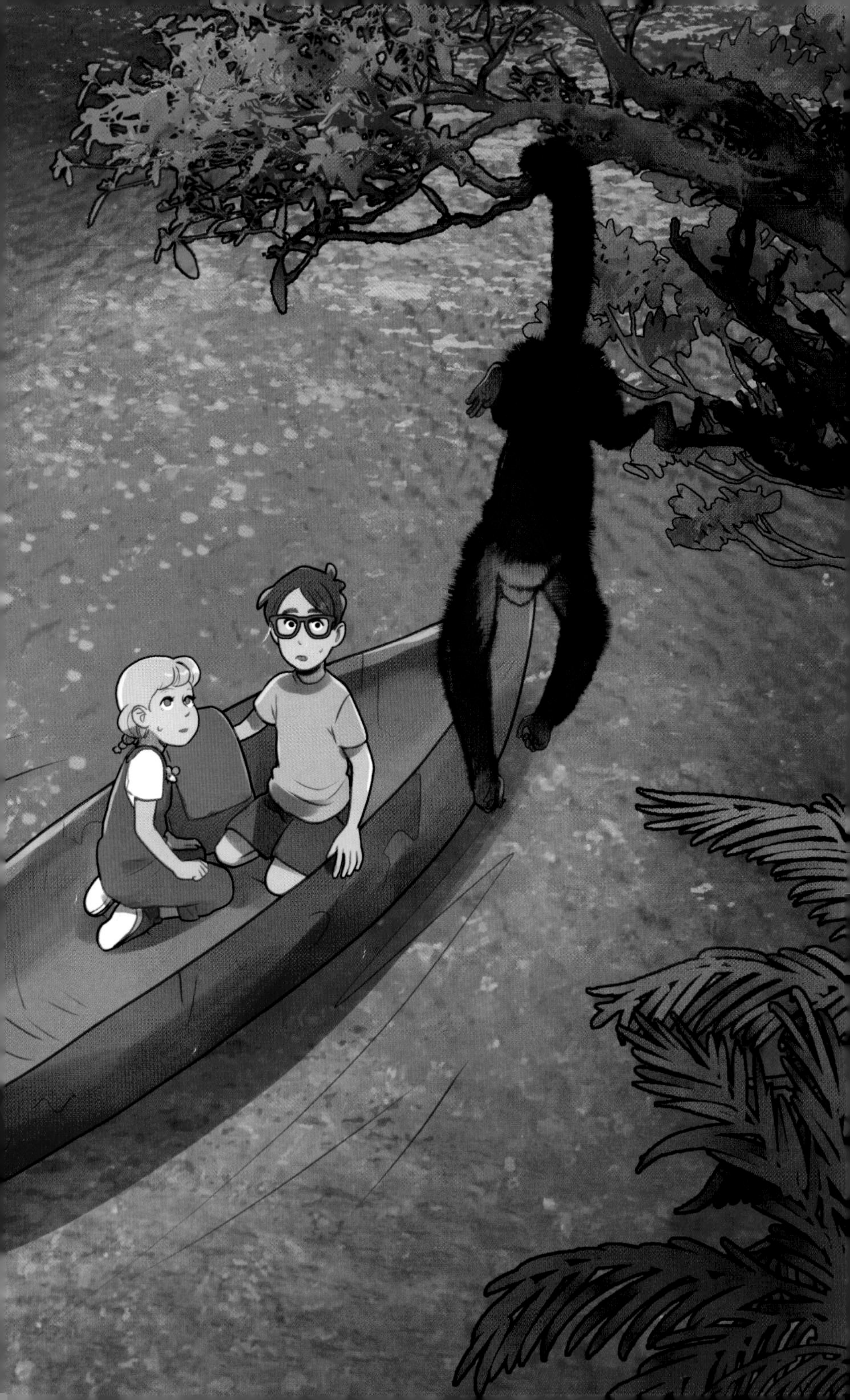

CHAPTER FIVE

Monkey Trouble

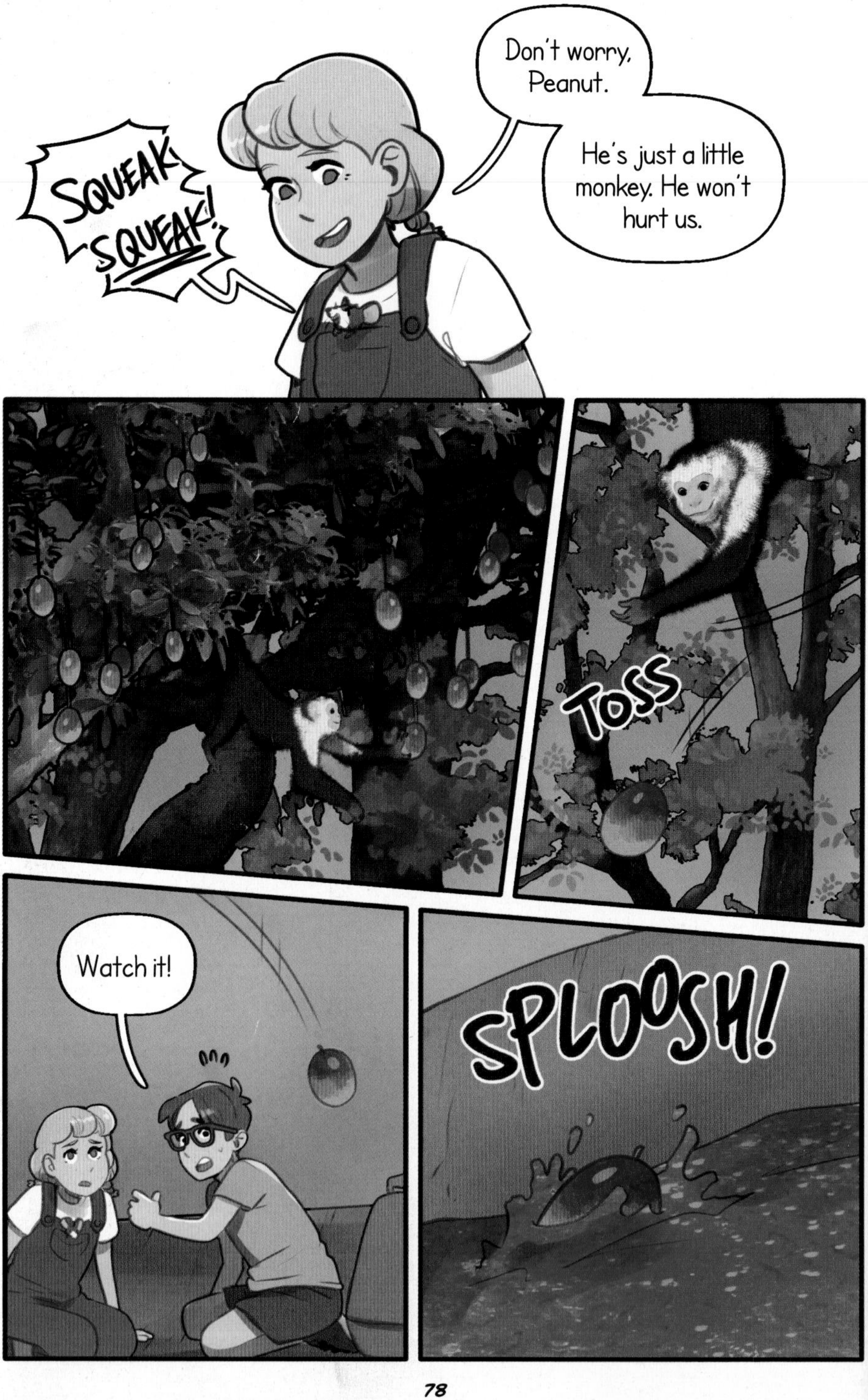
Don't worry, Peanut.
He's just a little monkey. He won't hurt us.
SQUEAK SQUEAK!
TOSS
Watch it!
SPLOOSH!

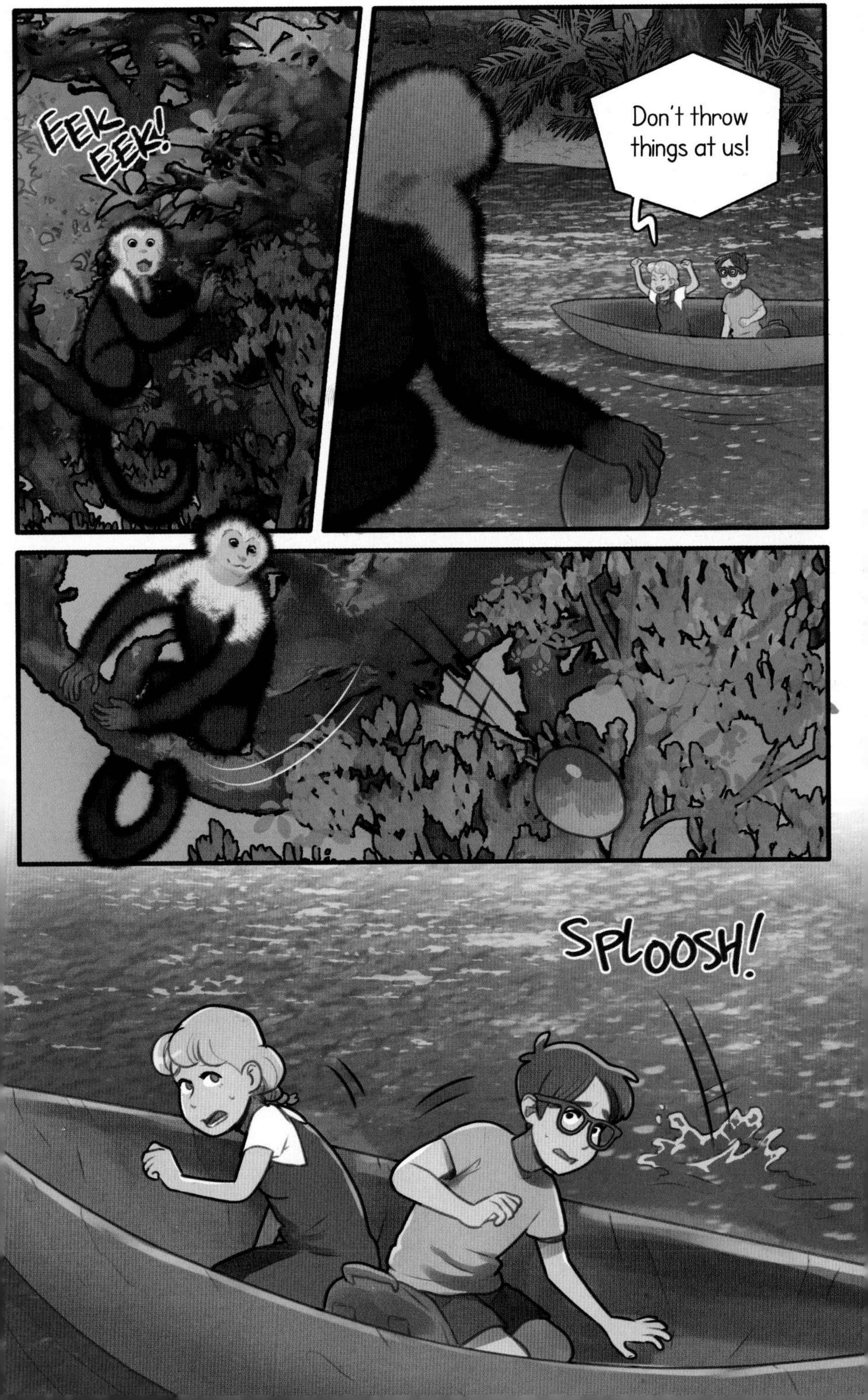
EEK EEK!
Don't throw things at us!
SPLOOSH!

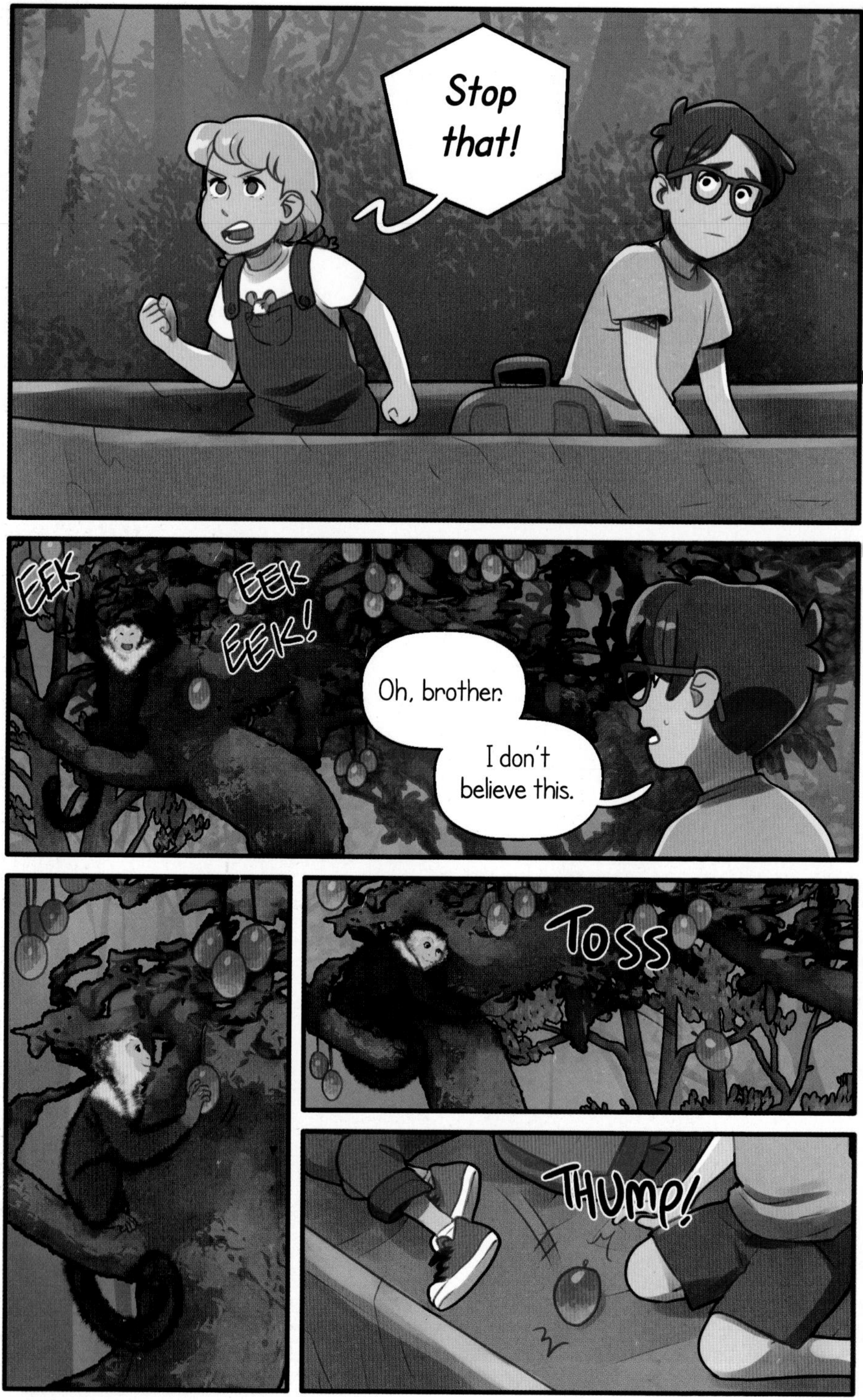
Stop that!
EEK
EEK
EEK!
Oh, brother.
I don't believe this.
TOSS
THUMP!

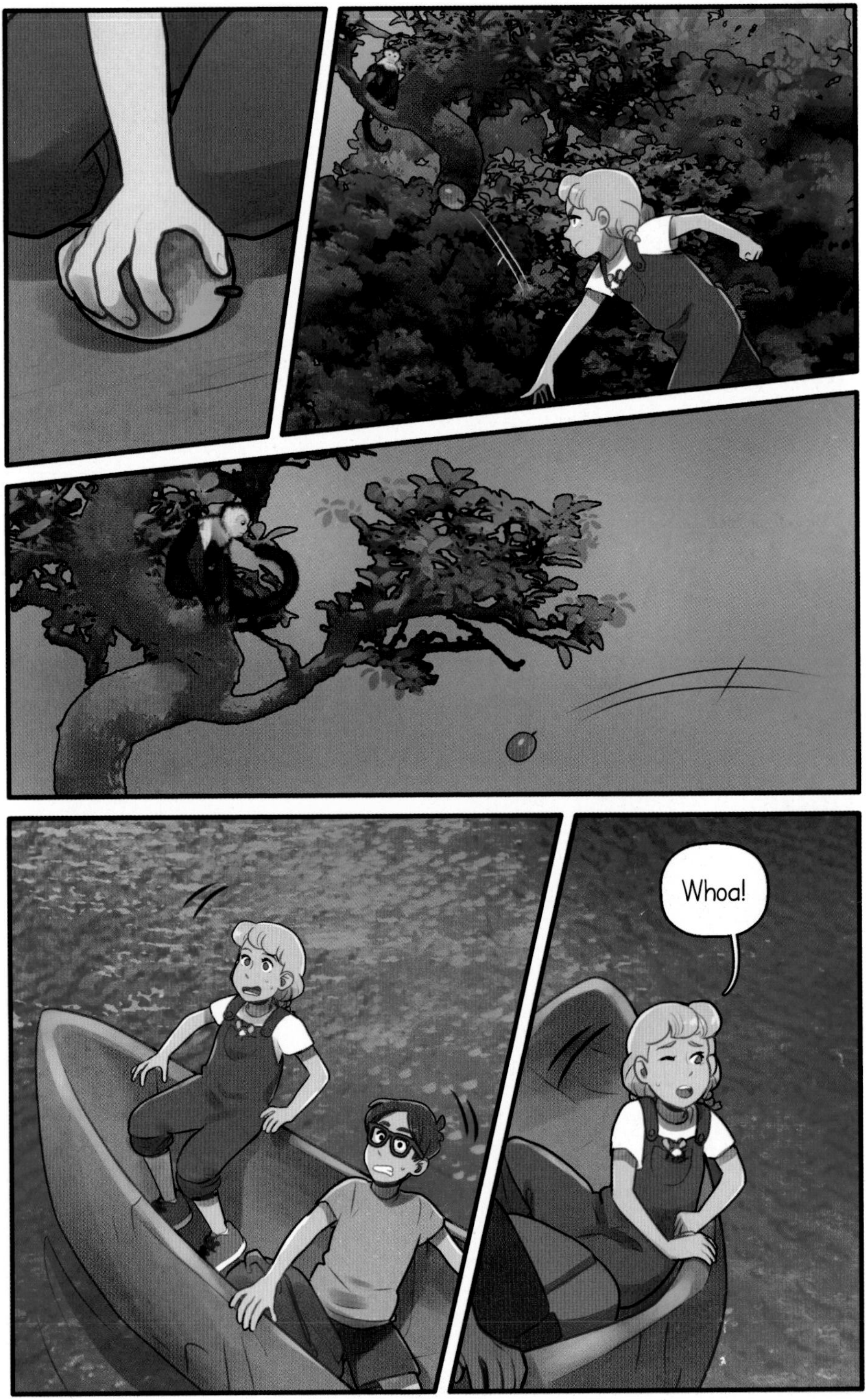
Whoa!

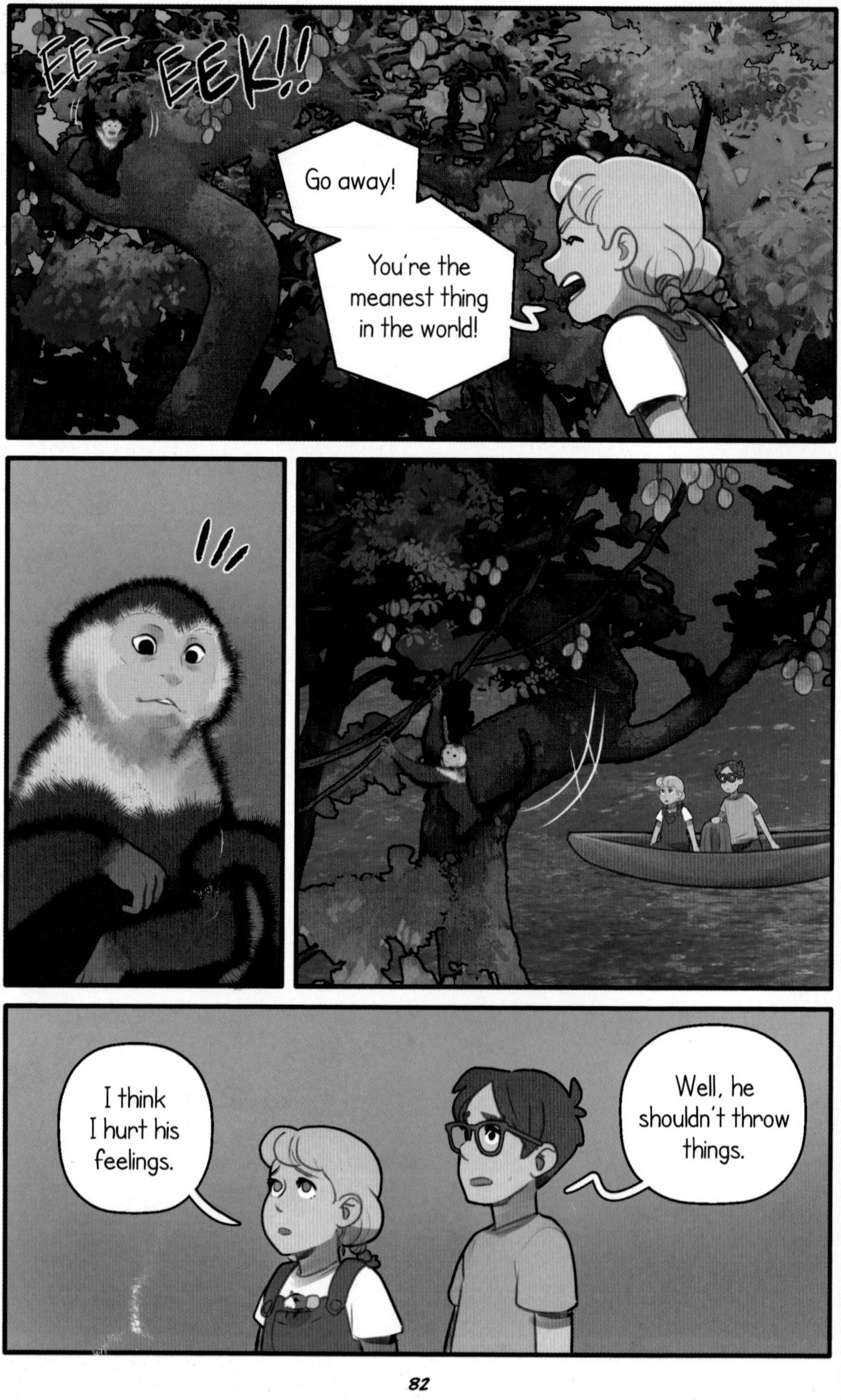
EE-EEK!!
Go away!
You're the meanest thing in the world!
I think I hurt his feelings.
Well, he shouldn't throw things.

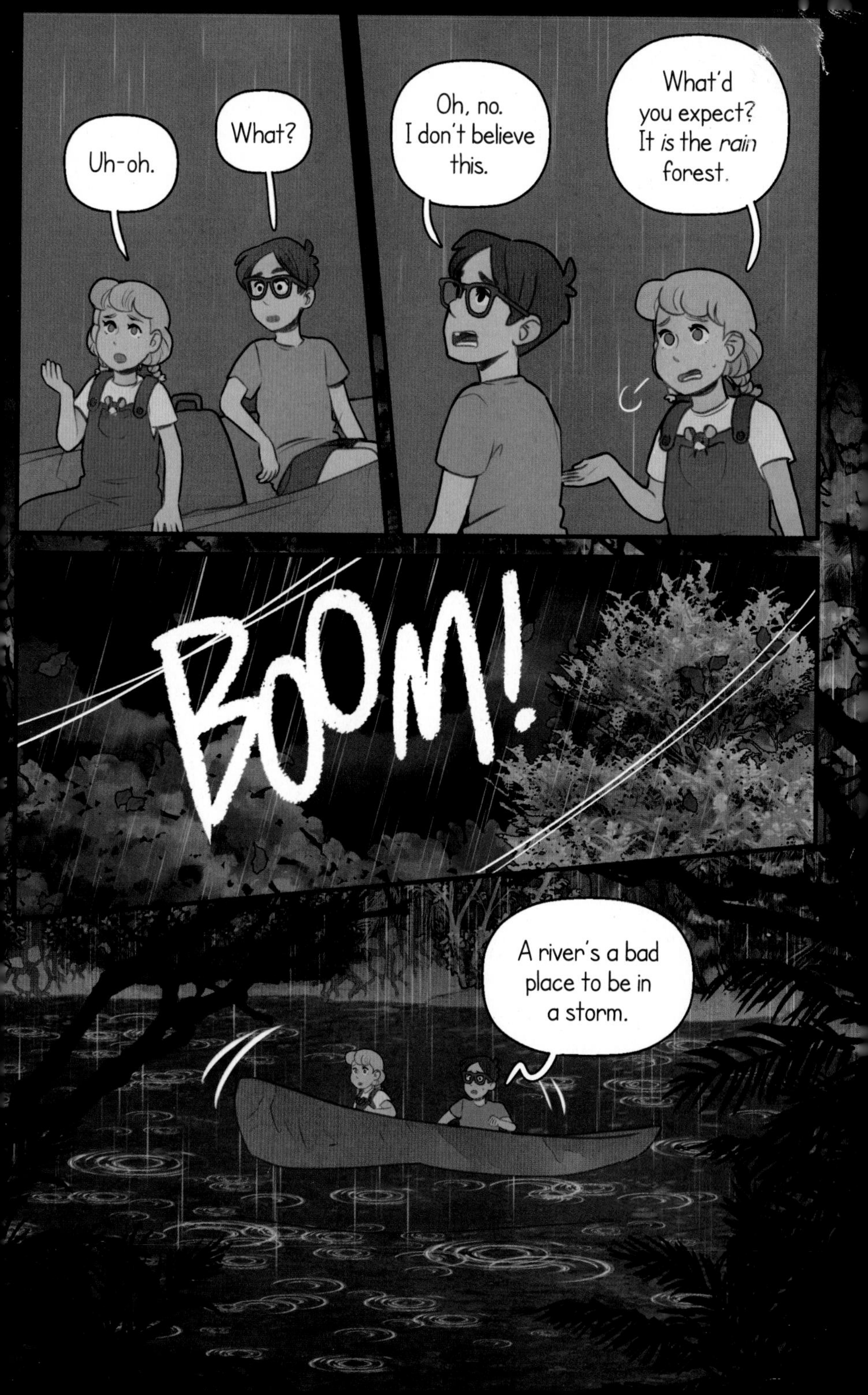
Uh-oh.
What?
Oh, no. I don't believe this.
What'd you expect? It *is* the *rain* forest.
BOOM!
A river's a bad place to be in a storm.

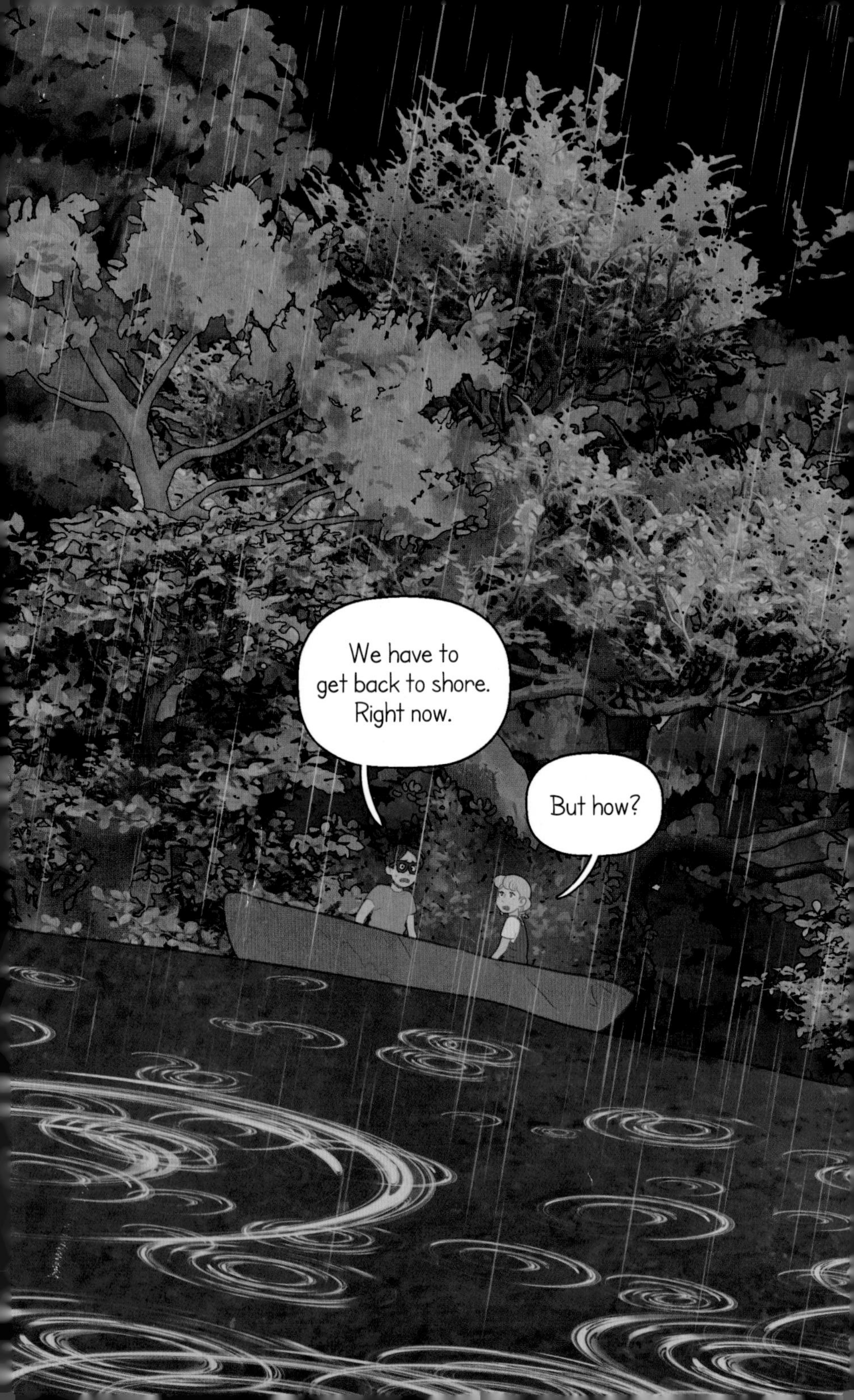
We have to get back to shore. Right now.
But how?

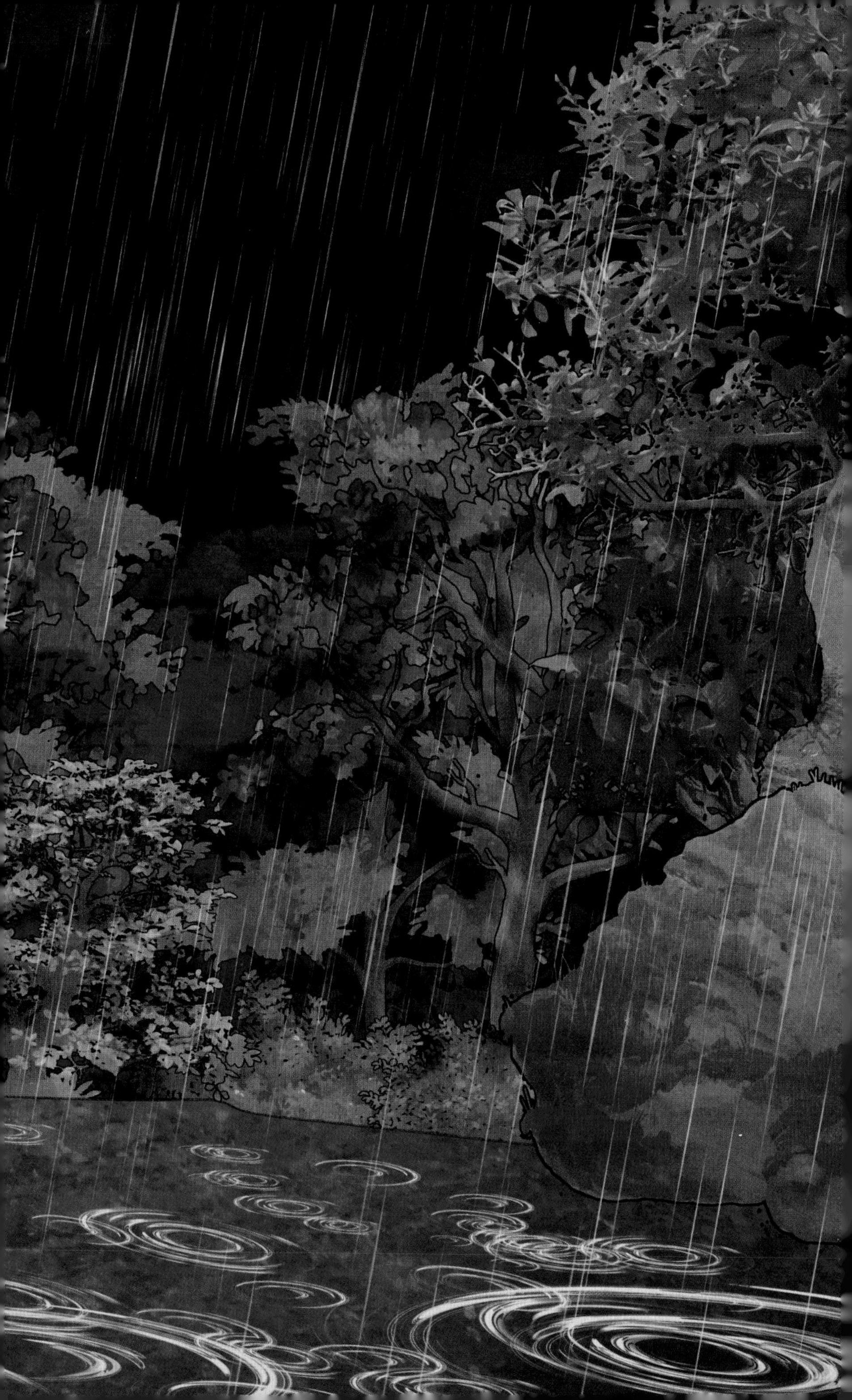

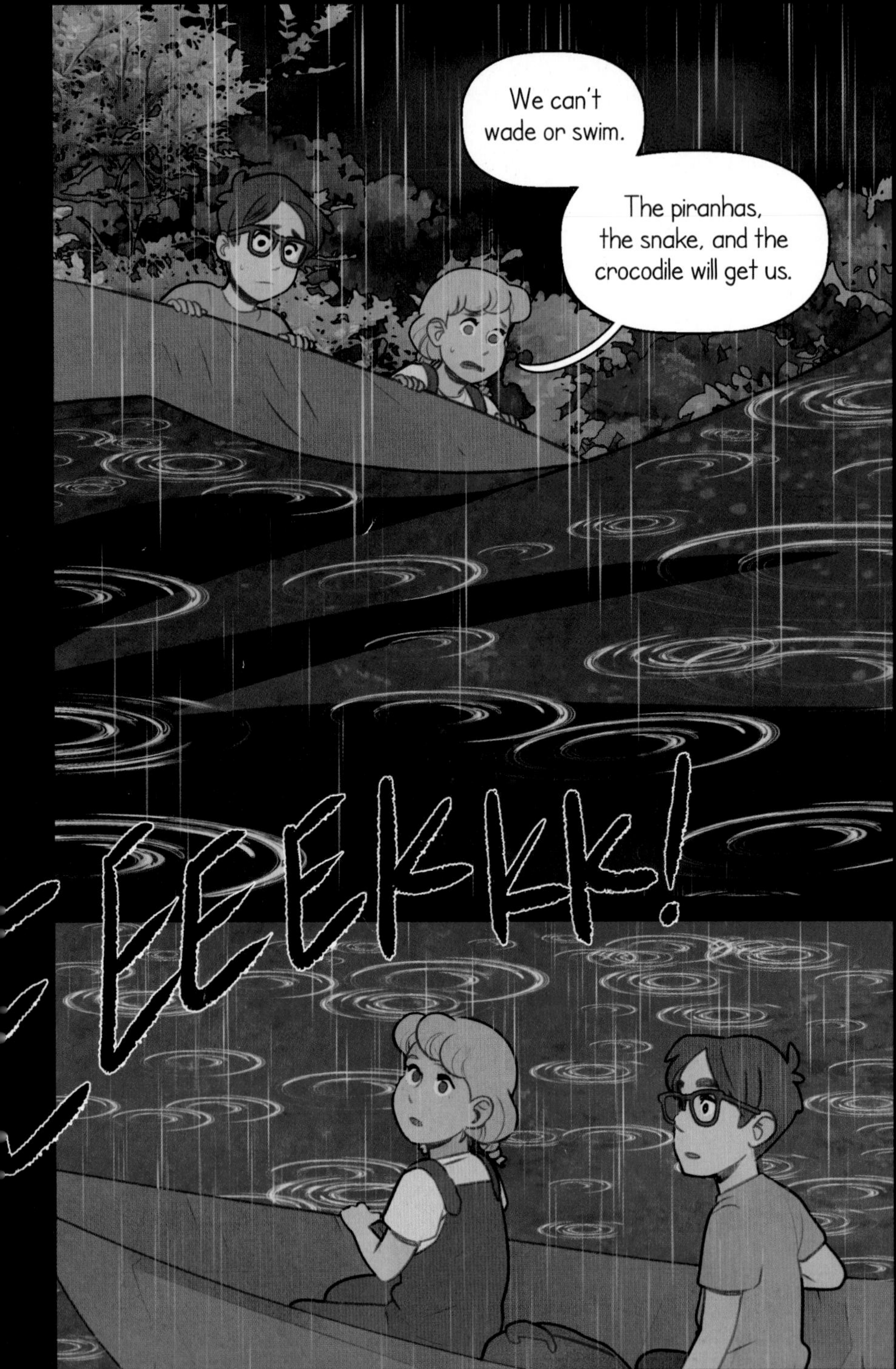
We can't wade or swim.
The piranhas, the snake, and the crocodile will get us.
EEEEKKK!

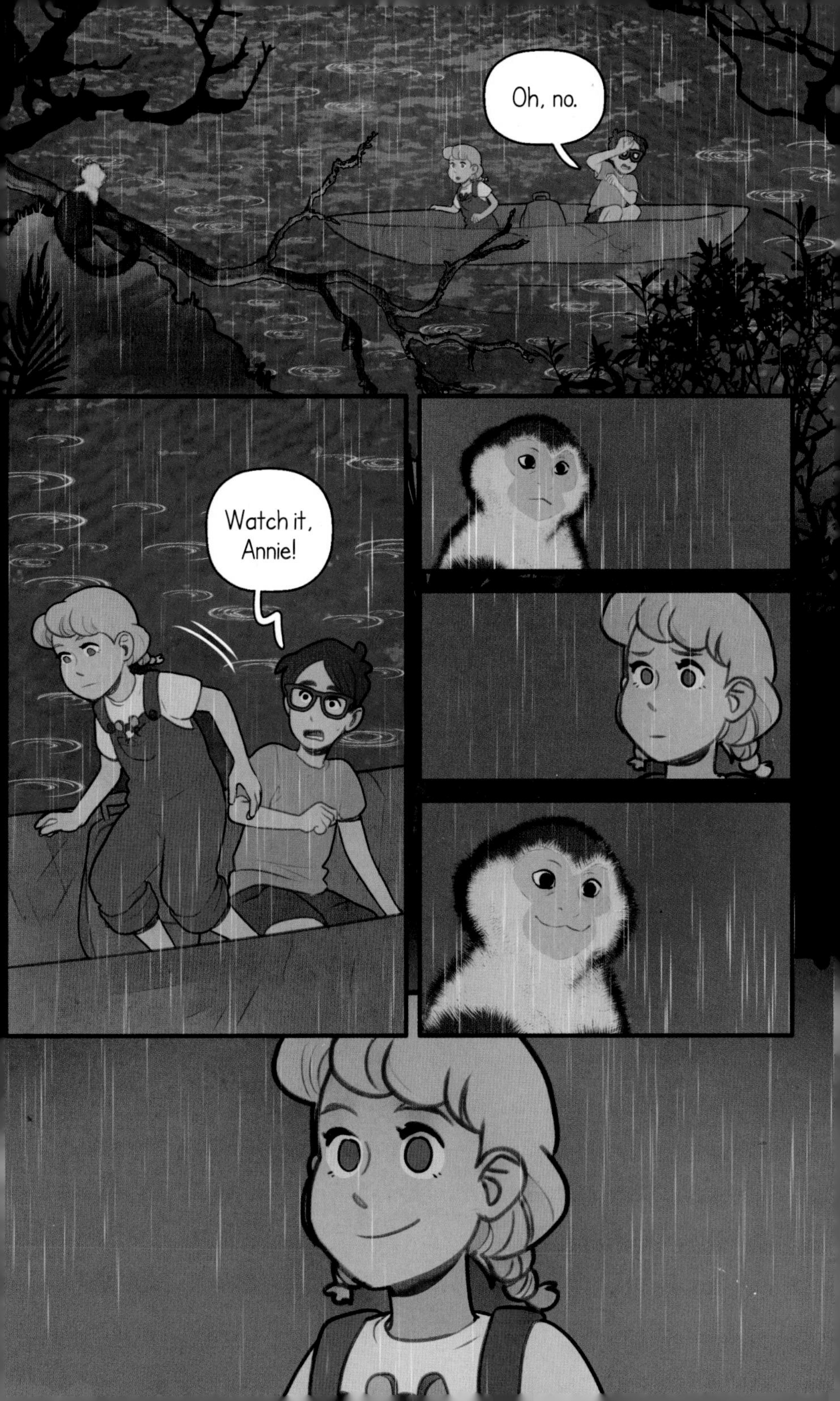
Oh, no.
Watch it, Annie!

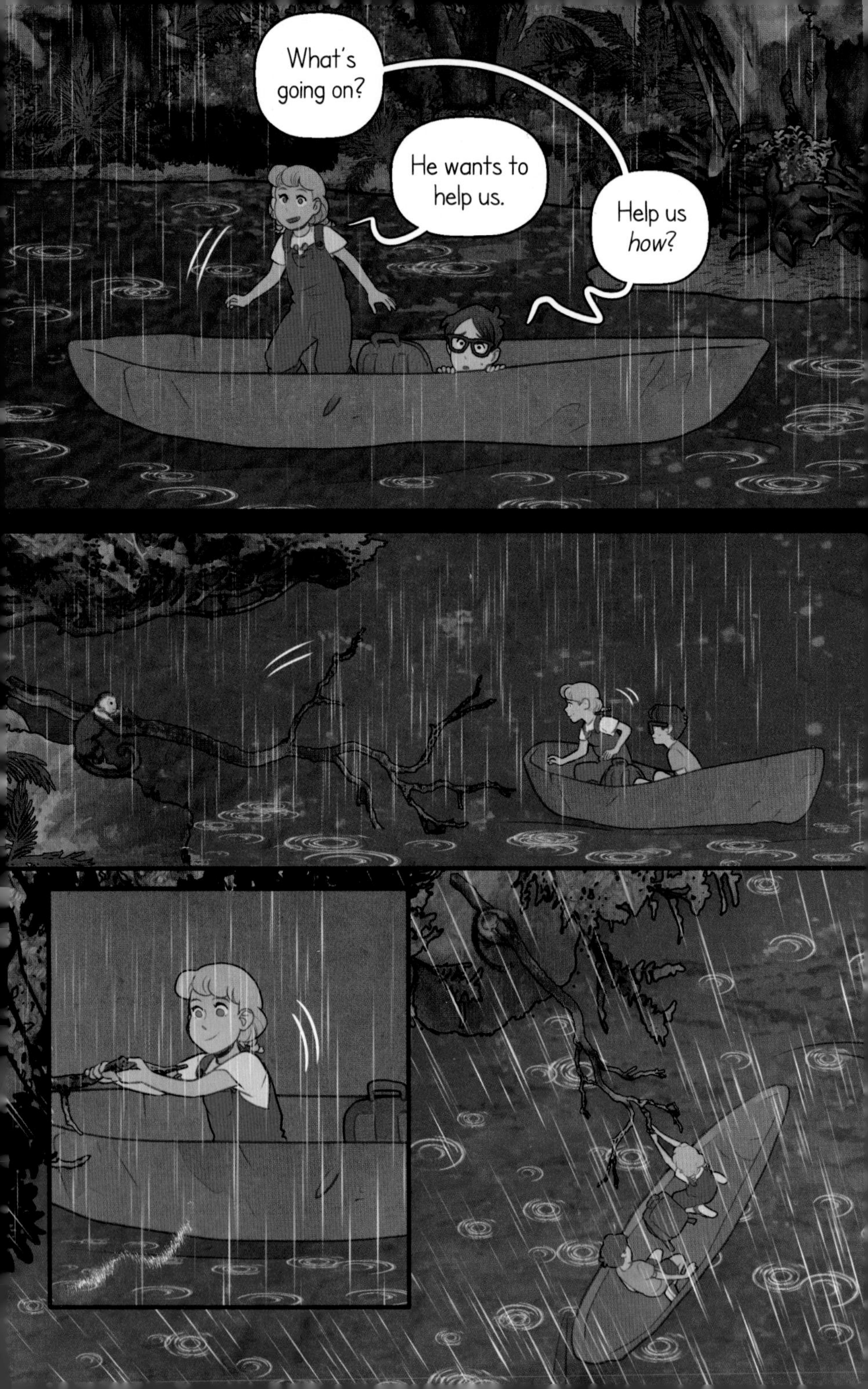
What's going on?
He wants to help us.
Help us *how?*

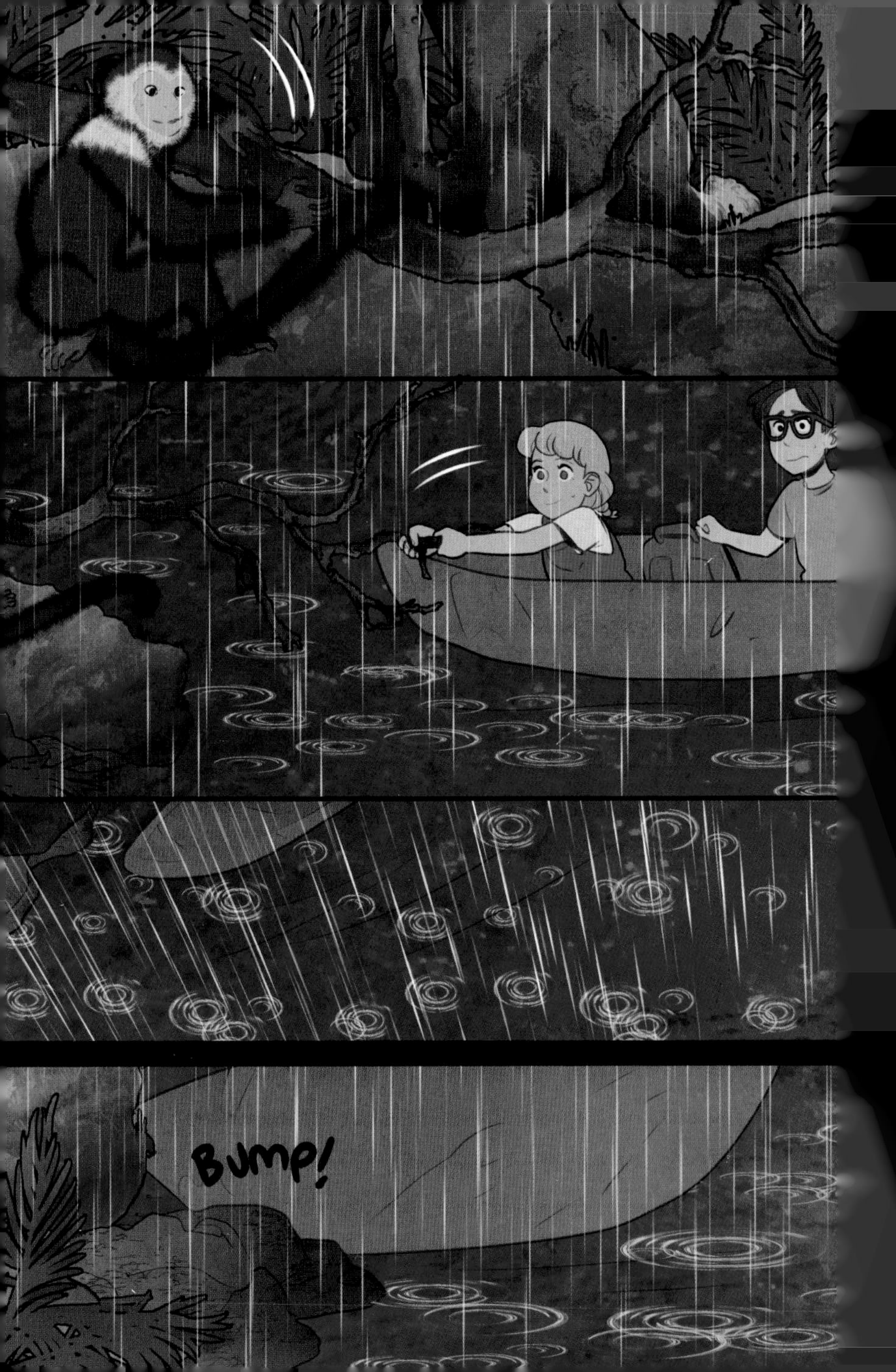
BUMP!

CHAPTER SIX

Freeze!

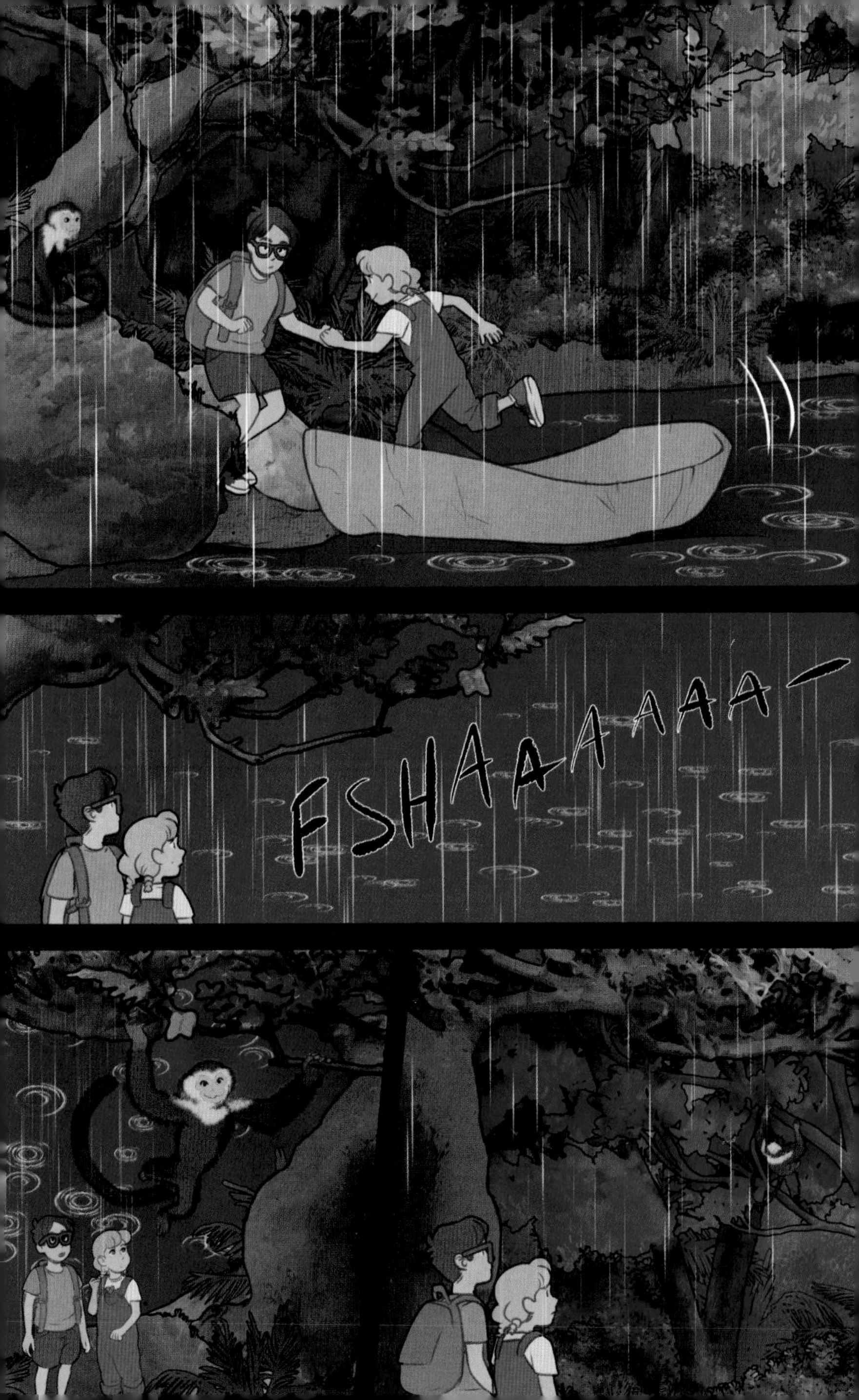
FSHAAAAAA

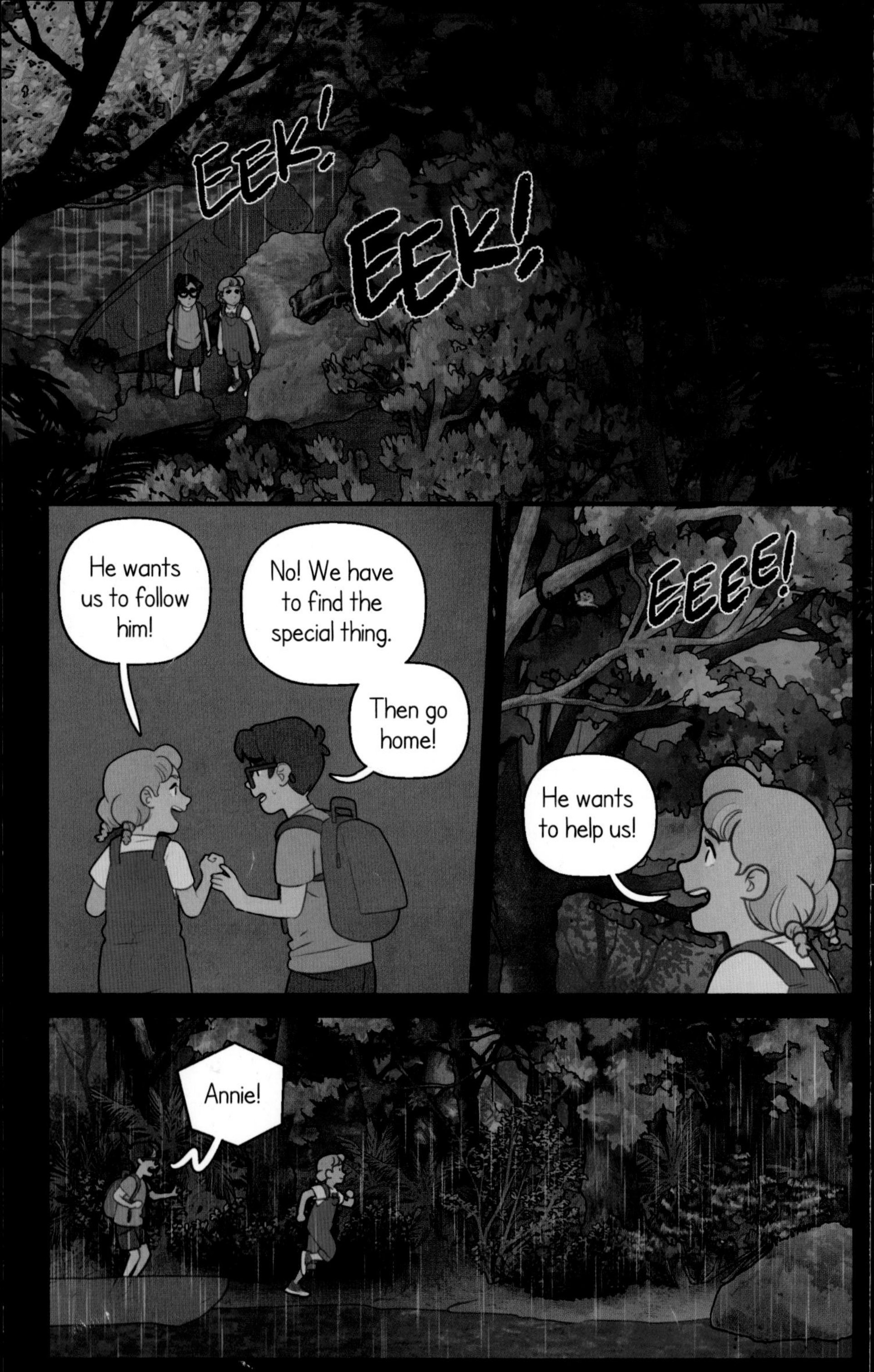
EEK!
EEK!
He wants us to follow him!
No! We have to find the special thing.
Then go home!
EEEE!
He wants to help us!
Annie!

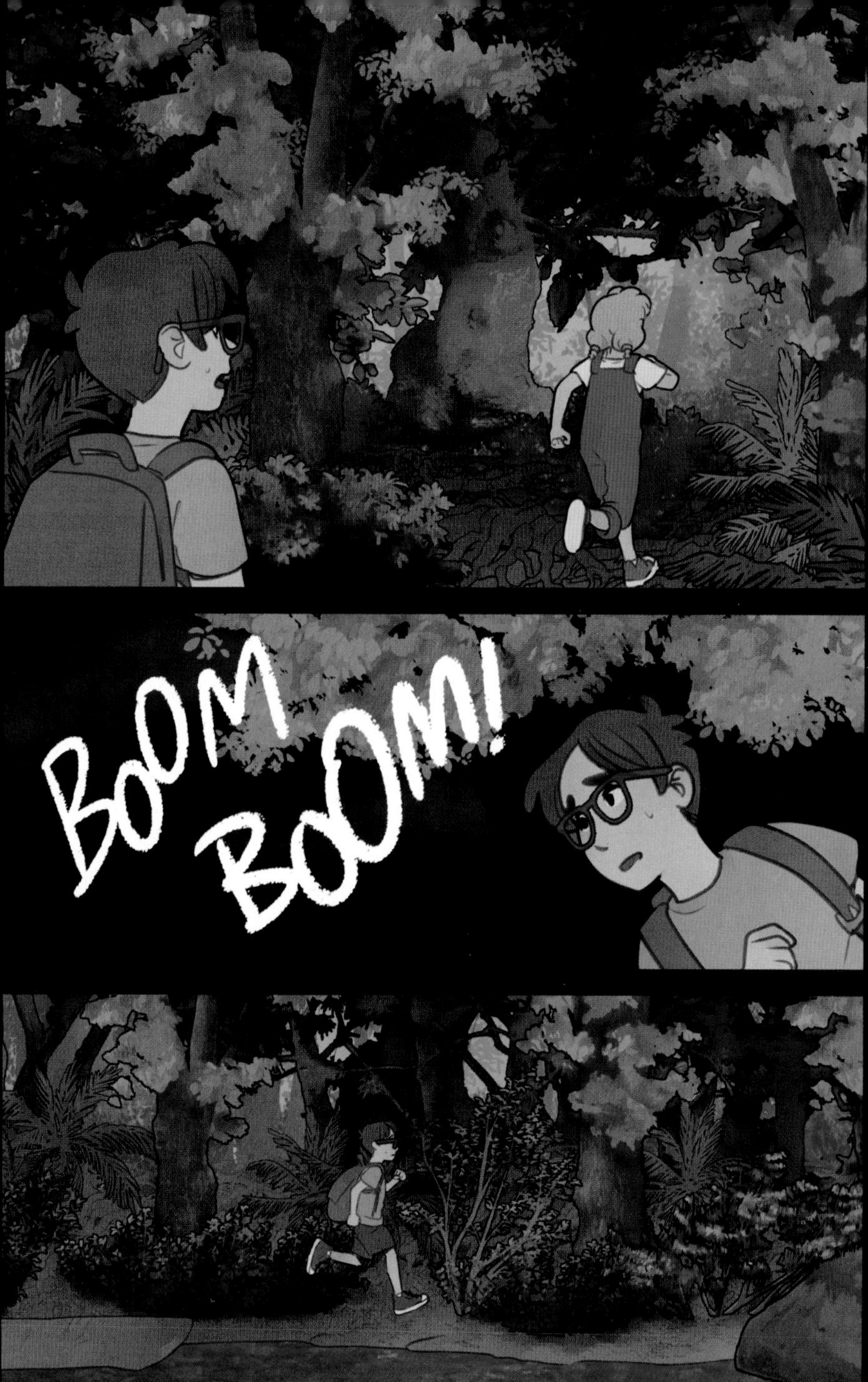
BOOM BOOM!

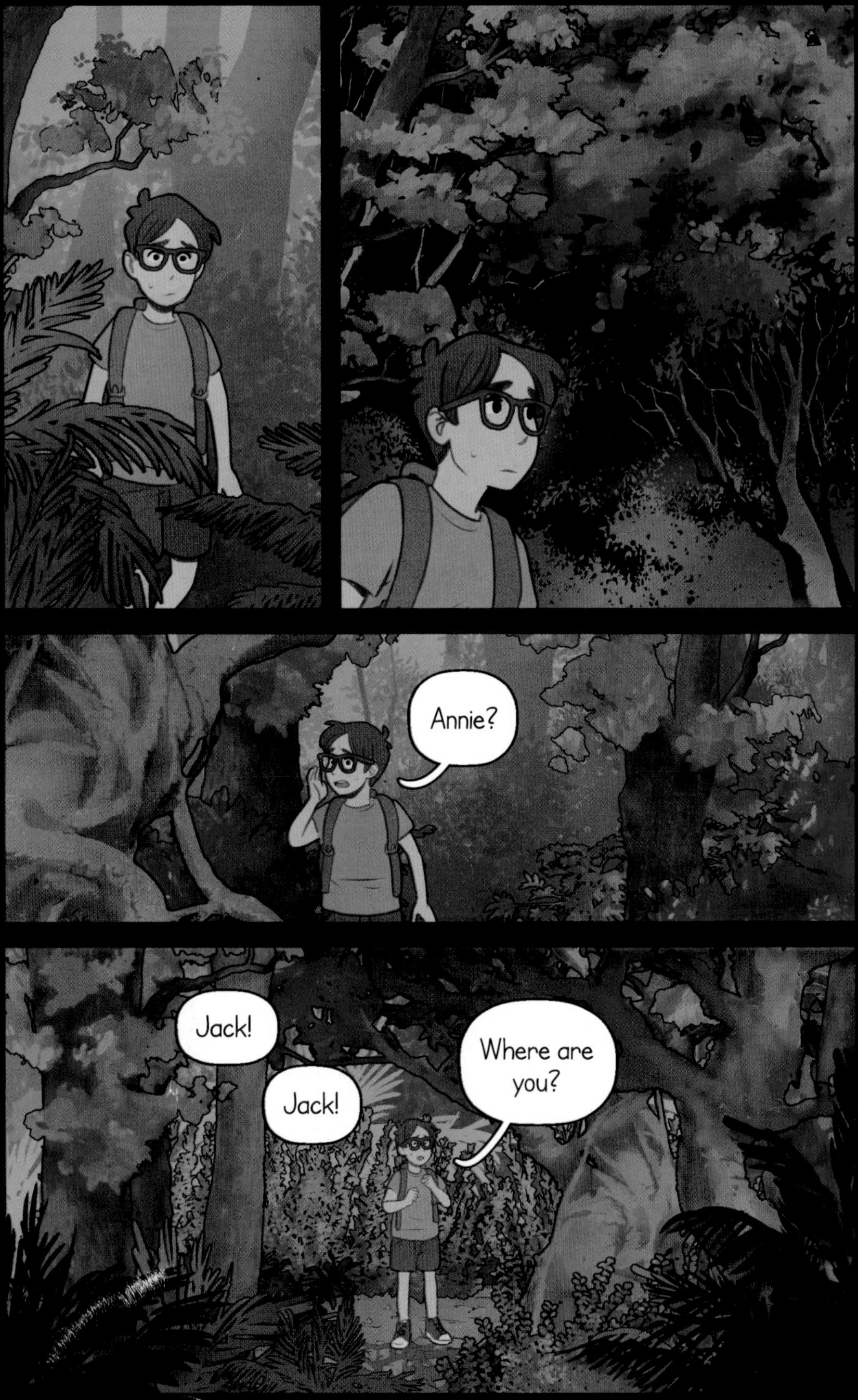
Annie?
Jack!
Jack!
Where are you?

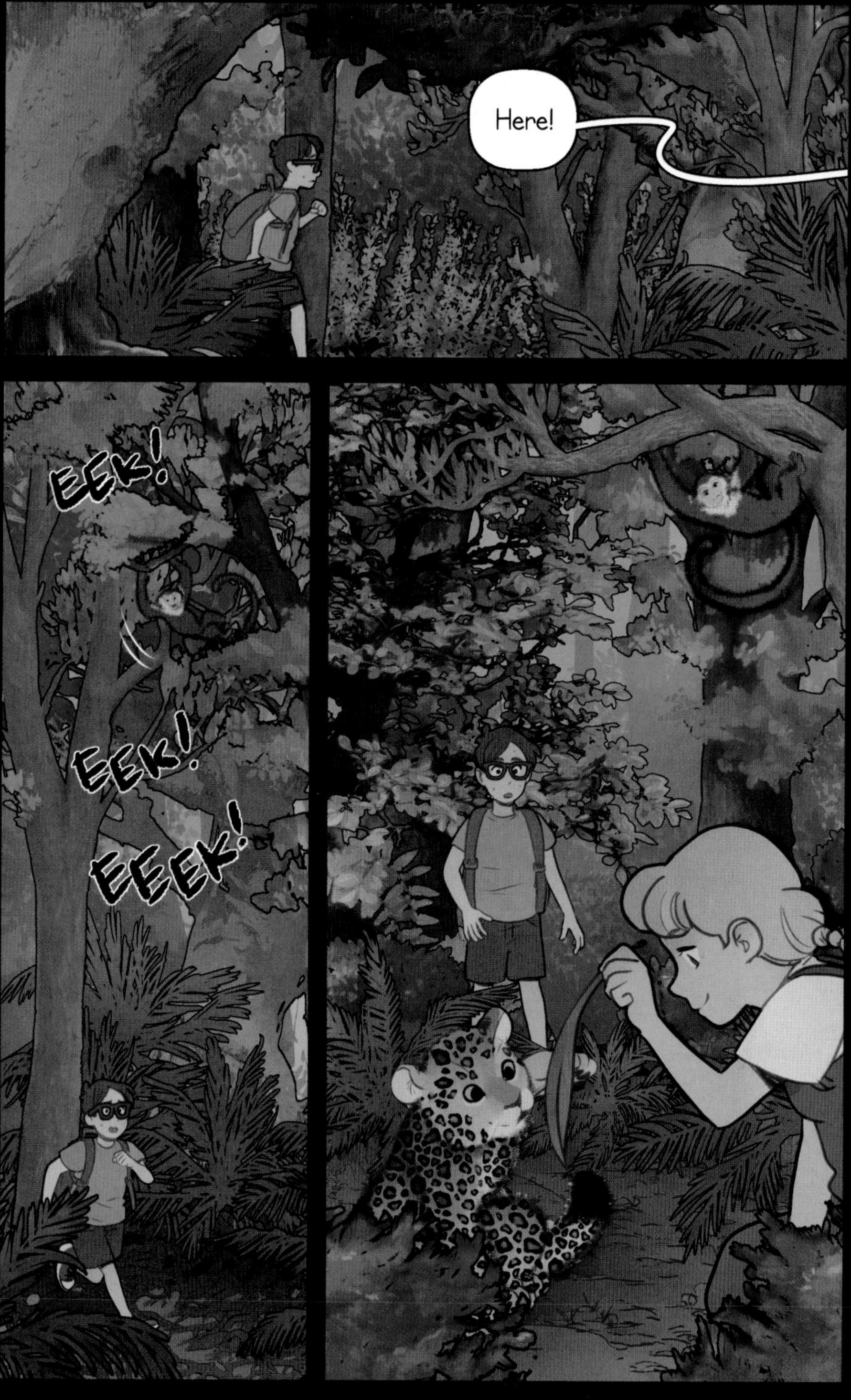
Here!
EEK!
EEK!
EEEK!

What's that?

I don't know, but I love it!

I'd better find out what it is.

Oh, it's so cute.

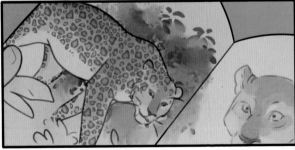

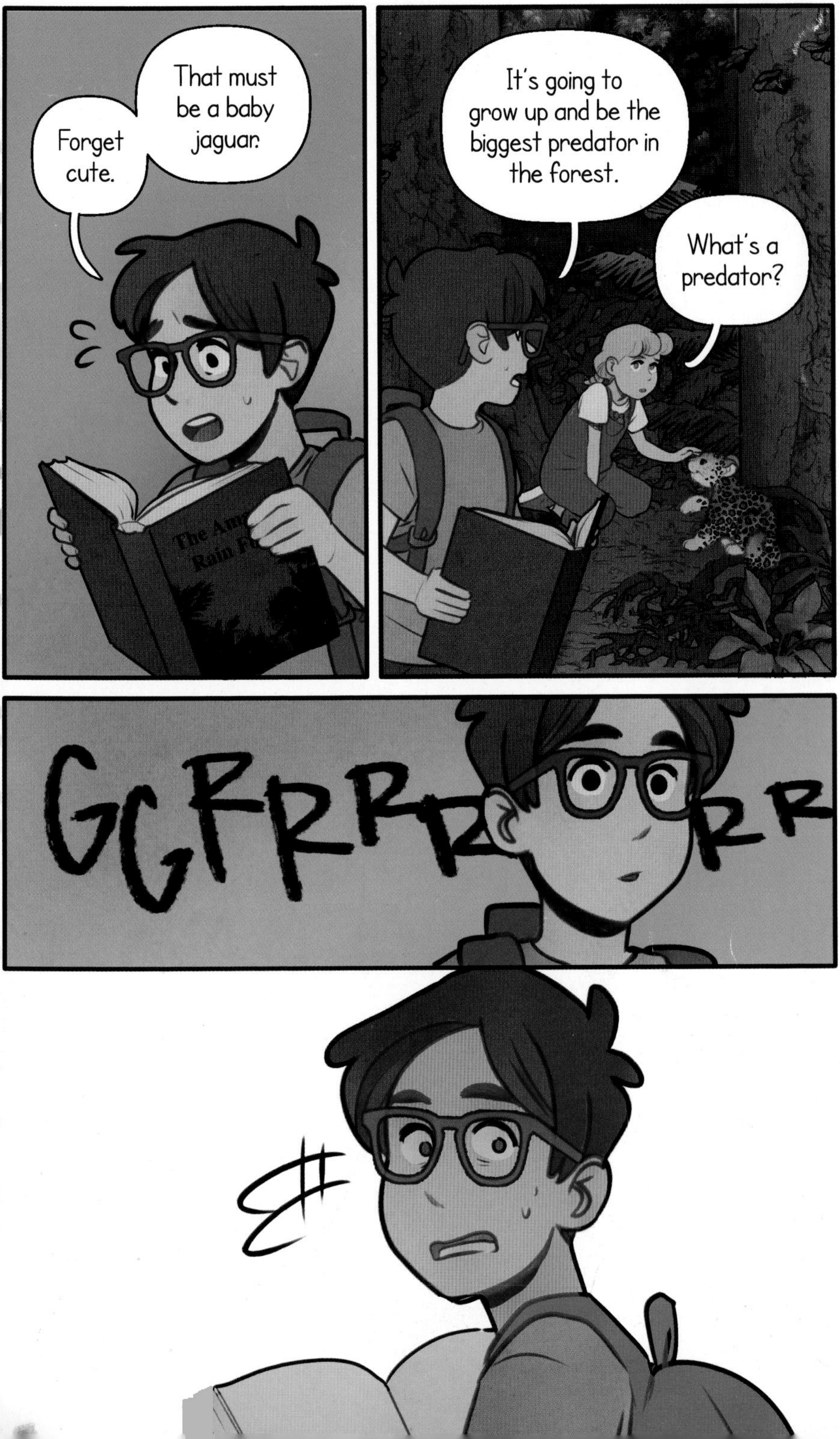
That must be a baby jaguar.
Forget cute.
It's going to grow up and be the biggest predator in the forest.
What's a predator?
GGRRRRRR

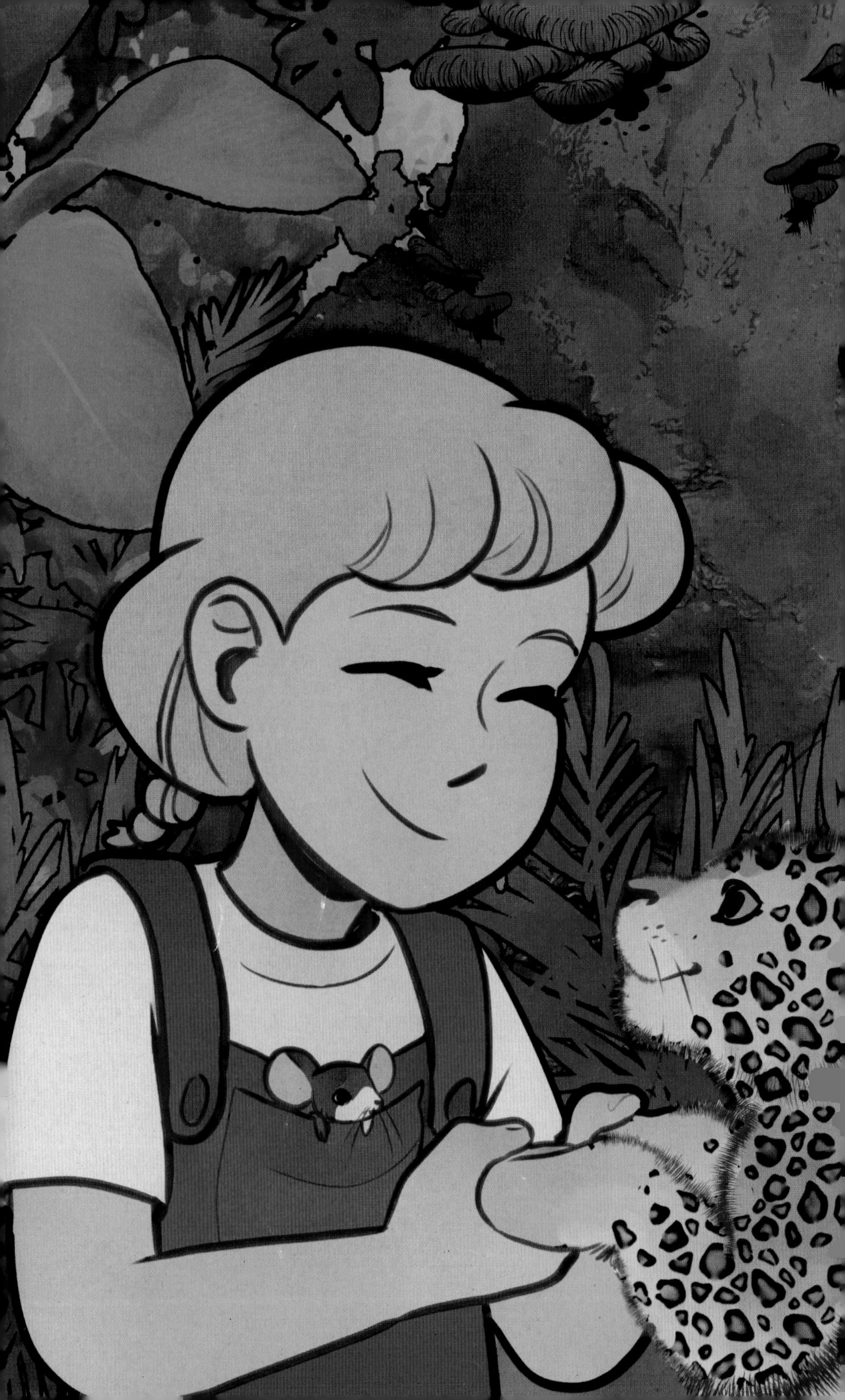

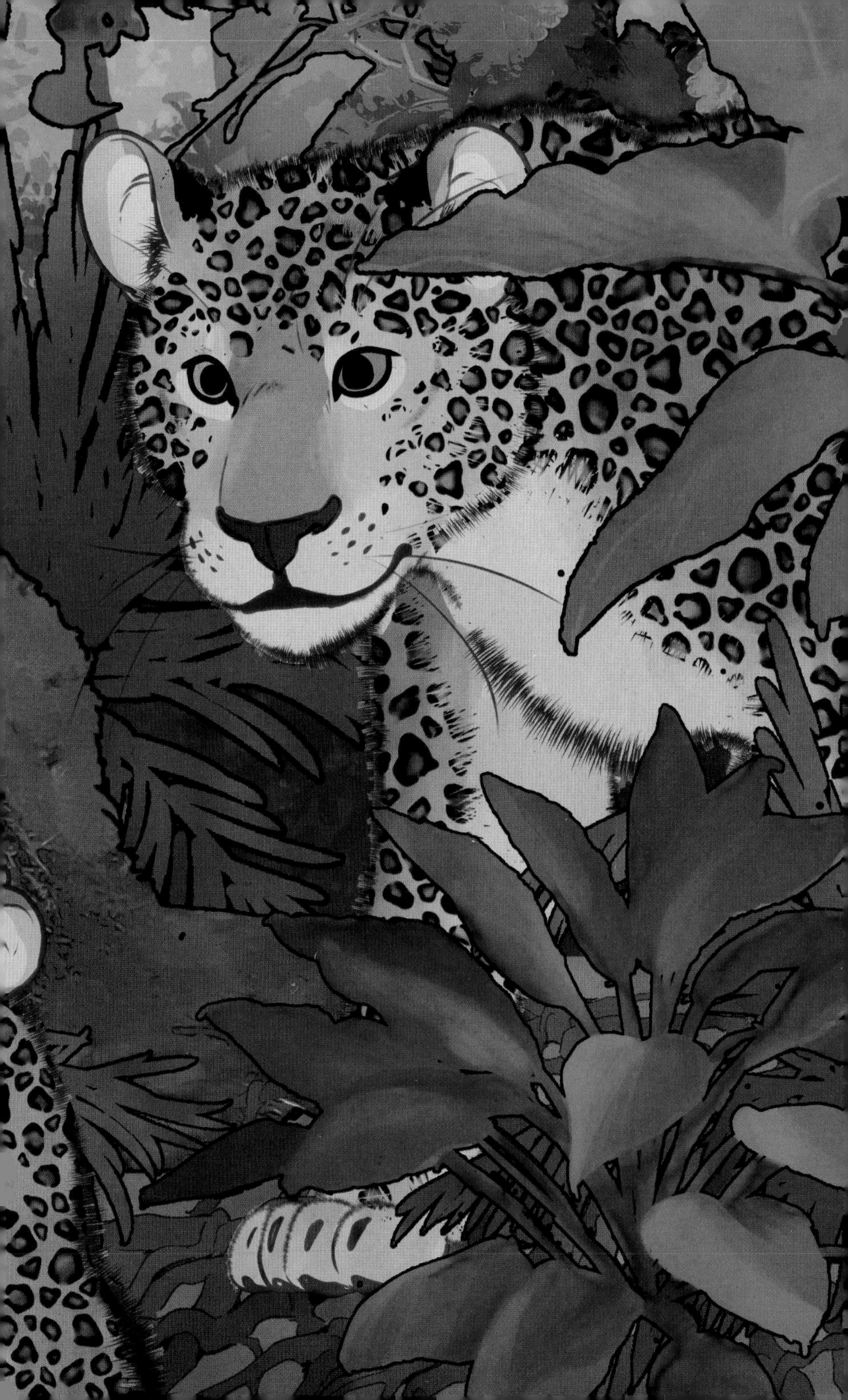

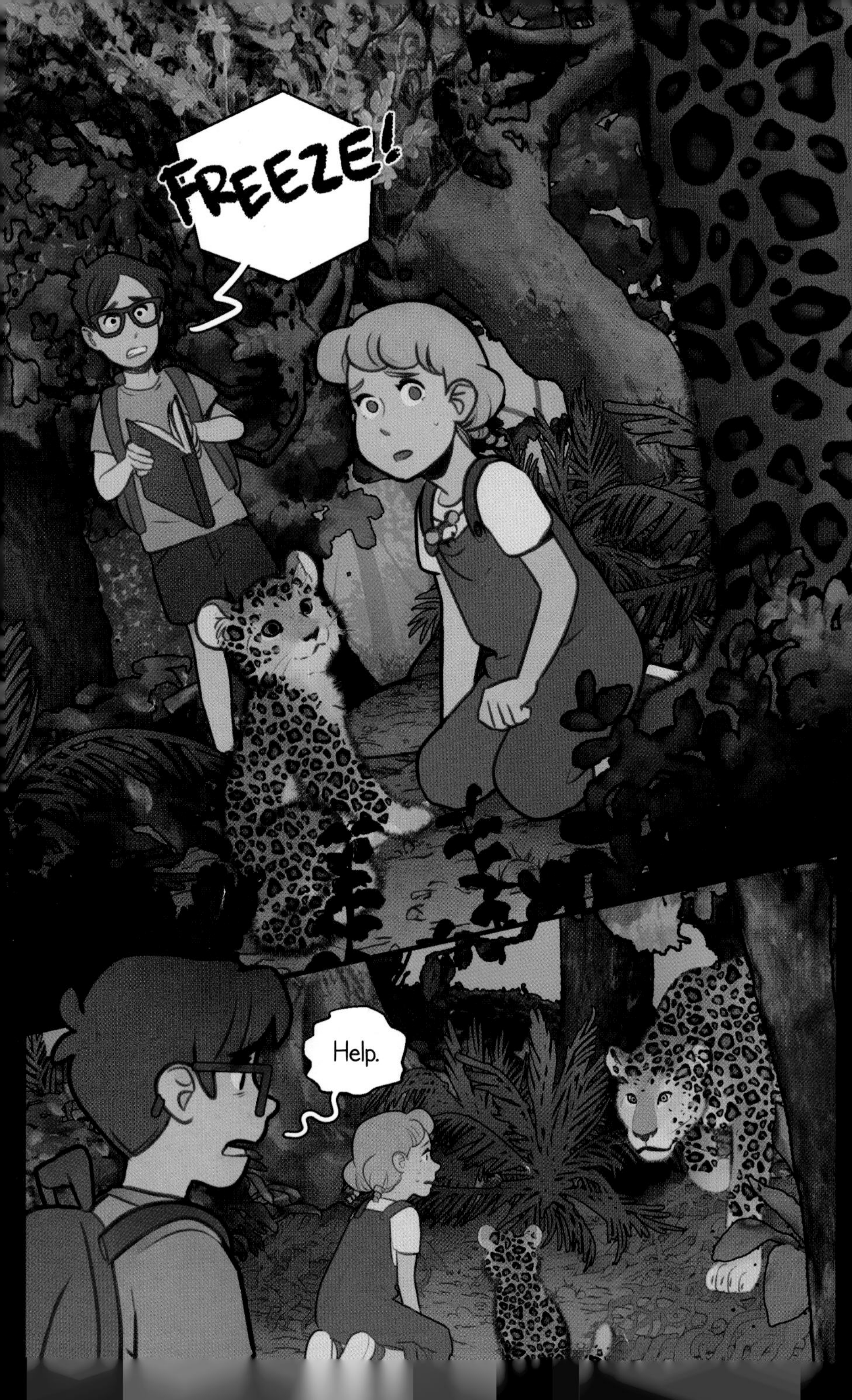
FREEZE!
Help.

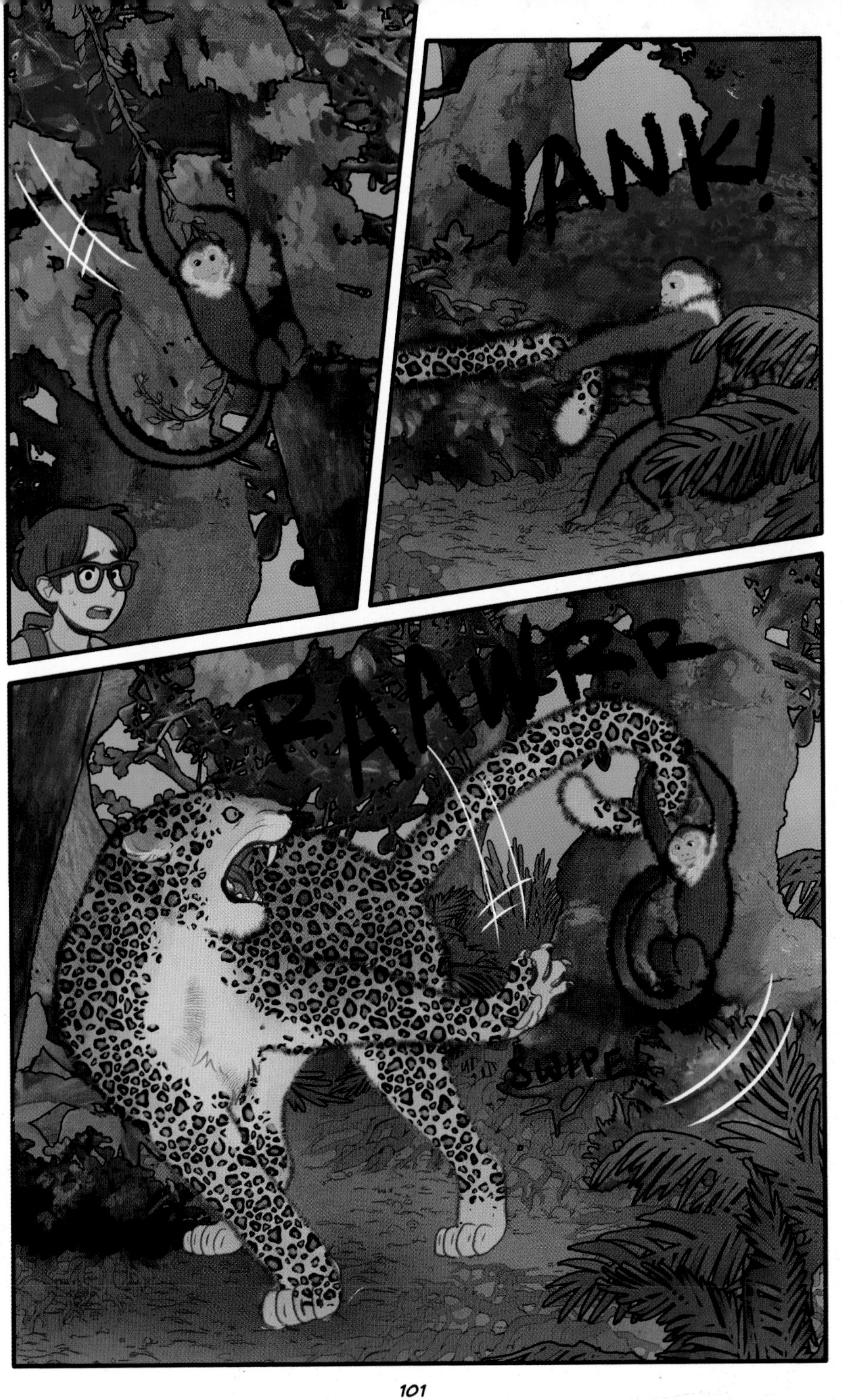
YANK!
RAAWRR
SWIPE

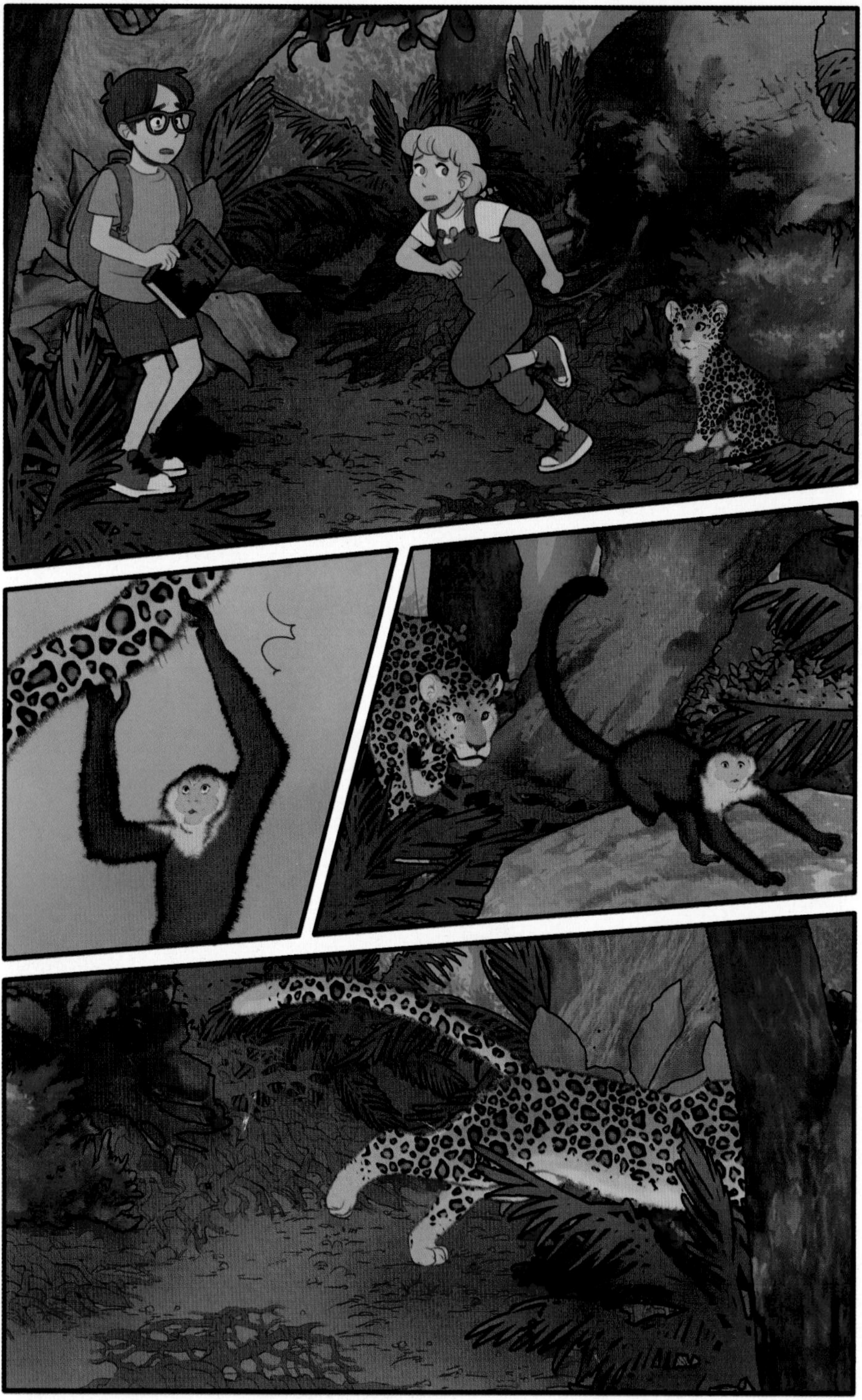

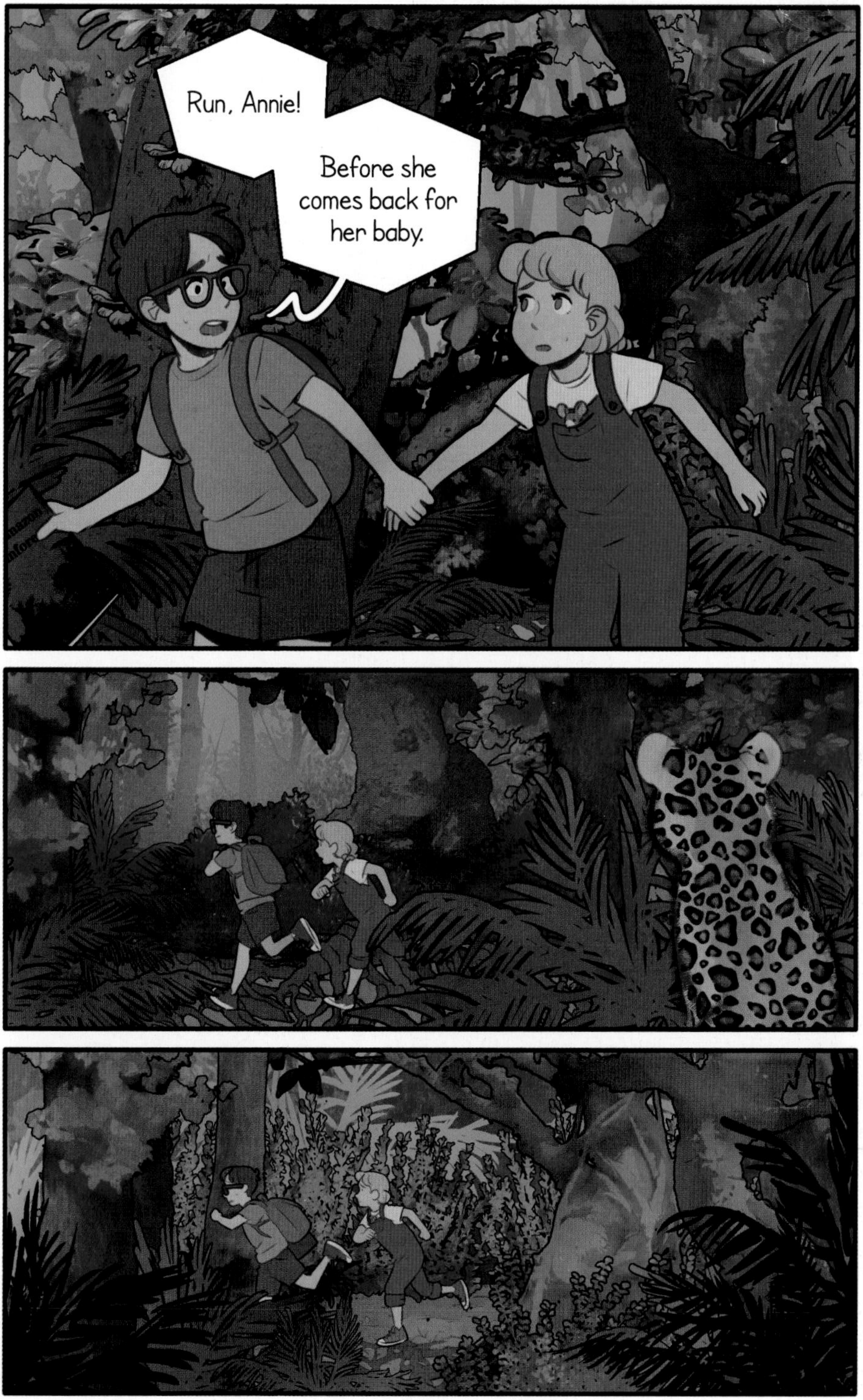
Run, Annie!
Before she comes back for her baby.

CHAPTER SEVEN

Vampire Bats?

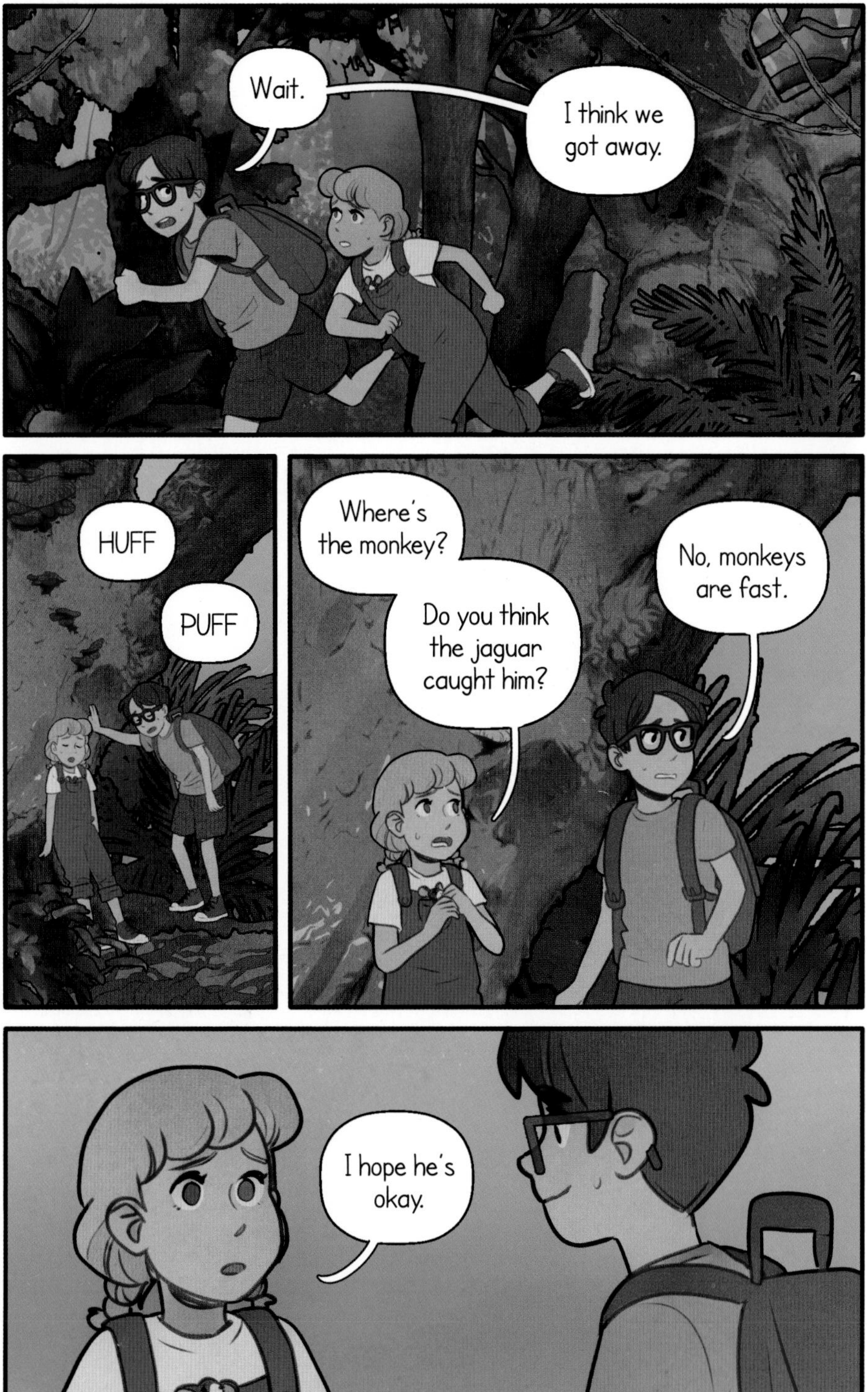
Wait.
I think we got away.
HUFF
PUFF
Where's the monkey?
Do you think the jaguar caught him?
No, monkeys are fast.
I hope he's okay.

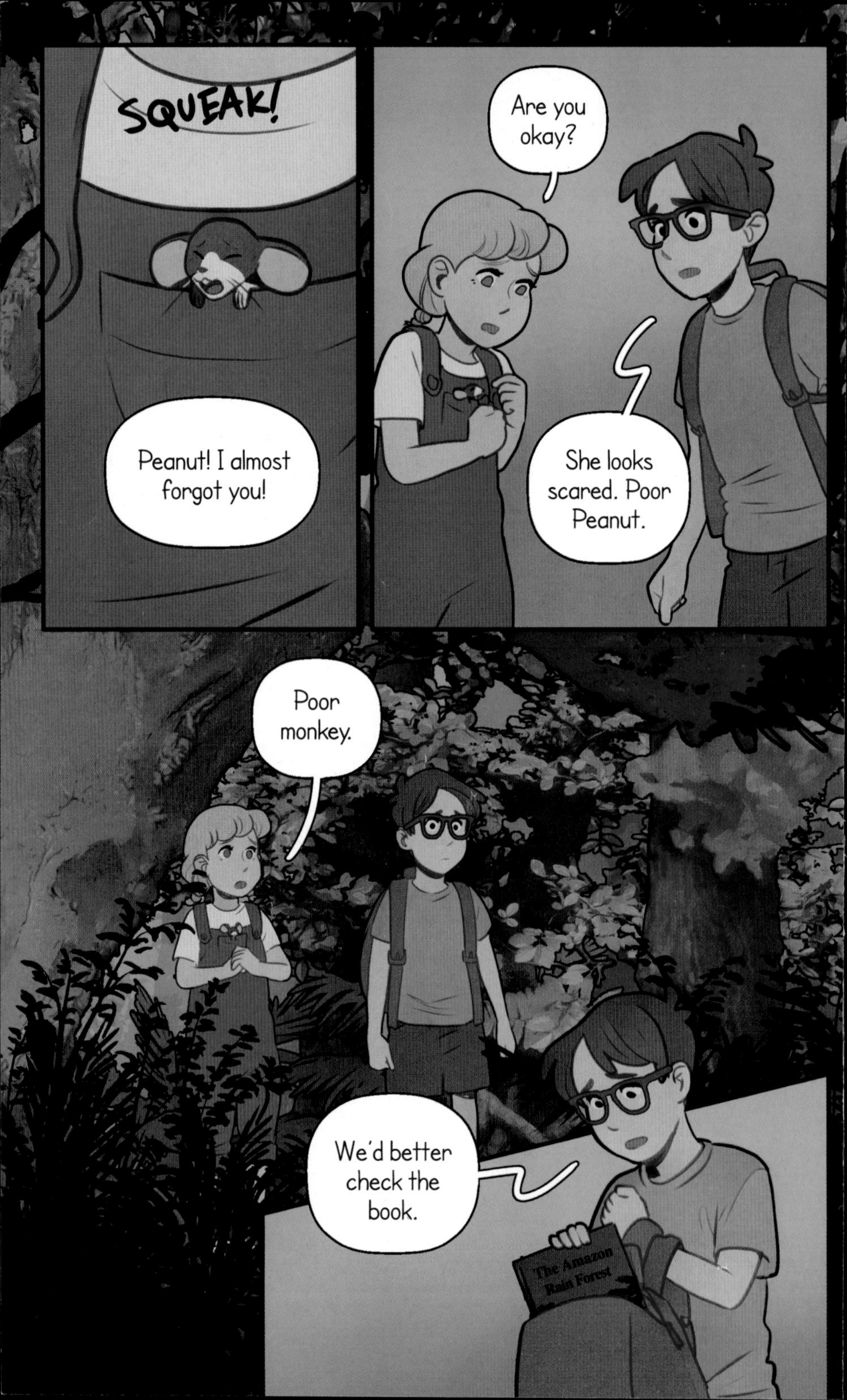
SQUEAK!
Peanut! I almost forgot you!
Are you okay?
She looks scared. Poor Peanut.
Poor monkey.
We'd better check the book.
The Amazon Rain Forest

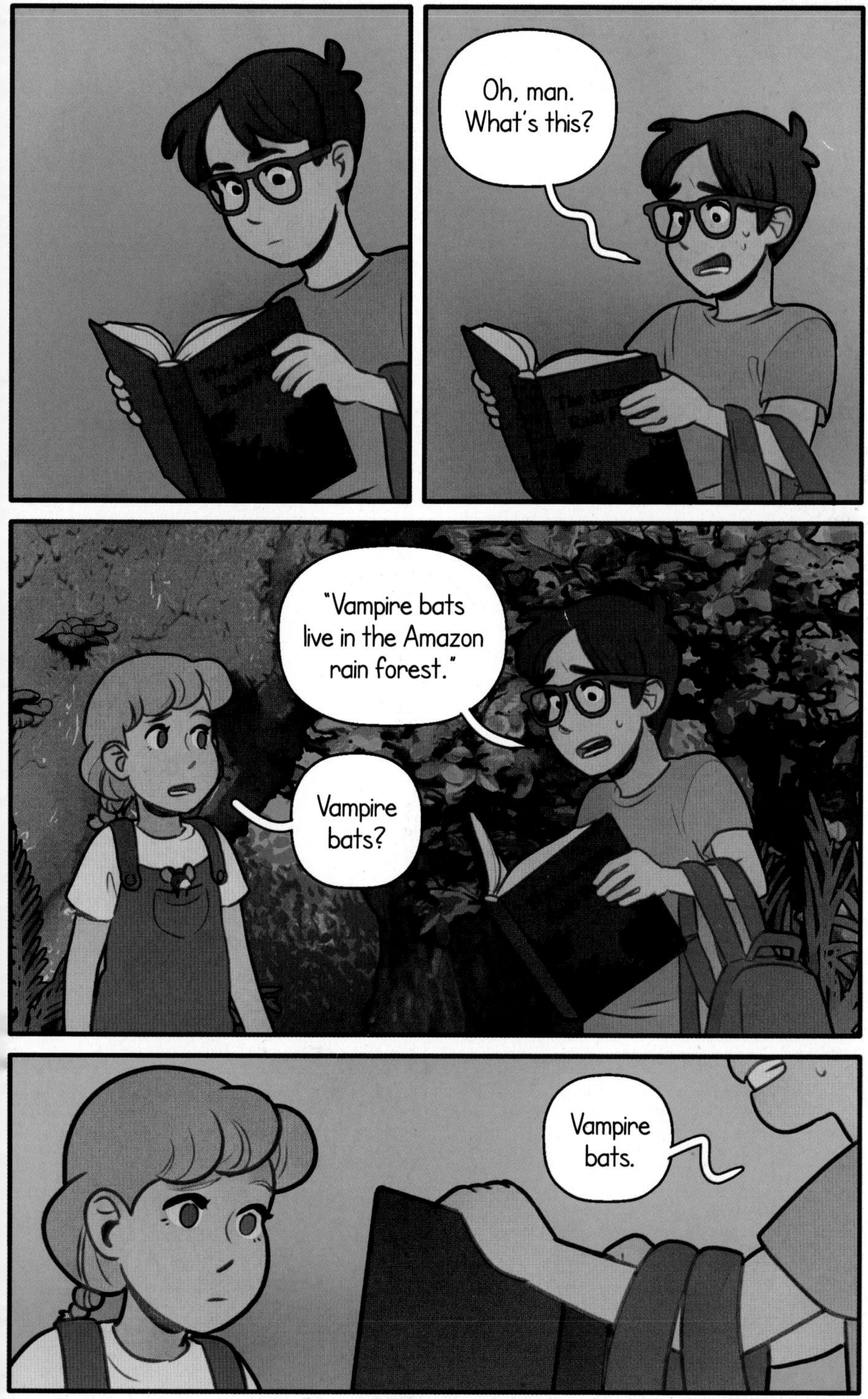
Oh, man. What's this?
"Vampire bats live in the Amazon rain forest."
Vampire bats?
Vampire bats.

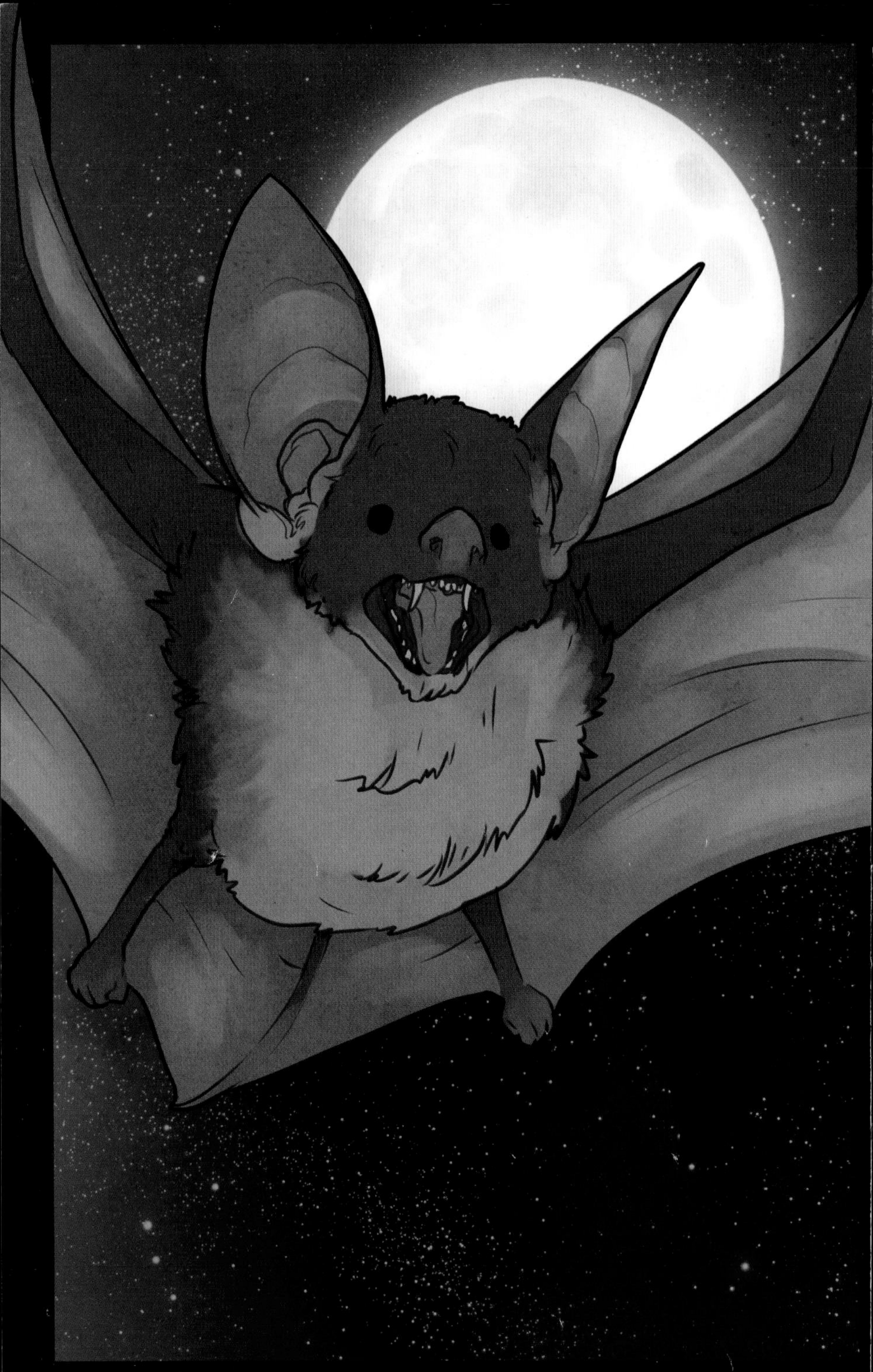

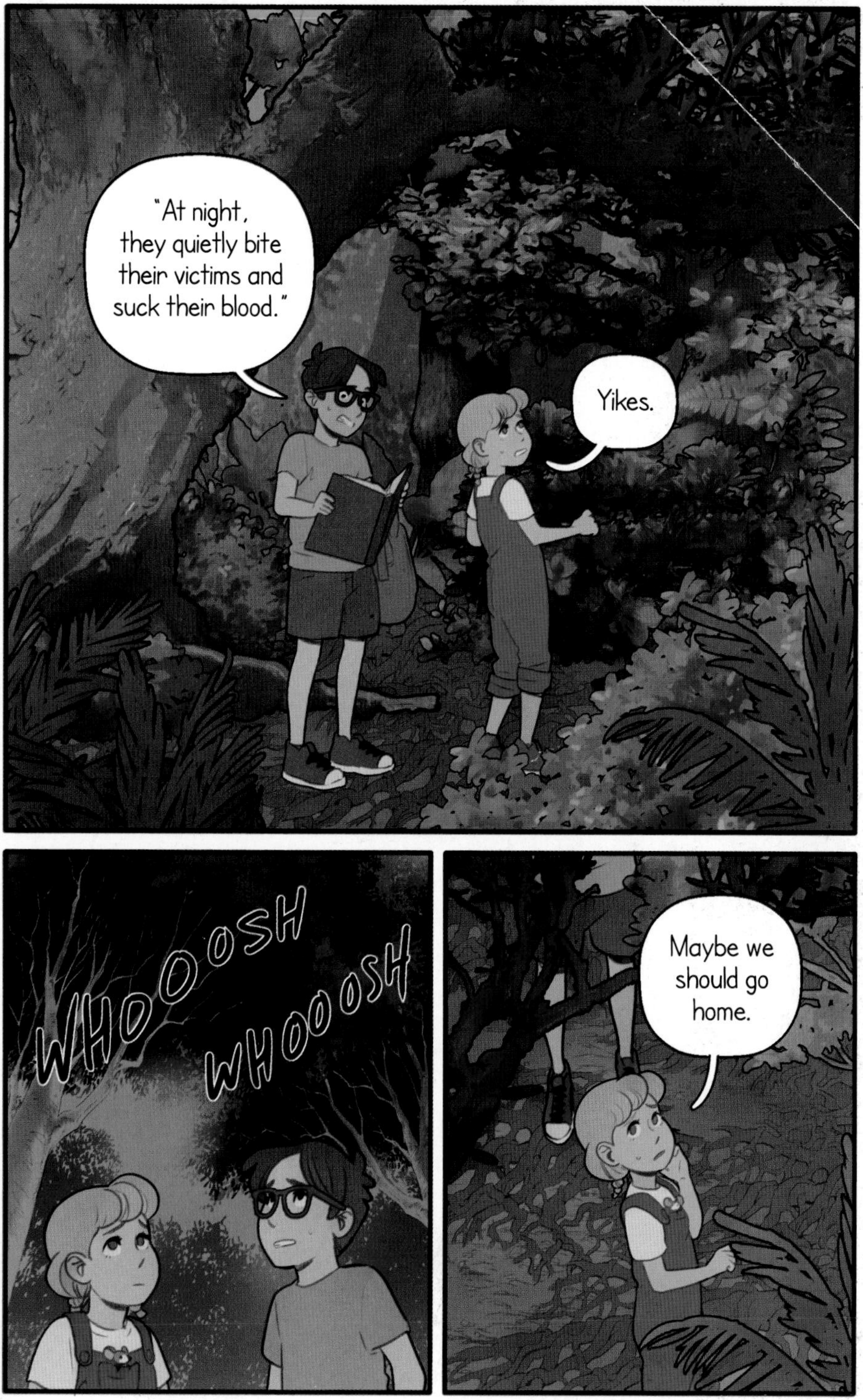
"At night, they quietly bite their victims and suck their blood."
Yikes.
WHOOOSH
WHOOOSH
Maybe we should go home.

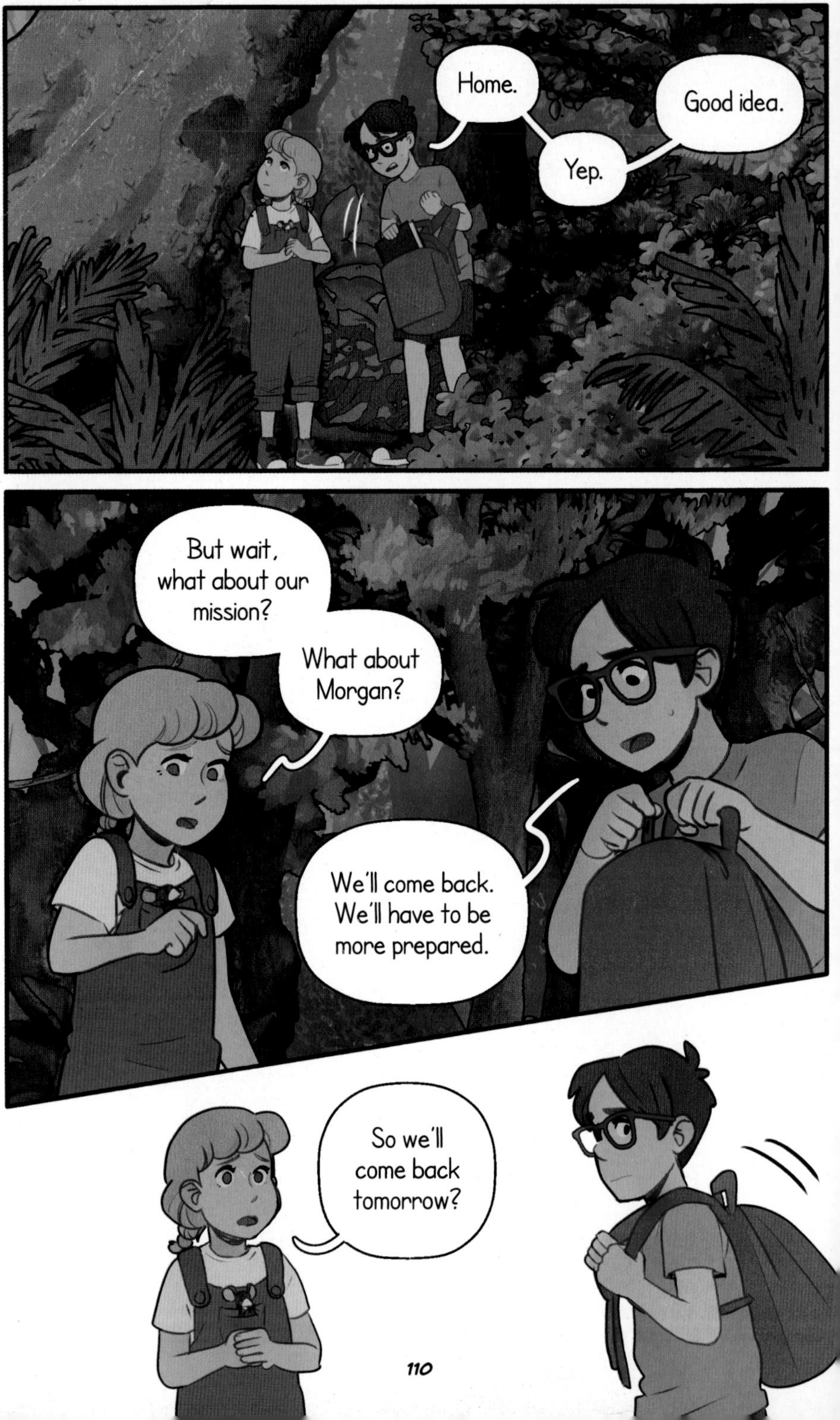
Home.
Yep.
Good idea.
But wait, what about our mission?
What about Morgan?
We'll come back. We'll have to be more prepared.
So we'll come back tomorrow?

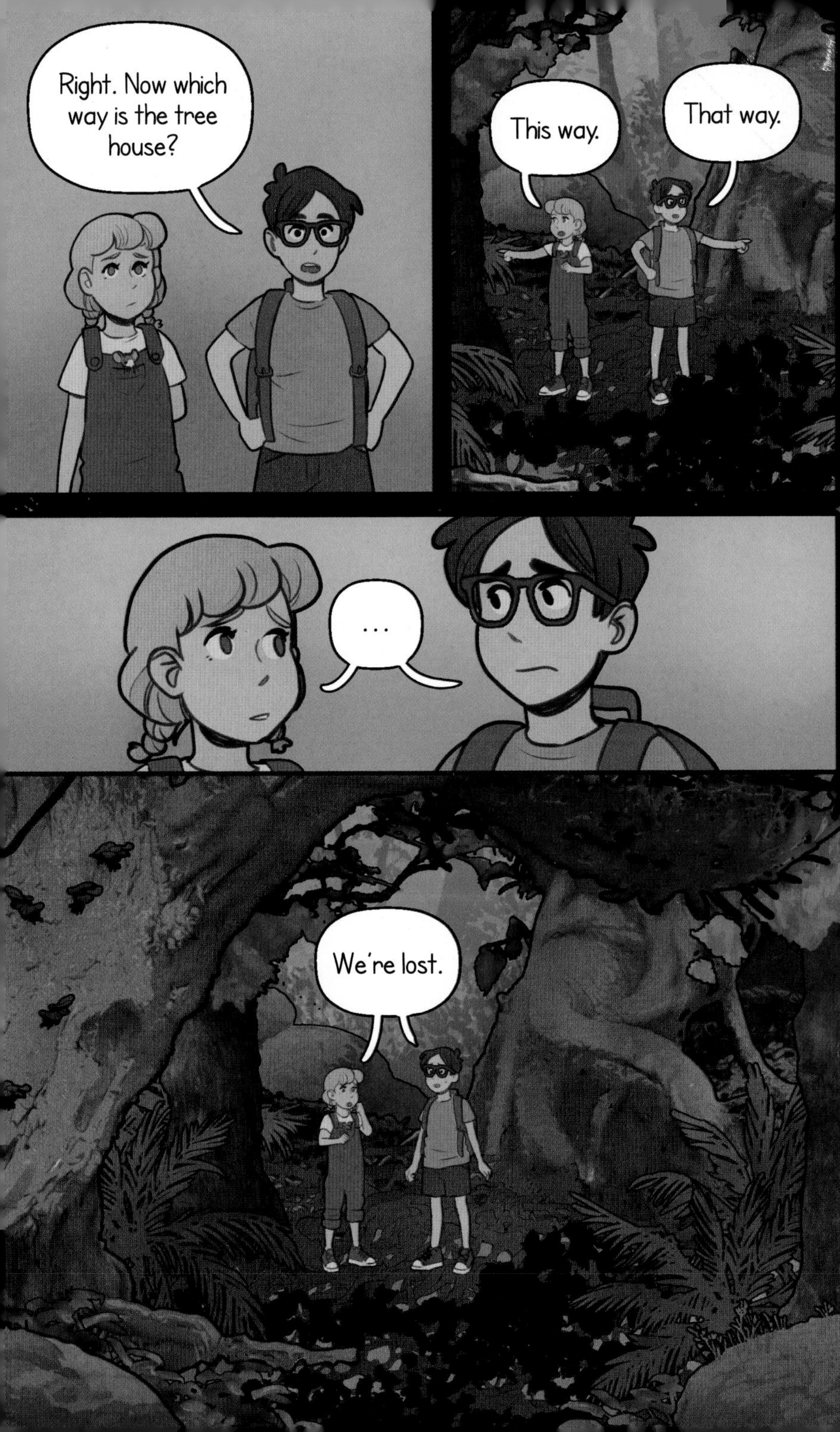
Right. Now which way is the tree house?
This way.
That way.
...
We're lost.

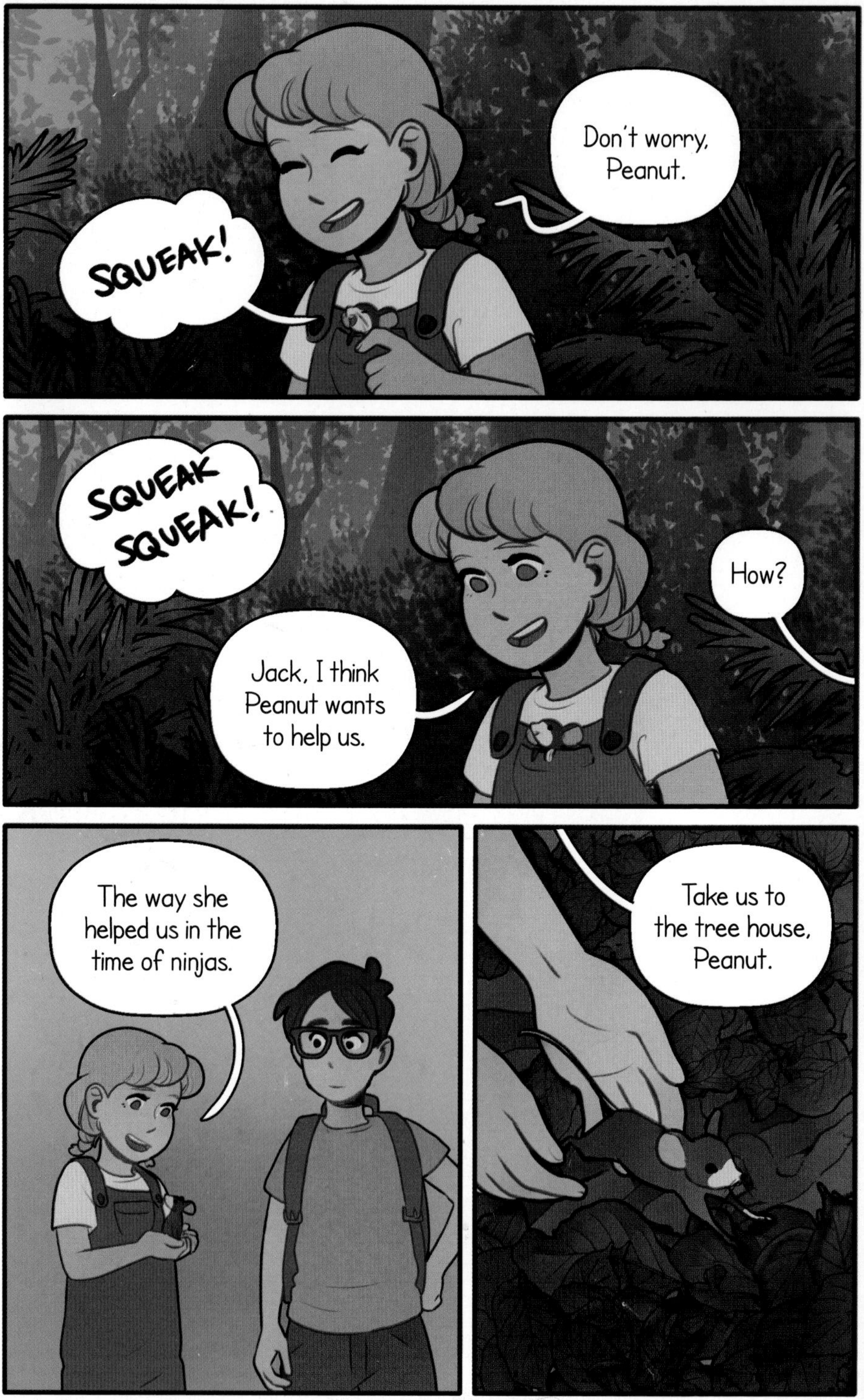
Don't worry, Peanut.
SQUEAK!
SQUEAK SQUEAK!
How?
Jack, I think Peanut wants to help us.
The way she helped us in the time of ninjas.
Take us to the tree house, Peanut.

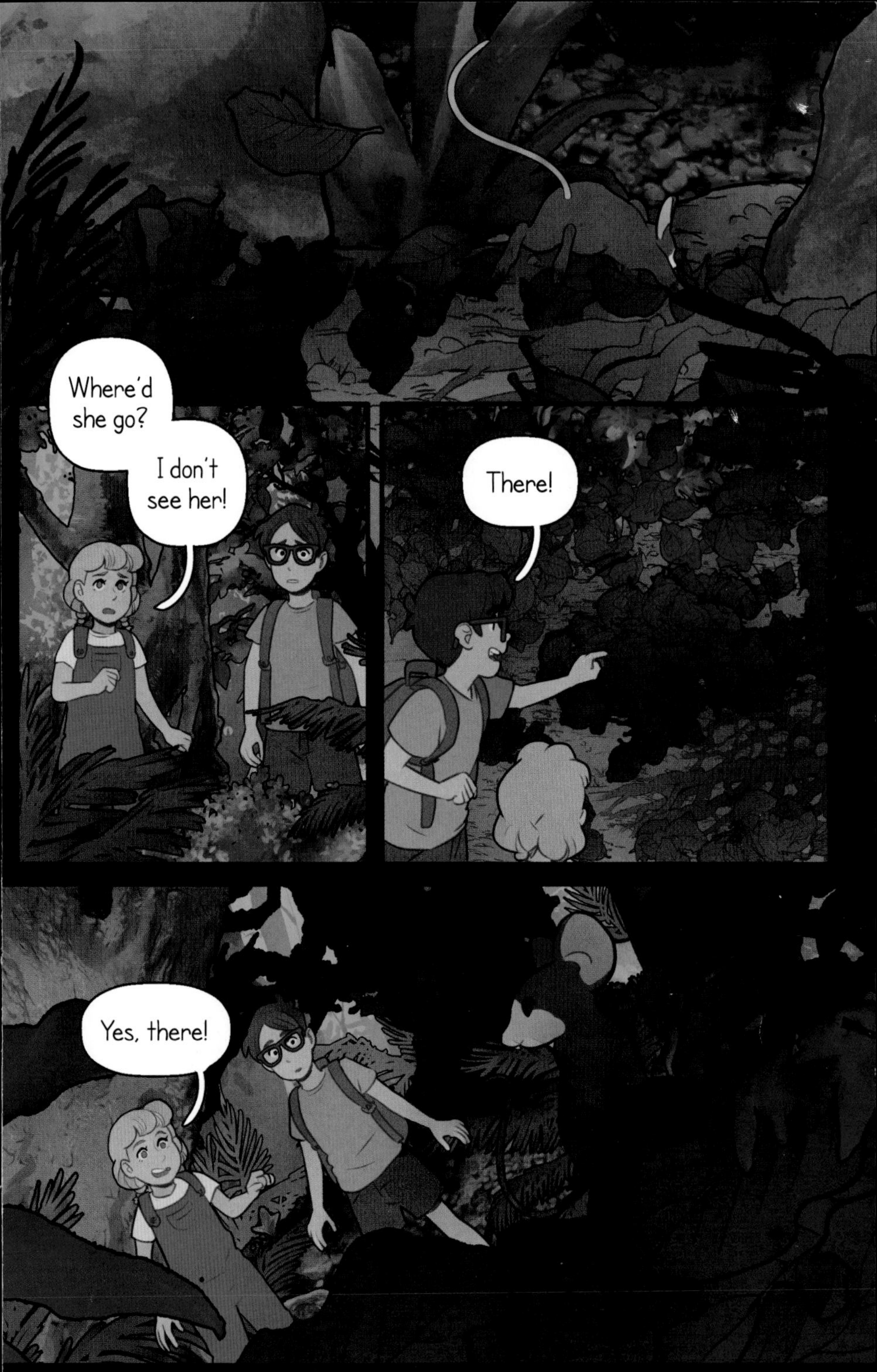
Where'd she go?
I don't see her!
There!
Yes, there!

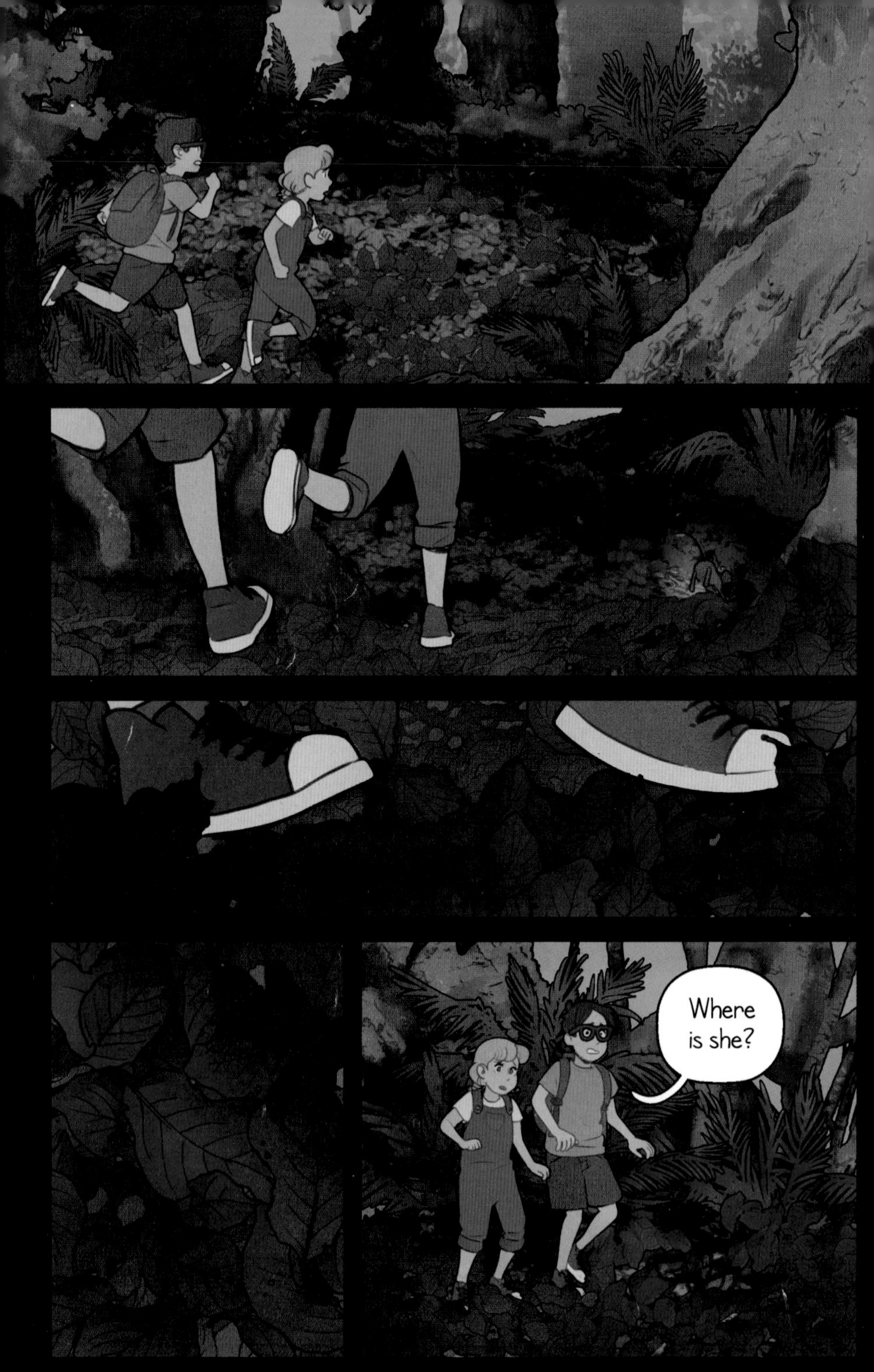
Where is she?

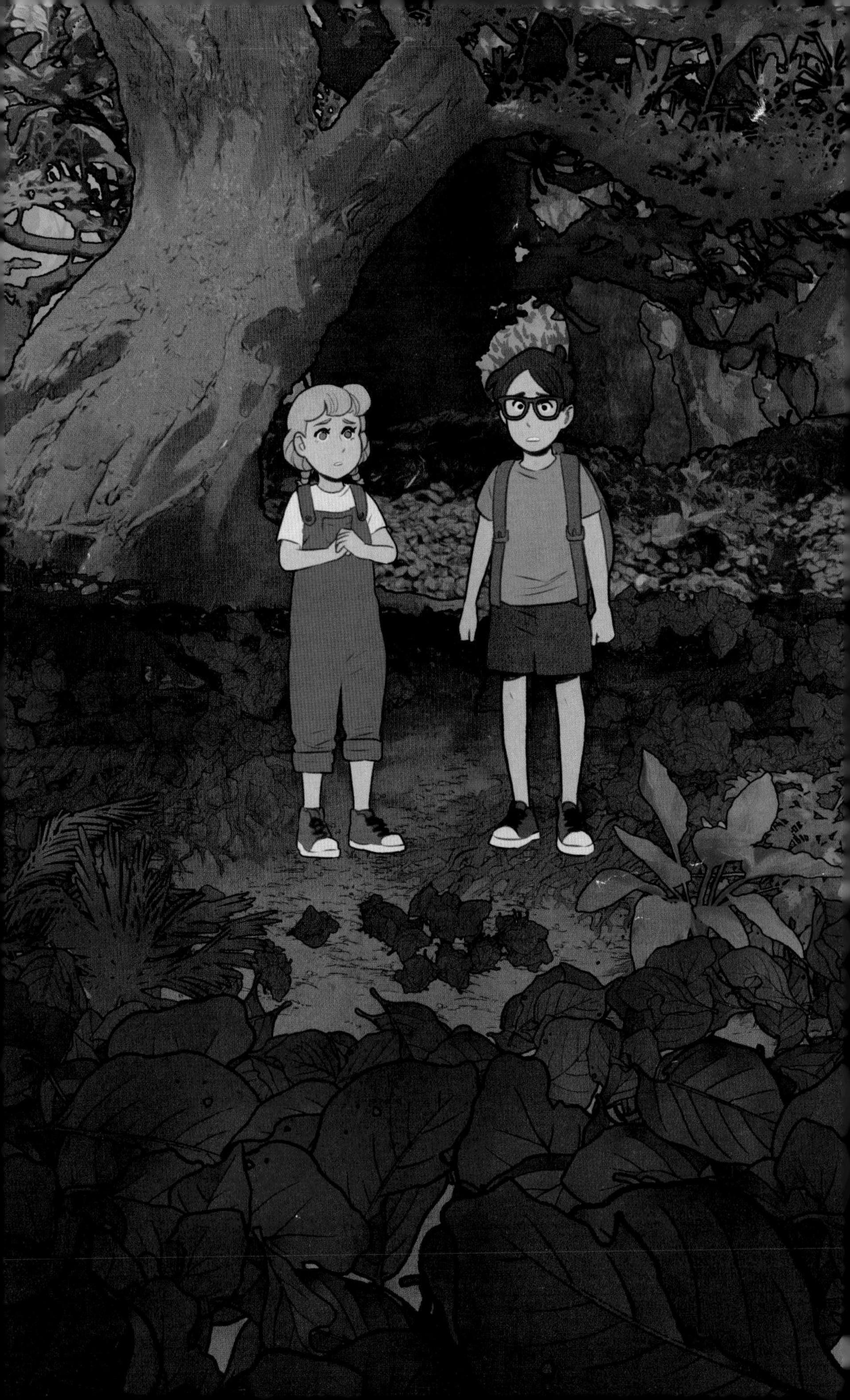

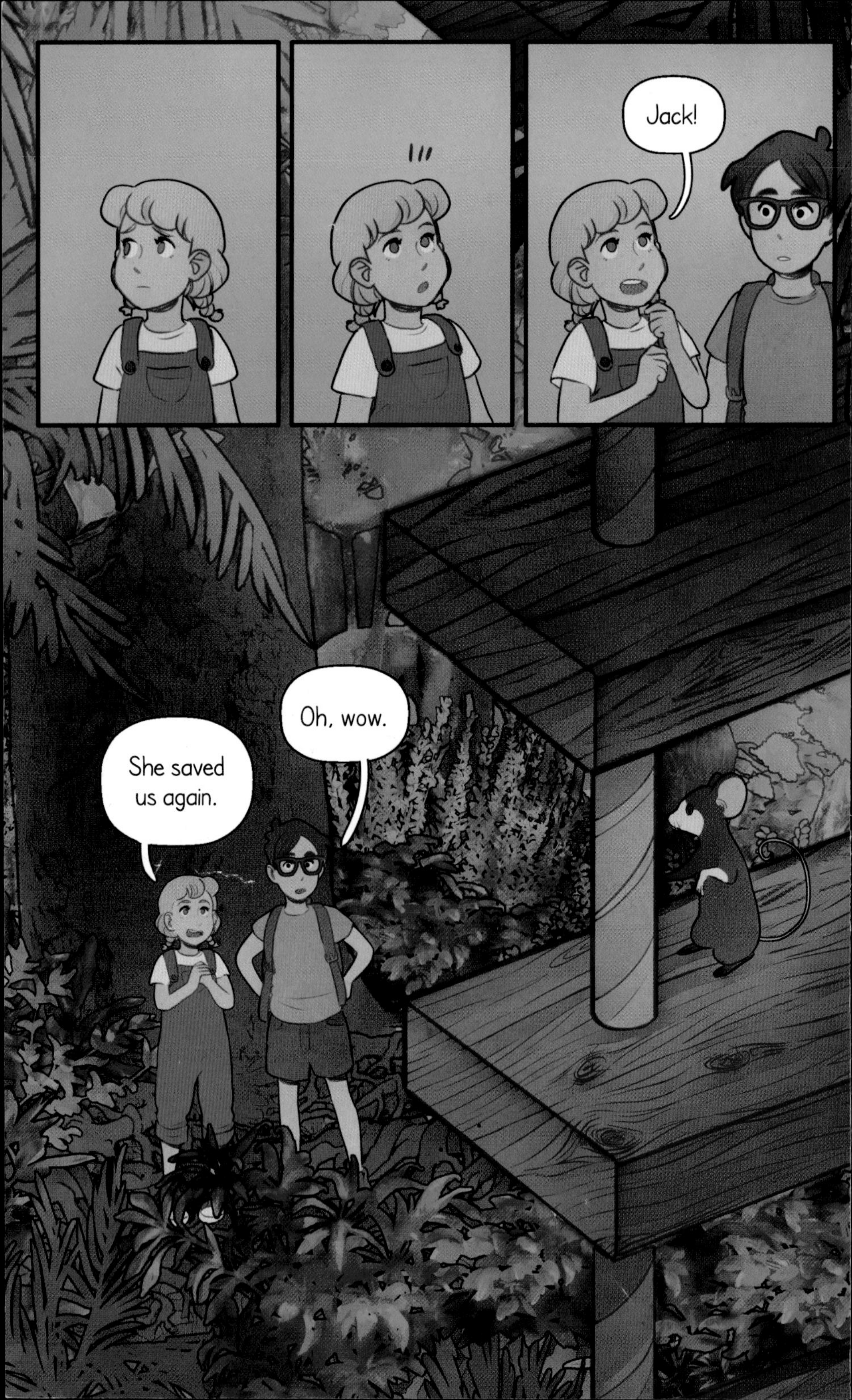
Jack!
She saved us again.
Oh, wow.

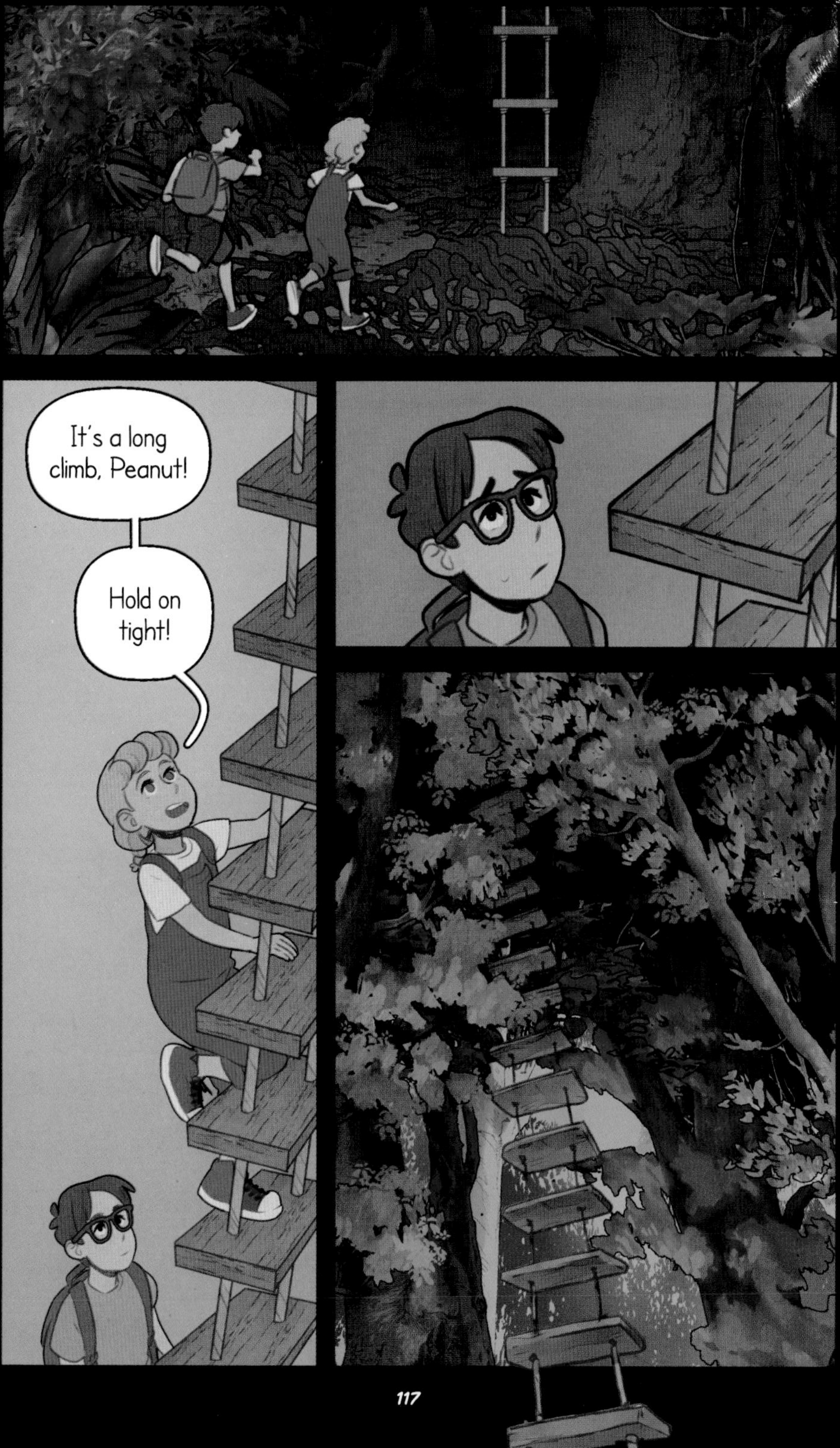
It's a long climb, Peanut!
Hold on tight!

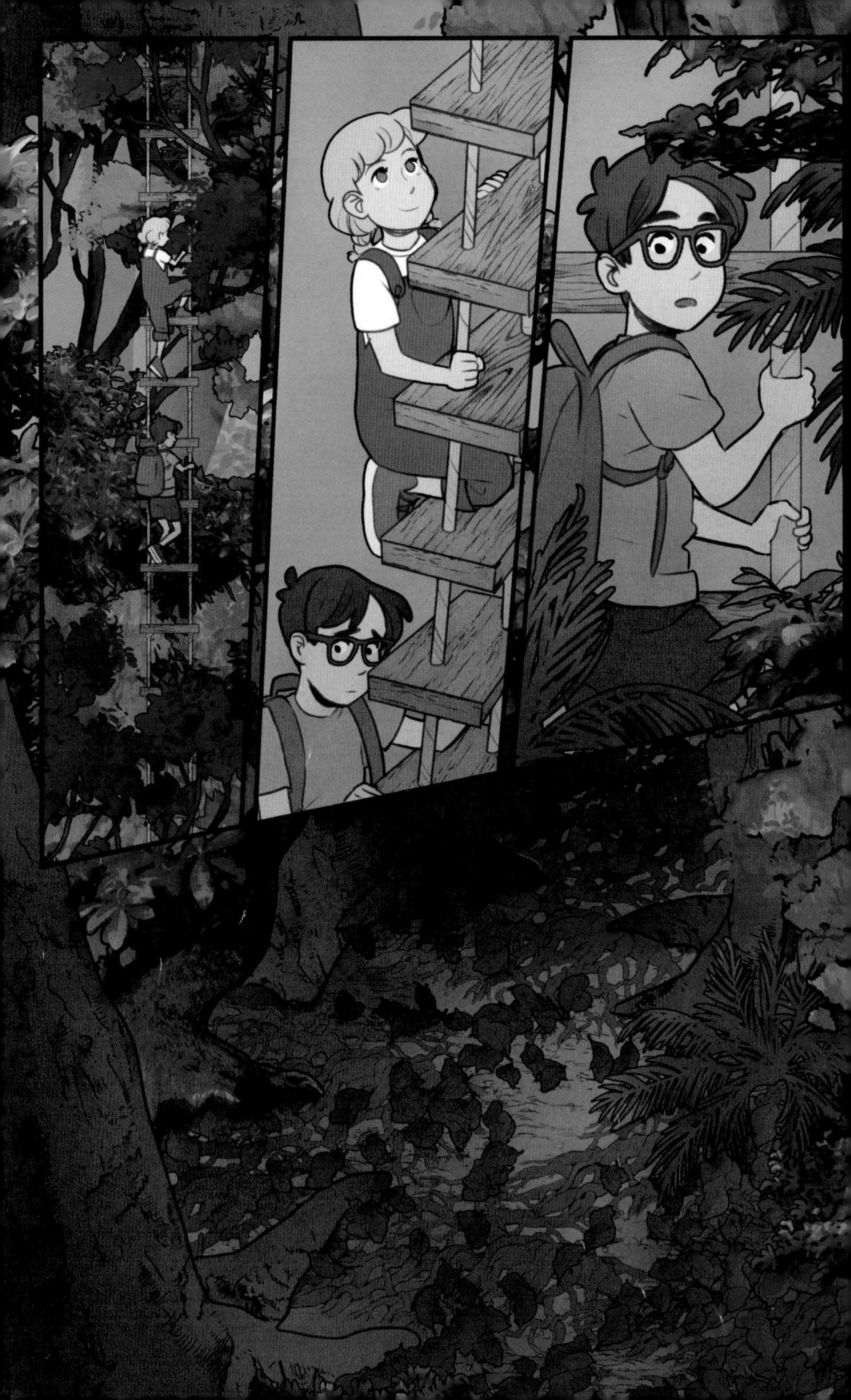

CHAPTER EIGHT

The Thing

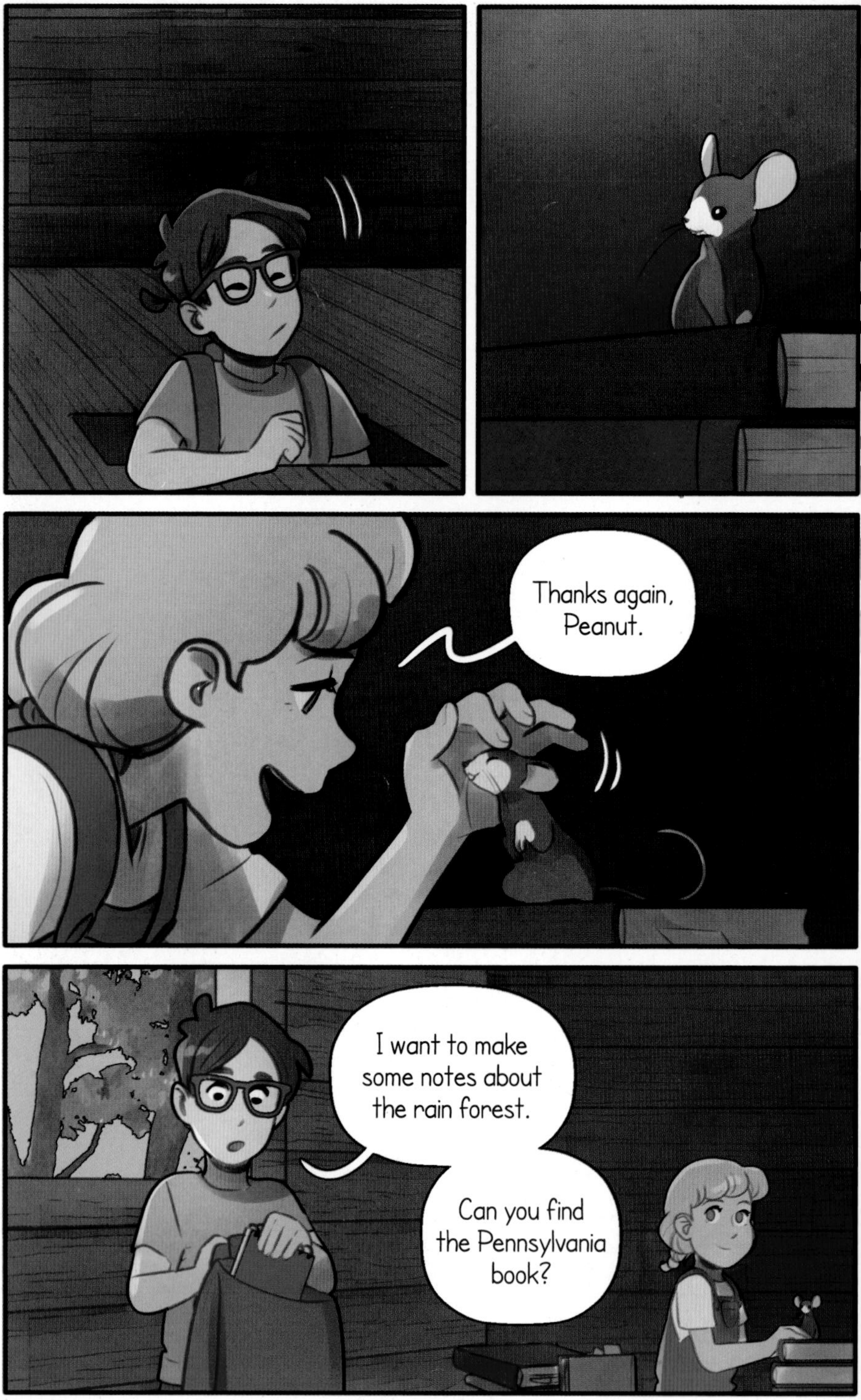
Thanks again, Peanut.
I want to make some notes about the rain forest.
Can you find the Pennsylvania book?

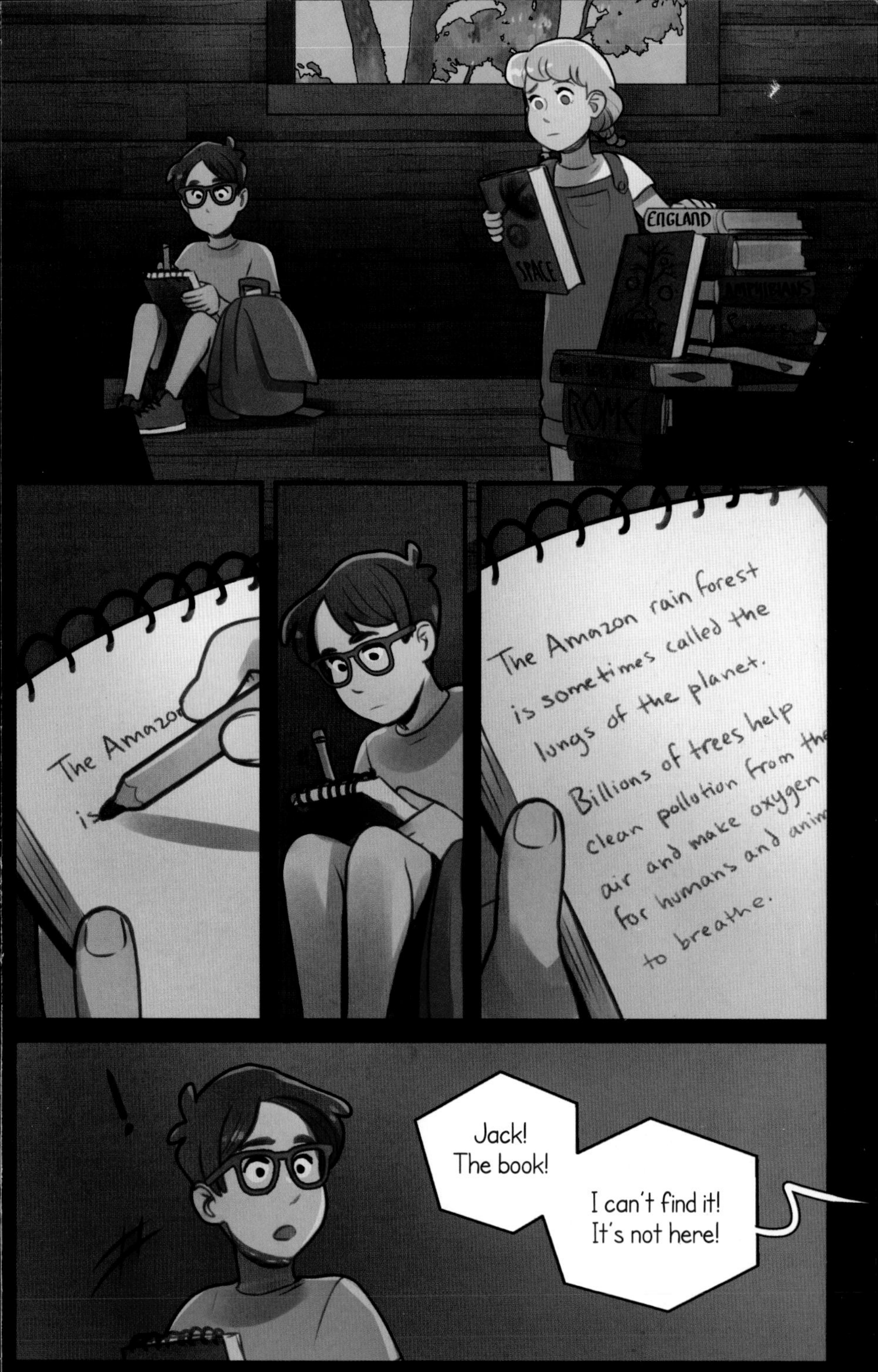
ENGLAND
SPACE
AMPHIBIANS
The Amazon
is
The Amazon rain forest is sometimes called the lungs of the planet.
Billions of trees help clean pollution from the air and make oxygen for humans and anim
to breathe.
!
Jack! The book!
I can't find it! It's not here!

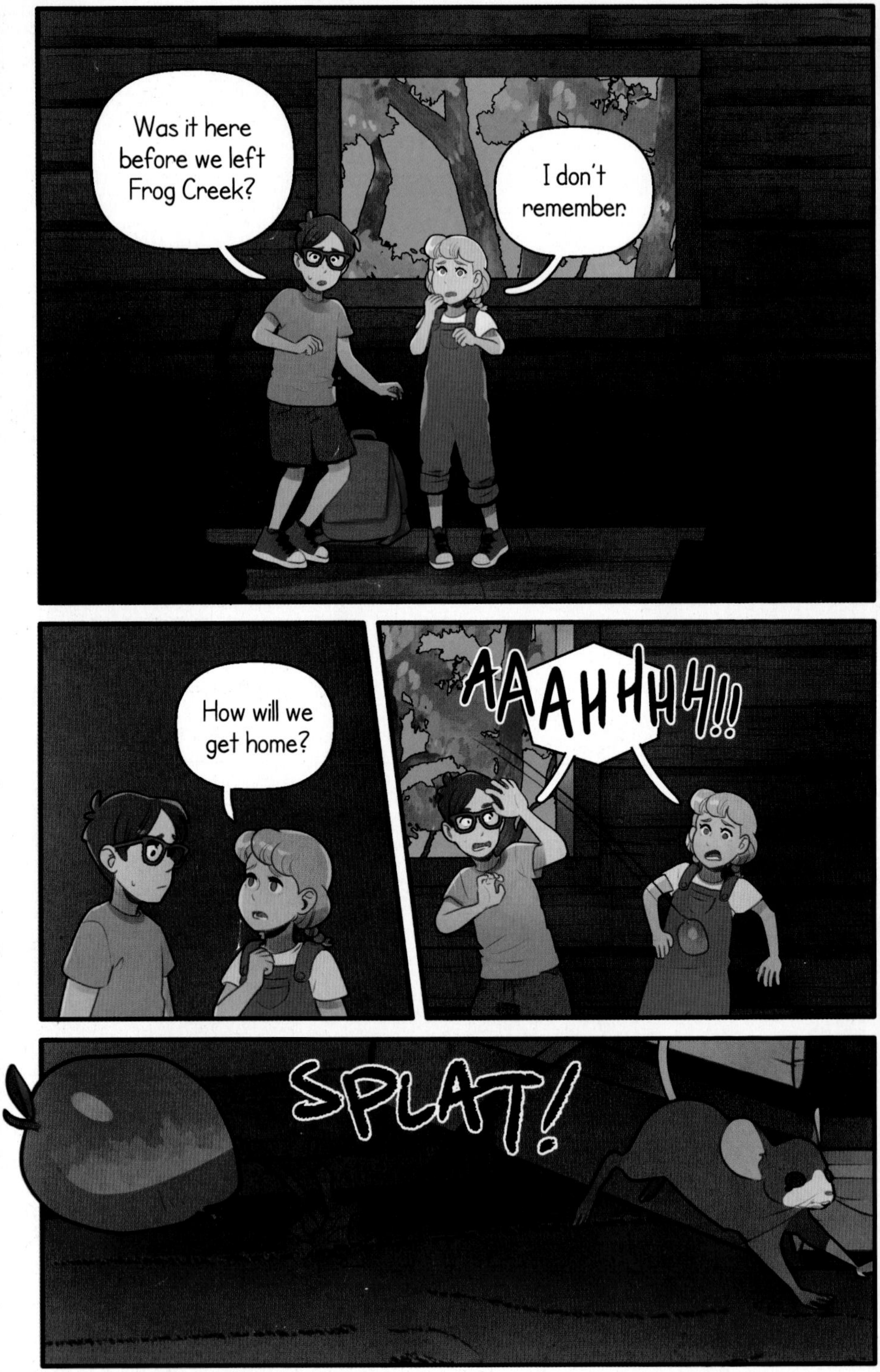
Was it here before we left Frog Creek?
I don't remember.
How will we get home?
AAAHHHH!!!
SPLAT!

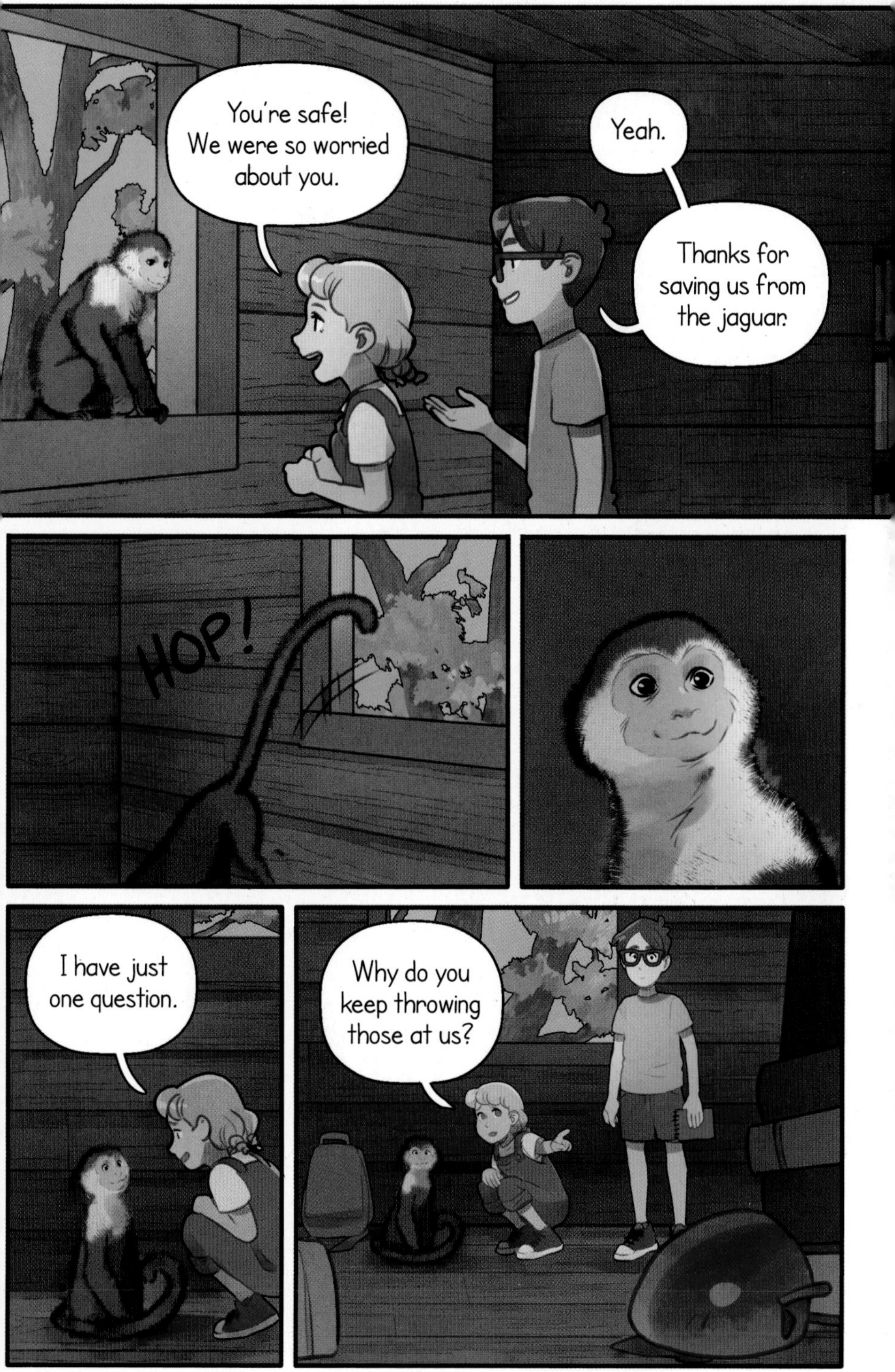

You're safe!
We were so worried about you.
Yeah.
Thanks for saving us from the jaguar.
HOP!
I have just one question.
Why do you keep throwing those at us?

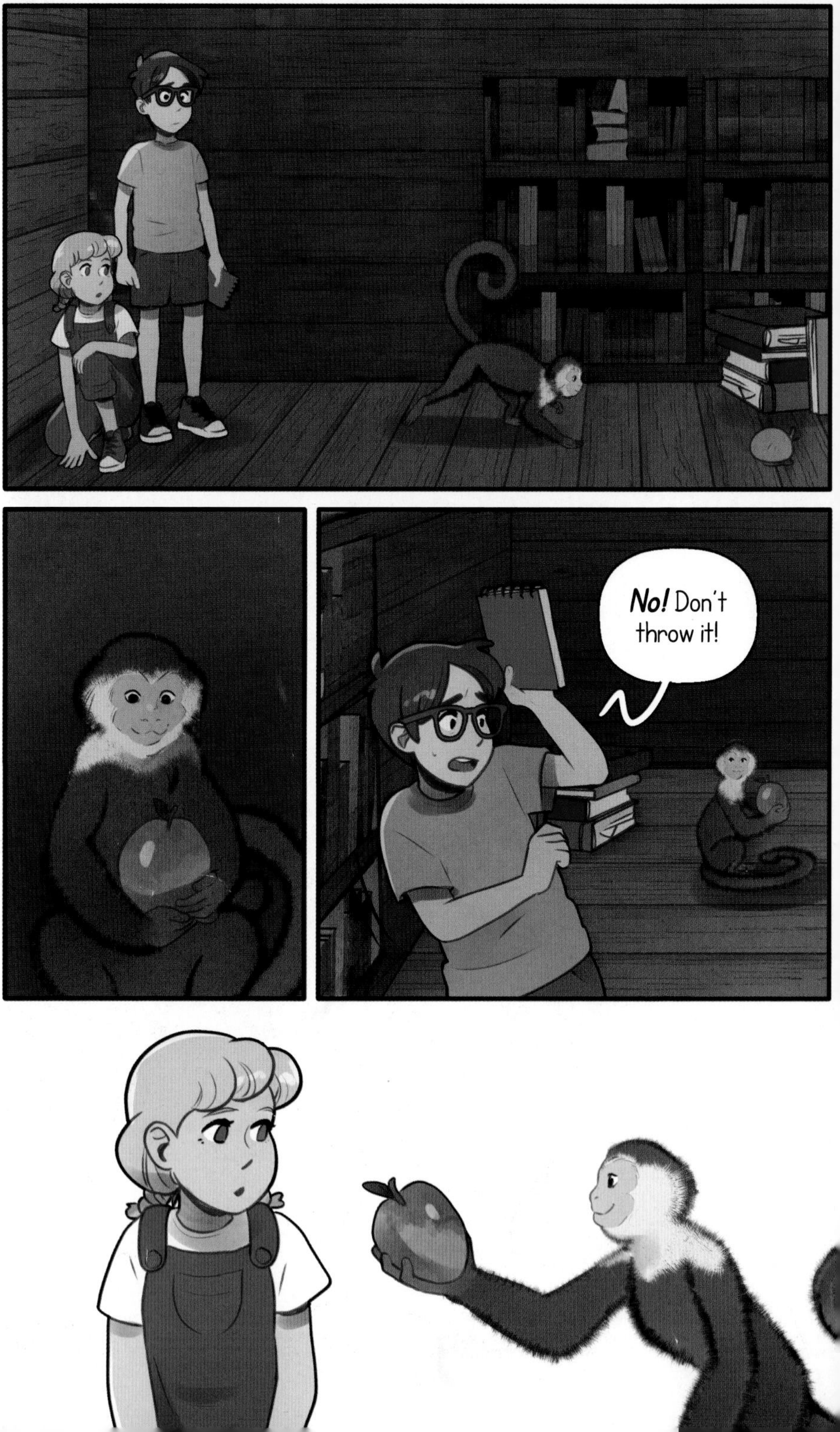
No! Don't throw it!

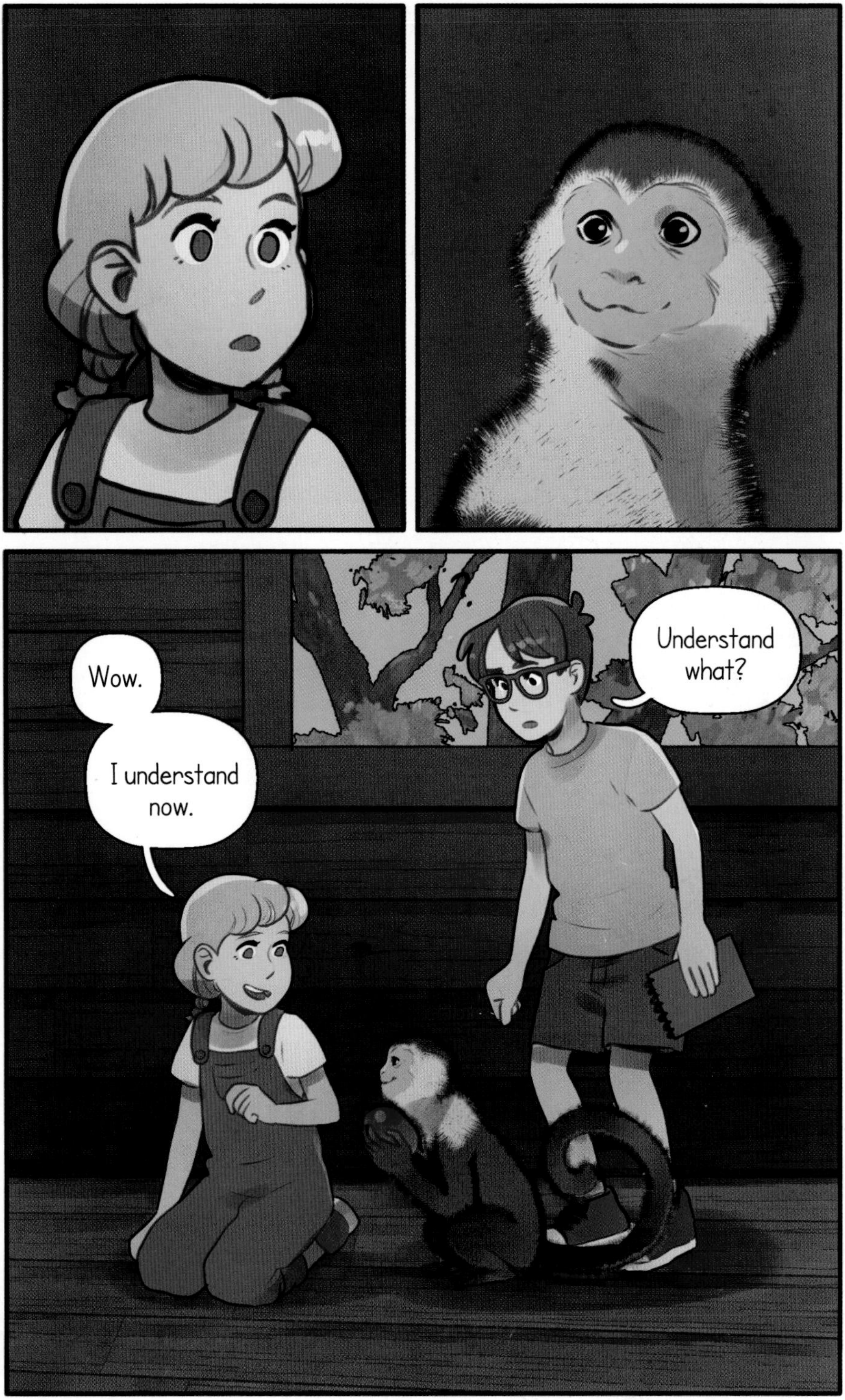
Wow.
I understand now.
Understand what?

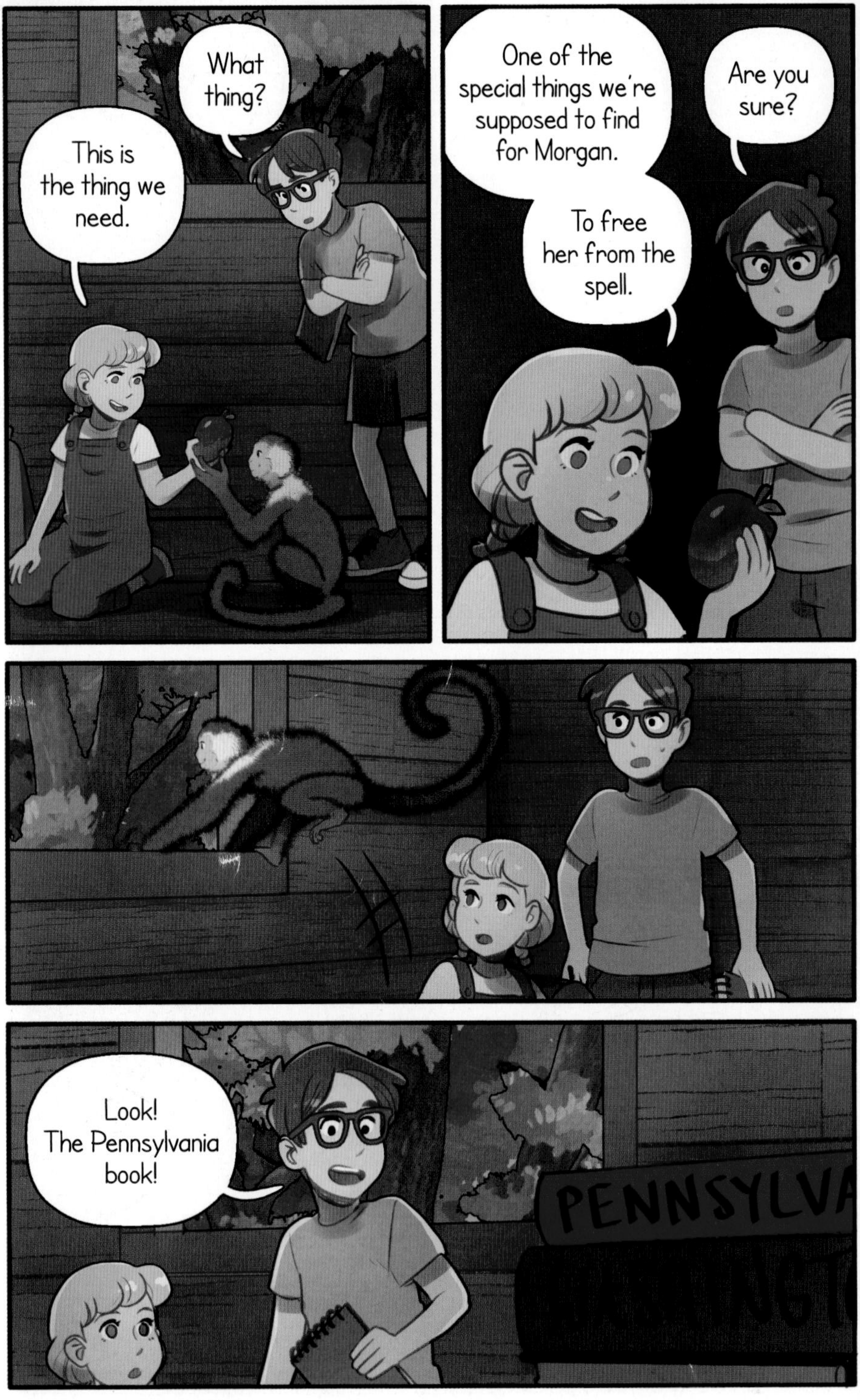
What thing?
This is the thing we need.
One of the special things we're supposed to find for Morgan.
To free her from the spell.
Are you sure?
Look! The Pennsylvania book!
PENNSYLVA

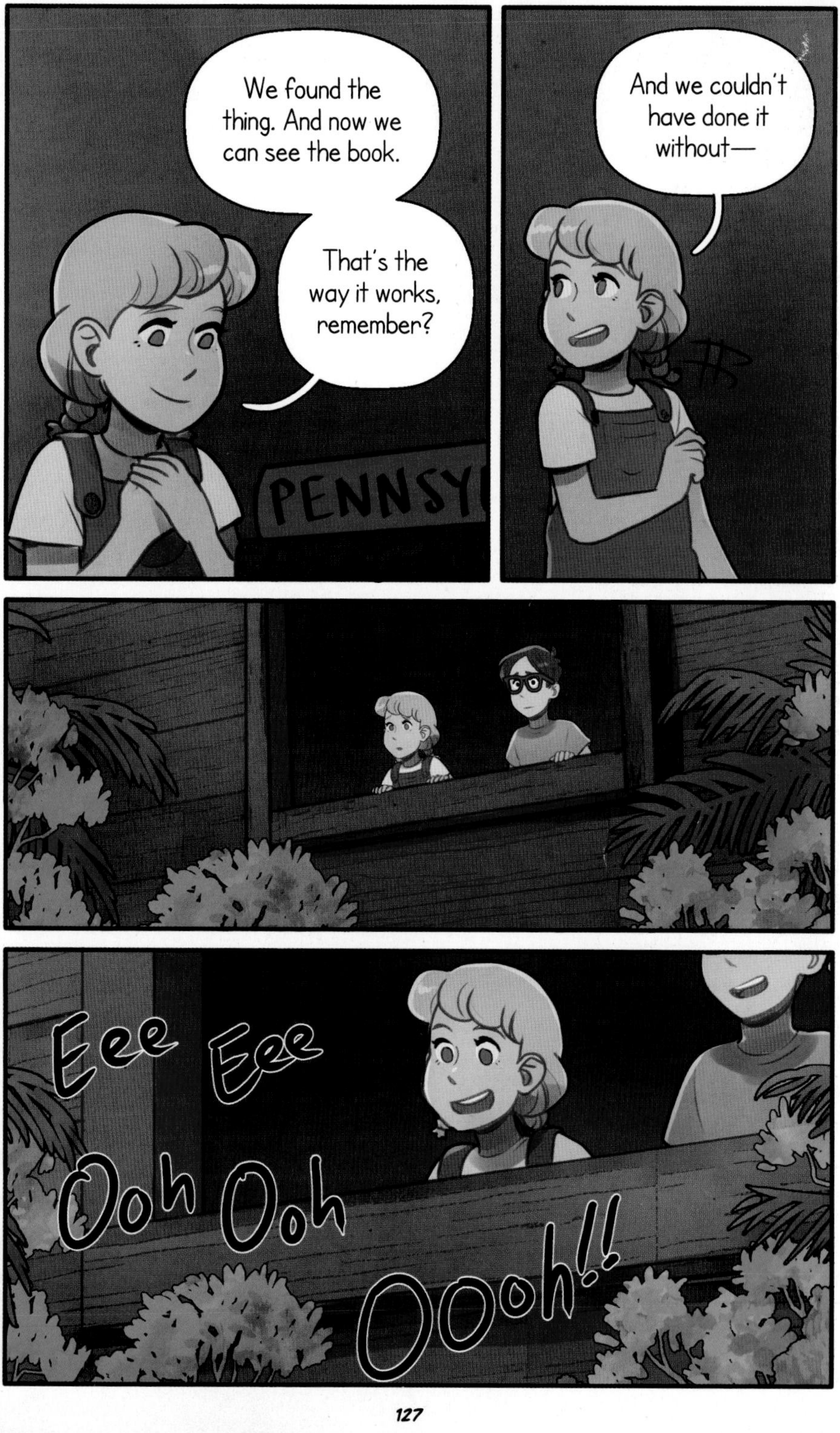
We found the thing. And now we can see the book.
That's the way it works, remember?
PENNSY
And we couldn't have done it without—
Eee Eee
Ooh Ooh
Oooh!!

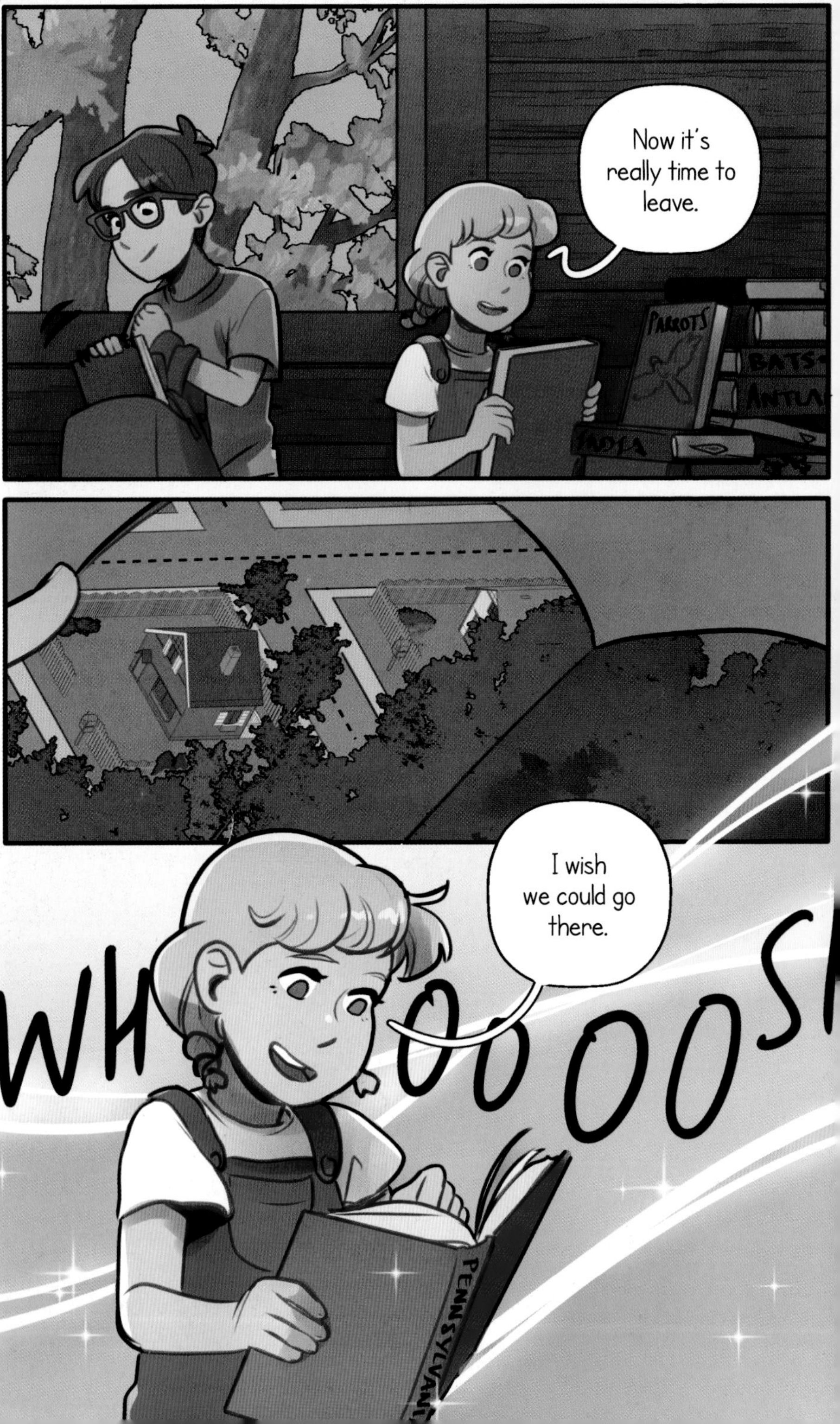
Now it's really time to leave.
PARROTS
BATS
ANTLA
I wish we could go there.
WHOOOOOS
PENNSYLVANI

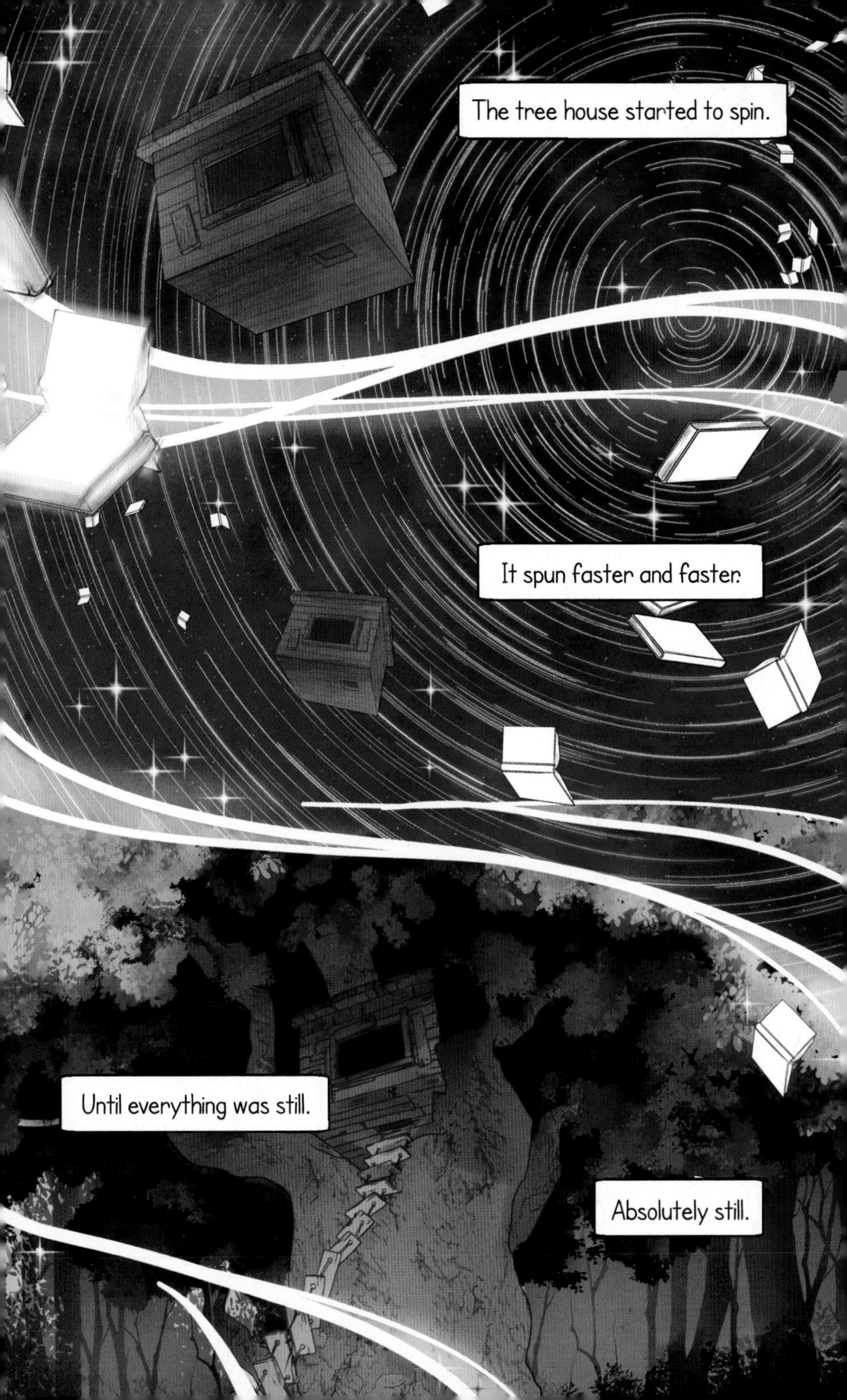
The tree house started to spin.
It spun faster and faster.
Until everything was still.
Absolutely still.

CHAPTER NINE
Halfway There

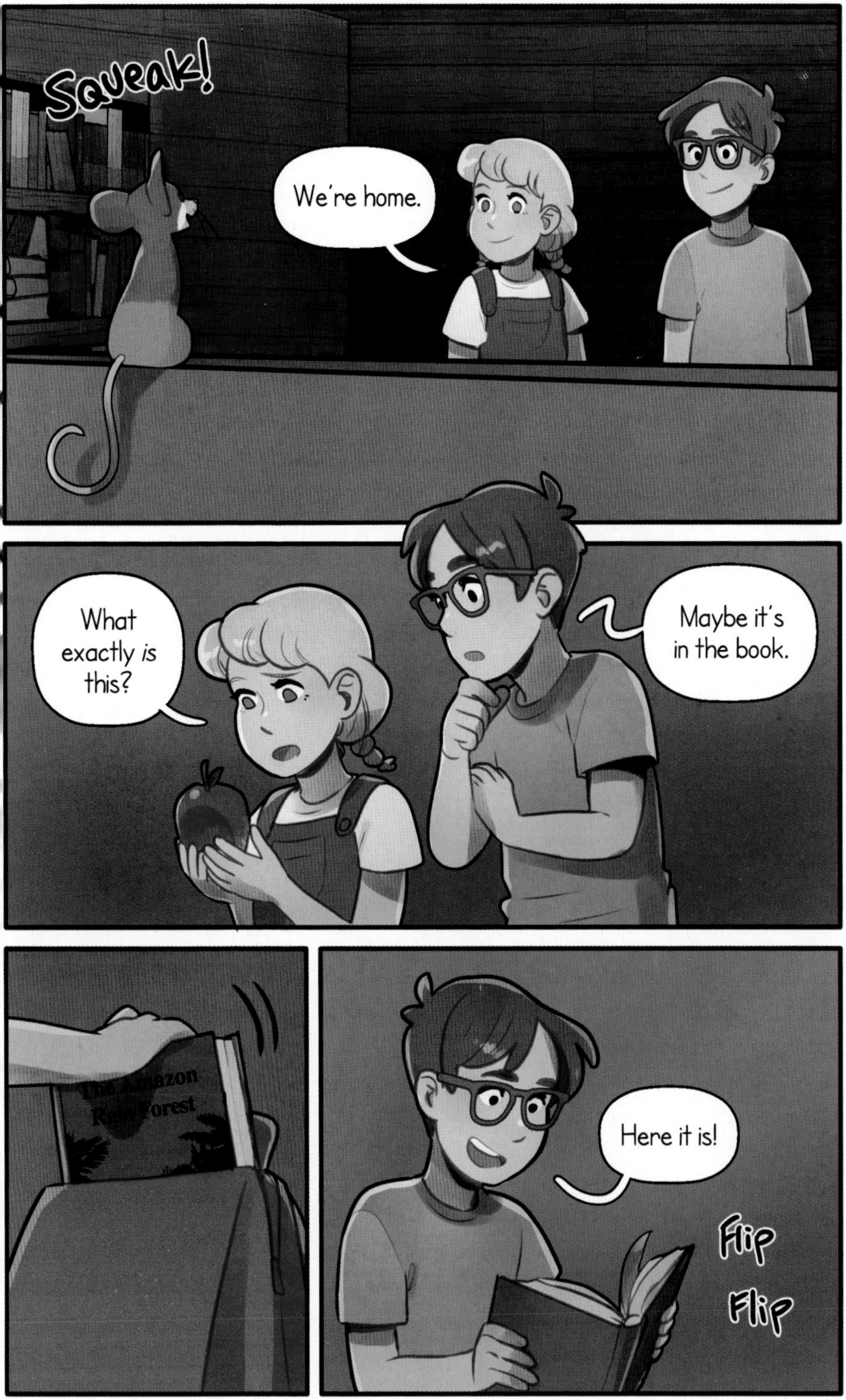
Squeak!
We're home.
What exactly *is* this?
Maybe it's in the book.
The Amazon Rain Forest
Here it is!
Flip
Flip

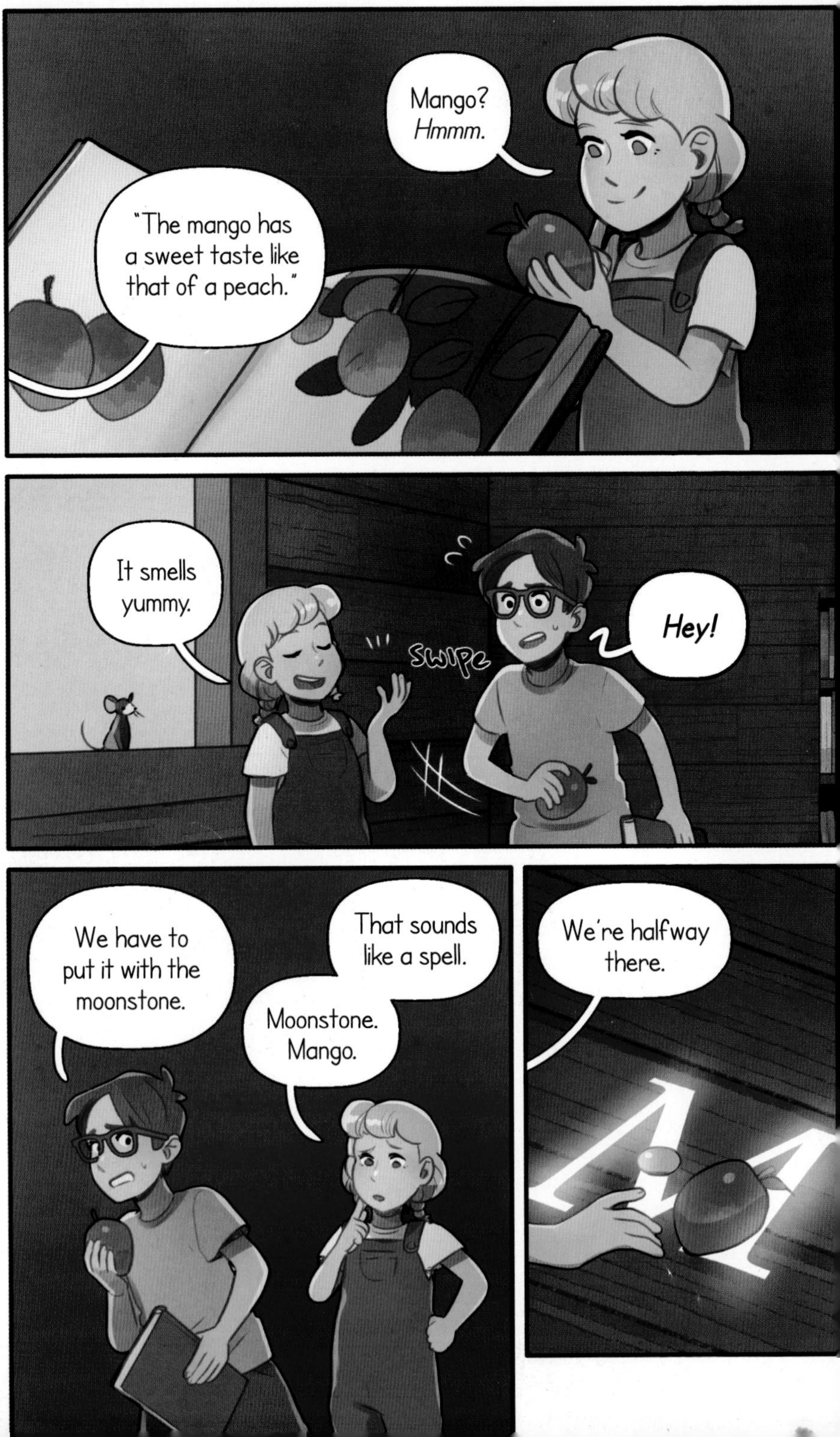
Mango?
Hmmm.
"The mango has a sweet taste like that of a peach."
It smells yummy.
SWIPE
Hey!
We have to put it with the moonstone.
That sounds like a spell.
Moonstone. Mango.
We're halfway there.

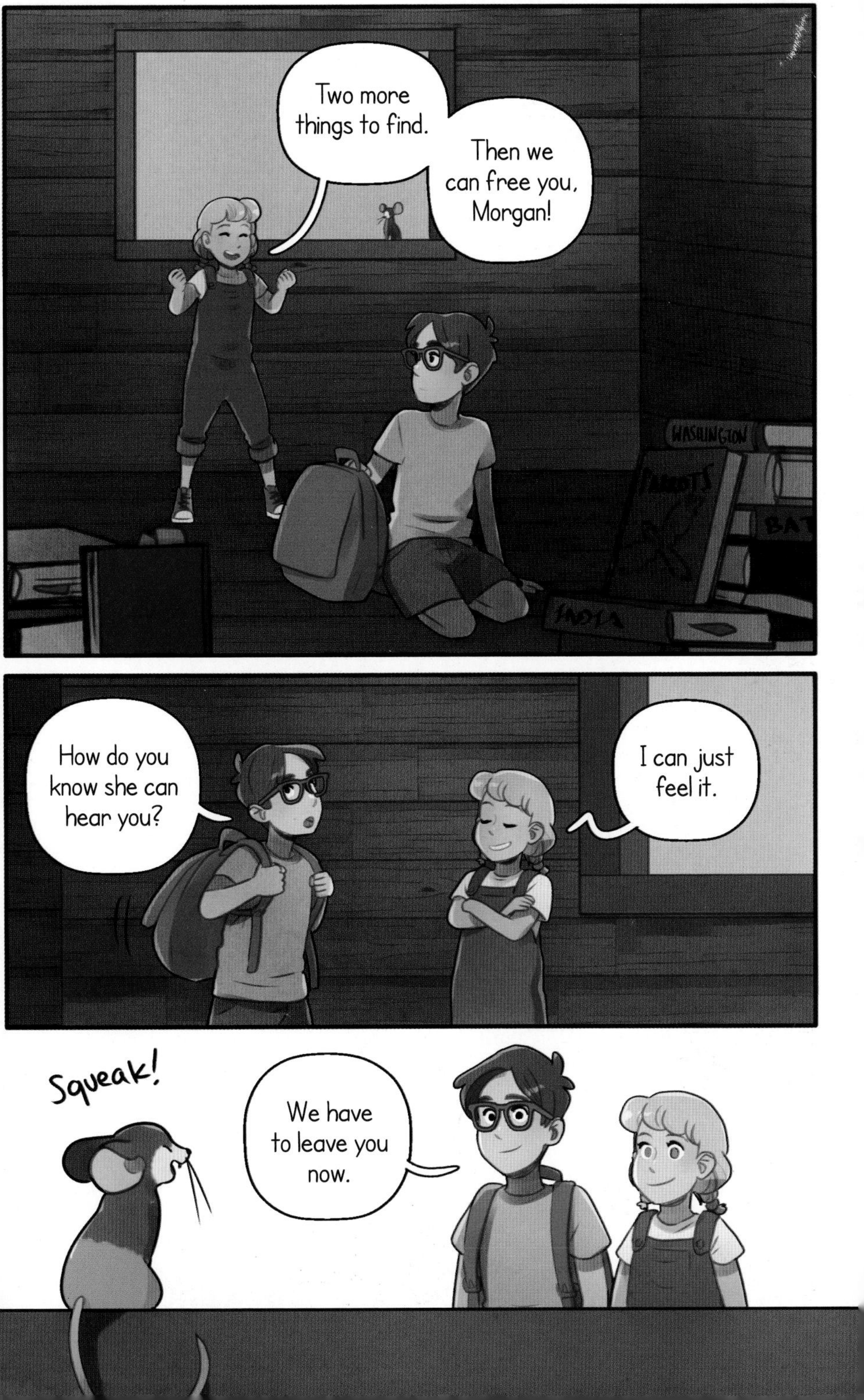
Two more things to find.
Then we can free you, Morgan!
WASHINGTON
PARROTS
How do you know she can hear you?
I can just feel it.
Squeak!
We have to leave you now.

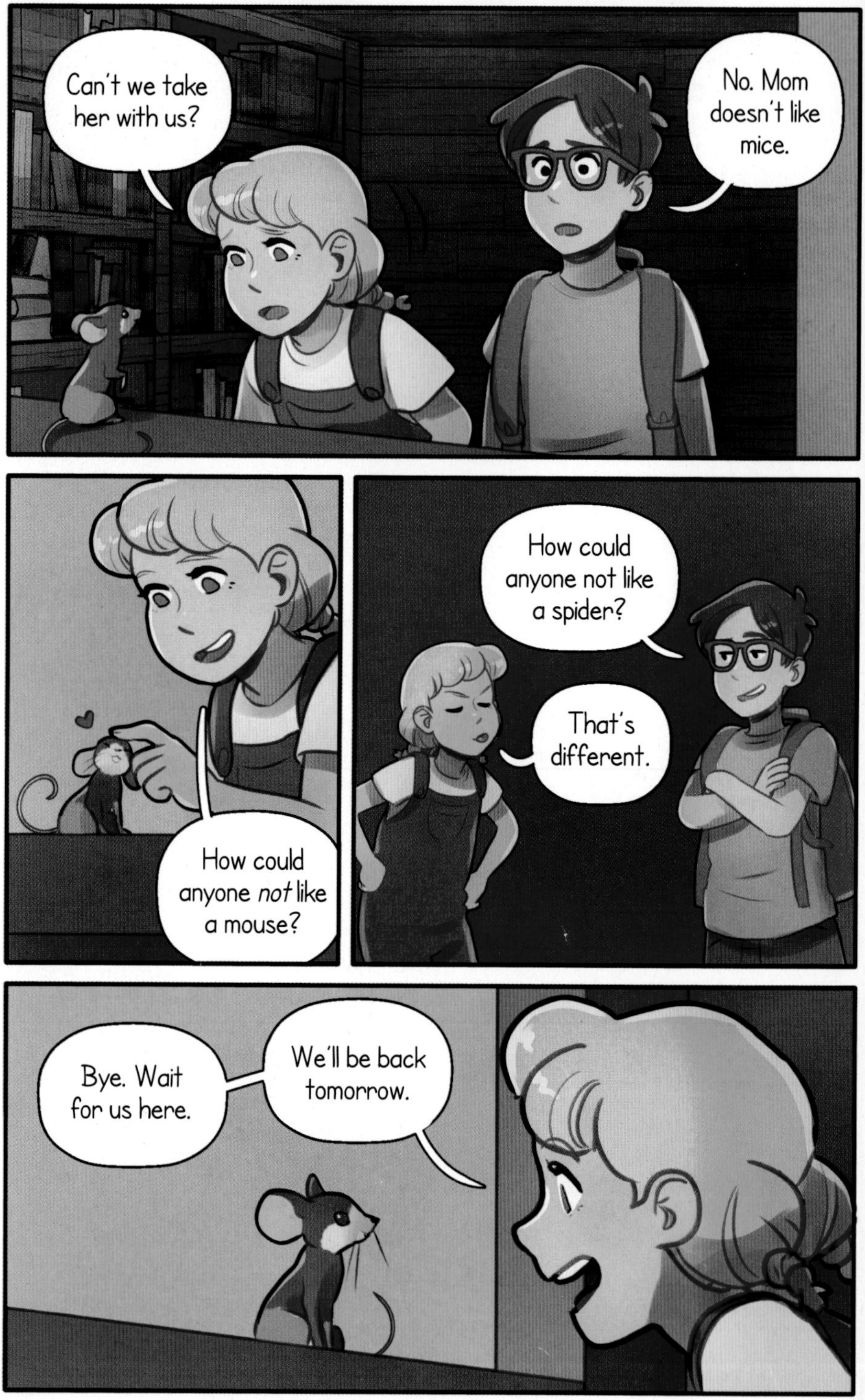
Can't we take her with us?
No. Mom doesn't like mice.
How could anyone *not* like a mouse?
How could anyone not like a spider?
That's different.
Bye. Wait for us here.
We'll be back tomorrow.

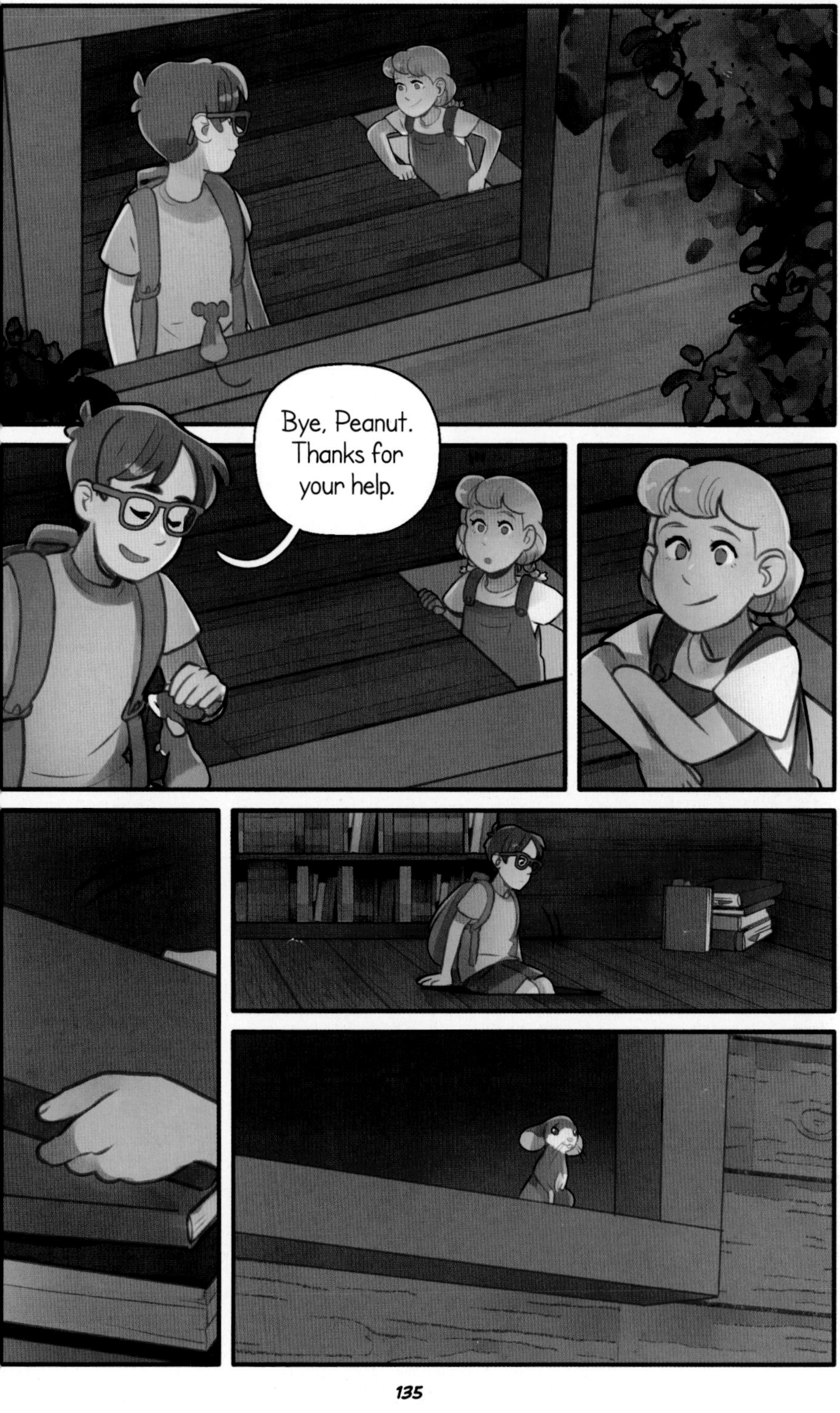
Bye, Peanut. Thanks for your help.

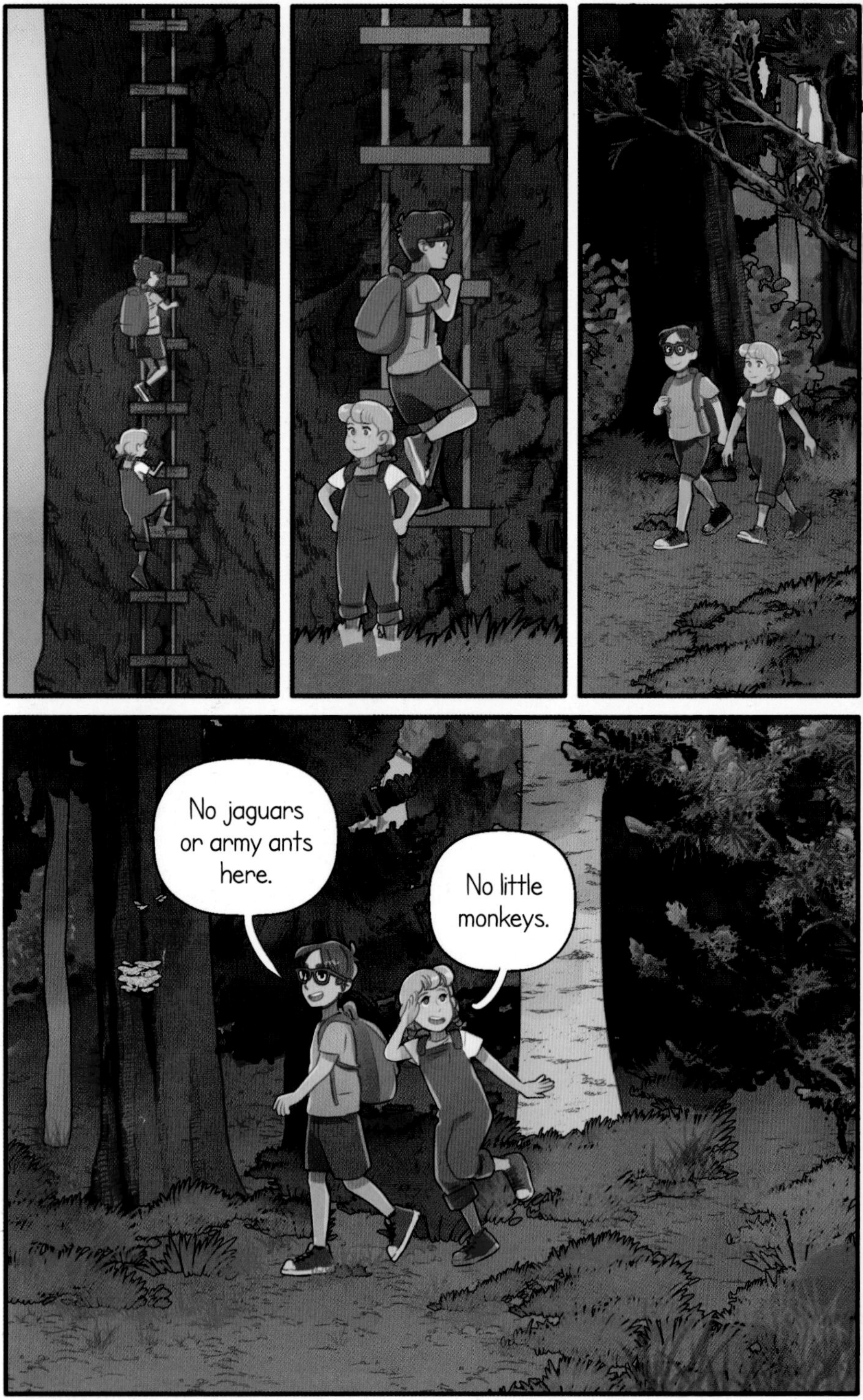
No jaguars or army ants here.
No little monkeys.

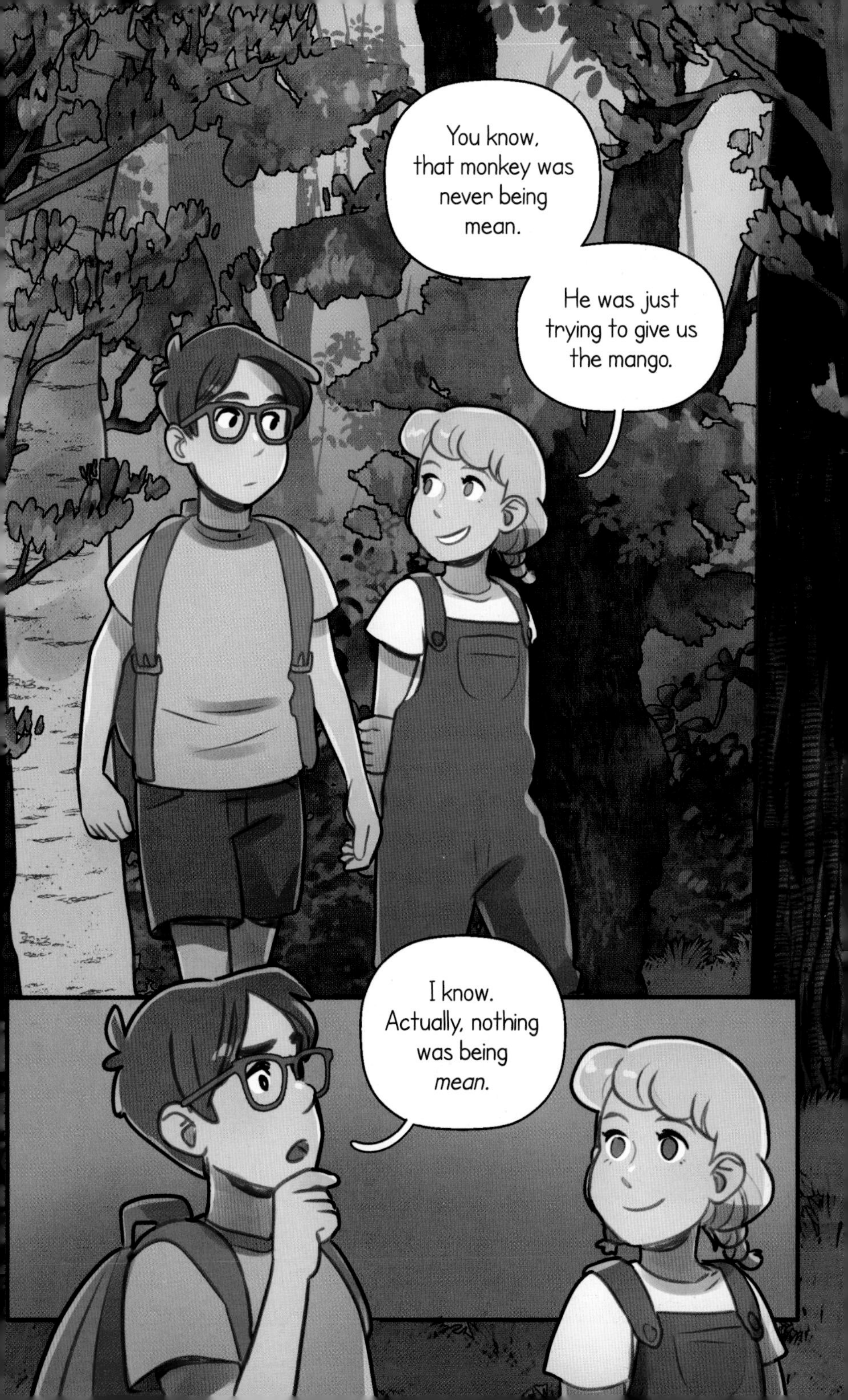
You know, that monkey was never being mean.
He was just trying to give us the mango.
I know. Actually, nothing was being *mean*.

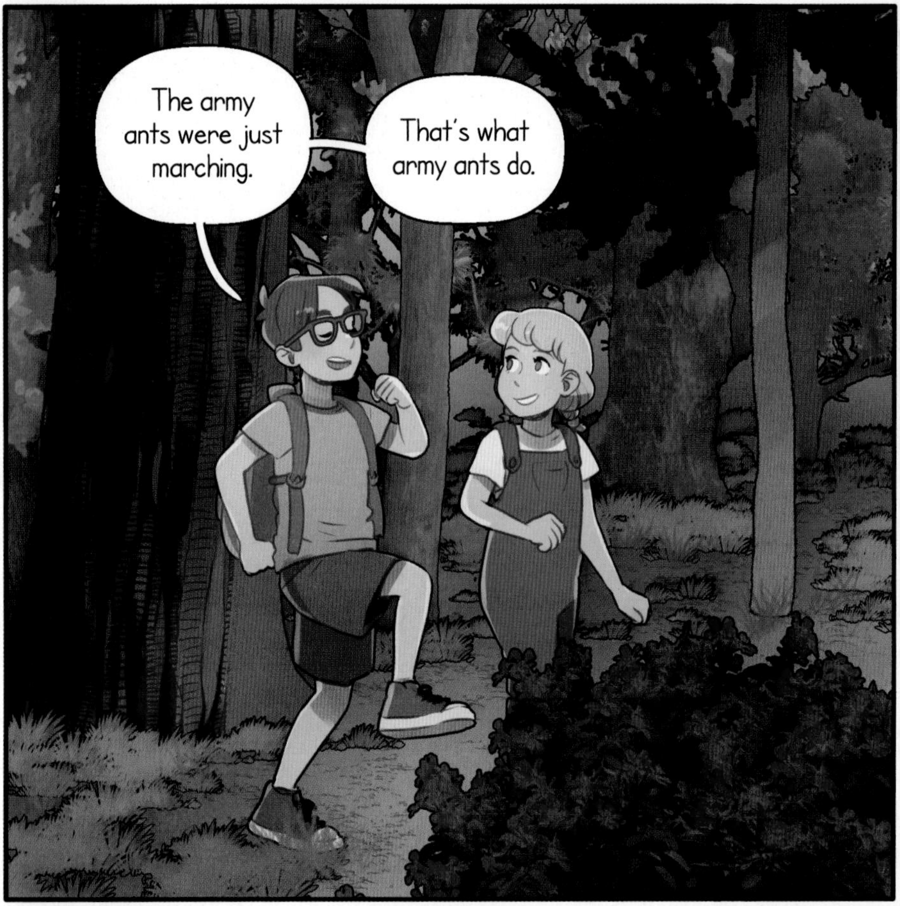
The army ants were just marching.
That's what army ants do.

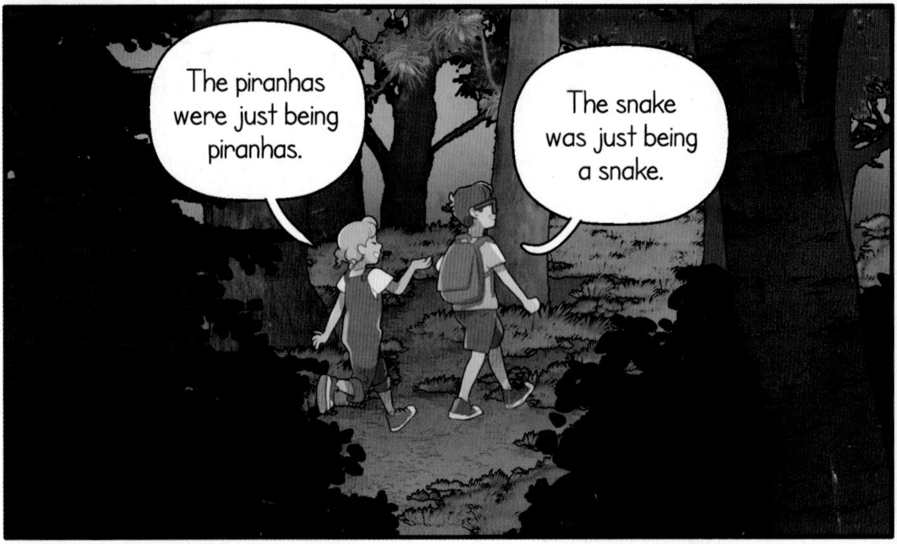
The piranhas were just being piranhas.
The snake was just being a snake.

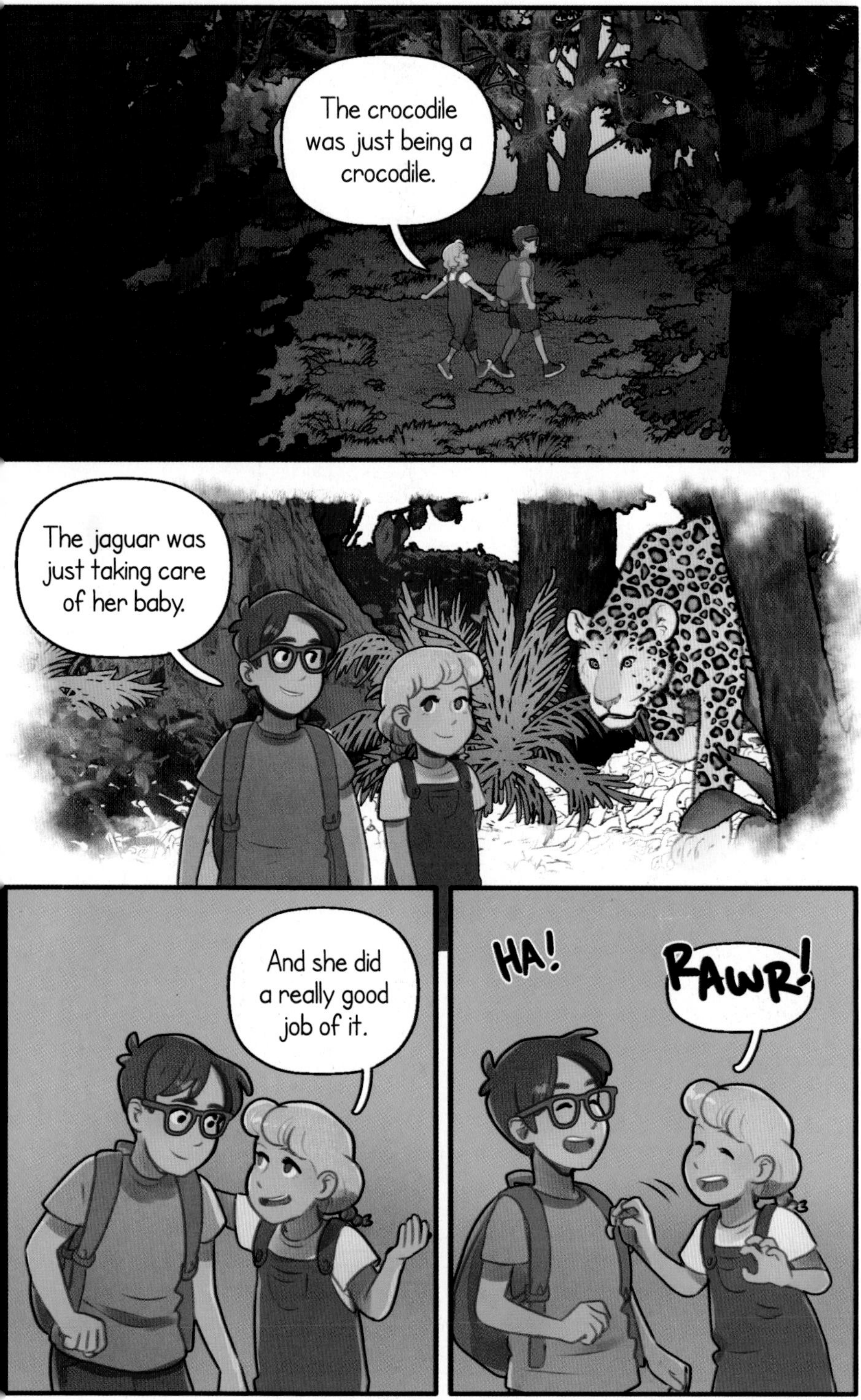
The crocodile was just being a crocodile.
The jaguar was just taking care of her baby.
And she did a really good job of it.
HA!
RAWR!

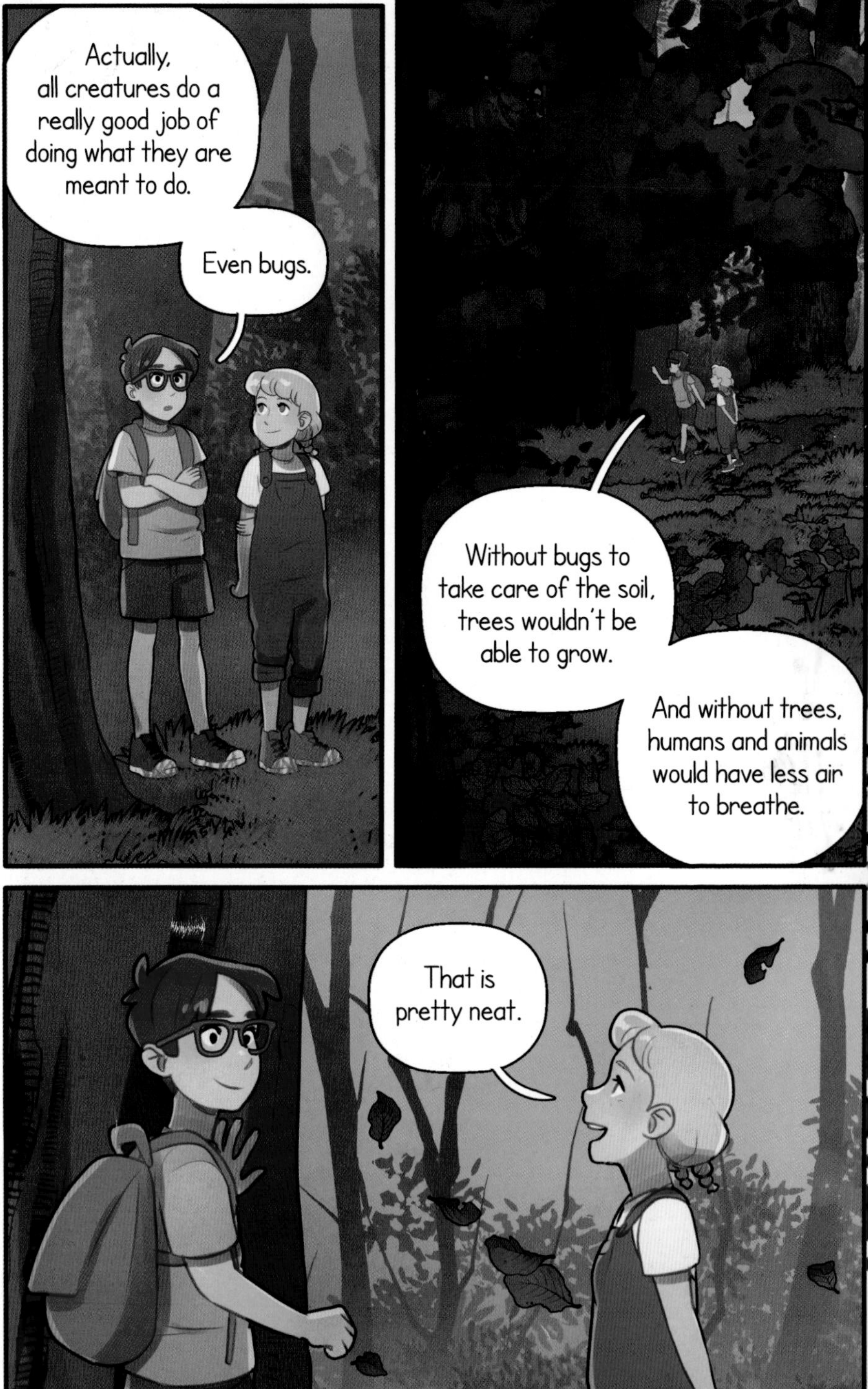
Actually, all creatures do a really good job of doing what they are meant to do.
Even bugs.
Without bugs to take care of the soil, trees wouldn't be able to grow.
And without trees, humans and animals would have less air to breathe.
That is pretty neat.

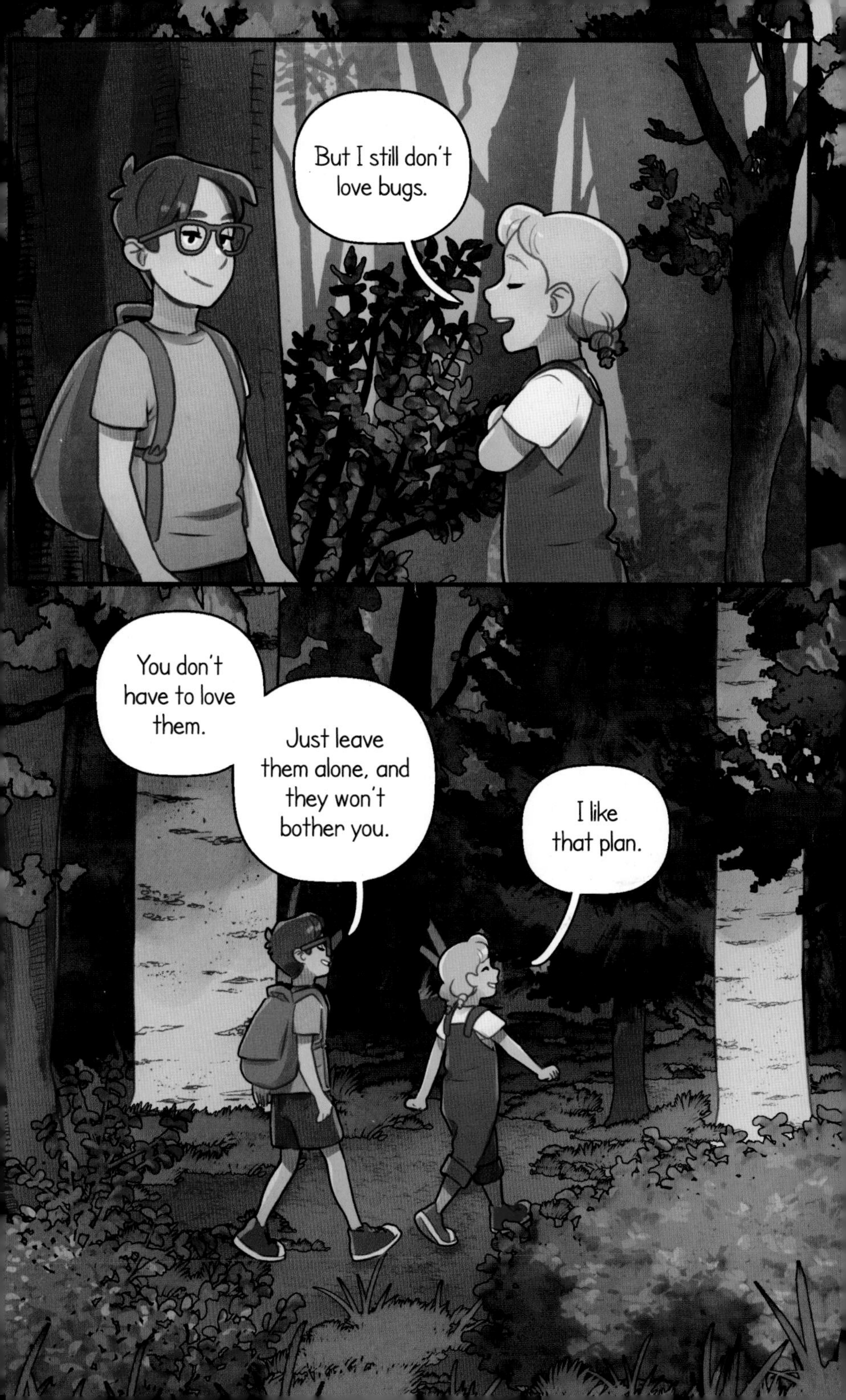
But I still don't love bugs.
You don't have to love them.
Just leave them alone, and they won't bother you.
I like that plan.

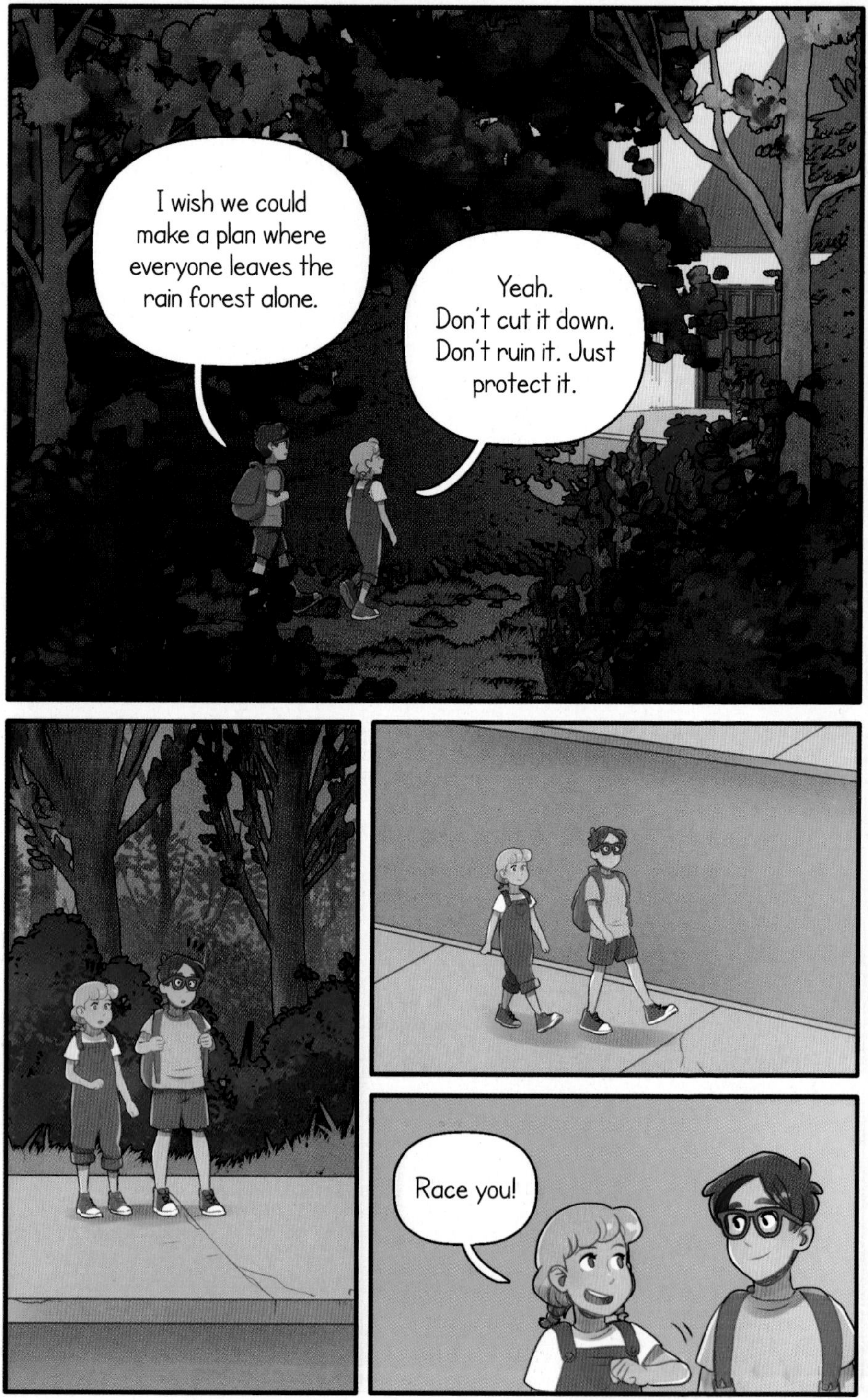
I wish we could make a plan where everyone leaves the rain forest alone.
Yeah. Don't cut it down. Don't ruin it. Just protect it.
Race you!

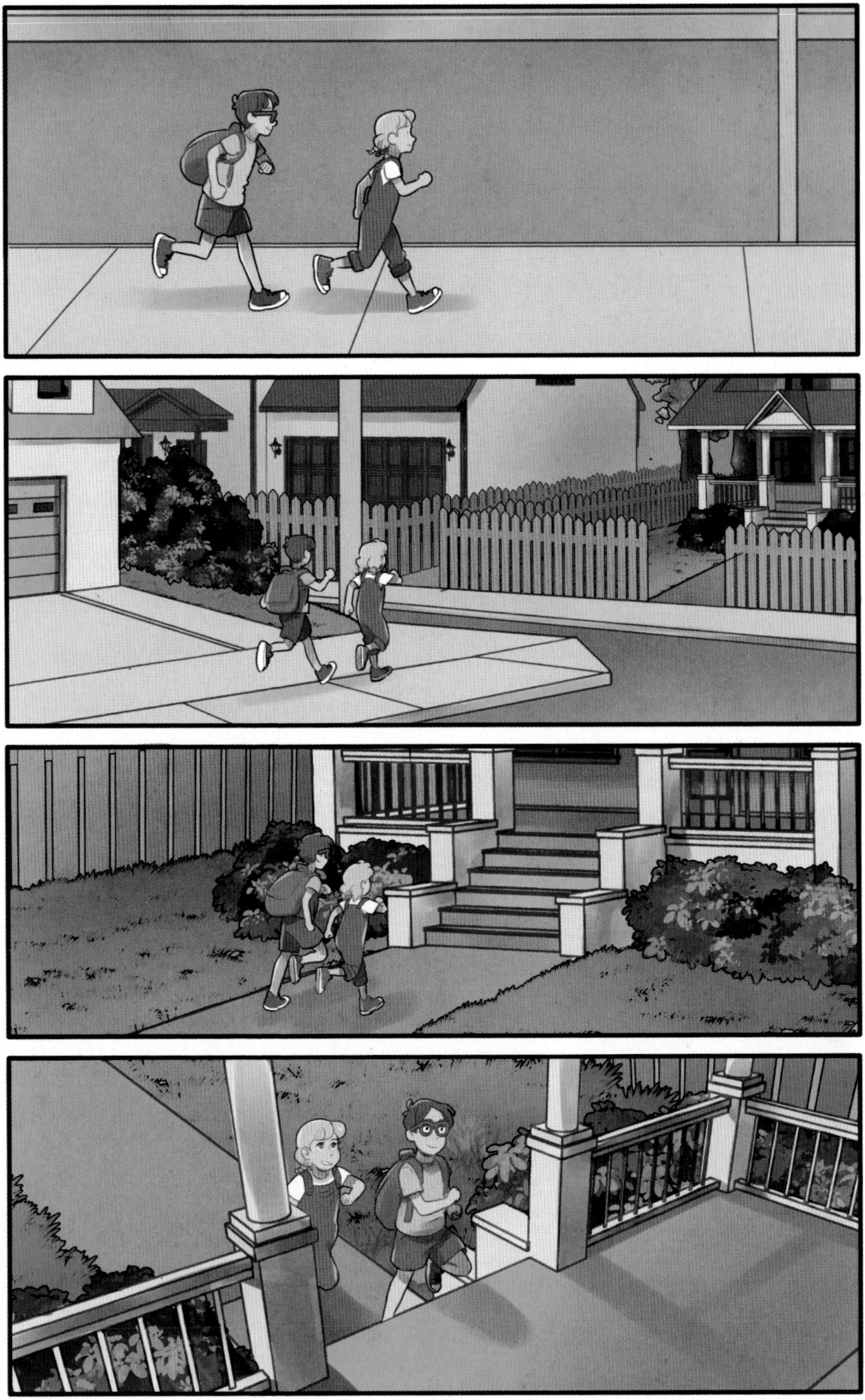

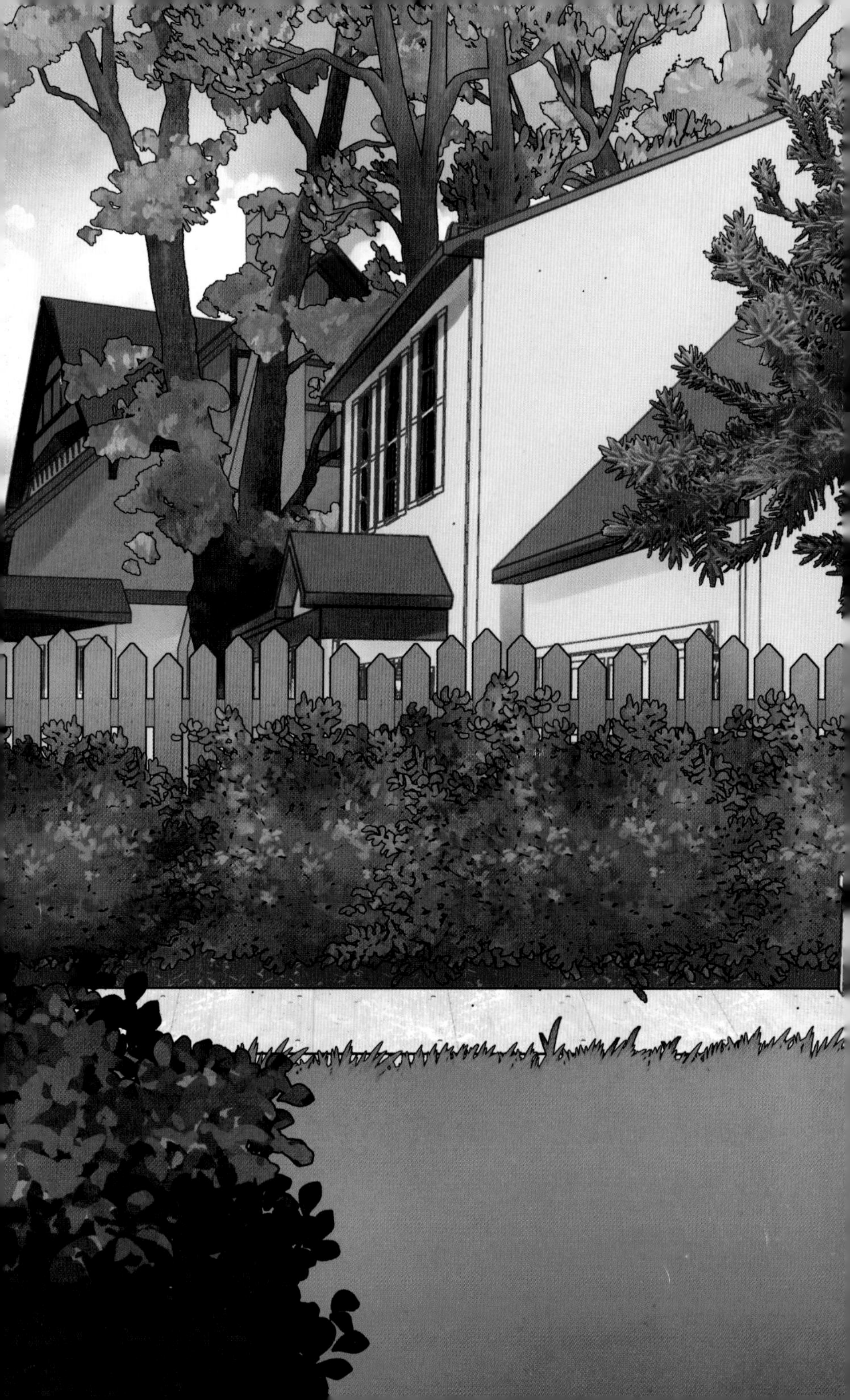

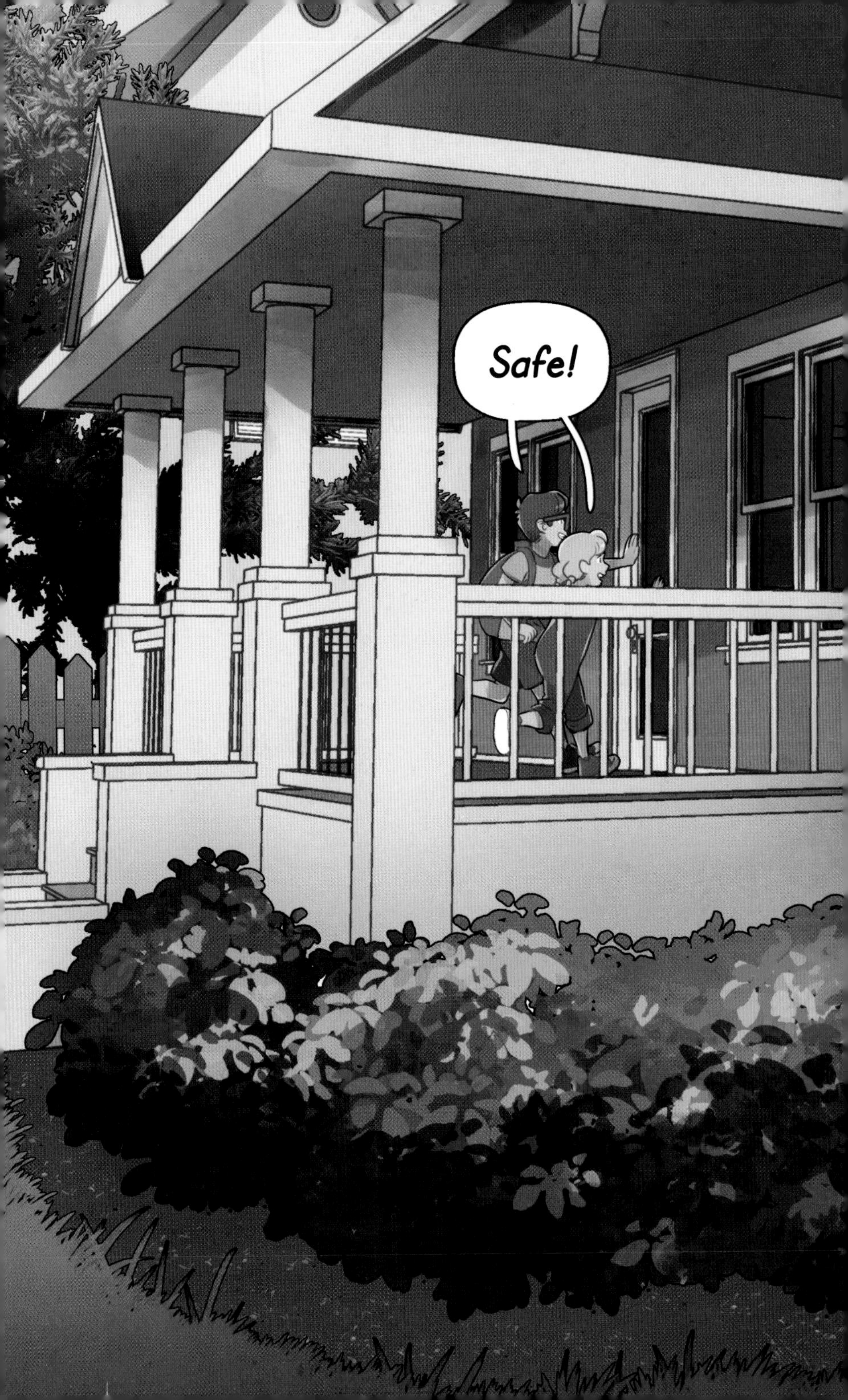
Safe!

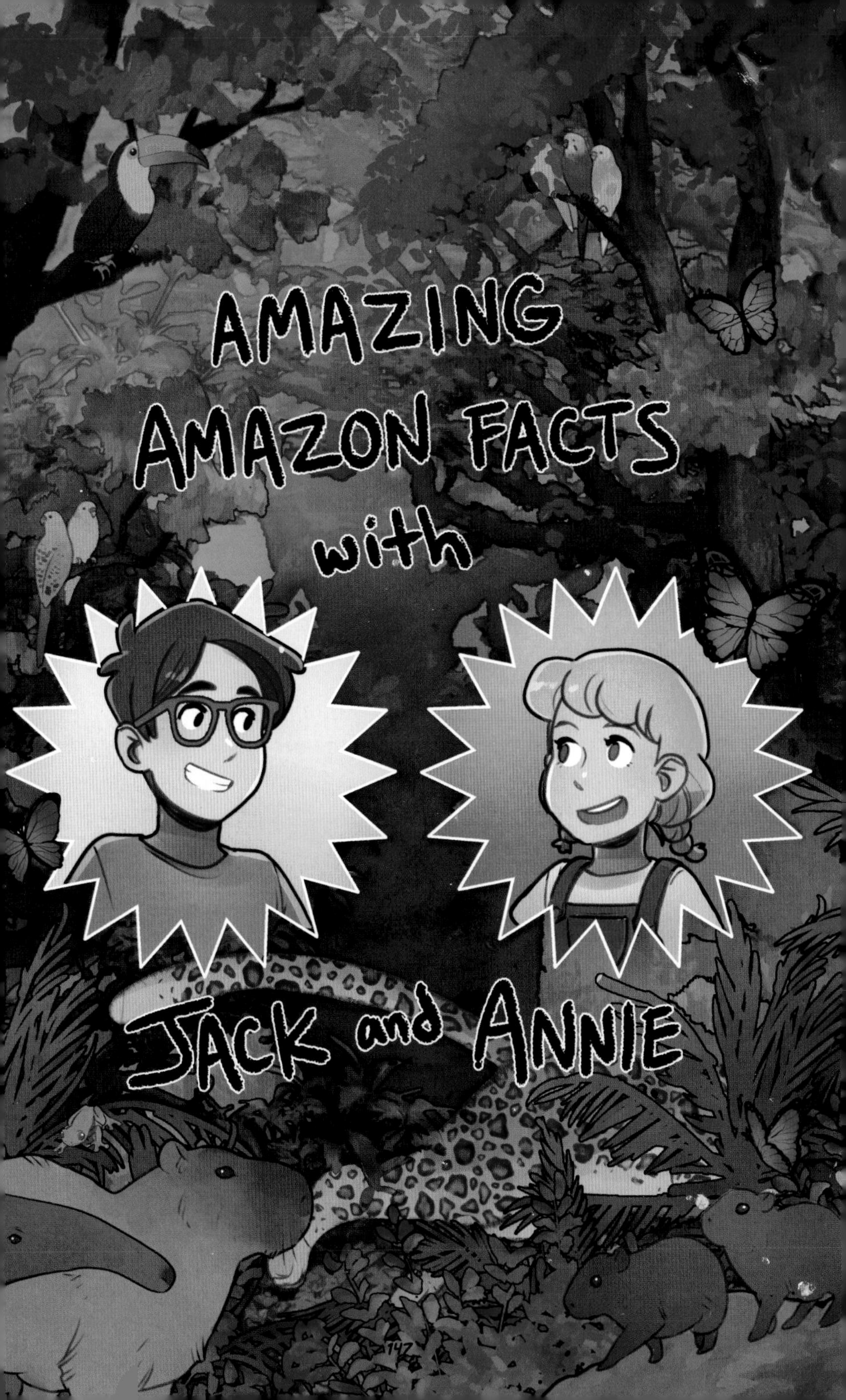
AMAZING
AMAZON FACTS
with
JACK and ANNIE

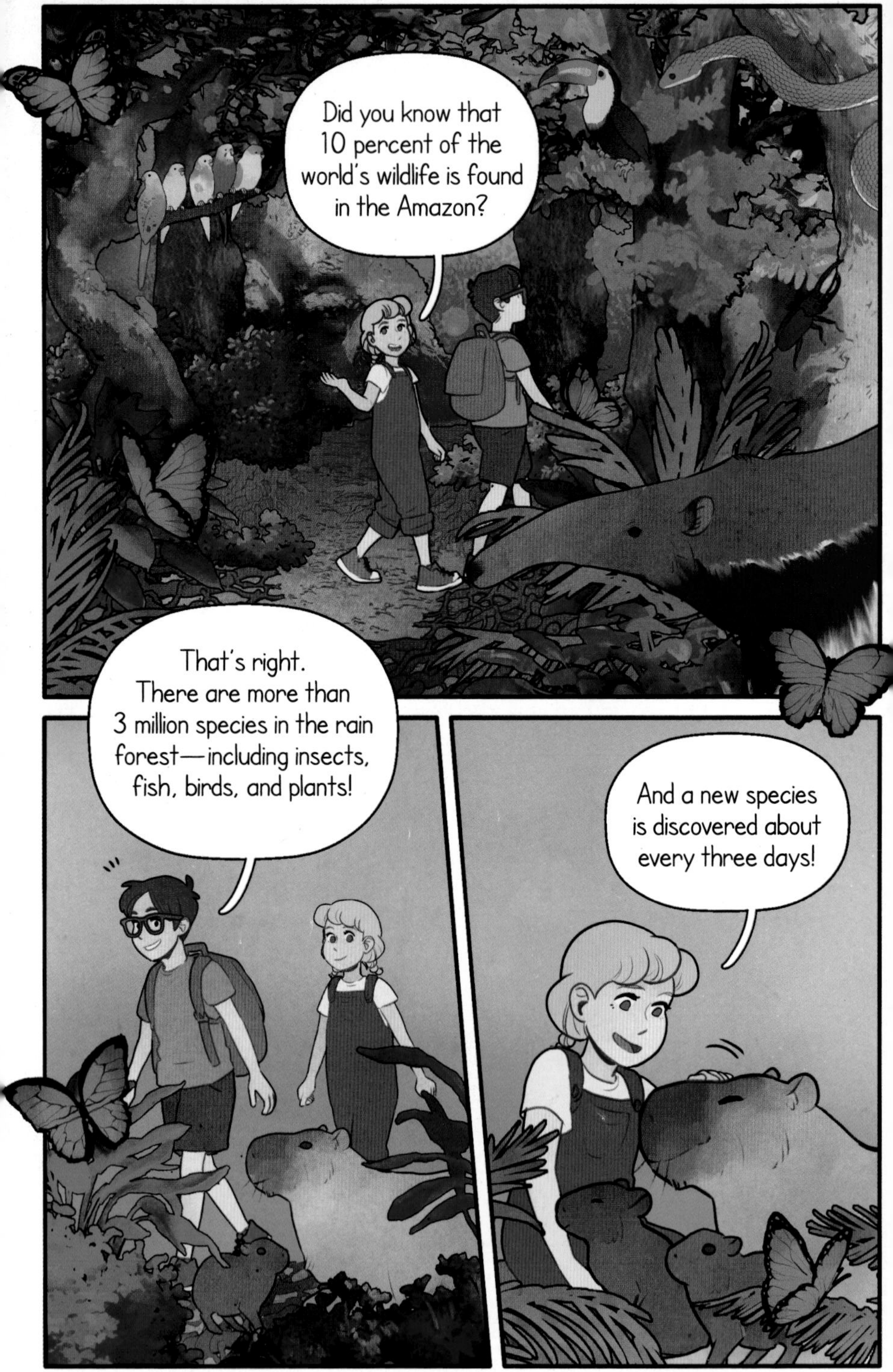
Did you know that 10 percent of the world's wildlife is found in the Amazon?
That's right. There are more than 3 million species in the rain forest—including insects, fish, birds, and plants!
And a new species is discovered about every three days!

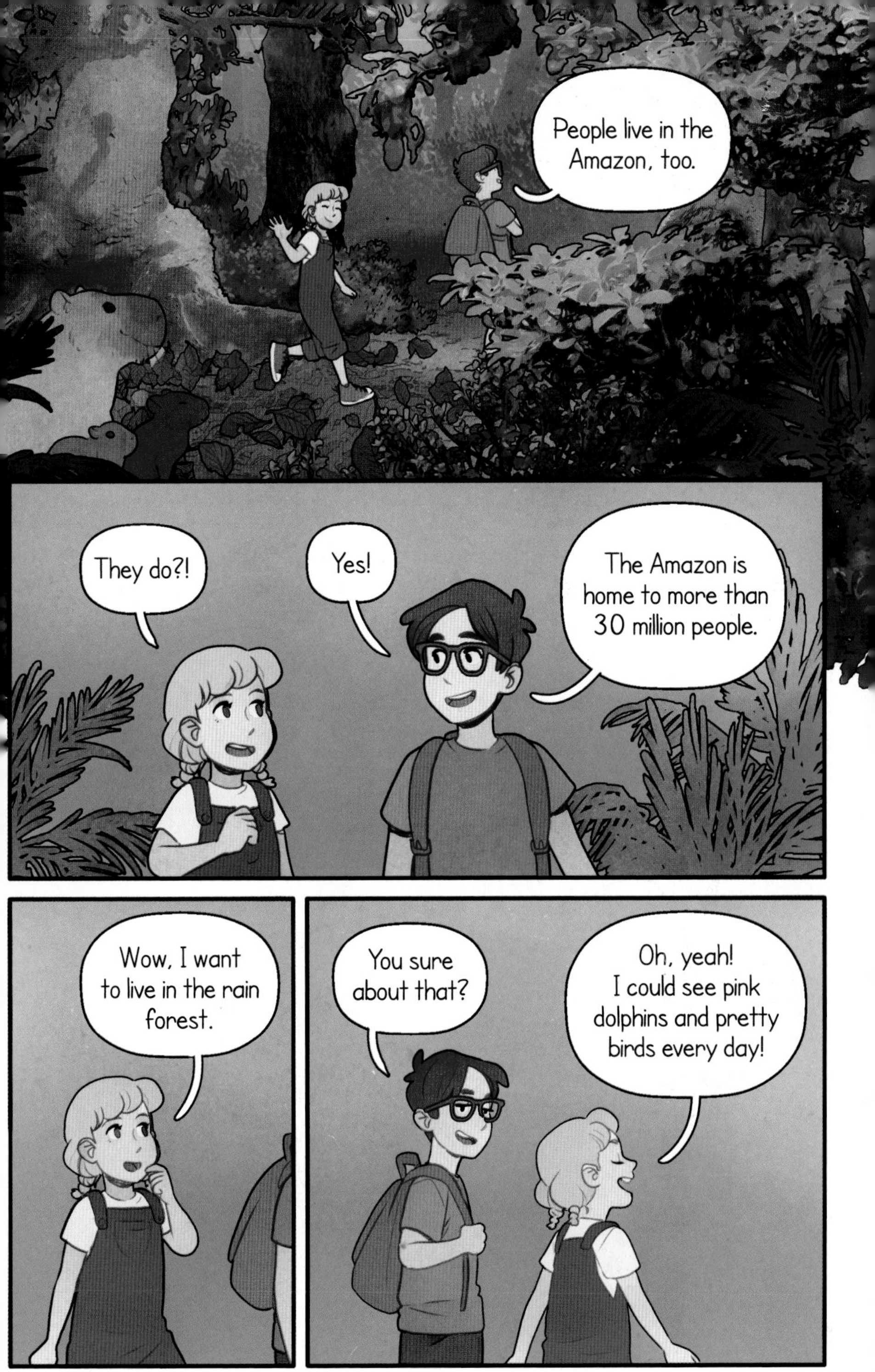
People live in the Amazon, too.
They do?!
Yes!
The Amazon is home to more than 30 million people.
Wow, I want to live in the rain forest.
You sure about that?
Oh, yeah! I could see pink dolphins and pretty birds every day!

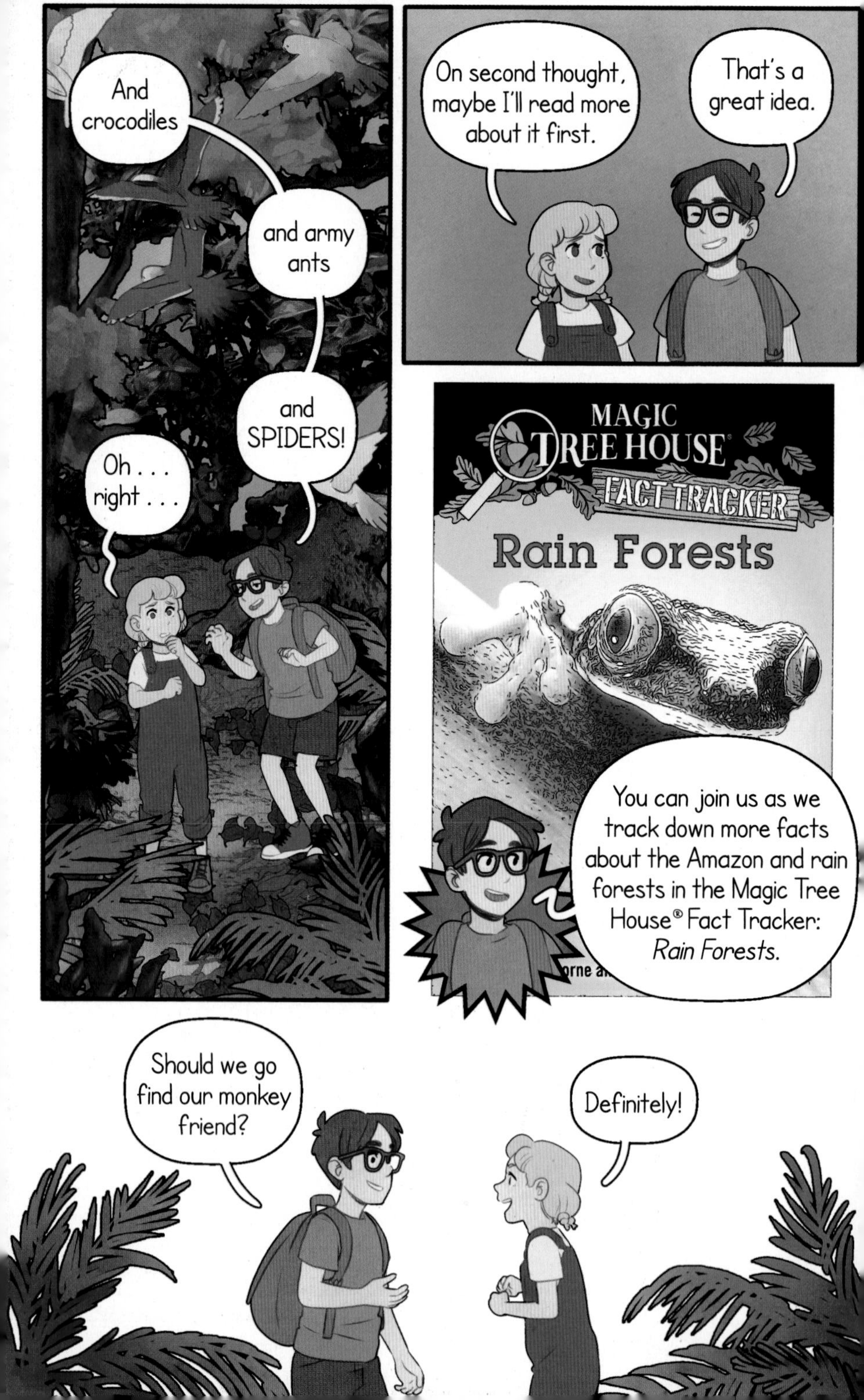
And crocodiles
and army ants
and SPIDERS!
Oh . . . right . . .
On second thought, maybe I'll read more about it first.
That's a great idea.
MAGIC TREE HOUSE
FACT TRACKER
Rain Forests
You can join us as we track down more facts about the Amazon and rain forests in the Magic Tree House® Fact Tracker: *Rain Forests*.
Should we go find our monkey friend?
Definitely!

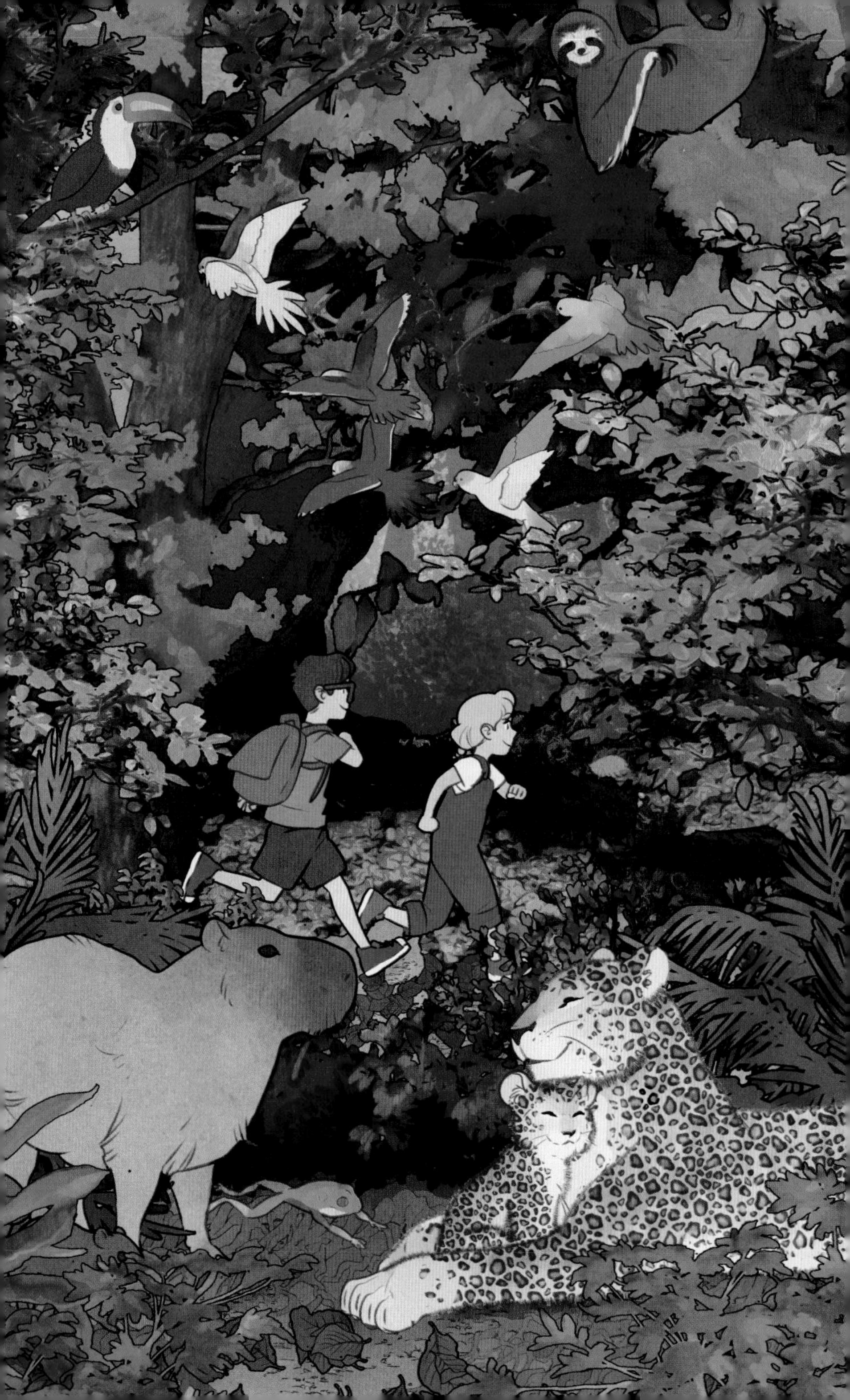

Don't miss another adventure in the Magic Tree House where Jack and Annie get whisked away to ancient Japan!

MARY POPE OSBORNE'S
MAGIC TREE HOUSE
THE GRAPHIC NOVEL
NIGHT OF THE NINJAS
ADAPTED BY JENNY LAIRD
ILLUSTRATED BY KELLY & NICHOLE MATTHEWS

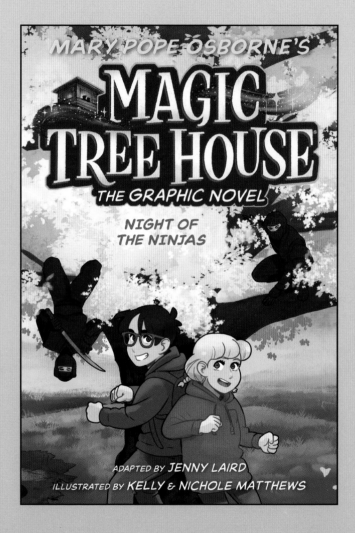

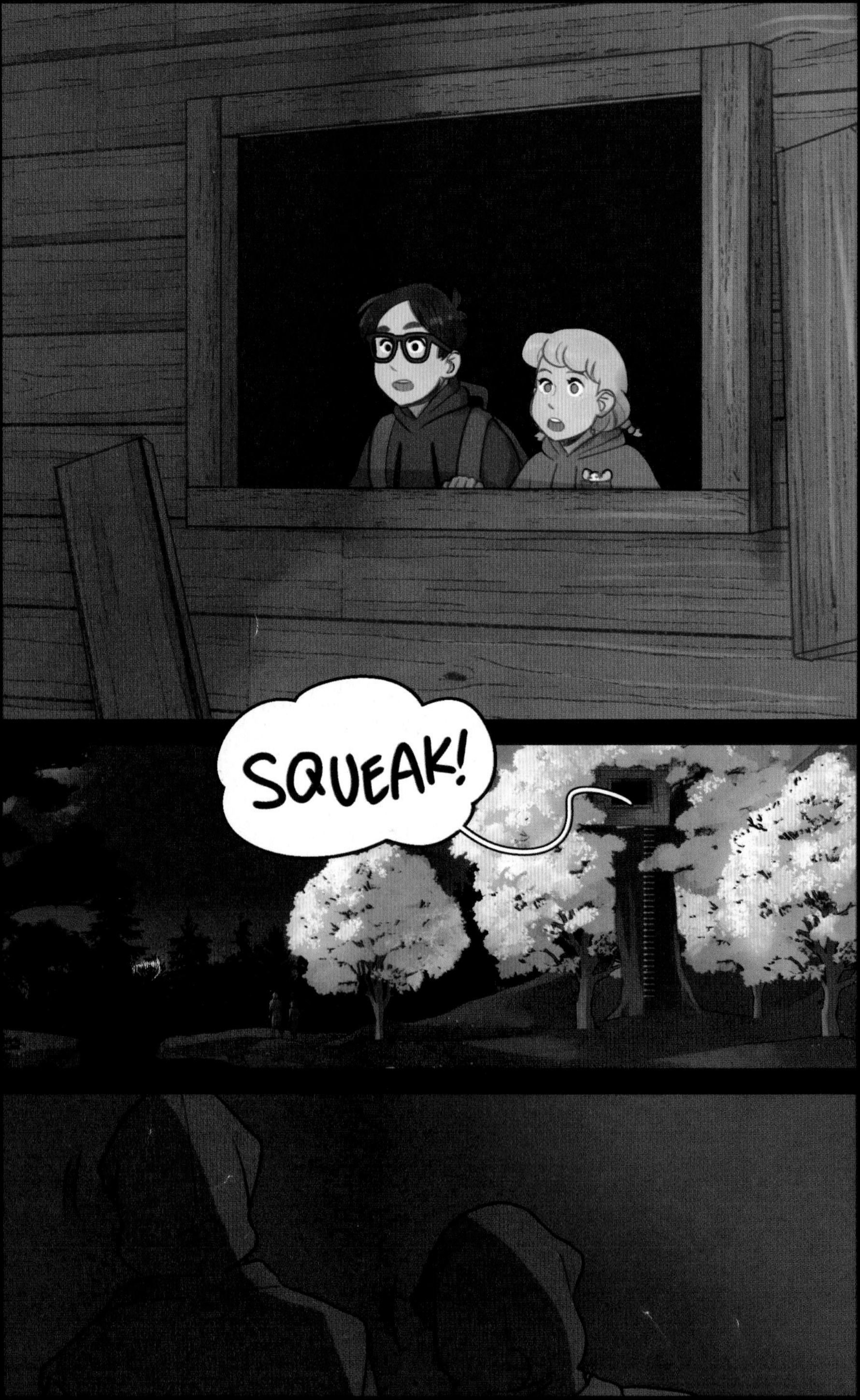
SQUEAK!

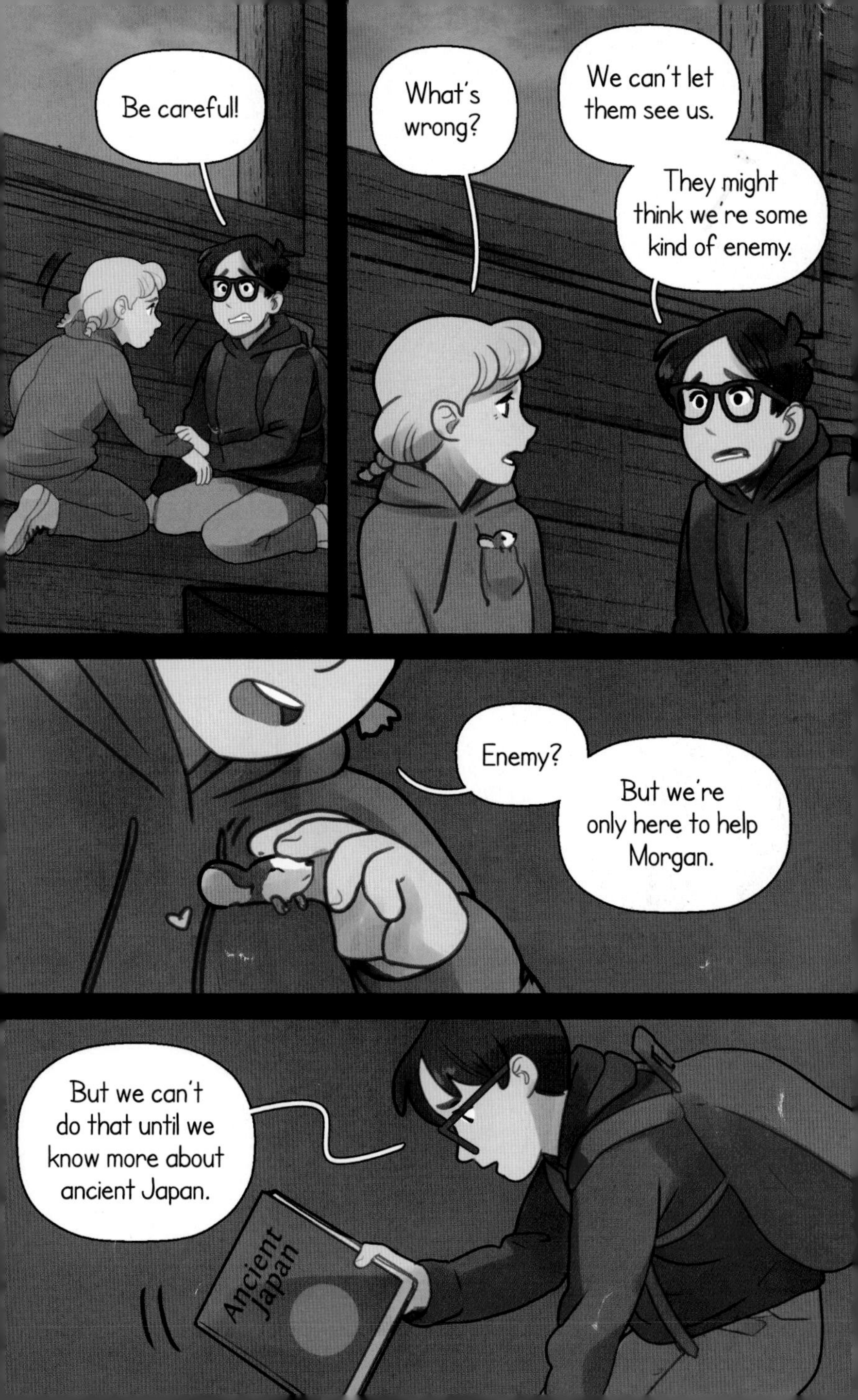
Be careful!
What's wrong?
We can't let them see us.
They might think we're some kind of enemy.
Enemy?
But we're only here to help Morgan.
But we can't do that until we know more about ancient Japan.
Ancient Japan

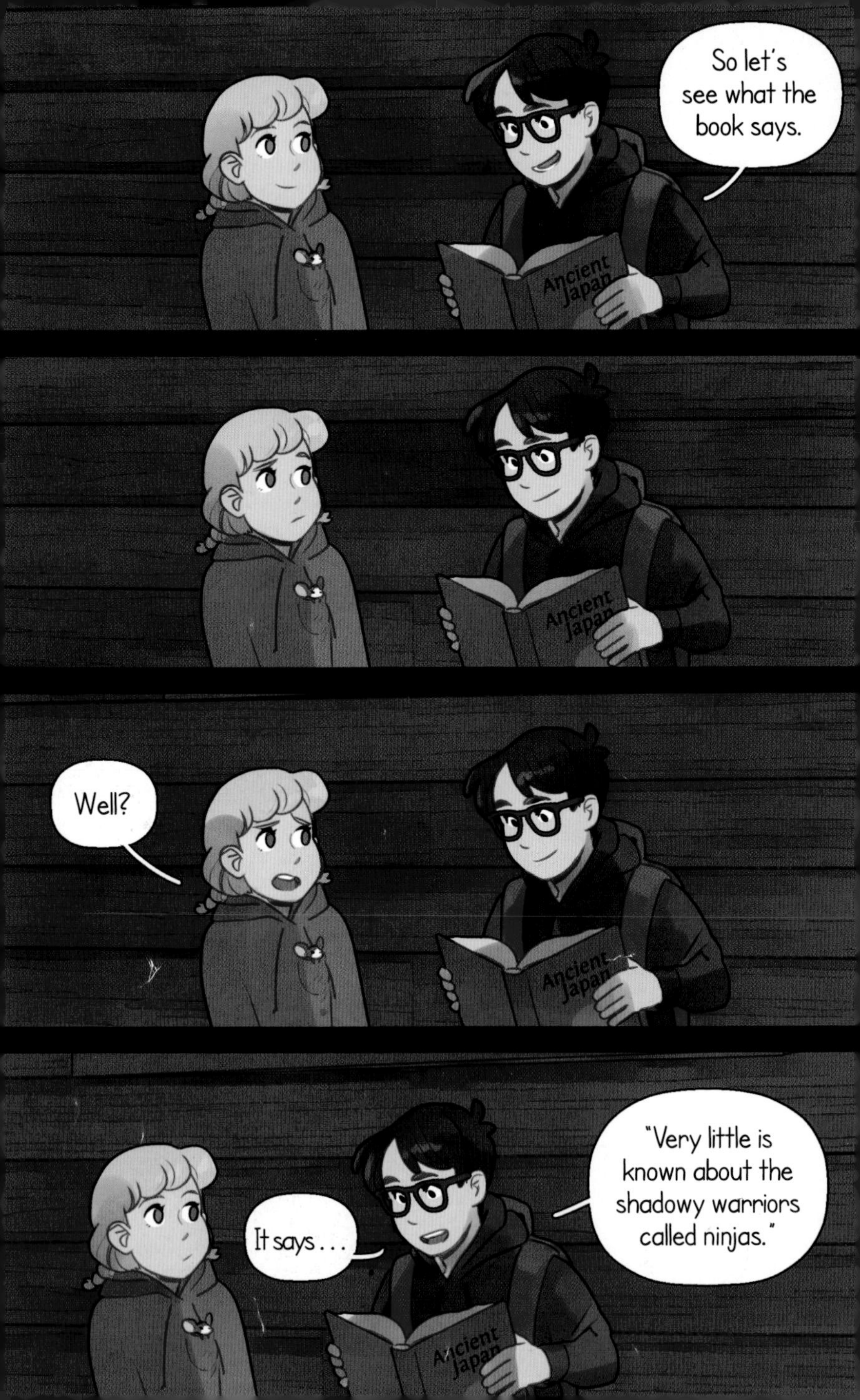
So let's see what the book says.
Ancient Japan
Ancient Japan
Well?
Ancient Japan
It says . . .
"Very little is known about the shadowy warriors called ninjas."
Ancient Japan

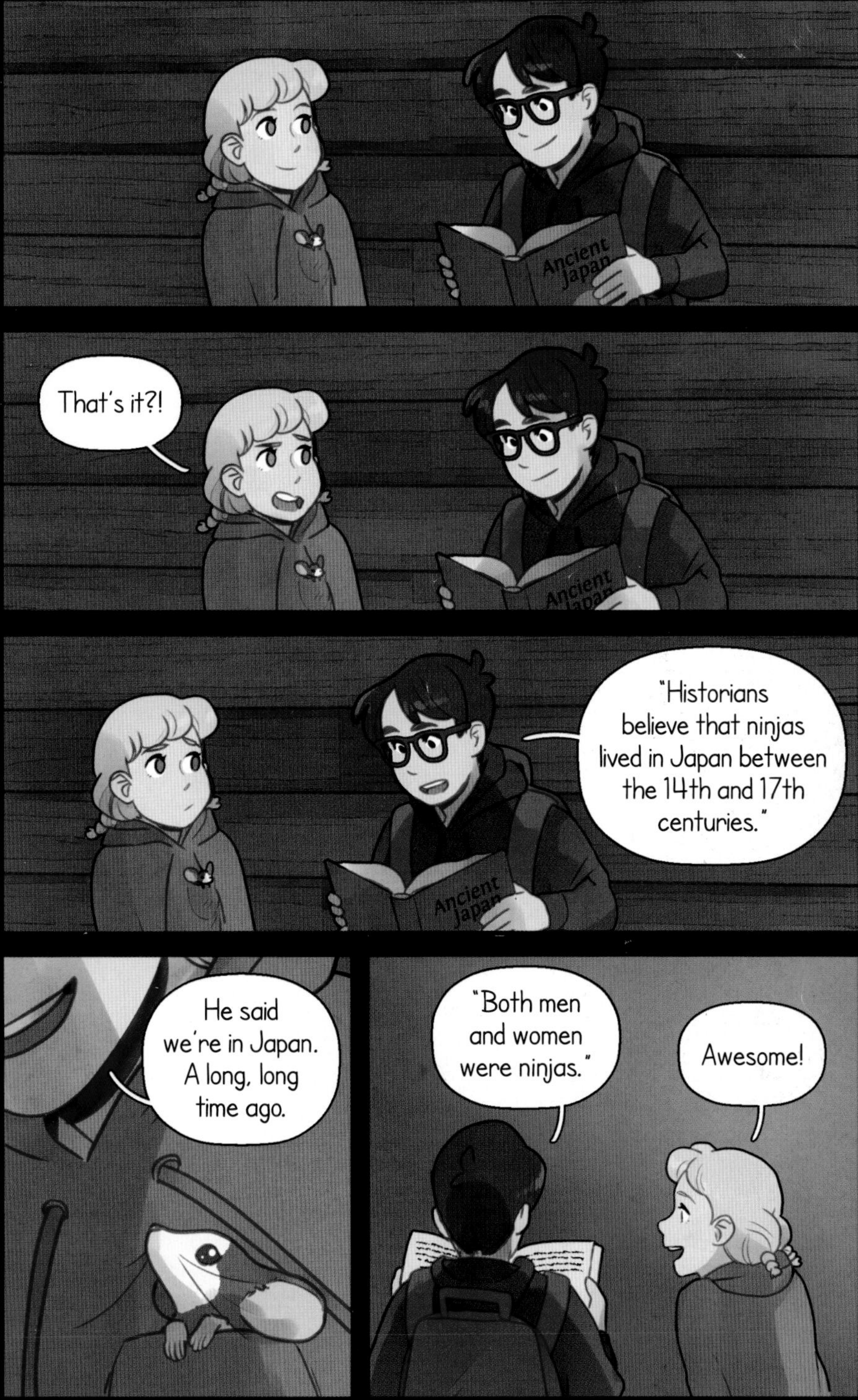
Ancient Japan
That's it?!
Ancient Japan
"Historians believe that ninjas lived in Japan between the 14th and 17th centuries."
Ancient Japan
He said we're in Japan. A long, long time ago.
"Both men and women were ninjas."
Awesome!

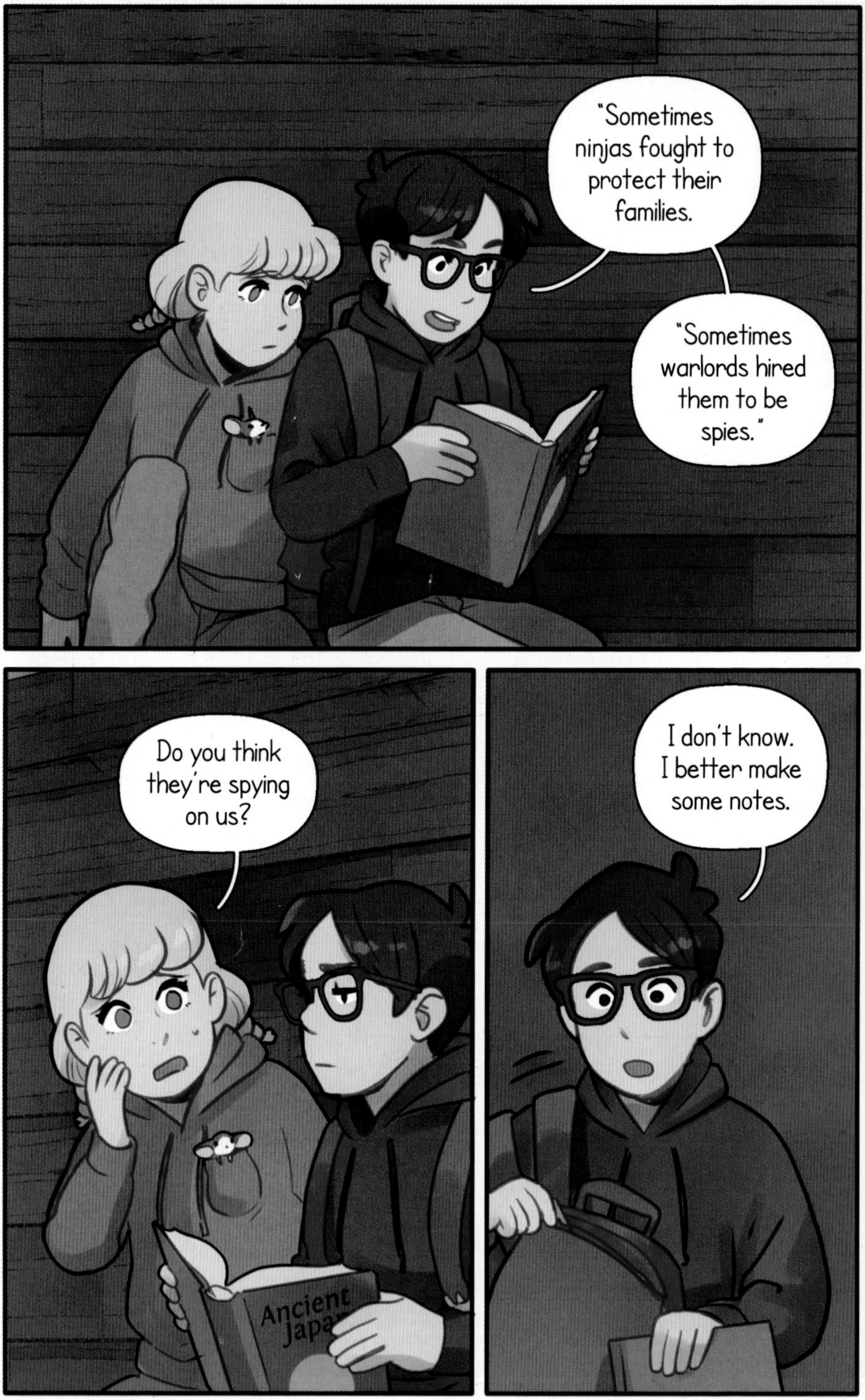
"Sometimes ninjas fought to protect their families.
"Sometimes warlords hired them to be spies."
Do you think they're spying on us?
I don't know. I better make some notes.
Ancient Japa

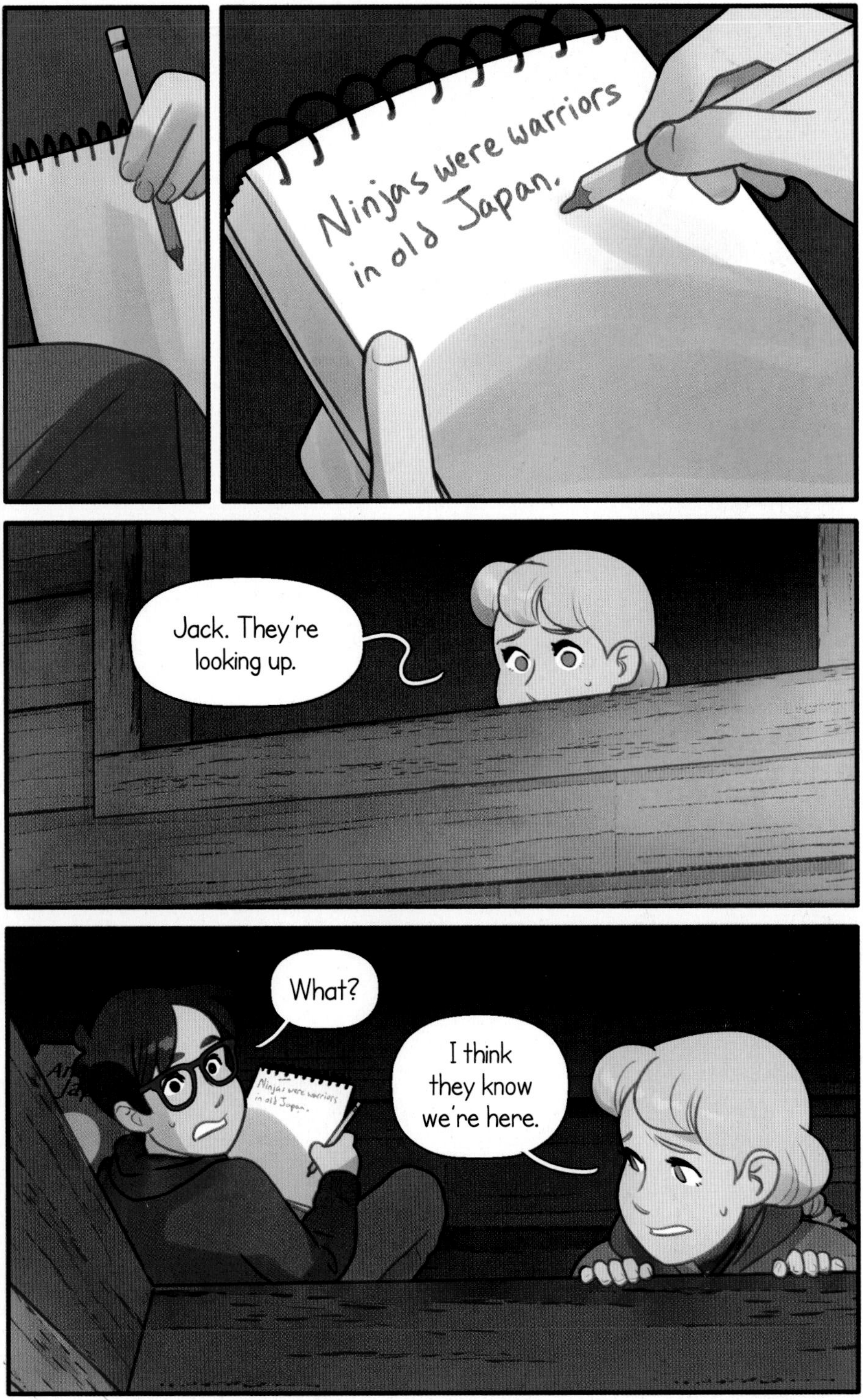
Ninjas were warriors in old Japan.
Jack. They're looking up.
What?
I think they know we're here.

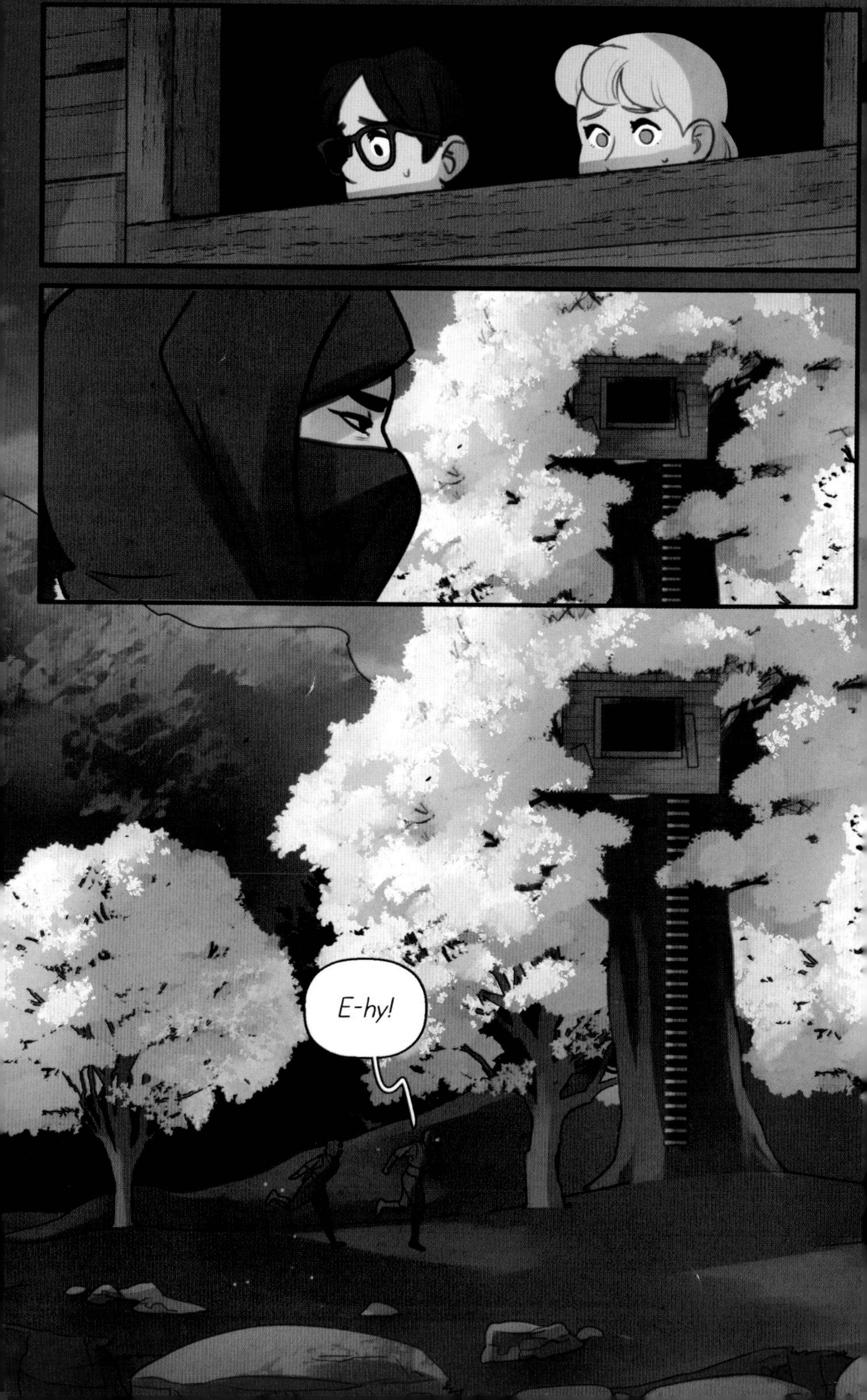
E-hy!

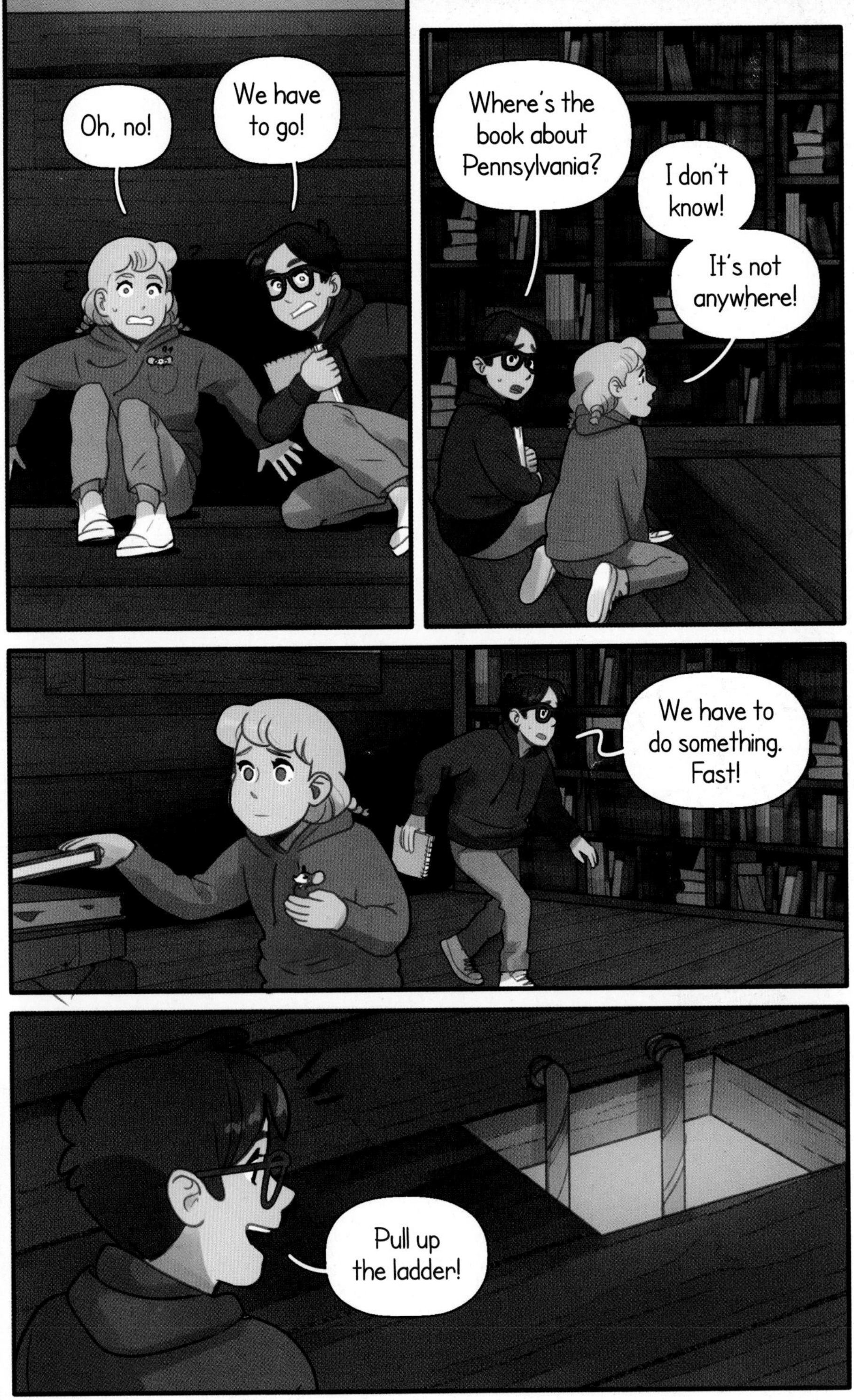
Oh, no!
We have to go!
Where's the book about Pennsylvania?
I don't know!
It's not anywhere!
We have to do something. Fast!
Pull up the ladder!

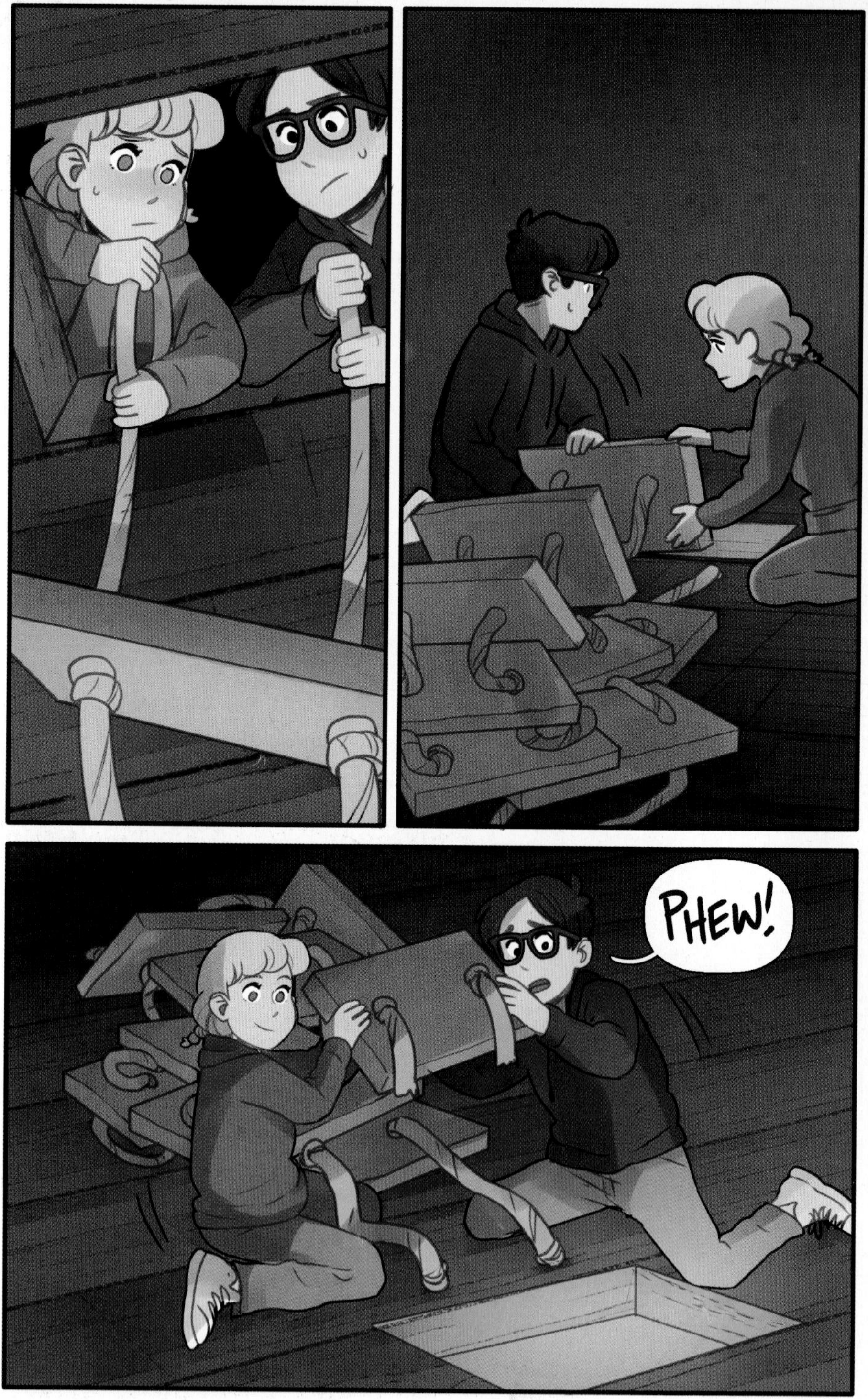
PHEW!

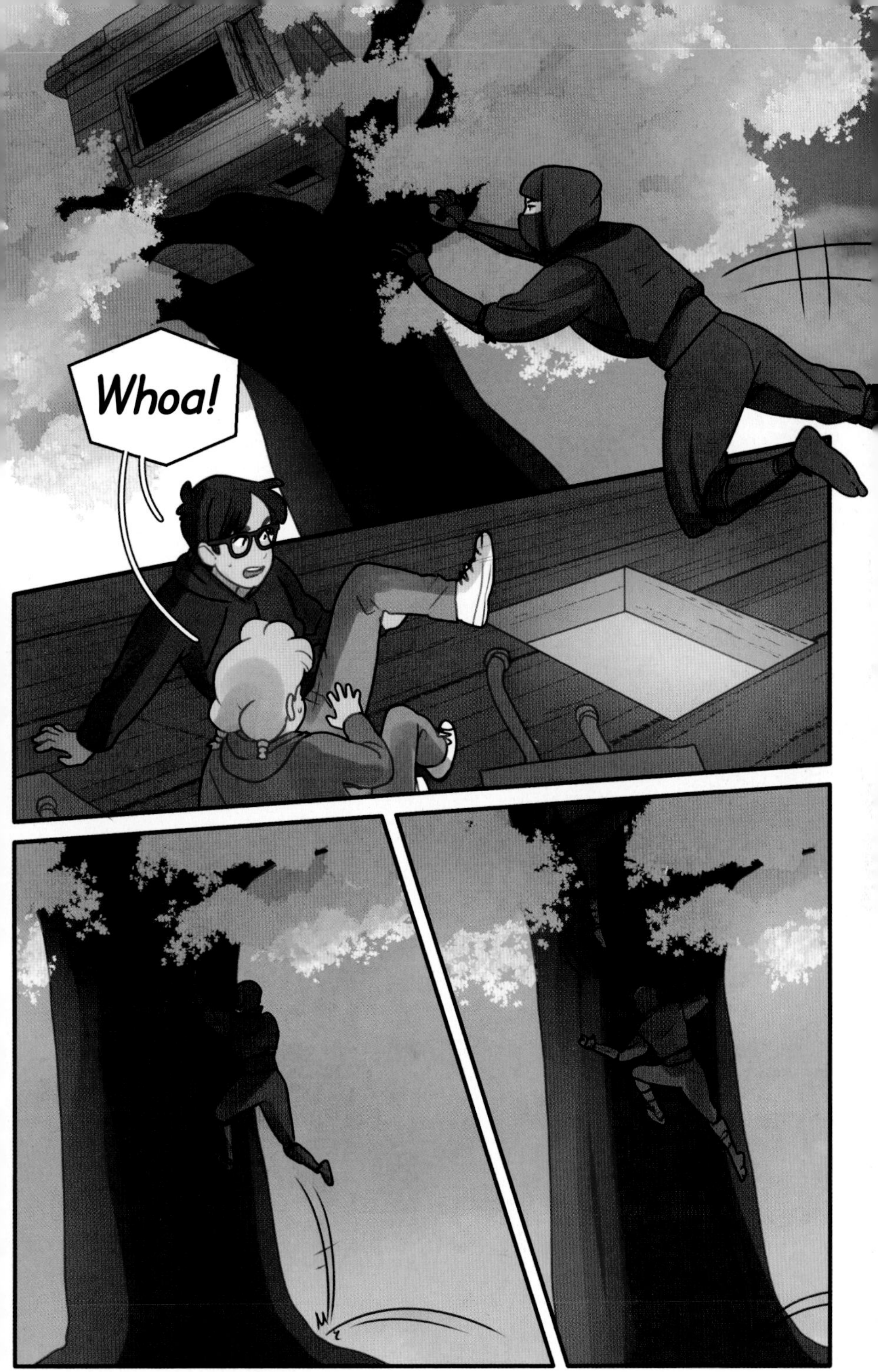
Whoa!

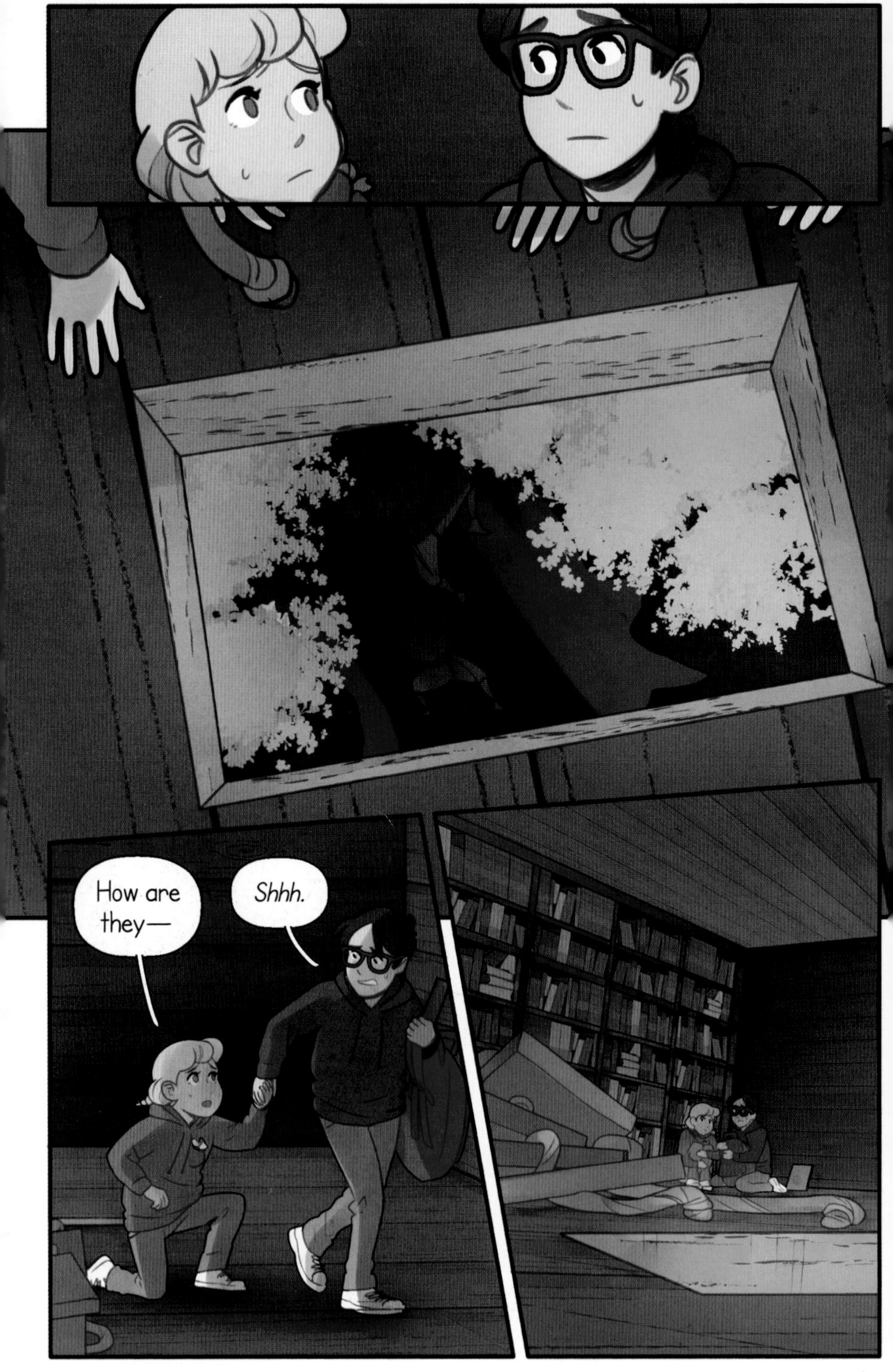
How are they—
Shhh.

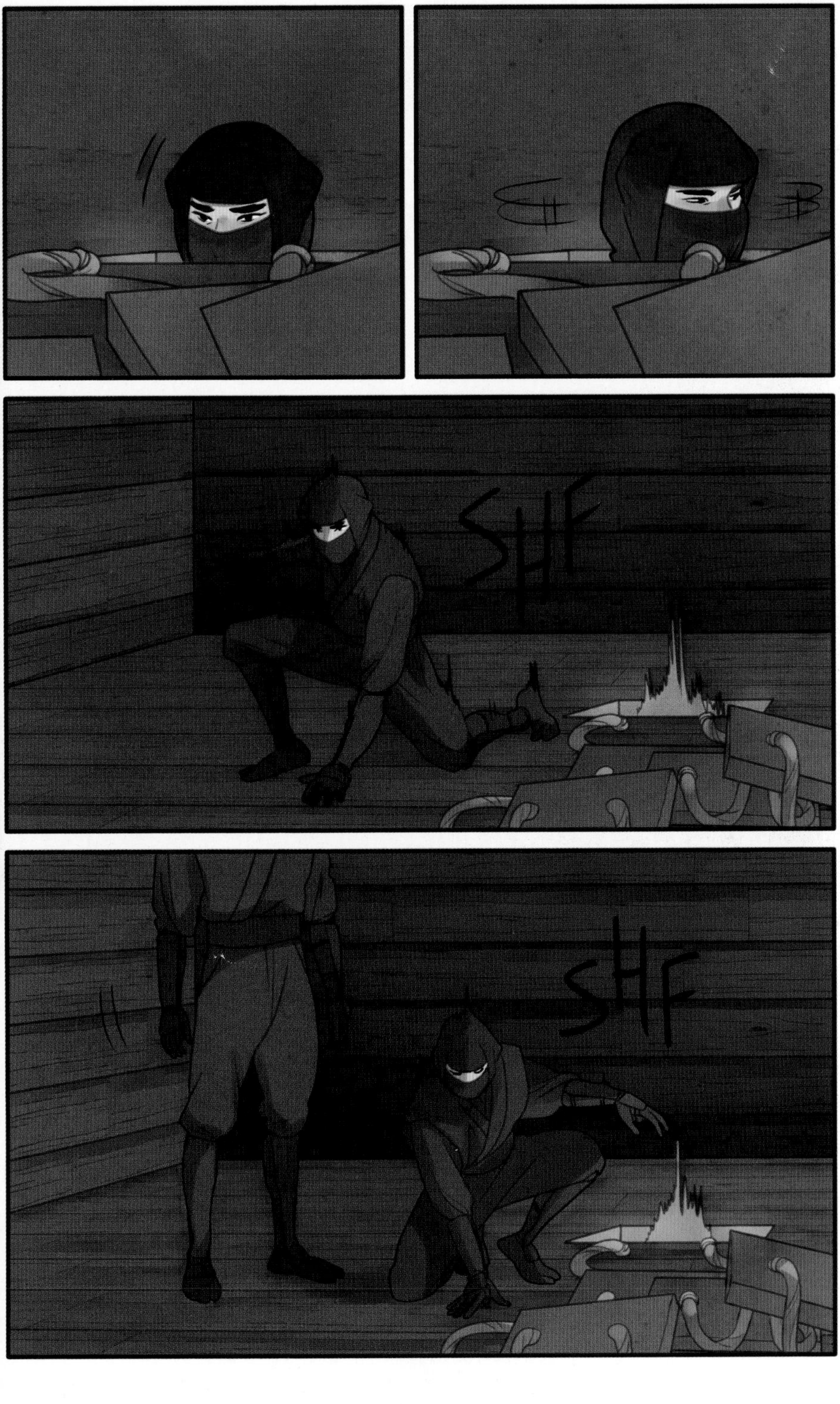
SHF
SHF

LET THE
MAGIC TREE HOUSE®
WHISK YOU AWAY!

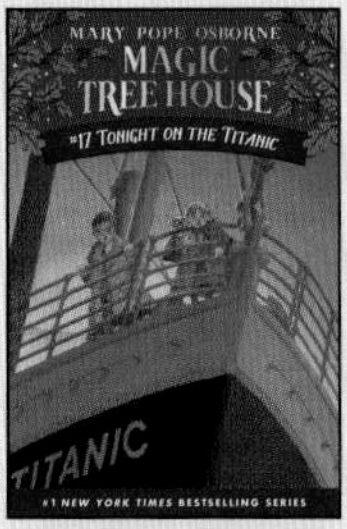
MARY POPE OSBORNE
MAGIC TREE HOUSE
#17 TONIGHT ON THE TITANIC
TITANIC
#1 NEW YORK TIMES BESTSELLING SERIES
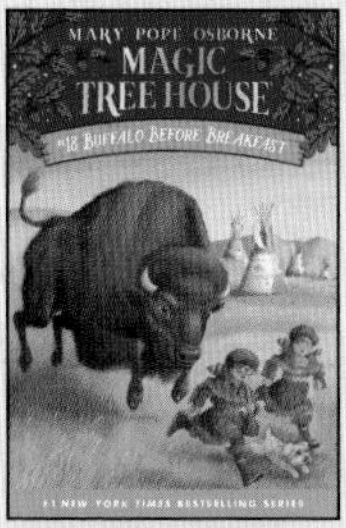
MARY POPE OSBORNE
MAGIC TREE HOUSE
#18 BUFFALO BEFORE BREAKFAST
#1 NEW YORK TIMES BESTSELLING SERIES
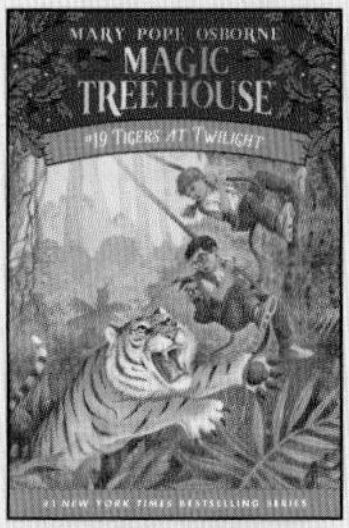
MARY POPE OSBORNE
MAGIC TREE HOUSE
#19 TIGERS AT TWILIGHT
#1 NEW YORK TIMES BESTSELLING SERIES
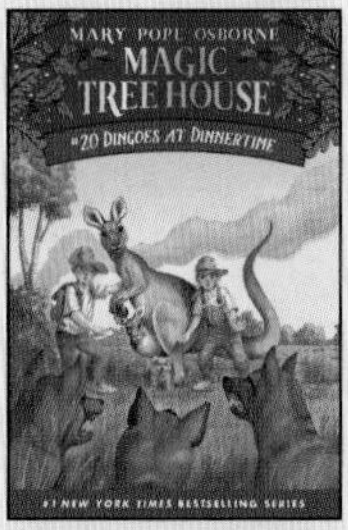
MARY POPE OSBORNE
MAGIC TREE HOUSE
#20 DINGOES AT DINNERTIME
#1 NEW YORK TIMES BESTSELLING SERIES
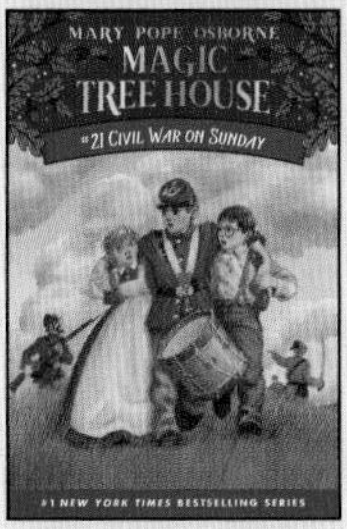
MARY POPE OSBORNE
MAGIC TREE HOUSE
#21 CIVIL WAR ON SUNDAY
#1 NEW YORK TIMES BESTSELLING SERIES
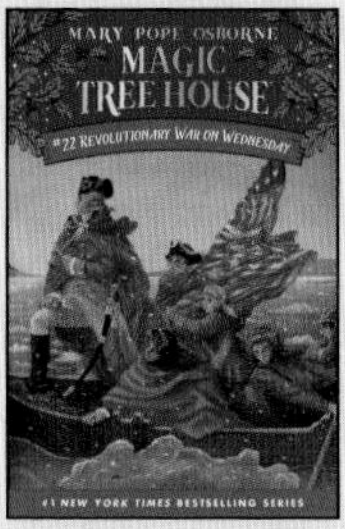
MARY POPE OSBORNE
MAGIC TREE HOUSE
#22 REVOLUTIONARY WAR ON WEDNESDAY
#1 NEW YORK TIMES BESTSELLING SERIES
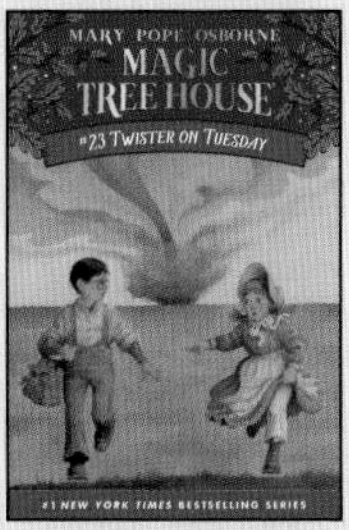
MARY POPE OSBORNE
MAGIC TREE HOUSE
#23 TWISTER ON TUESDAY
#1 NEW YORK TIMES BESTSELLING SERIES
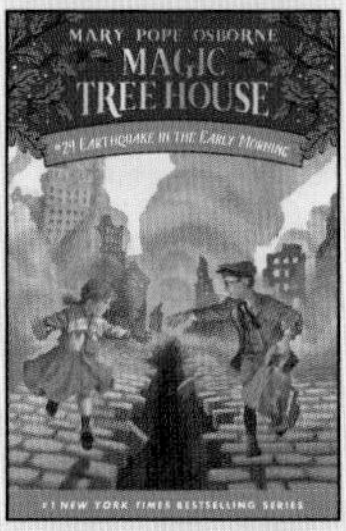
MARY POPE OSBORNE
MAGIC TREE HOUSE
#24 EARTHQUAKE IN THE EARLY MORNING
#1 NEW YORK TIMES BESTSELLING SERIES
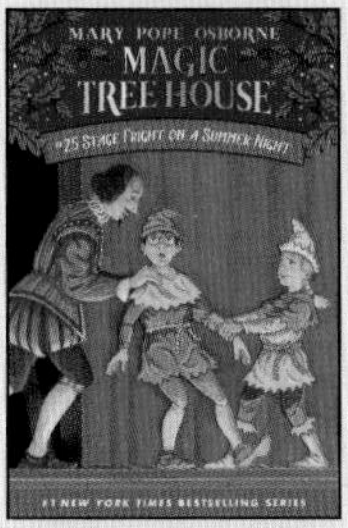
MARY POPE OSBORNE
MAGIC TREE HOUSE
#25 STAGE FRIGHT ON A SUMMER NIGHT
#1 NEW YORK TIMES BESTSELLING SERIES
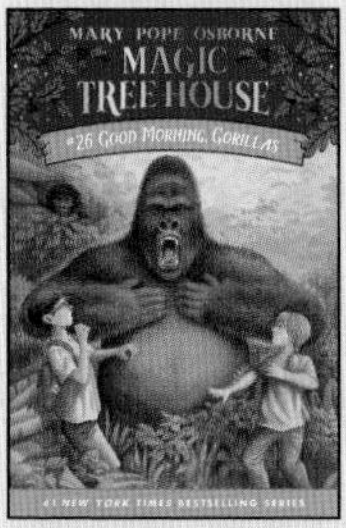
MARY POPE OSBORNE
MAGIC TREE HOUSE
#26 GOOD MORNING, GORILLAS
#1 NEW YORK TIMES BESTSELLING SERIES
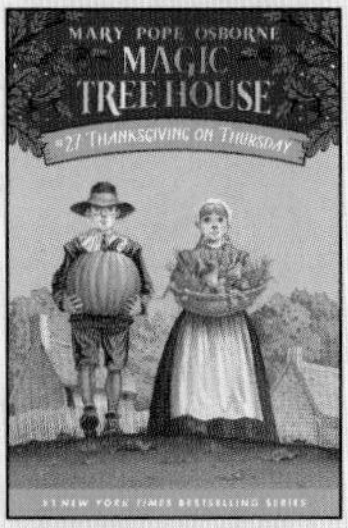
MARY POPE OSBORNE
MAGIC TREE HOUSE
#27 THANKSGIVING ON THURSDAY
#1 NEW YORK TIMES BESTSELLING SERIES
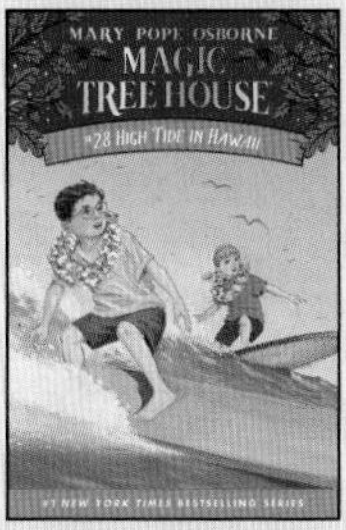
MARY POPE OSBORNE
MAGIC TREE HOUSE
#28 HIGH TIDE IN HAWAII
#1 NEW YORK TIMES BESTSELLING SERIES
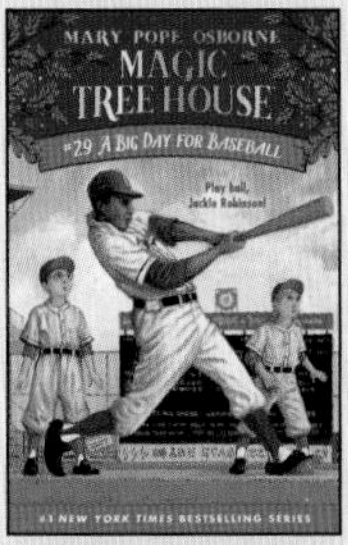
MARY POPE OSBORNE
MAGIC TREE HOUSE
#29 A BIG DAY FOR BASEBALL
Play ball, Jackie Robinson!
#1 NEW YORK TIMES BESTSELLING SERIES
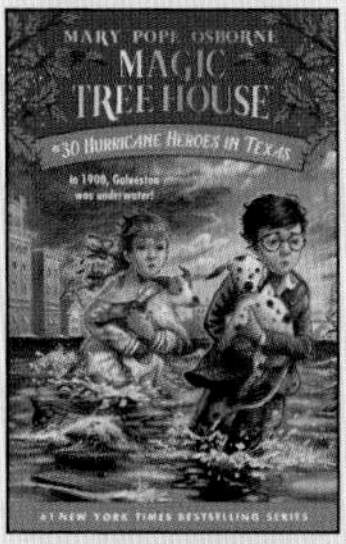
MARY POPE OSBORNE
MAGIC TREE HOUSE
#30 HURRICANE HEROES IN TEXAS
In 1900, Galveston was underwater!
#1 NEW YORK TIMES BESTSELLING SERIES
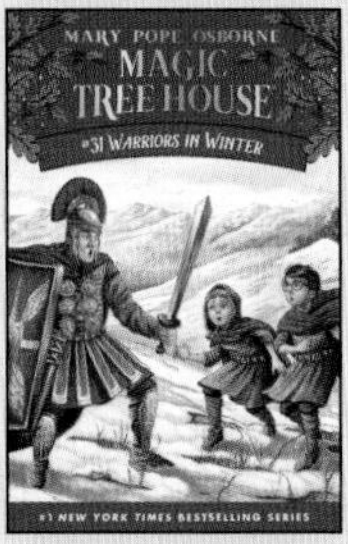
MARY POPE OSBORNE
MAGIC TREE HOUSE
#31 WARRIORS IN WINTER
#1 NEW YORK TIMES BESTSELLING SERIES
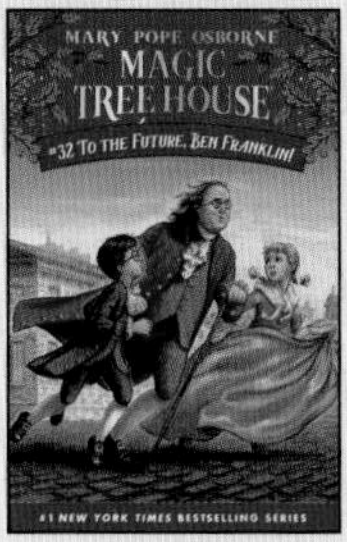
MARY POPE OSBORNE
MAGIC TREE HOUSE
#32 TO THE FUTURE, BEN FRANKLIN!
#1 NEW YORK TIMES BESTSELLING SERIES
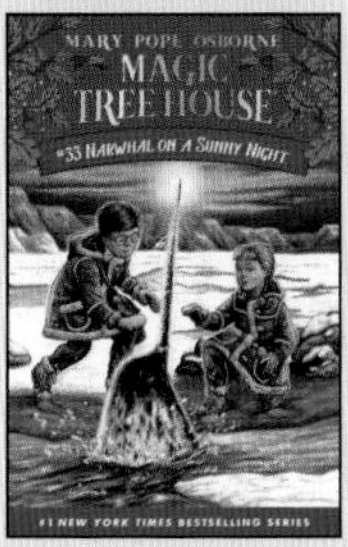
MARY POPE OSBORNE
MAGIC TREE HOUSE
#33 NARWHAL ON A SUNNY NIGHT
#1 NEW YORK TIMES BESTSELLING SERIES
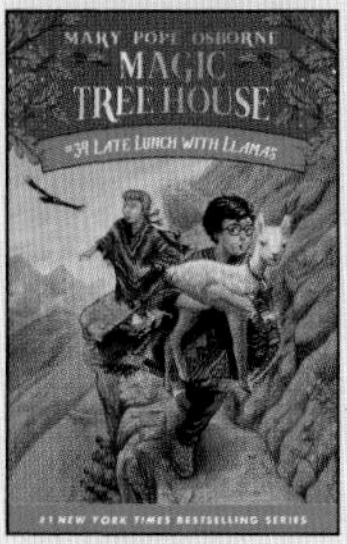
MARY POPE OSBORNE
MAGIC TREE HOUSE
#34 LATE LUNCH WITH LLAMAS
#1 NEW YORK TIMES BESTSELLING SERIES
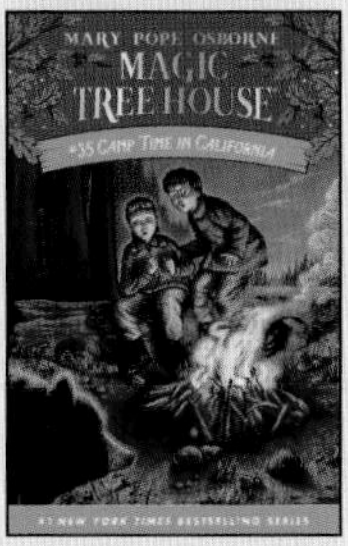
MARY POPE OSBORNE
MAGIC TREE HOUSE
#35 CAMP TIME IN CALIFORNIA
#1 NEW YORK TIMES BESTSELLING SERIES

TRACK THE FACTS WITH JACK & ANNIE!

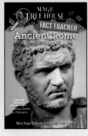
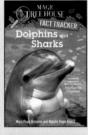

MAGIC TREE HOUSE FACT TRACKER — Dinosaurs
Will Osborne and Mary Pope Osborne

MAGIC TREE HOUSE FACT TRACKER — Knights and Castles
Will Osborne and Mary Pope Osborne

MAGIC TREE HOUSE FACT TRACKER — Mummies and Pyramids

MAGIC TREE HOUSE FACT TRACKER — Pirates
Will Osborne and Mary Pope Osborne

MAGIC TREE HOUSE FACT TRACKER — Rain Forests
Will Osborne and Mary Pope Osborne

MAGIC TREE HOUSE FACT TRACKER — Space
Will Osborne and Mary Pope Osborne

MAGIC TREE HOUSE FACT TRACKER — Titanic

MAGIC TREE HOUSE FACT TRACKER — Twisters and Other Terrible Storms
Will Osborne and Mary Pope Osborne

MAGIC TREE HOUSE FACT TRACKER — Dolphins and Sharks
Mary Pope Osborne and Natalie Pope Boyce

MAGIC TREE HOUSE FACT TRACKER — Ancient Greece and the Olympics
Mary Pope Osborne and Natalie Pope Boyce

MAGIC TREE HOUSE FACT TRACKER — American Revolution
Mary Pope Osborne and Natalie Pope Boyce

MAGIC TREE HOUSE FACT TRACKER — Sabertooths and the Ice Age
Mary Pope Osborne and Natalie Pope Boyce

MAGIC TREE HOUSE FACT TRACKER — Pilgrims

MAGIC TREE HOUSE FACT TRACKER — Ancient Rome and Pompeii
Mary Pope Osborne and Natalie Pope Boyce

MAGIC TREE HOUSE FACT TRACKER — Tsunamis and Other Natural Disasters
Mary Pope Osborne and Natalie Pope Boyce

MAGIC TREE HOUSE FACT TRACKER — Polar Bears and the Arctic
Mary Pope Osborne and Natalie Pope Boyce

MAGIC TREE HOUSE FACT TRACKER — Sea Monsters
Mary Pope Osborne and Natalie Pope Boyce

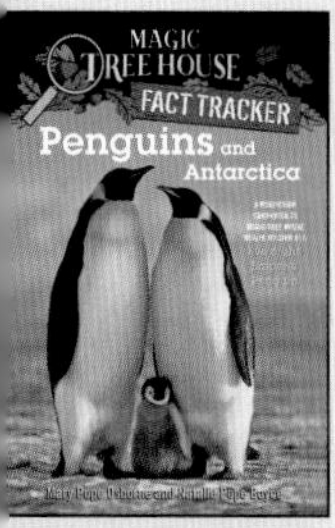
MAGIC TREE HOUSE
FACT TRACKER
Penguins and Antarctica
Mary Pope Osborne and Natalie Pope Boyce
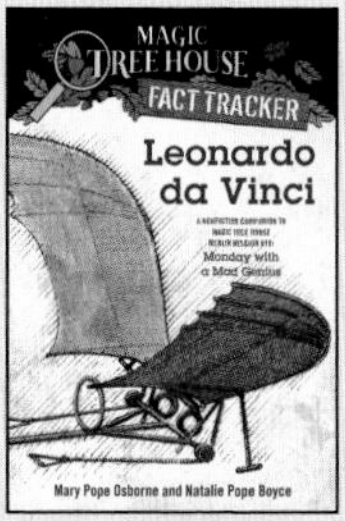
MAGIC TREE HOUSE
FACT TRACKER
Leonardo da Vinci
Monday with a Mad Genius
Mary Pope Osborne and Natalie Pope Boyce
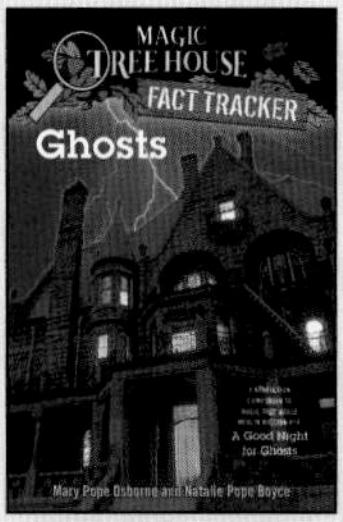
MAGIC TREE HOUSE
FACT TRACKER
Ghosts
A Good Night for Ghosts
Mary Pope Osborne and Natalie Pope Boyce
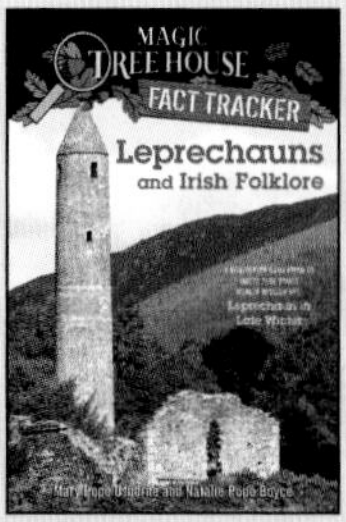
MAGIC TREE HOUSE
FACT TRACKER
Leprechauns and Irish Folklore
Mary Pope Osborne and Natalie Pope Boyce
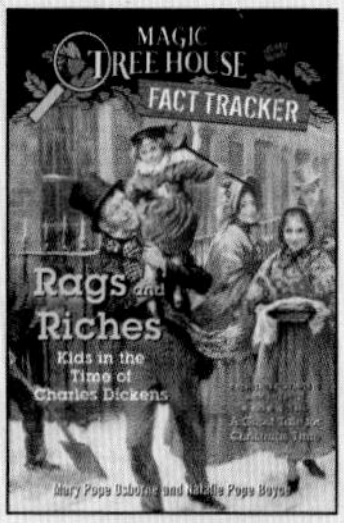
MAGIC TREE HOUSE
FACT TRACKER
Rags and Riches
Kids in the Time of Charles Dickens
Mary Pope Osborne and Natalie Pope Boyce
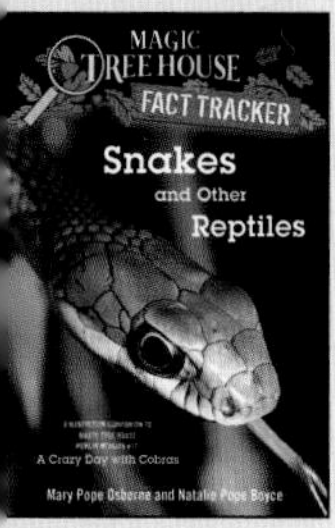
MAGIC TREE HOUSE
FACT TRACKER
Snakes and Other Reptiles
A Crazy Day with Cobras
Mary Pope Osborne and Natalie Pope Boyce
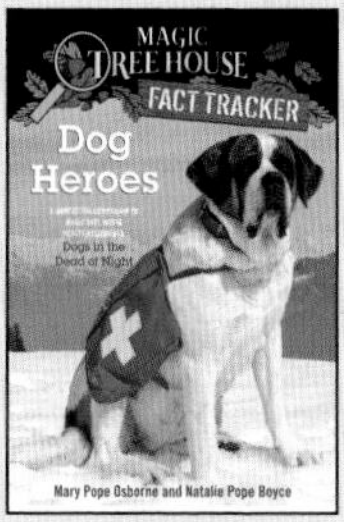
MAGIC TREE HOUSE
FACT TRACKER
Dog Heroes
Dogs in the Dead of Night
Mary Pope Osborne and Natalie Pope Boyce
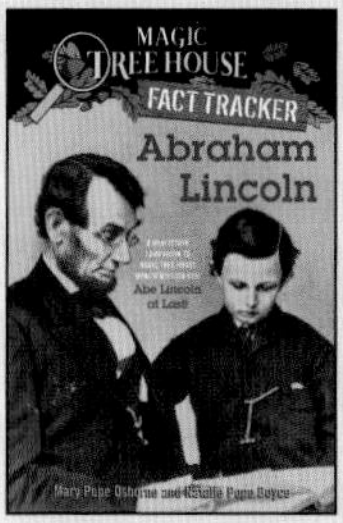
MAGIC TREE HOUSE
FACT TRACKER
Abraham Lincoln
Abe Lincoln at Last!
Mary Pope Osborne and Natalie Pope Boyce
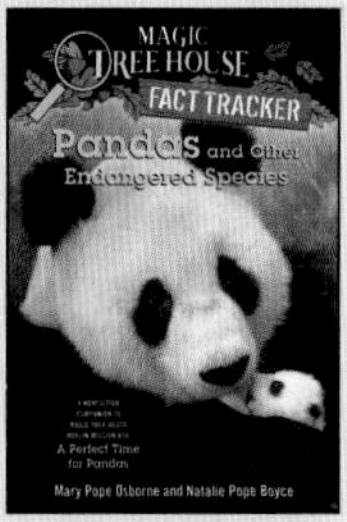
MAGIC TREE HOUSE
FACT TRACKER
Pandas and Other Endangered Species
A Perfect Time for Pandas
Mary Pope Osborne and Natalie Pope Boyce
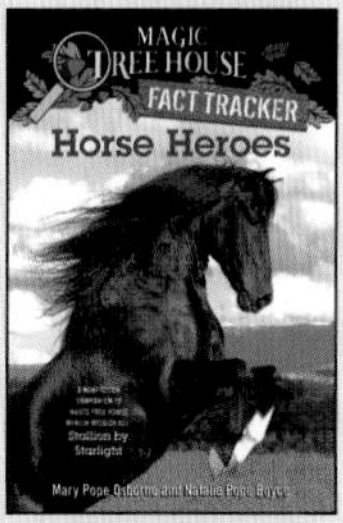
MAGIC TREE HOUSE
FACT TRACKER
Horse Heroes
Stallion by Starlight
Mary Pope Osborne and Natalie Pope Boyce
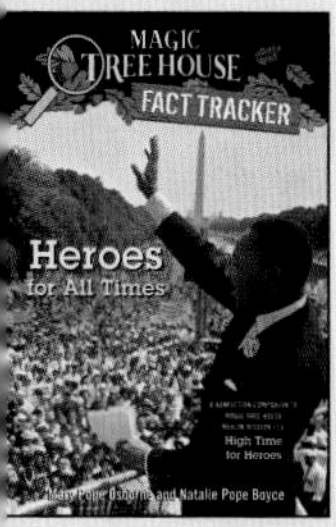
MAGIC TREE HOUSE
FACT TRACKER
Heroes for All Times
High Time for Heroes
Mary Pope Osborne and Natalie Pope Boyce
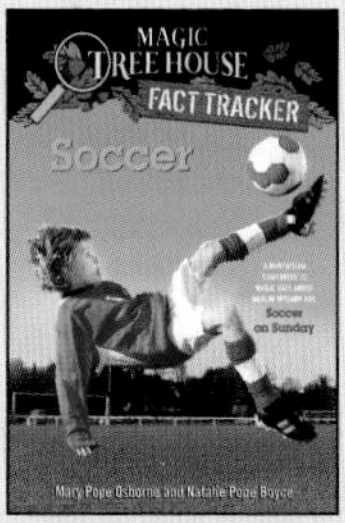
MAGIC TREE HOUSE
FACT TRACKER
Soccer
Soccer on Sunday
Mary Pope Osborne and Natalie Pope Boyce
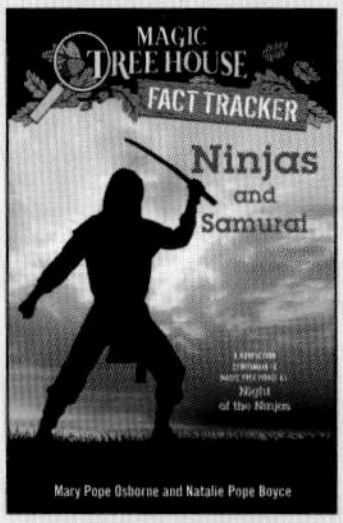
MAGIC TREE HOUSE
FACT TRACKER
Ninjas and Samurai
Night of the Ninjas
Mary Pope Osborne and Natalie Pope Boyce
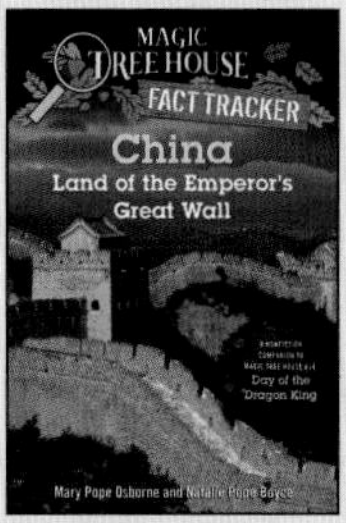
MAGIC TREE HOUSE
FACT TRACKER
China
Land of the Emperor's Great Wall
Day of the Dragon King
Mary Pope Osborne and Natalie Pope Boyce
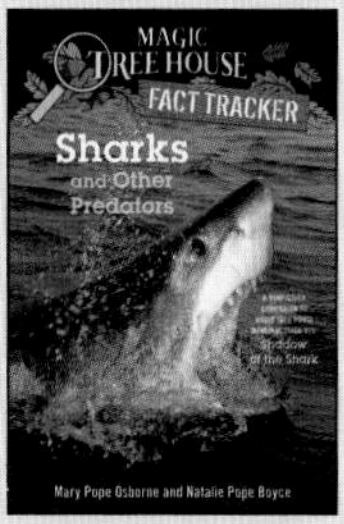
MAGIC TREE HOUSE
FACT TRACKER
Sharks and Other Predators
Shadow of the Shark
Mary Pope Osborne and Natalie Pope Boyce
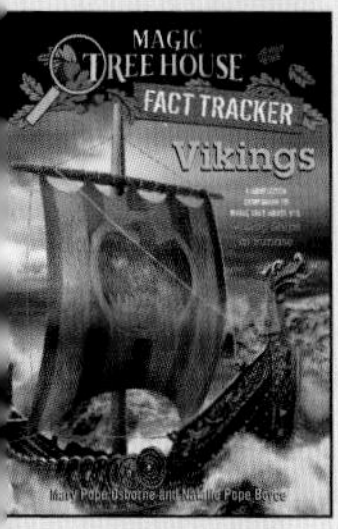
MAGIC TREE HOUSE
FACT TRACKER
Vikings
Mary Pope Osborne and Natalie Pope Boyce
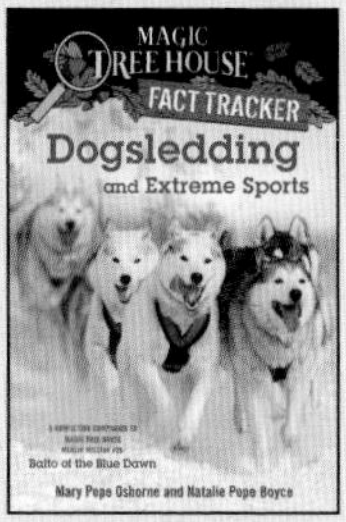
MAGIC TREE HOUSE
FACT TRACKER
Dogsledding and Extreme Sports
Balto of the Blue Dawn
Mary Pope Osborne and Natalie Pope Boyce
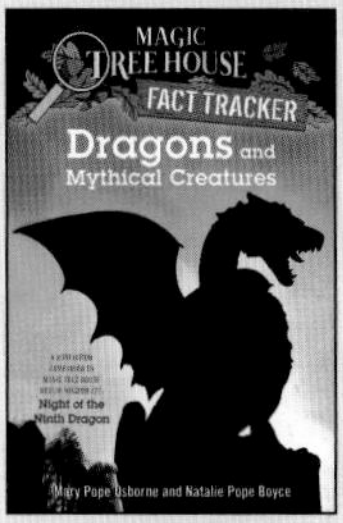
MAGIC TREE HOUSE
FACT TRACKER
Dragons and Mythical Creatures
Night of the Ninth Dragon
Mary Pope Osborne and Natalie Pope Boyce
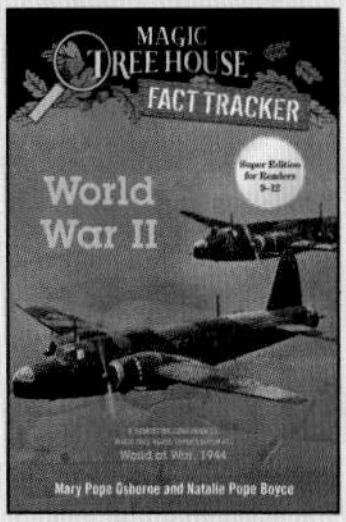
MAGIC TREE HOUSE
FACT TRACKER
World War II
Super Edition for Readers 9–12
World at War, 1944
Mary Pope Osborne and Natalie Pope Boyce
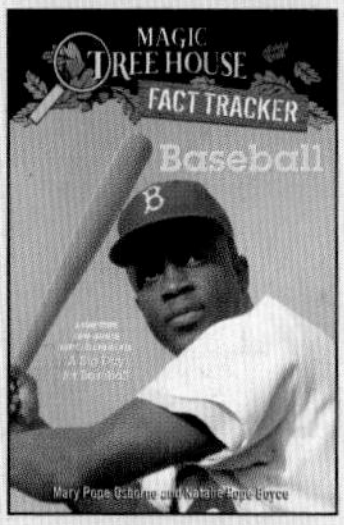
MAGIC TREE HOUSE
FACT TRACKER
Baseball
Mary Pope Osborne and Natalie Pope Boyce
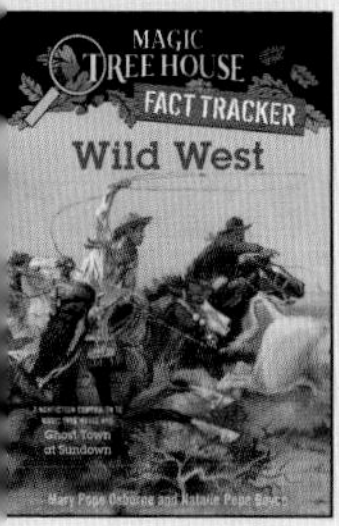
MAGIC TREE HOUSE
FACT TRACKER
Wild West
Ghost Town at Sundown
Mary Pope Osborne and Natalie Pope Boyce
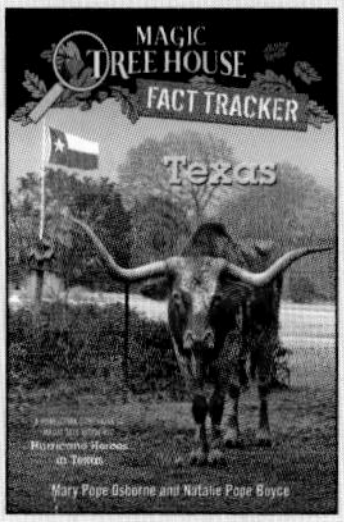
MAGIC TREE HOUSE
FACT TRACKER
Texas
Hurricane Heroes in Texas
Mary Pope Osborne and Natalie Pope Boyce
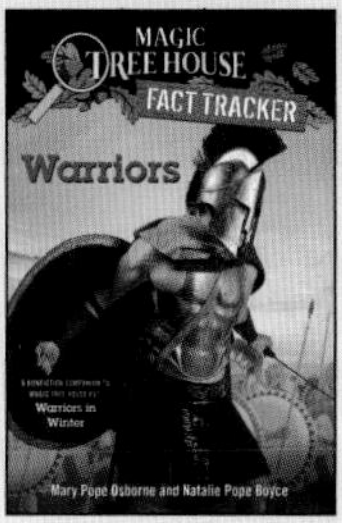
MAGIC TREE HOUSE
FACT TRACKER
Warriors
Warriors in Winter
Mary Pope Osborne and Natalie Pope Boyce
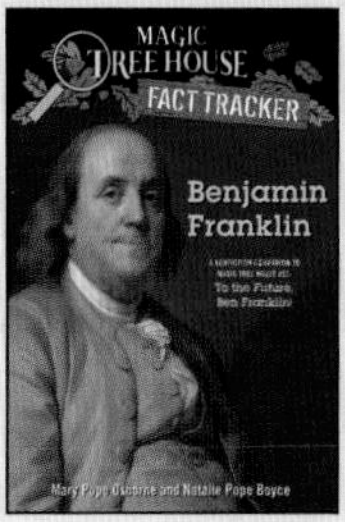
MAGIC TREE HOUSE
FACT TRACKER
Benjamin Franklin
Mary Pope Osborne and Natalie Pope Boyce
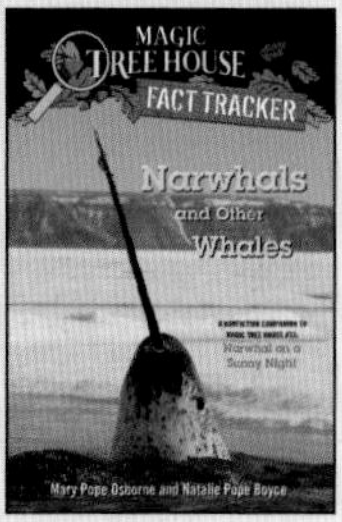
MAGIC TREE HOUSE
FACT TRACKER
Narwhals and Other Whales
Mary Pope Osborne and Natalie Pope Boyce

MARY POPE OSBORNE is the author of many novels, picture books, story collections, and nonfiction books. Her #1 *New York Times* bestselling Magic Tree House® series has been translated into numerous languages around the world. Highly recommended by parents and educators everywhere, the series introduces young readers to different cultures and times, as well as to the world's legacy of ancient myth and storytelling.

JENNY LAIRD is an award-winning playwright. She collaborates with Will Osborne and Randy Courts on creating musical theater adaptations of the Magic Tree House® series for both national and international audiences. Their work also includes shows for young performers, available through Music Theatre International's Broadway Junior® Collection.

KELLY & NICHOLE MATTHEWS are twin sisters and a comic-art team. They get to do their dream job every day, drawing comics for a living. They've worked with Boom Studios!, Archaia, the Jim Henson Company, Hiveworks, and now Random House!